UNWISE PROMISES

UNWISE PROMISES

Grace Thompson

This first world edition published in Great Britain 2002 by
SEVERN HOUSE PUBLISHERS LTD of
9–15 High Street, Sutton, Surrey SM1 1DF.
This first world edition published in the USA 2003 by
SEVERN HOUSE PUBLISHERS INC of
595 Madison Avenue, New York, N.Y. 10022.

British Library Cataloguing in Publication Data

Thompson,   Grace
    Unwise promises
    1.   World War, 1939-1945 --Social aspects - Wales - Fiction
    2.   Domestic fiction
    I.   Title
    823.9'14 [F]

    ISBN 0-7278-5852-1

Typeset by Palimpsest Book Production Ltd.,
Polmont, Stirlingshire, Scotland.
Printed and bound in Great Britain by
MPG Books Ltd., Bodmin, Cornwall.

One

As Audrey Thomas watched her husband Wilf walk away from her, she frowned slightly. He didn't complain, but she had the feeling that he was not well. It wasn't anything she could describe, just a slowing down, an extra tiredness, a lack of enthusiasm that he tried to hide from her. Either that, or something was deeply troubling him, something he felt unable to discuss with her. Neither possibility pleased her. They had always been able to tell each other everything and the idea of him being unable to include her in a problem was worrying. The other alternative, that he might be ill, was even more alarming.

He was not an old man, yet as she watched him turn the corner and give a final wave, she had a frightening feeling deep inside her that all was not well.

Although they were in their fifties, Audrey and Wilf Thomas had not been married very long. Their second anniversary had been celebrated the previous January, two months ago. Now, in March 1943, the fourth year of the war, she dreaded the thought of his health declining, of him becoming sick and unable to enjoy the years they could expect to spend together.

She wondered why her thoughts had immediately taken her to this gloomy possibility. He probably had nothing worse than an imminent head cold. The years of waiting to marry Wilf had left her aware of how few were the years they could enjoy together, but until now she hadn't felt the fear of that time being shortened by ill health.

Family commitments had kept them apart for most of the years before they married and before that, forbidding them to marry had been her family's punishment for her giving birth to Wilf's son. Bobbie had died and for the years that followed they had been refused permission to marry. So strong was

1

their obedience to the family, they had accepted that they would remain single until the deaths of Molly and Joseph Piper, Audrey's parents. The frustrations and the bitterness faded and they settled into a comfortable friendship, and it was only after the death of all four parents that they had finally become man and wife.

Sometimes she wondered why her obedience to the family had been so absolute. Her sister Marged had been allowed to marry Huw Castle, and Huw and his brother Bleddyn had been welcomed into the family and accepted like sons. Wilf had been treated like an interloper and even now he was excluded from much of the family discussions and plans. The family business, which was involved in much of what went on around the beach in the town of St David's Well, was the most important part of all of their lives, yet Wilf was excluded.

She remembered her mother, Molly Piper, telling her she was a member of a very important family. The Pipers of St David's Well were largely responsible for the fame of the town, she believed. 'In fact,' she often used to say, 'Pipers *are* St David's Well.'

Now the famous Pipers were gone; Audrey had been the last and once she had married Wilf she became Mrs Wilf Thomas. Huw and Bleddyn and their families were Castles and it was under their name that the business had continued, with the Castles of St David's Well, replacing the Pipers.

Yet, even though her father and mother were dead, she still heard their voices warning her to keep her promise never to leave the family; the Castles were great because of their closeness, and if only one person broke away it might be destroyed. 'The town needs us and we need each other,' her mother Molly Piper had repeatedly said, and Audrey had never considered disobeying.

Wilf had protested at her situation in the early years and occasionally his protests would re-emerge as they waited through the long years for the moment when they would be free to marry. He had tried to persuade her to leave, move away to another town, marry and raise children, but after a while the urgency left him and, like Audrey, he had accepted the half-life of waiting.

Her acceptance of her family's wishes had been absolute

and resentment had faded in the thirty-three years since the birth and death of little Bobbie. Now, with the fear of Wilf being ill and ruining their hopes of a few happy years, it bubbled up again. The promise, never to leave the family business and to stay to help her sister Marged run the business, had been an unkind one. It had been instilled in her that as the eldest, she had a responsibility from which there was no escape.

Still watching the corner around which Wilf had vanished, Audrey sorted out the books and leather moneybag she carried, made sure she had a couple of freshly sharpened pencils and her fountain pen, and set off on her calls selling national savings stamps. The spring weather was cold but thankfully it wasn't raining. The sticky-backed stamps got in a real mess if they became damp. She had worked hard, calling each week on an increasing number of houses, marking the amount she sold in her notebook and handing in the money each week. The round she had built up now took two and sometimes three evenings to complete, and she hurried to the point at which she intended to begin that evening's collections.

By this time she usually knew how many stamps each house would buy and that made it quicker. Some even left the money in a small Oxo tin into which she would put the stamps, avoiding the need to knock. It was seven o'clock when she reached 78 Conroy Street and knocked on the door. Morgan Price lived there with his daughter Eirlys and her husband Ken Ward, with their baby son, Anthony.

It was also home to Stanley, Harold and Percival Love, who had arrived as evacuees from London and stayed on in St David's Well after they'd been orphaned. After almost four years, they were accepted by most as local boys, particularly since they had developed a hint of a Welsh accent, mixed at times with strong verbal reminders of their roots, to the amusement of their friends.

There was a loud clatter of footsteps and impatient shouting as the three evacuees raced to be first to open the door. Audrey laughed as they thrust their hands out in front of her with their sixpences ready. Stanley, aged fourteen, and his younger brothers, Harold and Percival, filled the doorway until Morgan appeared and dragged them out of the way.

3

'Come in, Audrey, step over this lot,' he said cheerfully. 'Gang of hooligans is what they are.' He was smiling as he gently cuffed the head of whichever one he could reach and held them back for her to enter.

The business dealt with, Audrey asked to see the baby. 'It's amazing how quickly they change and I haven't seen young Anthony for a week,' she said.

'He's in bed and I'm in charge,' Stanley said proudly.

Morgan Price winked at her and agreed. 'The boys are wonderful with Eirlys's little one, insisting they're his uncles. Hang on a minute and see Eirlys and Ken, why don't you? They won't be long, they've gone for a walk and they've promised to bring back some chips for this hungry lot.'

'Thanks, Morgan, but I'll carry on. Perhaps Wilf and I will call at the weekend and see you all. The girls will be waiting for their supper and I haven't finished collecting yet. Say hello to your Eirlys for me.' She cut through their garden to save herself a few steps, intending to walk along the lanes to her next call.

As she walked down the path she heard voices nearby and she stopped, not wanting to interrupt what was clearly an argument. She waited near the fence, hoping they would move on, and as the emphatic statements continued, one against the other, she recognized the bickering couple as Morgan's daughter and son-in-law, Eirlys and Ken Ward.

Eirlys and Ken Ward had a very stormy marriage. Although everyone pretended not to know, it was fairly common knowledge that Ken had had an affair with Janet Copp, the girl who sang in concerts occasionally and had helped run the market cafe.

Ken travelled all over the country organizing concerts, some to entertain the troops or factory workers, others to raise money for charities to help the sailors, soldiers and airmen. Janet was often a performer in concerts organized by Ken and their work had drawn them together. Travelling to venues and rehearsals, Ken had relied on her help more and more. Frequently finding themselves far from home, in digs that would otherwise have been lonely, a friendship had grown, and from that it had been easy to slip into a more intimate relationship.

Being away from home for much of the time and, when he

was home, finding the house filled with the noisy evacuees and Eirlys out at work, Ken had become disillusioned with marriage. Eirlys had been at home for a while after the birth of Anthony, and he had hoped that was where she would stay. But ignoring his wishes, Eirlys had returned to her work at the local council offices on a part-time basis, insisting that as soon as she felt confident enough to leave the baby she would return to full-time. In Ken's mind, her idea of going back to work was wrong and she was being stubborn in recognizing the fact that she was needed at home.

Until Anthony had been born, Eirlys had managed a very responsible job working for the local council and for the past couple of years had organized the local 'Holidays At Home' entertainment, designed to persuade people to stay at home during the war and not travel great distances to enjoy their holidays. The idea was to save valuable fuel by cutting down on the use of public transport which was needed for servicemen and their requirements. Posters asked passers by 'Is Your Journey Really Necessary?' and every town had been asked to organize events to persuade people not to travel.

Since the birth of their child, Ken had tried to persuade Eirlys not to go back to the job she loved, and this was a constant battle between them. Both were unable to forget the humiliation of Ken's affair, and Eirlys needed to do something outside the home to fill the long days when Ken was travelling, afraid her thoughts would take her down unhappy roads unless she were happily occupied.

Since January, Eirlys had been going into the office for a few hours three times a week to help out and had been promised that if she could return without much more delay, the job would be kept open for her. Her friends, Hannah and Alice Castle, supported her and looked after the baby for the hours she was away. She was pleased to be back in the busy office and impatient now to return to full employment, while Ken hoped that the strain of the part-time hours would convince her she would be unable to manage.

Audrey stood, shivering in the cold garden listening unwillingly as the well worn arguments continued on the other side of the wall.

'I'm telling you, you can't go back to work!'

5

'Ken, it's what we agreed.'

'Well I don't agree now! Anthony and I need you at home.'

Carefully, slowly, Audrey moved back from the gate. She was unhappy at overhearing things she didn't want to know.

The previous November, when their son was born, Ken had sworn to Eirlys that the affair with Janet Copp was over. Audrey knew this and believed the troubled marriage was now on firmer ground, so it was with some alarm that she heard their increasingly bitter argument.

'So, in spite of my not agreeing, in fact begging you not to, you're going back to work and you're going to leave our son with strangers,' she heard Ken say.

'Don't be so melodramatic, Ken! He won't be with strangers. Hannah and Alice love him. They are capable and caring people, they'll share the hours, and when you're home he'll be with you.'

'I'd be afraid, Eirlys, to be honest. I might not know what to do,' he confessed.

'Then Hannah or Alice will manage. It isn't as difficult as you try to make out.'

'You can't do this to me or to Anthony. Please Eirlys. What happened to love, honour and obey? Do as I ask and stay home.'

'I can't obey you on this, Ken. It's for both of us and I'll need your help. Please support me in this.'

Audrey stood as close to the wall as she could, wondering whether to call out or stay still and hope she wasn't discovered. The couple had obviously stopped walking to continue their discussion and she knew she had left it too late.

Ken's voice became louder and more emphatic as he said, 'You don't *need* to work. What will people think of me not being able to keep my wife and child? It's humiliating, have you thought of that? And besides, there are plenty of people who can arrange the town's summer entertainment, what makes you think you're so indispensable?'

Eirlys had admitted to Audrey that she didn't have enough confidence in Ken – in their marriage – to place her future and that of her son in his hands. If he strayed again, she needed to know she would be able to earn enough for them to survive without him. Eirlys's heart gave a sudden leap as these thoughts reoccurred. If Ken knew how her thoughts were running he would be hurt, and temptation sometimes only needed a bit of a nudge to tip it over the edge from dream into desire and then fulfilment.

'Please, Ken. Don't fight me on this,' Eirlys pleaded. 'I loved my job and you have to admit that I did it well. Besides all the routine tasks of running the office, I set in motion all the town's summer entertainment. I was thrilled with the success, proud of what I had achieved and I want to do it again. This war can't go on for ever, even though it feels as though it might. Once it's over, everything will go back to how it was. Women will go back to running their homes and bringing up the children, and the jobs will be returned to the men.'

'Not you!' he retorted bitterly. 'There'll always be an excuse for you to do something different! I wouldn't mind if I were based at home, but I'm away for days at a time and Anthony ought to have you there as a constant face, a reassurance.'

'But he'll have that. He already knows and loves Alice and Hannah. Dadda works shifts and he's there for a part of every day. And I'll be there every evening.'

'No, Eirlys. I absolutely forbid it. If you really loved him you wouldn't even consider it.'

Pressed against the wall, the unwilling eavesdropper tried to move back the way she had come, through the garden and into the street. If only they would walk away. She didn't want them to know they were overheard and it was too late now to show herself. She stepped sideways, testing with her feet for any unlikely object that might trip her, her hands feeling the wall in the darkness. But no, it was impossible to move so far in silence. There was an apple tree in the opposite corner of the garden. If she could hide in its shadows until they moved, she might prevent them knowing she had heard them.

It was as she was feeling her way past the gate that a cobweb touched her face and startled her. She dropped a pen on to the concrete path and it sounded loud in the silence that she was desperately trying to preserve.

'Someone's coming,' she heard Eirlys say.

'Damn, now I'll never find it!' Audrey exclaimed loudly.

The gate opened and Ken and Eirlys appeared, carrying the unmistakable smell of chips with them, and she explained

7

about the lost pen. Using his own torch Ken bent down to search for it.

Keeping the pretence, Audrey said, 'There's lucky I am to meet you two. My own torch has become too weak to find a thing.'

The pen found, pleasantries were exchanged, Audrey went on her way. From what she had heard, she knew that the job at the council offices which had been kept open for Eirlys, was the bone of contention. It was an extremely demanding one with long hours and a great deal of overtime. Organizing the 'Holidays At Home' entertainment for the seaside town of St David's Well had taken all of Eirlys's time the previous year, and with the baby only four months old, no one had expected her to return to it. But it seemed they were wrong and Eirlys had intended to keep her promise to her bosses, Mr Gifford and Mr Johnston, to go back when the season began. Remembering the child she had lost so many years before, she wondered whether she would have done the same, and admitted that in the circumstances Eirlys found herself, she probably would. Although, being a part of the Castle family who ran the stalls and rides and cafes on the beach would have made a difference. Being involved in the family business wasn't the same as working for the council. All the Castles worked on the sands or close by, sharing responsibility for the care of the children as they came; the children themselves being given jobs as soon as they were able. It wasn't like a job, it was more a way of life.

Feeling inexplicably saddened by the quarrel she had unintentionally overheard, she abandoned the rest of her collections and went home. She and Wilf lived in the house that had been her mother's and she shared it with two girls, whom they had unofficially adopted, Maude and Myrtle. In the flat at the top of the house, Marged's son, Ronnie, lived with his wife, Olive, and their child. She was glad of the feeling of activity in the place, thankful for having Wilf, thankful of not being alone. Being a part of a family like the Castles didn't prepare you for being on your own. The shiver of apprehension passed over her and she hurried in to be reassured by Wilf, who stood up to greet her.

'Everything all right?' she asked.

8

'Everything's fine, my lovely girl. Maude has the cocoa mixed in the cups, the kettle's singing on the hearth and the bread is ready to toast for supper. Myrtle is at the pictures with Alice.'

She hugged him, glad of his familiar body pressed against her own, breathing in the well known scent of him, his warmth making her realize how cold she had become walking around the streets.

He whispered, 'I love you, Audrey Thomas. So much, that you can warm your feet on me when we get to bed! How's that for a declaration of love, eh?'

'You're daft,' she said with a chuckle.

'Daft about you, Audrey Piper.'

'Audrey Thomas and proud of it,' she amended.

Eirlys took the newspaper-wrapped package of chips into the house for the three boys and wondered whether she was doing the right thing by insisting on returning to work. Determination and guilt took her on a regular switchback ride as she tried to do what was best for everyone, including herself. She wanted – needed – the challenges of work, and, she reminded herself, she had promised her bosses.

She had tried to persuade Ken that her reason was to earn money for them to buy a house one day, but they both knew that she would never be able to leave her father or the three evacuees. No, she wanted this for herself, her peace of mind: her and Anthony's security.

Ken went to the phone box outside their house and spent half an hour arranging auditions and booking artistes for his forthcoming concert which was to take place in Cardiff. When he came in and started writing up his diaries and notebooks, she settled the boys, checked the baby and went to bed.

When Ken came up she lay still, and when he touched her she shrugged his hand away. Then guilt overcame her and she turned, put an arm around him and said, 'Sorry, Ken.'

He raised himself up on an elbow and looked down at her, the light from the landing – insisted on by ten-year-old Percival – making her face a confusion of shadows. 'Sorry? Does that mean you'll listen to me and tell Mr Gifford you won't be going back to full-time work?'

9

'No. It just means I'm sorry I pushed you away, sorry you're unable to understand. You know how much I want the job. I've made arrangements for Anthony to be looked after, so why do we have to quarrel about it?'

'Because you should be here, at home, waiting for me. Whenever I can escape for a few precious days, I don't want to sit in an empty house until you can spare a few moments of your valuable time. It isn't fair.' The quarrel, that had been interrupted in the lane by Audrey, went on. The fact that it was whispered didn't make it any less bitter.

They got up together the following morning, unrested after a night spent reliving their argument and thinking of fresh reasons to convince the other of the power of their opinion. Ken dealt with the ashes of the previous day's fire and re-lit it, while Eirlys made a pot of tea and began to set the table for breakfast.

As she stood to go and collect Anthony from his cot, Ken put an arm around her. 'Eirlys, my darling. Remember that however much we argue, I still love you. I know that I couldn't be happy without you and Anthony in my life. Whatever happens, there's nothing in the world that we can't sort out together.'

She reassured him and tried to accept his declaration of love and commitment, although there was always the little niggle of doubt. It would be a long time before her confidence in him and their marriage was fully restored.

While she bathed, changed and fed Anthony, Ken said, 'It would be different if we were on our own, just you, me and Anthony, but living here with the house filled to bursting, never having a moment's privacy, any time we have together should be special. With you out all day there'll be precious little chance of that. I hate coming home to an empty house, knowing you could be here with me.'

'There's no chance of us finding a place of our own for a long time. You know Dadda can't cope with the boys on his own, but one day we'll have our own home, I promise.'

'I admit I hated sharing with the three boys at first, but now I like the little beggars and I'd miss them if we moved away.'

Suddenly, the three boys themselves tumbled down the stairs, Stanley, cuffing Harold and Percival as they argued about who was to sit where. In an aside, Ken ruefully said he'd like to take back his last remark, and he and Eirlys shared a smile that was free from dissension.

'Shut yer eyes, brovers, they're going to kiss,' twelve-year-old Harold said with a groan of mock disapproval, slapping his hands over his eyes.

'I likes kissin',' the solemn Percival said and was rewarded by a look of absolute horror from Harold and a wink from Stanley.

Eirlys dealt with breakfast. There was very little fat left from the ration, but she managed to fry a few leftover boiled potatoes to fill their plates, sharing two poached eggs by giving them a half each. Sliding half of the softly cooked eggs from one plate to another, without giving one a greater share of the yolk than the other, called for a swift and confident movement, and Eirlys managed it with practised ease. Bread toasted in front of the now glowing fire on which they could have either butter or jam – not both – plus a cup of cocoa, filled them up and she put aside a round of toast for herself for later once the house was quiet and she could relax.

The noisy early morning activity reached its peak as the three boys dashed out of the house followed slowly by Ken leaving for his first appointment. The pulse of frenetic movement, the panic as the boys searched for various things they would need during the morning, mercifully slowed, relaxing into the promise of mid-morning calm. For a moment Eirlys enjoyed the silence. She looked around her, at dishes needing her attention, the sewing box overflowing with shirts needing buttons and trousers needing mending, and knew that it would never be enough. Running a home and looking after six people was hard, but if she did this and nothing more, there would always be something missing. She couldn't imagine ever not wanting to work.

Audrey wanted to give Wilf a surprise for his birthday. The chair he favoured was rather shabby – lace chair backs and cheerfully embroidered cushion covers could no longer disguise its dilapidated state. She would have liked him to have a new one, but it was almost impossible to buy from the limited display in the furniture shops of the town. Dockets were needed, to which few were entitled. Newly-weds were given priority, but even they weren't allowed sufficient dockets to completely fill a house without resorting to second-hand, even if they could find the money.

Furnishing a complete home was a problem for very few as most couples began their married life in either their parents' houses or with a neighbour, people helping by giving items they no longer needed. There was a cot and a highchair that had gone up and down the street, passed on as one child outgrew the need, on to others and back again when another baby arrived.

After discussing the problem with Maude, Myrtle and Marged, she decided to look around the sales rooms in the hope of finding a good second-hand chair.

With only a week to go, she managed to find a solidly built leather-covered fireside chair that seemed perfect. There was a handicraft shop in the town run by Eirlys along with Hannah Castle and Beth Gregory, two of Audrey's nieces. She went there to buy a couple of cushions and, carrying them, went to pay for the chair.

She'd had to borrow the money off Marged, because when she'd called at the bank to raise the money, she'd been told that there weren't sufficient funds. Alarmed at first, she'd argued, then decided that Wilf had probably sensibly taken any excess from the account and transferred it to their building society account.

'You spent all that money on me?' Wilf exclaimed when given his present. He didn't sound as pleased as she had hoped. 'Where did you get the money from? The bank?'

'Well, not exactly.' She told him about the embarrassing moment and borrowing the money from Marged.

'Sorry, I should have told you I transferred it. But I wish you hadn't spent so much on me. I was quite happy with the old chair. It's moulded itself around my body and it's a perfect fit.' He tried to laugh but Audrey was disappointed at his reaction.

'What I want for *my* birthday is a holiday,' she said lightly, hiding her face so he wouldn't see her disappointment.

'A good idea, lovely girl. Let's go and see about it tomorrow. We could go to Cornwall or Devon – I've never seen that area and it's supposed to be beautiful.'

12

'It will have to wait until the autumn,' she reminded him. 'The summer season will be starting soon and I won't be able to get away.'

'Always the same, no time for anything once the season begins,' he said softly. 'The Castle family business is a greedy mistress.'

'You aren't happy being a part of it?'

'I'm not a part of it and never will be, dear. But I'm happy as long as you're doing what you really want to do, you know that.'

'But you wish it could be different?' She frowned and asked, 'Is there something wrong, Wilf? You would tell me if something were bothering you, wouldn't you?'

'Nothing to worry about, but I do sometimes wish we could have the life we'd chosen instead of you having been born into this one. Don't you?'

'Sometimes. But being a member of the Castles isn't a bad life. My only regret is that we haven't spent the years together. Come on,' she coaxed, 'try out your new chair.'

He pushed it near the fire where the other one had stood for so long and settled into its comforting cushions. 'It's perfect, lovely girl. Just like you.'

'Marged and Huw are coming over later on. We have to try and work out rotas to cover all the stalls and cafe openings. And Huw and Bleddyn want to plan what questions they need to ask at the meeting of all those involved in "Holidays at Home" next week. Finding sufficient staff will be a problem once again. Won't it be lovely when our boys are back, and Alice and Maude can leave the factory and things settle back to how they were in 1939?'

'I don't think it will ever be the same, Audrey.'

'No, poor Bleddyn will never see his son Taff again. Our Ronnie's wounds won't let him do what he used to. All the young Castle boys loved working on the sands, didn't they? It seems a lifetime since we were all there together.'

'This war must end soon, the killing and the destruction can't go on much longer.' he comforted. 'Your two nephews, Ronnie and Eynon, will be back and grateful for the way you and Marged, Huw and Bleddyn have kept everything going for them.'

13

'Bleddyn and Hetty are coming to the meeting too. I thought we'd make a few sandwiches.'

'Already done and in the pantry under plates to keep them fresh,' he said. 'The big tray is set ready for teas.'

'Oh Wilf, what would I do without you?'

Again that little stab of fear.

Marged, Huw and Bleddyn were at the beach looking around to make sure nothing urgently needed fixing before the season began. The two brothers kicked the sand discussing where on the beach they would place the helter-skelter and the swingboats. Soon, the stalls would appear; stalls that had once sold ice cream and toffee apples, sweets and sticks of rock, but had changed to selling any items that could justifiably be called requirements for the sands. The powerfully built, bearded Bleddyn ran his heel around, gouging out a line in the sand to mark out the areas they would need. He and Huw discussed the men they would need to help when they took the prefabricated buildings out of store.

Before leaving the environs of the beach, they met Bernard Gregory with his string of donkeys, which gave rides to children on the beach throughout the summer months.

'You're too early, Bernard,' Huw shouted. 'There's no one on the sands yet.'

'I like to give them a walk now and then so they don't forget what they have to do,' Bernard said, lifting his trilby. 'I can check that the saddles are comfortable, too. Won't be long, mind. A couple more weeks delivering logs and firewood then their tips come off.'

The donkeys weren't allowed to give rides on the sand wearing tips or shoes, in case they accidentally trod on a child's foot. But a few of them worked during the winter and these needed shoes for walking the roads making deliveries. Removing them was the first sign that summer was about to begin.

Eirlys called in at the handicraft shop where she had arranged to meet Hannah and Alice Castle. Eirlys, Hannah and Beth Gregory ran the shop between them, each doing as many hours as they could spare, Alice also helping when she could. She shouted, and Alice came out and helped her carry the pram inside. Anthony was asleep and they were able to talk.

Taking a half-finished pair of gloves, Eirlys picked up stitches for the first finger and said, 'You *are* sure about sharing the care of Anthony if I go back to work full-time? I don't think we can rely on Ken for much. He's afraid of being in charge of such a young child. He'll be fine when Anthony's older, I'm sure.'

Hannah, who was married to Bleddyn's son Johnny, handed her a page of writing. It was a neatly printed timetable of how the shared responsibility would work.

'I can manage a few evenings, Eirlys,' Alice said, 'but Hannah's children mean that she can't. So if you need to work after five o'clock, you'll have to make sure I'm on the right shift at the factory.'

'Thank you,' Eirlys said warmly. 'I'm so grateful to you both. Dadda will help, of course, and between us I think we'll cope. If there are any problems, well, Anthony comes first and I'll have to learn the art of delegation.'

'You've talked Ken round, then?' Alice said.

'More or less. Although in truth it's more less than more, if you see what I mean,' Eirlys said with a laugh.

'Good luck,' Hannah said softly, her gentle face a little troubled.

Leaving the baby with her friends, Eirlys went to see her bosses and told them she was ready to return to her normal duties. Mr Gifford and Mr Johnston were delighted and promised to lend her one of the office girls for a few weeks while she caught up with what had been happening in her absence.

'There's the usual start-of-season meeting next Tuesday,' she was told by Mr Gifford. 'All the showground people and hotel and guest house owners have been invited, including the Castle family and others with businesses over on St David's Well Bay. I'll chair and you can take notes, that way you'll slip back into the swing of things with ease.'

Eirlys went home pleased, but apprehensive about telling Ken what she had done.

Meanwhile, in the handicraft shop, Alice took out a letter she had received that week from her husband, Eynon, one of Marged's sons. 'You can read it if you like, Hannah,' she

15

offered, so Hannah in turn opened her handbag and gave her friend a letter she had received from her husband, Johnny. Both letters were short, saying little more than that they were well, things were quiet and they hoped to be home very soon. In both, a sentence had been 'blue-pencilled' out and the letters ended with loving words that made them feel sad and empty.

'It's one I can show Johnny's father,' Hannah said as she replaced it in her handbag. 'I always share them when I can. The news is so precious.'

'They tell us so little. I wonder if we'll ever learn what these years have been like for them.'

'I doubt it. I think Eynon and Johnny will both want to forget and settle back into the pretend, fun and sun world of St David's Well Bay, don't you?'

'So will I,' Alice replied fervently. 'Children having fun, families all together, dads as well as mums. Laughing at nothing at all and enjoying the ordinary things. I can't wait to have Eynon home and to be a part of it all again.'

'Mrs Thomas?' Audrey heard as she bent down to pick up the milk one morning a few days later. She looked around and saw a neighbour pointing up at her roof. 'You got a slate slipped,' the woman informed her, pointing up to a place near the smoking chimney.

Audrey remembered seeing a man working on a roof in a street nearby and she went around and arranged for the builder, Keith Kent, to call and 'take a look'.

Keith went up and examined the fault. It wasn't a big job but it might be worth doing at a low price, or even for nothing. The Castles had several properties and this might lead to regular maintenance work if he did a good job.

When Audrey told Wilf that she had approached a builder, he didn't seem pleased. It was usual for her to deal with such things and she was surprised by his reaction.

'A man called Keith Kent is coming to look at the job this afternoon,' she had told him, and Wilf had nodded and said he would be there to deal with him. In fact, he sent him away. When Audrey asked him why, he explained that he would fix the slate himself. 'No need to waste money on a simple job like that.'

'We can afford it, so why risk a fall? Even Huw jibs at a repair on a high roof. Keith Kent is a builder and he's used to heights. You are not either.'

She said nothing more and when the slate was still out of place a week later, she went to find Keith, who was working on an extension and repairs at the local hospital. A brief explanation, a little subterfuge and she had arranged for him to come at a time when she knew Wilf would be out.

Keith came as promised and dealt with the repair quickly. If Wilf noticed that the work had been done, he didn't remark on it. She was puzzled by his refusal to deal with the small repair. She was more curious a few days later when she proudly told him she had saved enough clothing coupons for him to have a new suit, and to her surprise and dismay he refused that too, insisting it was an unnecessary waste of money.

She tried to persuade him to explain. 'Are you saving for something special? Is that it? The holiday I mentioned, maybe? We can't stop buying what we need to make sure we have a holiday, Wilf. Besides, we don't need to economise that much – we can afford a new suit and have repairs done and go on a little holiday. Once the season's over, that's what we'll do, all right? A few days in Devon or Cornwall, just as you wanted.'

'There's nothing to explain,' he said airily. 'I just don't think we should be spending money on things we can do without. Besides, I don't want one of these utility suits with a single-breasted jacket and no turn-ups on the trousers. No, forget it, Audrey love. I want to take you on a wonderful holiday and I want that more than I want a slate straightened or a new suit.'

'But we can afford all those things, can't we? Come on, love, we aren't young anymore and we have enough to see us through a comfortable old age, so why not enjoy ourselves?'

'Audrey, if anything happens to me, I want you to be comfortably off. I want you to be able to stop working if you feel you want to.'

'There is something wrong! I knew it! Tell me, Wilf, please.'

'There's nothing to worry about. I've been thinking about things that's all. My birthday is probably the cause. We're getting older. It's nothing more than that.'

17

'Promise me?'

'I want *you* to promise *me* something.'

'Don't, Wilf. Promises can be unwise, creating a burden that gets heavier as the years go by.'

'This isn't a promise like your mother made you give, tying you to stay and help your sister Marged for ever, and to never leave the business. That one should have been forgotten as soon as it was made, not been allowed to hold you back from what you wanted to do for all these years.' There was a hint of bitterness, then he smiled. 'All I want is a promise that you'll forgive me if I've done anything you disapprove of and that you won't waste the years you have left, that if I go first, you'll do something with your life, not spend the precious days grieving and being a slave to my memory.'

'We have to make those promises to each other, my love,' she said, hugging him to hide the fear that must surely show in her eyes. 'Please God, it won't happen for a long time yet.'

'Amen to that, lovely girl.'

Two

Myrtle pushed the heavy carrier bicycle wearily up Mill Lane, thankful that the delivery of groceries to Mr and Mrs Grange was the last. Since the age of thirteen she had helped whenever she could with the deliveries of weekly orders for the corner shop's customers. Now that she had left school and worked on the beach during the summer, the job was becoming tedious, and she was aware that most deliveries were undertaken by boys not girls, and all of them were much younger than herself. She was becoming more and more conscious of her mature status as an ex-schoolgirl. It was becoming a bit embarrassing, although the two shillings and sixpence she was paid was welcome.

As it was only April, the season was not yet underway in the small Welsh seaside town of St David's Well, and during the winter months she had done a variety of jobs, afraid to take on something permanent as that might mean she wouldn't be free to work on the sands when summer came. With the war into its fourth year, everyone was expected to do something to help the fight against Hitler. If she had been a little older, she would have been forced to take on work that helped the war effort and the Castle family would have lost another enthusiastic member of the team that worked on the sands.

It was only the fact of her young age and the continuing need for entertainment to help people to cope with the shortages and the losses of war, that enabled her to avoid factory or farm work. Myrtle loved the beach, and enjoyed helping the Castle family with their swingboats and helter-skelter and the various stalls and cafes they owned.

Myrtle, and her elder sister Maude, had been placed in a children's home when they were very young, after their parents were killed in a road accident. A belief that somewhere there

19

were people to whom they were related, had made them run away to search for them and it was while they were living rough, and Maude was seriously ill, that they had been found and taken in by Marged and Huw Castle. Now, they were regarded as part of the family and treated the same as the rest.

They lived in Sidney Street with Audrey and her husband Wilf. Running a business together meant the family was a close one and for Myrtle and Maude their belonging had brought them contentment, although Maude still had night-mares about their months living alone and surviving on what they could beg or steal. She constantly needed reassurances from Myrtle that she wouldn't be left to cope alone. Maude's greatest fear was that Myrtle, who was only fifteen, would find a boyfriend and abandon her. That fear made her act unreasonably at times, as nightmares of living alone and perhaps being ill and no one knowing or able to help, returned frequently to haunt her.

Myrtle was remarkably tough, showing no sign of their deprivation, while Maude had never recovered robust health after her adventurous weeks living out of doors during a cold, wet autumn and winter without proper food. Tall, with long, light brown hair and mischievous dark eyes, Myrtle was painfully thin and with the black woollen school stockings she still wore, was often teased; something with which she coped well, her bright mind returning insults with ease.

Riding along, her feet off the pedals now, allowing the heavy bike to freewheel down the hill below which she could see the blue sea, Myrtle sang and shouted, and thought she couldn't be much happier. Life would be perfect if only Maude would get out more and make friends of her own instead of depending on me so much, she thought with a sigh. She had been invited to spend an evening with Eirlys and Ken Ward. She'd had to refuse though, knowing how upset Maude would have been if she suggested leaving her on her own. If she weren't included in an invitation, Maude had a knack of making her feel too guilty to accept.

Maude gave regular but subtle reminders of the promises Myrtle had willingly given when Maude had been so ill. A promise never to leave her had gradually extended to only accepting invitations if Maude were invited too.

20

Clinging to each other throughout one long, cold winter, hiding away from authority while they searched in vain for someone they could regard as family, had made them abnormally dependent on each other, afraid to be apart, something the friendly Myrtle had quickly outgrown. Maude was just eighteen but she was utterly dependent on her young sister, and as she grew and wanted to enjoy a wider social life, Myrtle found the situation worrying. With increasing guilt for what Maude quietly implied was her selfishness, she wondered whether she would ever be free like other girls, to enjoy new friendships offered by girls – and boys. Or was she to remain forever tied to her unhappy and gently demanding sister?

As part of her weekly routine during the winter months, Myrtle also went each weekday morning to a children's home similar to the one in which she and Maude had lived. There, she helped with the cooking and earned enough to give something to Audrey for her keep. Most afternoons she went to help at Bernard Gregory's smallholding and she arrived there this afternoon in April to find Bernard's neighbour, Sally Gough, there.

Bernard and Sally were in serious conversation, so she waved and went through to where the tools were kept and began gathering the items she would need. Today, she had promised to hoe between the spindly carrots, spring onions – locally called gibbons – and radishes, all just showing above the earth in what had once been the old orchard.

Sally Gough owned the field in which Bernard Gregory kept his string of donkeys during the winter months. Bernard had built stables for them which were close to the boundary between Sally's land and Bernard's property. Sally had come to tell Bernard that the land was no longer hers.

'It seems the government insist the fields are used for growing crops, and as I'm too old, I have to let them out for someone else to work or they'll be confiscated,' she told Bernard. 'I wondered if you'd take them on. With your own field being so close, it seems the best solution.'

Bernard relit his pipe and looked thoughtful. 'It's a bit late in the year for starting new ground, mind,' he said, puffing on a recalcitrant pipe. 'It should have been prepared last autumn. And I'll need a bit of help, too. Tell you what, I'll think about

21

it and call you in the morning, when I've slept on it.'

'Don't leave it any later,' Sally warned. 'Powers they've got these days and the government can send men to come and take the field from me without notice.'

'I'll talk to young Beth, she's got a good head on her shoulders and she'll help me think it out.' He watched as Sally walked up the lane to where her small cottage stood, smoke climbing lazily upward from the chimney, and sighed. Sally had lived there all her life, as had three generations before her. Now it was nothing more than a neglected building surrounded by a couple of small, abandoned fields. She was lucky the land hadn't been taken from her before. The war had given the government necessary control, but at times it was frightening.

Myrtle worked until it was almost dark, the bright day lengthening the evening, so time slipped past with only hunger reminding her it was time to leave. She saw Beth coming home from her cafe in the local market, as she headed towards her bike. Beth was Marged and Huw Castle's daughter and was married to Bernard's son, Peter, and seemed to be in deep conversation with Bernard.

'Myrtle, sorry you're late, I forgot the time, but can you spare a couple more minutes?'

She stood, legs astride the ancient bicycle that Mr Gregory had found for her and waited curiously. Mr Gregory told her briefly what Sally Gough had said and he asked her what she thought about him extending his activities by taking over the fields.

'Best if you do, Mr Gregory,' she said politely. 'You won't know who your neighbour will be otherwise, and it might be someone who cares less about the land than you do. With some extra help you'd manage and it's all to beat old Hitler, isn't it?'

He smiled and nodded. 'I must admit I like the idea. It's something I've often thought of, but we're into April and the work of clearing the ground should have been started months ago.'

'You'll soon get ahead. Will it be potatoes to start with, to help clean the ground?'

'You're a quick learner, young Myrtle!' he said with a laugh.

22

'All right, I'll go and see Sally first thing in the morning and take things from there.' He looked at her thoughtfully. 'Would you be willing to work here full-time? I'll need extra help and I'd take on someone temporarily at first to deal with the heavy work of clearing the ground. I wouldn't expect you to do that, Myrtle, but afterwards I think you'd do well. What d'you think?'

'I like working here, growing things is fun, but I can't let Mr and Mrs Castle down. It's getting hard for them to find people to run the stalls and rides and things on the sands, with men and women called up or sent to work in factories.'

'I understand, Myrtle, but if you change your mind, let me know, right?'

Myrtle cycled back to the house in Stanley Street, where Audrey and her husband Wilf were standing on the doorstep anxiously looking up the street waiting for her to appear.

'Sorry, Auntie Audrey,' she called as she slid off her bike and pushed it into the hallway. 'Mr Gregory needed my advice about something,' she said jokingly. 'Wants me to work for him full-time, but I told him I'm needed on the sands until the end of summer.' She chattered happily as she went through to the kitchen to wash before sitting at the table, explaining about Sally Gough's field and her suggestion that Mr Gregory took it over.

Wilf laughingly said, 'Hush, lovely girl and start again, I can't make out what you're on about! You start talking the minute you're through the door. I've never known such a whirlwind!' He shared a smile with Audrey before adding, 'I wish I had your energy – and joy.'

'Go on with you, Uncle Wilf. Happy as a pair of larks you and Auntie Audrey.' She explained in more detail what Sally Gough had suggested, then asked, 'Well? What d'you think of Mr Gregory's extension then?'

'Marvellous, so long as he doesn't keep you there too often. As you say, we need you on the beach.'

'And that's what I told him, Auntie Audrey, when he asked if I'd work for him full-time. "The Castles are wonderful people, but they can't manage without me," I said.' Audrey and Wilf were laughing as the lively girl found her place at the table.

23

Myrtle's solemn-faced sister, was sitting at the corner of the table where the teapot, milk and cups stood. She poured the teas and handed her sister a cup. 'What a cheek,' she said. 'Working for him full-time would mean every hour God sends. As if you aren't doing enough already, the hours you put in and all for the few shillings the mean old devil pays you.'

'He's not a mean old devil. I was pleased, our Maude. In fact, I wouldn't mind the job, growing things is real satisfying. But it isn't as good as the beach in summer. That's magic,' she said to reassure Audrey that she was not about to let them down. 'St David's Well Bay in summer, yes, that's where I want to be, and coming home starving hungry for one of Auntie Audrey's dinners, eh, Uncle Wilf?'

Audrey began to serve helpings of steamed suet pudding with a small amount of meat at the bottom. Potatoes and some late leeks filled the plates and the lack of meat was disguised with helpings of Bisto gravy. As usual, the enthusiastic Myrtle was the first to empty her plate.

Later that evening, Audrey took the tablecloths from the cafe which she had freshly laundered, to Marged a few doors down the road and found Marged washing out some small meat-paste jars ready to fill with flowers for the cafe tables. Huw was chewing a pencil and making a list of jobs, then seeing Audrey, made the excuse that he needed to see his brother Bleddyn.

'Off for a pint they'll be,' Marged muttered.

'There's lucky we are to have Myrtle and Maude,' Audrey said, explaining about Mr Gregory's attempt to coax her away from the beach. 'Specially young Myrtle. She's so lively she'd revive a corpse!'

Work began almost at once on the field. A team of young boys was sent from the agricultural college, and with Bernard working with them for all the hours of daylight, the field was cleaned and dug during the last weeks of April and early May, and within a few weeks was ready for planting. Myrtle came regularly to help and was pleased to see she had been right about the potatoes.

'There's no magic involved, there's nothing in the potatoes to kill off the weeds and grass,' she told one of the students.

24

'It's the digging, and the earthing up and hoeing between the rows, then digging again to harvest the crop, all the time clearing weeds. All that digging and hoeing and weed-clearing helps to clean the ground.'

She knew that lifting the potatoes towards the end of summer was back-breaking work and admitted to Mr Gregory that she wouldn't be sorry to miss it. 'The beach is opening up and already the town is filling up as day trippers are coming to St David's Well to enjoy a day out,' she told him. 'So I won't be able to help much after this week.'

'Come when you can, you're welcome any time. A shaft of sunshine you are, young Myrtle,' Mr Gregory said and he nodded to Beth for her to add her agreement.

The cafes along the promenade and the gift shops had now shed their winter boardings, windows were cleaned and steps scrubbed. Windows were decked in whatever the owners could find to tempt customers into their shops and the smell of chips frying filled the air.

Audrey, who with Wilf had been delivering freshly baked scones to the Castle's cafe high above the beach, looked out at the golden sands of the bay and smiled. The beach was like a hibernating animal, waking and stretching its limbs.

'But it won't truly come alive again until Eynon and Alice are reunited, and Johnny comes home to his Hannah,' she said sadly. 'No matter how hard we try, behind the smiling faces there's the fear that threatens us all. A telegram, a letter from a friend, the feeling that the next moment will bring the news we all dread.'

'Try to be confident of their return, love,' Wilf said. 'I feel that we keep them safe with our thoughts and unhappy dread isn't what we want to go winging across the miles, now is it?'

'Perhaps this will be the last summer without them. Perhaps this year it will finally end.'

'Everything has to end sometime, lovely girl.'

Audrey glanced at him and saw that melancholy had settled on his handsome features and she regretted spoiling the mood.

'Don't listen to me, Wilf, dear. You're right. They'll be home again soon, and what a party we'll have then, eh?'

* * *

25

Maude worked in a factory but she was often absent from work because of illness. She had suffered more than Myrtle from the time they had been homeless and each winter brought on chest infections and almost continuous colds and coughs. Audrey had taken her to the doctor on numerous occasions, but he assured them both that it was nothing serious, and certainly not the tuberculosis they both secretly feared. So when she felt unwell, she would take to her bed and be fussed over by Audrey and Myrtle; Myrtle reading to her and spending as much time as she was able, although it was never enough to stop Maude from complaining about her neglect.

On the way home from her day at the beach cafe, Myrtle would go straight to Maude and ask about her day, which, she already knew, would never be as happy as her own.

'It's a shame you have to work in that factory, our Maude. If only the doctor would say you had to work outside then you could help on the beach and you'd throw off these colds as soon as you got them.'

'Auntie Audrey has tried,' Maude reminded her. 'Every time we see the doctor she asks, but he refuses, insisting I'm not sick enough to be excused from war work.'

'Thank goodness I'm only fifteen. Nearly sixteen, mind,' she added proudly, although with some exaggeration. 'The war's bound to be over before I'm old enough to be called up.'

'If only I'd passed the medical when I tried to join the Wrens,' Maude sighed. 'Not even the Land Army wanted me.

'Glad I am that you didn't. I'd miss you, Maude.'

'Yes, we must always stay together, mustn't we? Nothing must separate us, you promise?'

Willingly, as in the past, Myrtle promised.

Overhearing them, Audrey frowned. It was a wicked thing to make a fifteen year old promise. Myrtle wasn't able to think ahead to a time she might want to do something her sister begged her not to do, when Maude could remind her of a promise so solemnly and unthinkingly given. A spurt of anger flooded Audrey's mind. Once, she had been forced to take a path she hadn't wanted, and it was something she would always regret. While she had been in a vulnerable state, she had been persuaded that she had no right to her dreams, no

26

right to be happy. She had given up on a great many dreams because of a similar promise, a decision forced upon her when she was too young and vulnerable to realize that such a promise could, and perhaps should, be broken.

Resentment, so long hidden in Audrey's mind beneath layers of guilt and obedience and a sense of duty, was coming to the surface more frequently, and seeing the willingness of Myrtle to accept her sister's subtle domination, hardened her heart more strongly.

Audrey Thomas and her sister Marged were not equals, because their mother had deemed it so. One had been more dominant since they'd been children. Although Audrey was the elder, she had deferred to her sister for the whole of her life. Now, at the age of fifty-two, with a worrying suspicion that her darling Wilf might be ill, Audrey was aware of a growing dislike towards her sister. For too long she had allowed Marged – and before her their mother, Molly Piper – to tell her what to do. Looking around her at people the same age as herself, who were sharing the fun of children and grandchildren and being an important member of a growing and loving family, she was aware of just how much she and Wilf had missed, how cruelly her sister had robbed them by emphasizing the extent of their shame and making her keep to her unwise promises.

She didn't want Myrtle to suffer in the same way, but didn't know how to warn her without causing a rift between herself and the sisters. Perhaps even that was wrong; to worry so much about offending someone so that you were unable to be honest.

The Castle family's business was a complex one including cafes, a shop, plus the stalls and rides every summer. Audrey rarely became involved at the beach; it had been her role to keep house for her mother and deal with the housekeeping side of the business, and, until Granny Molly Piper's death, she had accepted that.

When she and Wilf Thomas had married, so late in their lives, she had expected things to change and when they did not – she had been expected to continue to deal with the domestic side of things, besides look after Maude and Myrtle – her bitterness had slowly grown. She said little to Wilf who was more philosophical, thankful that they had at last married and grateful for every day they spent together.

Sitting in the quiet kitchen, waiting for Wilf to return from his afternoon stroll, she began to wonder if they would ever find a way of breaking away from the responsibilities that had crowded everything else out of her world, and make a different life for themselves. She was unaware that Wilf, sitting in the weak sunshine of the early May afternoon in 1943, was mulling over similar thoughts.

In spite of the sun, there was a weariness on many faces of the people wandering around St David's Well. Beth Gregory, who owned the cafe in a corner of the town's market, felt saddened as she looked around at the neat, clean, but poorly-dressed shoppers. They would flop down on one of her chairs and order a cup of tea that was pale and for which she felt like apologizing, if it weren't for the fact that there was nothing she could do about it. Rationing affected cafes as well as the housewife.

She saw her mother approaching and called her over. Marged thankfully put down the heavy basket containing some newspaper-wrapped packages and a bunch of bluebells picked from the woods near the town, and Beth handed her a cup of tea. 'Sorry it's so weak, Mam, but it's the end of the week and I have to make it last until Saturday evening,' she apologized.

'Wet and warm'll do for me, love. I've brought you a lot of knitting wool. Mrs Denver gave it to me. It will do for making some toys and small garments for you to sell in your shop.'

Whenever she found a spare moment, Beth helped to keep the shop well stocked with handmade items. Working what hours they could, she and Eirlys and Hannah kept the shop open, sitting sewing or knitting between attending to customers.

'Mrs Denver thought our Lilly would like it to knit for little Phyllis,' Marged went on with a tut of disapproval, 'but there's more chance of a man walking on the moon than our Lilly doing something useful!'

Beth's sister, Lilly, had escaped from family commitments

28

by marrying an older man and she lived comfortably in his house with her daughter, Phyllis, who was just about to celebrate her third birthday. Lilly's husband, Sam, was wealthy enough to have paid help in the house and many of the tasks that Lilly might reasonably expect to do were performed by Sam himself. Although everyone in the Castle family helped with the various businesses, particularly during the summer season, Lilly had never been willing. Marriage to Sam Edwards had given her a life free from worries and she loved it. As long as she managed to avoid having another child, she foresaw years of idle contentment.

Thinking of this, Marged looked at her daughter Beth and smiled. 'Lucky I am to have you, Beth, love.'

'I feel guilty working here when I should be helping you and Dad on the sands. And there's the time I spend helping my father-in-law as well as taking time to help Eirlys and Hannah in the shop. Do you mind very much, Mam?'

'It is difficult,' Marged admitted. 'Temporary strangers aren't as committed to giving the customers a happy time. For us Castles it's more than a job, isn't it? But don't feel guilty about managing a business of your own, we're proud of you. Weekends and summer evenings when you could be doing other things, you come when you can and serve in the cafe or help out on the stalls. Grateful we are, your dad and me.'

'I know what I do isn't enough. With our Ronnie round the corner on the vegetable stall and our Eynon serving out in the desert, I try to do what I can, but wish I could do more.'

'It's strange, isn't it, that those two girls Maude and Myrtle who are no relation at all, are more use to us than your sister Lilly has ever been?'

Beth didn't want to get into a discussion about her lazy sister and she was glad when the conversation was interrupted by a group of customers needing to be served.

When they had been supplied with sandwiches and a pot of tea, Marged went on as though the interruption hadn't happened. 'Wonderful girls they are. Did you know Myrtle was offered a full-time job helping your father-in-law? Since Bernard has taken over Sally Gough's field he's desperate for extra help and I know she was tempted, but she has enough family loyalty to stay with us on the beach. Lovely girls they

29

are.' As an alarming thought struck her she asked, 'You aren't going to help on the smallholding more now, are you? Instead of helping us on the sands?'

'No, Mam. Helping in the fields isn't for me!' she said, with an eloquent shudder. 'I help in the house, and with the paperwork, that's all. I'll be with you and Dad whenever I'm free. Bernard understands that.'

'Good on 'im,' Marged said with an approving nod.

Beth smiled but inside she was worrying how she would manage. When her husband Peter came home he had priority over everything, but when he was away, there was the cafe, the gift shop, helping her father-in-law and trying to give a few hours to the activities on the beach. She felt sometimes that she ought to give up the cafe, but it earned a reasonable profit and when the war was over, and Peter started to develop the employment agency business he was already planning, she wanted to present him with a sum of money to start him off, as well as continue to support them both until the agency took off.

During a previous engagement, to Freddy Clements, she had learned the hard way of the importance of money. Freddy had cheerfully spent everything she had saved. His affair with Shirley Downs, who was now Bleddyn's step-daughter, had ended their engagement and although it had been a shock, she was now grateful and bore Shirley no ill will. She wondered how he was. He still wrote to her occasionally and under-standing how important letters were to men serving overseas, she wrote back to him. Peter had no objection and, apart from Shirley Downs and the occasional duty letters from his mother, she guessed he had very few.

With a last comment about the laziness of Lilly, Marged left, automatically taking her dishes into the area of the stall where dishes were washed. Beth wondered whether to call and see her sister. Perhaps she would pop in on the way to the beach one evening and suggest that their mother would appreciate a visit. Her little niece Phyllis rarely saw her grand-parents and Beth knew how Lilly's indifference hurt them.

Myrtle continued to deliver groceries twice a week during the early evening, then she would dash back over the beach to help clear up at the end of the day. The stalls were quickly boarded up and the swingboats and helter-skelter locked to prevent them being used after hours. It was the cafe that presented the most work. There, overseen by Marged's critical eyes, any remaining food was either taken home for supper or placed in the special bins provided for pig food. Nothing was left to be sold the following day and Marged had the cooking to a fine art so there was usually very little wasted. Sometimes they would take home a few cakes to have at supper time with their regular cup of cocoa before bed.

At the end of each day, the counters and tables and chairs were washed, the tables reset with clean tablecloths and cruets, plus the glass meat-paste pots placed ready for a few flowers when they were available, leaves and grasses when they were not. The tea urn was washed out and dried, and the cheerful gingham tablecloths that had been used were packed to take home for Audrey to wash and iron.

Marged always stood at the door for a moment before leaving and looked around to satisfy herself that everything was immaculate and ready for a fresh start the following morning. They usually crowded into the van for Huw to drive them home, but today he was out of town buying supplies and they had to walk.

Marged and Beth and Myrtle shared the things to be taken home and they set off. Marged looked tired, and Beth was content to take her slow pace, only Myrtle was showing no sign of the long day; she skipped like a small child, impatient with their slow crawl.

The three Love brothers were walking to the beach for an evening stroll, Stanley and Harold escaping to avoid being asked to help on Uncle Morgan's allotment. When they saw the group from Castle's, they volunteered to help carry the collection of empty tins and the bundle of washing. Thankfully, Marged agreed.

Percival, who was ten years old, took Marged's hand. He was still in need of mothering. The boys' mother had died in a London air raid and Morgan Price's wife, Annie, was also dead, so although Eirlys did what she could, they welcomed the attention of an older woman who would talk to them in the affectionate tones of a grandmother or aunt, although in fact they had experienced little of that luxury until they had come to St David's Well.

Stanley walked beside the lively Myrtle and when they reached Sidney Street and he relinquished his burdens, he said, 'Fancy coming to the pictures with us tomorrow? Saturday morning pictures is for kids, but we could go, just for a laugh.'

Myrtle was so surprised at the unexpected invitation – her first from a boy – that she became flustered, one second wanting to go, the next wanting to run away and hide. She hid her embarrassment behind a haughty laugh.

'Me go to the children's matinee? I'm far too old. Look at me. Long as a beanstalk. I'd never pass for fourteen!'

'Wearing them black stockings and with your hair all over the place like it usually is, you could pass for twelve, no trouble.'

'Well, I don't think so. I'm almost sixteen, mind,' she said with her regular distortion of the truth.

'I'm too old, too,' he retorted huffily. 'Just crouch down as we go in and I'll hide you. In that crush who's going to notice us? Who'd care, so long as we paid our sixpence?'

He smiled at her then, his eyes seeming to melt into her own in a rather delightful way. Perhaps it would be nice to go out with him one day. He didn't look like one of the kids anymore. At that moment she recognized not the familiar boy, but a young man, and the cheeky remark she was about to impart didn't leave her lips.

'Sorry, Stanley,' she said in a softer manner. 'I couldn't go with you anyway. I have to help over the beach. Saturday's one of our busiest days, remember, with the town full of day trippers.' She hesitated a moment, her hand on the door through which the others had disappeared. 'You can come and help if you want to. No fooling about mind, the Castles haven't got time to bother with idle time-wasters. It's work or nothing, right?'

'Come on in, Myrtle,' Wilf called. 'You too, Stanley, Harold and Percival. There's a drink of pop here and a couple of Welshcakes going begging.'

Giving an exaggerated sigh, Stanley said, 'Work it is then. About half past eight?'

'Can I have one without currants, Uncle Wilf?' Percival wailed. 'Them currants bover me.'

32

Marged, thinking of how few currants and sultanas the Welshcakes now contained, knew that wouldn't be a difficult task.

Maude was sitting in the corner of the big couch and she beckoned to Myrtle. 'What did he want?' she asked, gesturing to Stanley who was reaching for one of the flat, spicy cakes being offered by Marged.

'Invited me to the pictures, he did. You know, the kids' programme in the morning, but I told him I'll be working.'

'Cheek. As if you'd bother with someone like him.'

'He's nice enough. He's coming to help us on the sands tomorrow. It's your day off, so are you coming?'

'Only if you get rid of him!'

'He won't bother you. I expect Uncle Huw will put him on the hoopla stall. Uncle Huw'll have to do it himself if he doesn't come. We're terrible short of help.'

'And you aren't going to the pictures with him later?'

'The grown-up pictures?' she joked. 'Of course not, Maude. By the time we've cleared up it'll be too late! Pity, mind. I'd have liked to go with him. He's nice.'

'Don't be silly, Myrtle. He's not from round here, remember,' she said warningly. 'We don't know anything about him.'

'Enough to know that I like him.'

'You're too young to be thinking about boys. Just look at yourself. You're only fifteen and that's a child!'

Myrtle went to her bedroom and looked at her reflection in the wardrobe mirror. She pulled her long hair back and piled it on top of her head, she pouted her lips and bent her head to glance upward in what she imagined was a sultry expression. Then she stepped back and pulled a face. She pulled off the hated black woollen stockings that Audrey insisted she wore until the end of the month, and hid them in the wardrobe, intending to throw them later into the bag of rags intended for the scrap collection. She looked down at her skinny legs, as white as bones in the butcher's shop.

Taking a brush, she pulled it through her untidy mane of dark-brown hair and with scissors, cut a good two inches off the ends, shaping it into a curve instead of the straight line that had made it easier to plait. Biting her lips and slapping her cheeks to redden them, she wondered how soon she might

33

dare to try a lipstick, the faintest pink, no more, but she determined that if Stanley or any other boy were to ask her out again, it wouldn't be to a picture show for the under fourteens.

She went back downstairs in some trepidation, waiting for the gasps of horror, but Aunt Audrey came up to her, hugged her and told her she looked lovely.

'If you like, we can arrange for a good hairdresser to cut it for you, as a late birthday present.'

'No makeup, mind,' Marged added sharply. 'You're too young.'

'I hates makeup. Too much and you look like someone different,' Harold said.

Marged guessed he was thinking about their mother, who had dressed to attract men and had left her children on their own whilst she'd go out on the streets to find them.

Myrtle looked at Stanley and he smiled as though they were already sharing secrets. Perhaps not lipstick just yet. The haircut and saying goodbye to those black stockings were enough for the moment. The invitation from Stanley, although refused, had made her aware of a change in her, a restlessness, a hint of something exciting about to happen. Childhood was over. Free and easy innocent delights like riding down hills on her bike with her feet off the pedals would be a delight no more. The look in Stanley's eyes hinted at pleasures of a different kind.

Then Maude spoilt it as she whispered, 'Be careful, Myrtle, you don't want to make a fool of yourself with the likes of Stanley Love, do you?'

When the three boys were leaving, having helped clear away the surplus food Marged had brought home, it was Maude who offered to see them to the door.

'Don't bother to come to the beach tomorrow,' she whispered to Stanley. 'We've more than enough people hanging around as it is, thank you.'

'Why not? I was looking forward to it. I'll work hard and I don't want no money. It's nice to get away from my brothers for a while and they'll be happy enough with Uncle Morgan on his allotment.' He deliberately stood aside and beckoned to Myrtle who was standing watching them. 'Go on, Myrtle, say I can come.'

'Maude said you weren't to come,' Myrtle admitted.

'Oh, I see, Maude says what suits her and you have to agree.'

Myrtle looked back at her sister, who had moved away and was watching her through the open door of the living room. There was little chance of Maude complaining once Stanley was put to work, and she knew Uncle Huw and Auntie Marged would be grateful for an extra helper. 'All right, then. Come at half eight and talk to Uncle Huw.' She closed the door and, to avoid an immediate confrontation with her sister, ran past her and went to the kitchen to help Marged prepare their supper. She was unable to suppress a smile at her small victory.

When it was time for the boys from the agricultural college to leave Bernard's smallholding, now with its extra fields, he negotiated with their tutor and the ministry for them to stay another couple of weeks and help him build a greenhouse against what had once been the wall of the orchard. The trees had become too old to produce a worthwhile crop so they had been removed and the area cultivated and was now used for smaller produce like beetroot and carrots and radishes.

As he was marking out the area before preparing the footings and building the low wall, Bernard noticed that the rhubarb was ready for its first picking under its protection of a bucket filled with straw. He asked Myrtle to gather some and take it to Ronnie Castle's stall in the market. He dropped her and the two boxes of rhubarb off at the entrance to the market, and she carried one to Ronnie and went back for the second.

Ronnie was pleased with the colourful sticks of fruit. He would have no trouble selling them, in fact, before Myrtle had returned with her second armful, there was already a queue forming with women dreaming of a fresh, nutritious treat for their families.

'Go and tell our Beth to give you a cup of tea, Myrtle. I'll pay for it later,' Ronnie said. 'I appreciate Mr Gregory thinking of me when he had this to sell.' He put the paper showing the amount he owed into his folder to be settled at the end of the month. 'I'll call at the weekend for some duck eggs and some bundles of firewood, if he has any.'

Myrtle made a note of the transaction and Ronnie's Saturday

requirements, then went to the market cafe to see Ronnie's sister to beg that cup of tea.

Beth was packing up to close the cafe but when she saw Myrtle, she willingly provided her with a hot cup of tea and a couple of leftover sandwiches. Myrtle was skinny but her appetite matched that of Beth's brother Ronnie.

'I asked Stanley to help on the beach whenever he's free, Beth. He offered to help on the stalls. That's all right, isn't it?'

'Of course, why shouldn't it be? Mam and Dad are pretty desperate these days and he's the right type, full of banter that pleases the customers, and I'm sure he'll work hard.'

'Maude doesn't think I should.'

'Because he's a boy and you're a pretty girl,' Beth teased. 'You and Maude are so close she's bound to be a bit jealous of anyone who tries to take you away from her.'

Blushing furiously, Myrtle said, 'Maude, jealous? That's a laugh. Stanley's just a kid!' Her outrage and the colour in her cheeks made Beth regret her teasing. It seemed that the time for teasing was over. Stanley had awoken something in Myrtle that was changing her from a gangly schoolgirl into a young woman. Impulsively, she hugged the embarrassed girl and said, 'Lucky he'll be, if he has you for a girlfriend, Myrtle.'

'He's just a kid,' Myrtle repeated, before hiding her face in a huge bite from a doughnut that Beth had placed before her.

The weather that weekend was not good and a fine drizzle kept people off the beach, and instead they crowded the shops and cafes. Stanley hung about on the empty sands for the few enthusiasts who insisted on riding the swingboats in the rain, puzzled by their determination to laugh and defy the steady, cold downpour that continued for most of the day. He kept up what Huw called his cheeky chat when there were any girls about, flirting and making them laugh, but at heart he was disappointed. Although Myrtle was working in the cafe above the beach, with Marged and Huw and her sister Maude, she hadn't once stopped to talk to him.

The rain increased and was coming down in sheets, and when Huw came to close up at three o'clock he didn't pretend to hide his relief. 'Thank Gawd fer that! I'm perishing cold and perishing fed up, Mr Castle.'

'Myrtle said you wanted to go to the pictures,' Huw said as he started dragging the wooden boards over to close the stall. 'Just give me a hand with this, then if you go up to the cafe, Myrtle will give you a cup of tea and a bite to eat and you can pack it in for the day.'

Encouraged by the promise of food and a meeting with Myrtle, Stanley hastily closed down the stalls and rides and ran up the metal steps leading from the beach to the cafe on the cliff path.

The cafe smelled strongly of wet clothing and everywhere was damp. The windows were steamed up, coats were spread hopefully around chairs to drip-dry before being put back on. The few remaining customers sat in bedraggled heaps, slumped on the tables hugging a cup of tea, trying to drag out the drinking of it as an excuse to stay in the dry that little bit longer. The floor was puddled by the passage of dozens of day trippers, many of whom had come in coaches, hoping for a day on the sand and who had been driven to the cafe to find shelter until it was time to leave.

Many of them had a long wait before their bus came to take them home. Most of those who had come by public transport had already left, some still queuing at the bus stops or the railway station, standing in soggy groups, coats held out over their heads and sharing with each other their gloomy opinion of the weather.

Stanley bounded in and went to where Myrtle was wiping down the front of the counter and polishing the glass with a dry cloth.

'I'll do that,' he offered, taking the bowl of water and the cloths from her. 'You go and find me the plate of food Mr Castle promised me, is it?'

Myrtle laughed. 'Is it?' she teased. 'Stanley, half the time you're Welsh and half the time you're a Londoner.'

'A mongrel, that's what I am. Fancy coming to the pictures with a mongrel, do you?' He turned to call to Marged. 'All right if Myrtle and me goes to the pictures, Mrs C?'

'Oh, Myrtle! You promised to help me finish that sock I'm knitting,' Maude said at once. 'You know I can't remember how to turn the heel.'

Seeing Myrtle's disappointment, Marged said. 'Bring it

37

down to me and I'll help you, Maude. It'll be a nice change for Myrtle to go with Stanley and he'll look after her, won't you, Stanley?'

Maude turned away to hide the anger she felt. Myrtle had promised they'd stay in and finish the socks they were knitting for the airforce parcels.

'Thanks, Auntie Marged,' Myrtle said. 'It's one of Auntie Audrey's nights for collecting national savings or she'd help.'

She knew she was blushing again. Silly really, it wasn't like a proper date. It was just Stanley going with her to the pictures, but it was exciting to be going with a boy for the first time. Stanley might be only fourteen but he was tall and quite handsome. Her mind wandered into thinking about the back row and perhaps a stolen kiss or two, and her blush deepened as she noticed Huw staring at her and giving her a wide, knowing wink.

At the cinema, once they were settled into their seats, she didn't find it easy to relax, she felt oddly aware of Stanley close beside her, shouting and laughing with the rest.

Self-conscious, trying to hide her discomfort, she laughed when he laughed, groaned when he groaned but was unable to become involved in the plot; her mind was in a tangle of unrecognizable emotions that made thought difficult. She was relieved when it was time for them to leave.

The chip-shop black out restrictions had forced the proprietor to add an entrance which was a wooden passage with a corner half way to prevent light escaping, so it was difficult to see whether it was open and if so, whether there was a queue waiting to be served. Stanley took her hand and pulled her inside, insisting he was starved and couldn't walk another yard without food. In the isolated darkness of the blacked out entrance, he leaned towards her and kissed her cheek. It wasn't as embarrassing as she might have feared, this first hint of affection. Its simplicity, with no need to worry about the response was almost matter-of-fact, but it made the evening more special and her slight unease drifted away leaving her pleasantly content.

He bought her a rissole and chips with some of the money Huw had paid him for his day's work and they walked through the chilly, damp streets huffing as they tried to chew the hot snack, swapping burning chips from one side of their mouths to the other in their impatient hunger, discussing the film between scalding mouthfuls.

The companionship gave Myrtle a frisson of happiness that was different from the usual pleasures. She enjoyed the hours they had shared and hoped, firstly that Stanley would invite her again, and secondly, that Maude wouldn't find a way to spoil it if he did.

Audrey and Wilf were sitting by the fire when Myrtle went in, the kettle singing its lullaby at the side of the fire. Maude was in an armchair and appeared to be sulking.

As she rose and reached for the kettle to add boiling water to the cocoa cups standing ready on a tray, Audrey whispered to Myrtle, 'Take no notice of Maude, she's your sister, not your jailer, remember.'

Maude heard the comment and left the room. Audrey went on, 'We all have our own way to make and if we try to please too many people we please no one. My advice is do what's best for you and let everyone else's wishes fit around that.' She reached for Wilf's hand and added with a hint of sadness, 'Sometime, sooner or later, you have to make a stand. And when we do, most of us regret not making it sooner.'

Three

The day was dull with a threat of rain. Flags on the stalls and around the cafes hung limp, windmills and funny hats adding a false gaiety. Bright dresses were half hidden by towels, brought for bathing, being draped around shoulders for warmth. Huw Castle and his brother Bleddyn, were checking the paintwork on the outside of their beach cafe. It was situated high above the sands with metal steps leading up to a doorway with another door opening out onto the cliff path. After the winter months, in spite of efforts made each autumn, the place always looked shabby. Heavy rain and freezing temperatures had worn the paint away and removed some of the putty holding the glass in place. Gusts of chill wind rattled the panes threatening disaster if the warning went unheeded.

The cafe was already open for business but on this Saturday morning when the weather would discourage many prospective customers, they had decided to add to the work already done and treat the wood to another coat of paint before it became weakened to the point at which it would need replacing.

It was still early and Bleddyn looked down at the beach, where a few people were already settling on the sands, spreading their belongings, building banks of sand, unfolding deck chairs, draping towels around as meagre protection against the unkind wind. They were determined to enjoy their day out whatever the weather.

On the promenade, Sarah, the gypsy fortune-teller, had set up her tent with its mysterious symbols adorning the sides, her several shawls worn for warmth as well as effect. The beach photographer was prowling around in the hope of an early patron. He wasn't very hopeful and wouldn't have been out so early if his landlady hadn't discouraged him dallying

40

in the warmth of the breakfast room. Her impatient movements had left him in no doubt that he was in the way of important work.

Two men were spreading out deckchairs for hire, their ticket machines hanging over their shoulders, their eyes – like those of the photographer – looking for a prospective customer. The people working the stalls and rides were decorating their walls with flags, windmills and a few balloons.

Bleddyn sighed. There were few men to be seen and he thought of his two sons, Taff who had been killed and his other son, Johnny, for whom he feared. This war was a long way from finished and every day the town heard of yet more of its sons being lost for ever. He turned to his brother, trying to shake off melancholy thoughts.

'It's going to be difficult to find staff again this year,' he reminded Huw. 'With Alice sent to the factory, and your Beth running the market cafe, we'll have to employ strangers again.'

'Who'd have thought it, eh? With your two boys and my four, we believed we were set up for all the help we needed. But there's our Lilly as useless as ever, and Ronnie and Beth working in the market. Pity your stepdaughter turned out to be such a wonderful singer, or we might have persuaded her to help. Wonderful voice she's got, your Shirley.'

'Shirley's talented all right, but thank goodness for her mother. Hetty has been a godsend.'

'Lucky devil you are, our Bleddyn, a lovely wife and a talented stepdaughter.'

'Lucky beyond,' Bleddyn agreed, turning away as his thoughts returned to his dead son. 'Now, what are we going to do about staff?'

'I'd like to employ young Stanley Love. What d'you think? He came here from London yet you'd think he'd lived in St David's Well all his life. He loves helping on the stalls and he's good at it.'

'I know we shouldn't ask him knowing that if he gives up the shop he'll be out of work once September comes, but it's tempting.'

'I think he'll complain about being too sick to go to work more and more as the summer progresses, and we might as well make it legal!'

Before the war, with their six children, the Castles had coped well with their various activities, as everyone had helped, with the exception of Lilly, who had never taken to the family firm and found days on the beach utterly boring. With the war causing the departure of their children from the family business, the brothers were faced with the problem of staff every summer. Finding help was difficult. Everything closed down at the end of September and didn't reopen until the following summer. Most of their summer staff found something permanent at the end of the season and were not available to help after their first year. Now, with Beth running the market cafe and Ronnie having a market stall too, and Lilly as idle as ever, the situation was worse than last year.

As the month of May brought warmth and longer days, the activities in the seaside town increased and the holiday season expanded in importance to involve the whole town. Small hotels and guest houses offered full board, or room and breakfast only, some families moving out of their bedrooms to sleep in ancient caravans or even their kitchens, to pack more paying visitors into their homes.

Buses and trains brought excited families: mothers, children and grannies, often plus a couple of dogs and mountains of luggage. The shops searched the warehouses to find items to sell to them, while landladies scurried about trying to find something to fill their plates. Marged saw queues stretching out of sight along the cliff path as customers waited to be served with trays for on the beach, or a sit-down meal in the small cafe. She knew there were too few family members to cope. Something had to be done.

To sort out some of the logistical problems, Marged called a family conference. She and Huw ran the cafe at the beach and the stalls and rides on the sand but it was Bleddyn who dealt with the fish and chip shop and restaurant that was open throughout the year. He was assisted by his wife, Hetty, and, along with Shirley, they came to the meeting called for Sunday evening at Audrey's house.

The Castle family business had been started by Marged and Audrey's grandparents and, until Huw and Bleddyn had insisted, the cafe and the other businesses had been called

Piper's. When it was pointed out that most of the work was being done by Huw and Bleddyn, both Castles, an argument ensued after which the name had been changed. On occasions such as this first meeting of the new season, Marged sometimes found it difficult to remember that the business belonged to them all. She rustled papers and prepared to open the discussion, but Bleddyn ignored her obvious intention to take the meeting and stood to address them all himself.

'Right, then,' he began. 'No seaside sweet and rock shop this year because of sweet rationing, but everything else the same as last year. Now, any suggestions about what we do with the sweet shop?'

Audrey had always taken responsibility for the sweet shop and everyone looked at her for her opinion.

'I'd like to take it on full-time instead of me doing what hours I can between all the other chores and having to find someone to do the rest. Now Alice is no longer free, having been called up to work at that factory, it might be difficult to find someone to help out, but I want to work in the shop and only the shop this year.' Allowing no time for the objections to be raised, she went on quickly, 'We ended last season selling postcards and small gifts. Shall we try that this year? It's still possible to get those and visitors are always looking for something to take back as a memento of their holiday.' Aware of the shock registering on her sister's face she looked at Huw for support. He nodded approval.

'What d'you mean, work in the shop full-time? How can you? Your job is dealing with the laundry and cooking, as you've always done,' Marged said. 'Now Alice's been sent to work in a factory, we have to find someone else. You can't be spared from what you always do.'

'We can advertise for someone to run the shop for us,' Huw said. 'It shouldn't be too difficult to find someone. Easier than finding people to run the stalls.'

'Of course it's difficult,' Marged snapped. 'It's bad enough if we all pull our weight, but . . .' She glared at Audrey.

There was the usual groan. Whereas before the war, the whole Castle family was involved, and few outsiders were needed, the prospects for a family run season looked bleak.

'All right,' continued Marged, 'if we let the shop out to

43

rent, you'd be able to stay home and do what you've always done.' Marged suggested, 'Rent instead of sales wouldn't be too bad.'

It seemed a fair answer, but to everyone's surprise the normally compliant Audrey looked adamant. 'It's someone else's turn to do the housekeeping. I want to run the shop. I want to open it at ten every morning and find someone to take over at three so Wilf and I can go out sometimes. I've had years of being tied to the house cooking and cleaning, plus filling in at the shop when there was no one else, as well as spending hours every week helping in the beach cafe for six months of every year. I've had enough. It's time Wilf and I had a bit of freedom.'

'But you're a Piper,' Marged said, proudly reminding her of their maiden name.

'Not anymore. I married Wilf Thomas, remember? And I want to spend more time with him. I think I'm owed it.' The gentle, unassuming Audrey had never once complained and now they stared at her as though she had accused one of them of murder.

'You what?' Marged said with a glimmer of anger. 'Are you saying we've taken advantage of you all these years?'

'No, not really,' Audrey replied quietly. 'Wilf and I haven't been married very long and we want to enjoy some time together, instead of being tied up with the beach activities all through the summer. Is that unreasonable?'

Huw and Bleddyn muttered that it was not, but Marged said, 'Yes, it is! This is a family business and we all have to do what we can.'

'Of course, Marged. And I will run the shop on the promenade. On most days, that is. There will be times when Wilf and I will need a few days off. We're going to defy the government's request to avoid using transport and travel a little, while we can.'

'There's nothing wrong, is there?' Marged looked concerned. 'You aren't ill or anything?'

'I'm fine, but I am past fifty and Wilf's getting to an age where he'll have to slow down. It's time we had a bit of freedom. I looked after Mam until she died and Wilf looked after his mother. Now it's time for us.'

Bleddyn glanced down at the notes he had made before coming to the meeting and said, 'Right then,' – his usual opening remark – 'if Audrey takes on the shop we'll need someone for the housekeeping and cooking, plus some lads to help on the beach. Any suggestions?' He glanced at Audrey and she gave him a grateful smile.

'We were thinking that young Stanley Love might help some evenings and at weekends; he's energetic and full of cheeky patter, just what we need,' Huw suggested. 'In fact we wondered whether to offer him a full-time job.'

Marged said very little. She stared at her sister, looking away when Audrey tried to meet her gaze. She was upset and wanted Audrey to know it. After a few more suggestions and a discussion of the few who had applied for work, they moved from Audrey's front room into the more cosy living room. Wilf was there and the kettle was simmering on the side of the coalfire. He was five feet six inches tall and as round as a barrel, and with a white beard and overlong white hair, his face rosy in the glow from the fire, he looked like Father Christmas, a nickname he was often awarded by the local children. He got up and began to spread out cups and saucers, and uncover the snacks Audrey and he had previously prepared, his bright blue eyes crinkling into a huge smile as he looked at Audrey.

'Everything sorted?' he asked cheerfully.

'Some might think so,' Marged sniffed. 'I don't know how we're going to manage now Audrey is refusing to do her share.'

'Refusing to do my share?' Audrey said, her voice louder than usual. 'I—'

'What say I try again to talk to the doctor about getting Maude back full-time?' Bleddyn interrupted, aware of the danger that the disagreement could break into an argument. 'It's clear that factory work doesn't suit her and a job out of doors is obviously what she needs. If we count up the days she's been sick this winter, that might convince them.'

'I've tried and they won't release her from war work to help on the sands; you know that,' Marged told him.

'Then let's try again,' Huw said. 'This time Bleddyn and I will go. Perhaps they'll listen to us.' Marged shrugged making it clear that if she couldn't persuade them, she didn't think Huw had any chance at all. Huw pointed to her handbag and said, 'Letters, Marged?'

Marged opened her handbag and took out the letters they had received that week. With a son and a nephew plus friends serving in the forces home and overseas, reading letters were treasured moments. Within the family and often among neighbours too, letters were shared, read out for everyone to enjoy. When news was slow coming through, it helped to hear the news of much loved absent friends and family. Even someone else's news helped to ease away the feelings of dread that the lack of contact brought.

Marged and Huw had received letters from their son Eynon and Bleddyn's son, Johnny. The letters were read and the minimal amount of news they contained was dissected. A general discussion on the progress of the war went on for a while. Only Marged and her sister Audrey were silent, animosity darting from one to the other as resentment and defiance battled in the air around them.

Marged had always been the strong one, dominating her sister and making sure Audrey did what she wanted. Only twice had Audrey surprised her by digging her heels in over something Marged wanted. The first time was two years ago when she had married Wilf Thomas without even telling her. When Lilly did the same thing, ten months later, Marged blamed Audrey for giving her daughter the idea. She was convinced that Lilly wouldn't have come up with the plan if Audrey hadn't shown her how. Now this refusal to run the housekeeping side of the Castle business. It was a large, unwieldy business, and with few of the family able to help, and so many restrictions, life was difficult enough without Audrey being uncooperative. It was so unfair.

Needing someone to blame, she accused Wilf, but not to Audrey's face; she knew that wouldn't go down very well. Instead, she complained to Huw and Bleddyn. To her surprise they supported Audrey. Defeated, she sat down to decide on the best way of using the staff they had and work out how many more people they needed.

Her and Huw's son, Eynon, and Bleddyn's Johnny, had always enjoyed the beach. They had been involved since they were small. Eynon's wife, Alice, would have helped but she

46

had been called up to work in a factory making the instruments of war. Johnny's wife, Hannah, was a dressmaker with two little girls, so although both daughters-in-law wanted to help, neither was able to do more than an occasional hour or two. Marged wondered how they could keep it all going. And now Audrey was making things worse.

Audrey and Wilf went for a walk the following morning, and without discussion their feet took them to the cemetery. There, against an ivy-clad wall, they stopped and replaced the bedraggled flowers with a fresh posy of bluebells and primroses they had gathered on their way. The tiny grave belonged to their son who had died in November 1910 when he was only ten weeks old.

'Why was I so obedient, Wilf? 'Audrey asked softly. 'Why didn't I defy Mam and Marged and marry you all those years ago? I did what Marged and Mam said I should, even though I knew they were wrong. I put obedience to the family before my love for you.'

'With today's attitude and the knowledge we have now, it's impossible to understand how we were then, or why we did what we did. Everything was different. We were young, too young to walk away from the family and take hold of our own life.'

'It was such a waste.'

'Not a complete waste, dear. We've had a lifetime of friendship and love. We're still together and we've had a couple of happy years as man and wife with many more to come.'

'It was a terrible time,' she said trying to pull a piece of ivy away from hiding Bobbie's name. 'That was when my mother made me promise never to leave Marged to cope on her own. Foolishly, so wracked with guilt, I gave that promise willingly, hoping that if I did the recriminations would cease.'

'Promises like that should never be taken literally, but at the time we didn't know that, dear.' He knelt down and with a pocket knife teased the colonizing ivy and grass from around the grave. 'Now,' he said briskly, 'where shall we go for our first little holiday?'

They wandered off hand in hand through the peaceful cemetery and planned their future travels, their laughter ringing out

47

occasionally as Wilf made more and more outrageous suggestions. When they went to the beach cafe for a cup of tea, Audrey's face was glowing and Wilf's eyes were bright with laughter in his handsome face, and Marged felt a pinch of envy at the happiness they showed. Guilt made her turn away in case they recognized the unpleasant emotion.

Myrtle had arranged to meet Stanley Love and go for a walk. He had promised to show her where a blackbird was nesting. Myrtle said nothing to her sister, telling her she was going to see Shirley Downs to ask about the concert in which she had performed the previous week.

'It was a Worker's Playtime programme and was on the wireless,' she told Maude. 'Dying to hear all about it, I am. Imagine, Shirley Downs singing on the wireless. She'll be famous soon and we're sort of related. There's exciting!'

'I'll come with you, if you like,' Maude offered and at once Myrtle shook her head.

'No, best you sit and rest. Working in that smelly ol' factory, what you need is a quiet afternoon listening to the wireless. I'll make you a cup of tea before I go and I'll tell you all about it when I get back.' She dashed out of the room before Maude insisted.

She went first to Brook Lane to call on Shirley. She was not a natural liar, but had quickly learned that the closer to the truth you stayed, the less chance there was of being caught out. Shirley was there alone, Bleddyn and her mother Hetty were at the beach, manning the helter-skelter since it was Sunday and the chip shop was closed.

'Such a busy family, the Castles,' Myrtle said as she was invited in. 'I bet they wake up some mornings unable to remember where they're supposed to be! Beach cafes, shops, rides and stalls. Wonderful, isn't it?'

Shirley had been involved in an accident but with determination and a great deal of help from both family and doctors she was now able to walk short distances unaided.

'If I weren't so busy I'd like to have helped. It must be fun sharing the pleasures of the beach with the visitors.'

'That's exactly what it is, sharing the fun. There's clever you are to realize that. Why don't you come over sometimes

48

and sit and watch? Marged will find you something to do, mind, she never misses a chance of some help, and will have you buttering bread then scraping it off again like a good 'un. Expert, you'll be in no time. Come and see us, you'd love it.'

'Perhaps later on. I'm busy with rehearsals this week. I've been asked to sing a couple of solos in a concert next week, and I'm going to sing at the school. I'll show you my new dress, shall I? Not new, of course. It's second hand, altered to fit by Hannah.' They admired the midnight blue dress to which the clever Hannah had added sequins and some lace. They sat discussing which of her shoes she should wear. 'I usually wear sensible strong shoes as I'm afraid of falling with my legs still so weak. But I might be tempted to wear a little heel. What d'you think?'

'Sensible and safe,' Myrtle replied emphatically.

'I've been invited to go on a tour organized by Ken Ward,' Shirley went on. 'Factories mostly, but there are two concerts in army camps and one RAF camp and a fund-raising event in a church. I'll be away for more than a week.'

'You'll do it?'

'Yes, I want to, but Mam and Bleddyn think I shouldn't unless I have someone with me in case I need some help. Nice idea but it isn't possible. Mam can't come, they're so busy trying to fit everything in at the beach, so if I do go I'll have to manage on my own. I find it a bit frightening, but anyway, it isn't until July and who knows what will happen by then?'

'You'll be playing leap frog in a few more months,' Myrtle said encouragingly.

'I'd be happy just to walk.'

'I'd better go. To tell the truth, I've got a few hours off and I'm meeting Stanley and we're looking for birds' nests. I haven't told Maude. She worries about me so much,' she confided.

'Don't worry, I won't remember what time you left here.' They shared a conspiratorial smile as Myrtle picked up her coat and left.

Stanley was waiting at the corner of Brook Lane and they went through the fields to a large park where people sat in the May sunshine, and watched as children played games and dogs chased excitedly around them.

'How's Shirley?' Stanley asked. 'Pleased to see you, was she?'

'Of course. Half-sisters we are.'

'Some would be resentful, her dad scarpering off with your mother. You're lucky she ain't.'

'She's been on the wireless. Imagine that. Singing for the whole country. And now someone has asked her to join a group of artistes travelling around the country giving concerts for the troops and the like. She's wonderful.'

'I bet your Marged would think she was more wonderful if she could do something to help out on the beach! She's Bleddyn's stepdaughter now, and that makes her a part of the Castle family. That lot expect everyone to do their bit.'

'She's too important for that! She'll be a famous singer one day, even more than she is now.' She frowned and added, 'Talking about doing their bit, Auntie Marged is upset with Auntie Audrey. Terrible short of help they are and Auntie Audrey told them she doesn't want to do the housekeeping side of it anymore. Talk about a flap! Auntie Marged is having to advertise for help and that's something they'd never have done before the war. Auntie Audrey has always dealt with the tablecloths and all that, besides helping with the cooking and running the sweet and rock shop.'

They walked in the park, ambling around without any real purpose, and it was five o'clock when they decided to head back home. Stanley left her at the end of Sidney Street and stood watching as she let herself into Audrey and Wilf's house. She popped back out and waved before closing the door and walking in, calling to let them know she was home.

'Where have you been?' Maude demanded. 'Auntie Audrey's been looking for you.'

'I told you, I went to see Shirley.'

'That's what you said. That's why Uncle Wilf went there to fetch you!'

'What's happened?'

'Auntie Marged's cut her hand that's what, and they needed you to help in the cafe.'

'I'll go straight away, now this minute.' Throwing off her coat, she rushed into the kitchen to find an apron and then go back out, but she was stopped before she reached the door. First Audrey came in, then Huw supporting a white-faced Marged, whose arm was thickly bandaged and in a sling.

50

'Auntie Marged, what can I do to help?'

'If you could go over to the cafe with Huw and help clear up, love, that would be wonderful. Sorry your afternoon off was spoilt.'

'Forget about afternoons off! I'll do anything you want me to.' She looked at her sister. 'Maude'll help too, won't you, Maude?' Without any hesitation Maude stood up and both girls waited outside the door for Huw to take them in the van. At the top of the street, Myrtle saw Stanley talking to Ronnie Castle and his wife and baby girl and she ran to tell Ronnie about his mother's accident and said to Stanley, 'Fancy earning a few shillings helping clear up in the cafe?' He joined them as Huw opened the van door after telling Ronnie briefly what had happened.

Explanations were given as they drove through the town out to the sandy beach. Marged had left the cafe early and been cutting up old pillow cases to patch sheets. Impatiently, she had used a carving knife to cut open the seams. The knife had slipped and had cut her hand deep enough for it to need several stitches. A neighbour had cycled across to tell Huw.

Myrtle explained her absence and made no secret of her meeting with Stanley. It was only Maude who disapproved, and she knew there was no need to hide it from the rest. The cafe had been hastily closed and the four of them tackled the cleaning with enthusiasm, anxious to get back to Marged.

Once everything was clean and tidy, Stanley offered to go to the smallholding to tell Beth about her mother's accident, and with nothing more to do, Myrtle went with him. When they got there, slightly out of breath after their walk, they saw Beth arm in arm with a tall, slim, rather handsome man. Walking behind them was Mr Gregory.

Beth's husband was in the casual, rather shabby clothes he wore when helping his father on the land, and Beth too was wearing ill-fitting, muddy trousers and a sloppy jumper. Mr Gregory looked even more untidy, his ancient corduroys stained and tucked into boots that had seen better days.

'Gawd 'elp us, a fashion show!' the cheeky Stanley called and the three turned and smiled.

'It's a bit late for a visit. Is something wrong?' Beth asked at once.

51

'Well a bit,' Myrtle said. 'Don't panic, Beth, but your mam's cut herself and she's had to have stitches.'

'Oh, I'll go at once.'

As she turned away, Myrtle said, 'No, your mam said not to go, she's all right and she'll see you in the morning.'

'But—'

'Yeh, she's all right but she'll want to rest. The shock,' Stanley explained airily. 'And she wants to sit quiet and work out who's going to do what over at the beach.'

Peter asked questions about what had happened and agreed that it would be best for Beth to wait until the morning before disturbing her. 'Stanley's right, it's rest she needs, not people crowding around and making her explain all over again what happened.'

'When you going back?' Stanley asked Peter.

'Stanley! It's more polite to ask how long he's going to be home!' Myrtle admonished.

'I have five whole days, and I suppose your next question is, can I help over on the sands?' Peter's eyes glistened with amusement.

'Well, if you're offering, I bet Marged wouldn't say no to a bit of a hand.'

'Beth will be at the cafe all day and unless Dad has something important for me to do, I'll come and do what I can.' He tilted his head quizzically and Mr Gregory shook his head.

'Nothing important son,' he said. 'You go and help, you'll enjoy a day or so on the sands.' He took off his cap and from the lining eased out a small notebook. 'I have three deliveries tomorrow,' he said, scratching his head with a stubby pencil, 'but one of the college lads is coming to lend a hand. He'll be here all day. There are more lettuce and radish to sow, and there's an extra lot of runner beans to transplant against their sticks. They're a bit late but they'll catch up,' he muttered as though to himself, his teeth clenching his pipe.

'Tell Mam I'll come in the evening to help clean,' Beth promised. 'So long as she rests.'

'Fast asleep she'll be,' Myrtle said confidently.

When she walked into the house in Sidney Street, she went in on tiptoe afraid of disturbing Marged, but she needn't have bothered. Marged was in the kitchen, listening to the comedy hour on the wireless and ironing, struggling to fold the cafe's tablecloths, using her teeth to compensate for the lack of a left hand as she finished them, placing them carefully over the back of a chair. 'There's awkward it is using only one hand,' she said with a deep sigh.

'Auntie Marged, I thought you'd be in bed,' Myrtle scolded. 'Or at least resting.'

'Since she hurt herself, she's even more energetic than usual,' Maude called. She appeared, her hands and forearms covered with flour. 'Shames us all she does. She's got us all that busy, you wouldn't believe. Making the mixture for Welshcakes I am, because Auntie Audrey isn't going to do it anymore, and Uncle Huw's gone to ask Mrs Denver if she'll spare a couple of hours to help in the cafe. It's a mad house.' She shook her head in mock despair and told her sister that the fire needed more coal as it looked as though they were going to be up half the night.

Somehow the cafe survived. Marged was there like the captain of a ship, refusing to stay home, standing with a permanent look of disapproval on her features as she watched the activities of the staff, complaining occasionally and tutting frequently. Peter Gregory found himself running the hoopla stall and at the same time taking money for rides on the swingboats. Customers that day had longer rides than usual as he simply couldn't remember to time them.

Raising money for the many charities was something with which everyone was involved. The list of needy causes grew each month and most weeks saw either a concert or a dance or a sale of work advertising for people's help. Concerts were popular and the halls were filled beyond sensible capacity, in complete disregard of fire regulations, as more and more people handed over their money and were herded in. At some concerts, professional entertainers came, but more often it was local people who stood on a stage and gave enthusiastic, if not talented performances.

In a week during which she had no bookings, Shirley was feeling a little bored. Remembering Myrtle's remarks about helping in the cafe and aware that her mother was at the fish and chip restaurant with Bleddyn, Shirley took her walking

53

stick and caught the bus to the beach.

The bus was crowded, passengers carried heavily laden bags filled with picnic requirements plus awkwardly held spades and buckets. She didn't find it irritating, but instead was taken back to a childhood where, like these children, she was with her mother with no sign of her father. Not because he was fighting a war, or had been tragically killed. Far less honourably, he had been absent because he had left them to live with another woman.

When Maude and Myrtle had been searching for a mythical brother they had found Hetty, who was now married to Bleddyn, and to her dismay she had learned that their father had been her father too. He had left her mother and herself, to live with their mother, which made them Shirley's half-sisters.

Any anger Shirley had felt was long gone and she liked having Maud and Myrtle call her their sister. So she was pleased when the first person to greet her when she went into the busy cafe was Myrtle.

'Eating or helping?' the lively Myrtle called out and Shirley said she could spare an hour if they needed her.

'Lovely girl, will you sit at the till while I go back for more supplies?' Huw asked at once. 'Desperate we are, this crowd shows no sign of easing.'

With Marged, Maude or Myrtle shouting out the totals, Shirley took the money and gave the change and a warm smile, staying almost until closing time.

'I've enjoyed it,' she told a grateful Marged and Huw. 'It'll be something to put in Freddy's letter when I next write. But I wouldn't like to do this every day – I'd be worn out,' she admitted.

She went home and once she was rested, decided that, if she was needed, she would do the same the following day. In fact, she spent most days for more than a week helping in the cafe. They usually gave her a sitting job, aware of the difficulty she had with standing for long periods.

At the end of the week she wrote to Freddy. She told him of the almost party-like atmosphere the family managed to build, making their customers feel welcome for the short time they were there, even though they were very rushed and tired.

54

'Teasing sometimes and making jokes – the same ones day after day I suspect, mind – adding a smile and a pleasant remark to almost everyone, admiring the children, sympathizing with those suffering sunburn. They are wonderful,' she wrote. 'Compared with what they do day after day, going on a stage and singing is a life of ease.'

A few days later, Myrtle called in to see Marged and found her trying to write a letter. Being unable to hold the paper steady with her left hand was making it impossible to write neatly and she gladly accepted Myrtle's offer to help her.

Myrtle stayed, and when the letter was done she began totalling the amounts in Marged's weekly accounts book. Marged was amazed at the girl's efficient speed and accuracy. Her eyes darted up the columns and she had worked out the total before Marged was no more than halfway up, muttering the amounts as she went, pausing sometimes to tap with her fingers on the table. When Marged reached the total and added it over the amount Myrtle had already pencilled in, she smiled ruefully.

'Where's that little girl who came to us a few years ago unable to read or write, Myrtle?'

'She grew up, thanks to you and Uncle Huw and Auntie Audrey.'

While Marged's hand healed, Myrtle continued to help with the bookkeeping and her neat figures filled the pages in a way that impressed Marged, Huw and Bleddyn.

'She ought to go to night school and learn the job properly,' Bleddyn said one evening after they had looked through the month's accounts and checked Myrtle's totals. Myrtle told Stanley what had been said and he nodded wisely in his wise old man manner. 'Clever you are, Myrtle, an' I think they're right. You should get some proper learning.'

Walking back from the cinema that evening, he reached for her hand as they crossed the road and didn't let go when they reached the other side. It was pleasant; a mild feeling of belonging and a new sensation about which she wouldn't tell Maude. A clumsy kiss on the cheek when they parted made her confident in their unexpected friendship, and when she was delivering the dreaded groceries a day later, she went to 78 Conroy Street after her deliveries were done, to see if he was free to go with her to help at the beach for the last couple of hours.

The sound of a crying baby met her and she hesitated before knocking at the door. Perhaps it wasn't a good time to call. She turned and retreated back up the path, but the sound of the door opening made her turn.

Harold had seen her coming and he invited her inside, explaining, 'That's young Niblo yelling. Good an' loud, ain't 'e?'

Stanley appeared carrying a very angry baby who was fighting against having a dummy stuck into his mouth. 'Come on, Anthony, I've dipped it in the condensed milk for yer. Lovely that is, you lucky little fella.'

Eirlys returned home shortly, so they set off on their bicycles; Myrtle still using the heavy carrier bike on which she had made her deliveries They sped towards the beach, where they were in time to help close the cafe and clean everything away ready for the next day.

'When are you going to pack up that delivery lark?' Stanley asked. 'You're better use in the cafe, I'd have thought. Specially as that Auntie Audrey's gone on strike.'

'I suppose so, but it's pocket money and I don't earn much yet.'

'Thought any more about evening classes?'

'Hardly. The summer's too busy to think about anything else but work. Perhaps, when they start in September. It's a bit scary, mind, not having proper schooling.'

'I might go and do something myself. English maybe, reading, writing, I enjoy that.'

'And poetry?' she teased.

'Why not?' he said. Then asked, 'Have you seen the poem on the door of Castle's cafe? It was Piper's cafe when it was written there and now it's hard to read. Your Auntie Marged told me what it said:

> Teas for trippers, donkeys and dippers
> Sunhats, hoopla and tides
> Piper's kingdom, cloths of fresh gingham
> Fortunes, windmills and rides

Good ain't it?'

* * *

56

Myrtle was pleased that with the season underway and show-ing signs of developing into a busy one, she had been able to give up her morning work at the children's home and work full-time on the beach. That week she told the grocer her days as a delivery girl were over.

Huw had found a few young boys looking for temporary employment while they waited to be called into the forces. They were happy to enjoy a few months of relaxed, unin-volved employment during which they could forget the horrors to come.

Stanley skived from the shop as often as he dared, complain-ing of bad headaches, and bad nights being disturbed by Eirlys and Ken's baby son, and bad stomach aches and anything else he could describe as bad. Apart from one or two incidents when he saw customers who might recognize him and had been forced to hide, he was a reliable assistant on the rides and stalls, shouting to attract custom, flirting with the girls and giving cheek to the rest with a cheery grin that drove away any offence. Huw and Bleddyn were still undecided about whether to persuade him to leave the shop and work for them full-time, but aware that winter would mean unem-ployment and having to accept work he might not enjoy, they let things stay as they were, grateful when the boy could find an excuse to join them on the beach. They carefully avoided questions about why he wasn't at work.

For Stanley, part of the attraction was the fun of the crowds and the freedom of the work, but a greater part was working with Myrtle. For Myrtle too, her first thought on arriving at the cafe high above the sands was to look down to see whether Stanley had managed to wangle himself a day off from his employer to help. She would smile and wave when she saw him helping Bleddyn open up the rides and stalls, dragging away the heavy canvas and wooden shutters from the stalls, and unlocking the rides.

He was young enough to find the rides irresistible and as soon as they were unlocked, he would climb up the twisting steps and slide down the helter-skelter with a brief 'Just test-ing' as an excuse.

The hours went fast, the cafe a popular venue for visitors and locals alike, but when Myrtle could look down to see

Stanley, the day was always brighter. There was an air of fun about him and the way he flattered her with a look both startled and warmed her. She said nothing of this to Maude, knowing her sister would not welcome her thoughts about someone who might destroy their closeness.

Despite her sister's obvious disapproval, Myrtle did occasionally go out with Stanley, but his brothers were usually with them. It was rare for them to be alone and when they were, they did nothing but talk, sharing stories about their lives before they had arrived in St David's Well. Hand in hand they would walk through the fields behind the town, or wander through the streets, stopping on occasions to sit in a cafe and drink tea, eat cakes and compare them unfavourably with those that were sold at Castle's cafe.

Myrtle dreamed of kisses, but her immaturity made her joke when Stanley tried, running away, laughing and afterwards imagining how it might have been.

Since her marriage to Wilf after more than thirty years of waiting, Audrey tried to feel free of involvement in the business, conscious of feeling a restlessness that was for the most part guilt. All she achieved was a simmering anger. Stifled for so many years, it had grown and was gradually replacing the guilt. For many years, she had done what the family had asked of her, putting aside her own dreams of a home and family of her own, accepting that her role was to support the rest. Living with her and Marged's mother, Granny Piper, had made it impossible to think of rebellion. Moll Piper had been strong willed and Audrey was not. Although that was now changing.

It was after the death of their mother that the relationship between Audrey and her sister changed. Audrey was finding it increasingly easy to say no; something that had been unimaginable in earlier years. Her life had been swallowed up by the seaside entertainment businesses and the demands of the family, until now, at last, she felt she was strong enough to find a life of her own; her and Wilf, enjoying what was left of their lives. She had been forced into believing that obedience to her mother was immutable and it had taken years for her to realize that obedience to a younger sister was not. It was this realization that had begun the change in her, a change that Wilf applauded.

She would never be free of guilt. She knew that the freedom she sought would be less than perfect, that the feeling of letting her family down, of ignoring the promise she had made to her mother would never leave her. She would have to live with it, accept it as a part of the payment for escaping. It was particularly hard knowing she was letting them down at the beginning of the busiest months of the year, but somehow she found the strength to ignore Marged's unsubtle hints.

At odd moments, she imagined her mother staring at her with disapproval out of one of the photographs of her that were scattered around the house that had been hers. Now, the house was Audrey's, even though she and Wilf shared it with Myrtle and Maude, and Ronnie and his family lived in the top flat. The house belonged to her and Wilf and the others were there because she wanted them to be. Yet there was still a feeling that she should be asking her mother's permission for the few changes she had made.

She heard the door open and called, 'Wilf, dear? Is that you?'

'It is, and I have the booking for the week in Devon. We go the week after next for seven whole days.'

At once Audrey started gathering the laundry and put it into piles for the various stages of the washing day chores.

'Now, dear, don't fuss.' He took hold of her hands. 'All we have to do is tell Marged where to find the linen, and pack our cases. Don't try to deal with every situation that might happen while we're away or you'll be exhausted before we get to the railway station. You have given warning that you will no longer be responsible for all this, so let it go, let them cope. It will do them good. Your Marged is always telling us how efficient she is, and Maude is eighteen, remember.'

'You're right, as usual, Wilf. Let's go and see what we need to take and what we have to buy. We mustn't forget the ration books if we expect to be fed.' Chattering happily, they went upstairs and took the suitcases down to be dusted and filled.

Wilf put an arm around her and sighed happily. 'When we finally married, it was a new beginning and I thought I couldn't be happier, but telling Marged you won't be able to help with the housekeeping any longer was an even greater one. Today we're starting the best days of our lives, you and me. Lucky man that I am.' They kissed, then stood with their arms around each other for a very long time, remembering the years of disappointment, grateful for the final end to their unnecessary separation.

'She's going away? Now? When the season is building up to its busiest weeks?' Marged shouted. 'What's got into that sister of mine?'

'Hang about, Marged,' Huw shouted back. 'Don't shout at me, it's Audrey and Wilf who're leaving, not me!'

'But she can't!'

'Oh, but she can. And stop *shouting*, woman!'

'Sorry, Huw, but I don't know what's got into them.'

'Don't you think they might be trying to make up for all the past years? We've had thirty-one years together and they've only had two and a bit. Fifty-one she is. Time to start living before it's too late. All those years they wanted to marry and you and your mother stopped them. I can't forget that if you can.' There was a glint in his eyes, a warning of disapproval.

'You're right. I shouldn't begrudge them a week in Devon. I'll go and tell them I'm pleased and wish them luck.'

'Good on you.' Huw allowed the anger to ease away, anger he always felt when Audrey's late wedding was mentioned. At least Marged was trying to make up to her sister, even if she did need a lot of persuasion.

Audrey opened the door to her and stepped back to allow her to enter. 'You've heard then? About Wilf and me taking a holiday?' There was aggression in her eyes as though prepared for confrontation, but her expression softened, just for a moment, as her sister spoke.

'Huw just told me and I'm here to wish you both a good time and to ask if there's anything you want me to do while you're away.' Marged tried to relax her smile but failed. The words were honest and kindly meant but tension held back the warmth that should have been there. 'Pleased I am that you're taking a little break. Devon too, it sounds wonderful. I'm really glad.'

'I expect Huw said that too and here you are repeating his words like a parrot and expecting me to believe they're generously offered.' Audrey's face was rosy with simmering anger.

'Audrey. What's made you so bitter? What has brought all this on? You and Wilf, you're all right, aren't you? You can tell me if you have a problem.'

'Wilf and I are fine. The only problem is the Castles.'

'If you want to retire from helping with Castles, that's fine. My only disappointment is your timing. If you'd only waited until the end of the season, or told us earlier and given us a chance to find people to help.'

How could Audrey explain that it hadn't been until a few weeks ago that she'd felt brave enough to make the decision? She stood there unable to reply and was surprised when Marged stretched out her arms and took hold of Audrey's hands, pulling her reluctant sister towards her.

'When you and Wilf married, you went on doing what you've always done. Why has everything changed now?' To her alarm she saw tears fill her sister's eyes. 'Audrey?'

'I'm tired. That's all. Tired of doing the same thing, day after day, washing and ironing the tablecloths, boiling the tea towels. Doing the shopping and most of the cooking, and cleaning the house. There's never time for Wilf and me.' Her voice hardened as she went on: 'Well, all that's going to change. Two years is all we've had and I want to make every minute from now on really special. I want us to have wonderful memories of our life together so when we're old we can think back on it and forget how brief it was.'

'Then I'm your friend as well as your sister and whatever you want me to do I'll make my priority. I owe you and I promise to remember that.' Cautiously they held each other, both doubtful about the possibility of such a promise but both hoping it would happen.

Four

Maude was beginning to feel neglected. She and Myrtle had always been very close. Losing their parents while they were so young and believing they were alone had made them closer than the normal ties between sisters. Now Myrtle was leaving her alone more and more frequently – and for that stupid Stanley Love.

Evening after evening, when she came home from the factory she would face hours sitting alone in an empty house. With Audrey and Wilf in Devon the house rattled around her as she sat waiting for the sound of her sister's key in the door. Even the wireless sounded different: hollow, distant, more as though she were eavesdropping on something she wasn't entitled to share. Laughter and the delights of music were meant to be enjoyed with someone else. To look across at someone and see the same pleasure on a companion's face was a large part of the enjoyment.

A cup clattering on its saucer, the kettle being filled, a door squealing as it closed, all sounded excessively loud in the empty rooms. At the top of the house, Ronnie and Olive were separated from her by the extra staircase, in a world of their own far removed from the solitude of hers.

She looked into a future where she would repeatedly glance across at an empty chair, the laughter dying before it reached her eyes, snuffed out by lack of joyful reciprocation. She was only eighteen but social skills eluded her. In the early years after their parents' deaths, her mind had been filled with memories of happy times spent with them, but now, life in the children's home overlaid those memories and saddened her.

Years of not truly belonging anywhere or with anyone, except Myrtle; years of being a face in a sea of faces had made it difficult for her to respond to overtures of friendship. In the years following the death of their parents, life had been a rigid soulless routine, with no room for impromptu moments. Obedience had been the goal; life was considered successful if the rules were obeyed and nothing was done to disrupt the activities of others. Being 'good' was something at which she excelled.

Yet, despite being brought up in identical circumstances, Myrtle had not been affected in the same way. She made friends wherever she went. The reason she wasn't in touch with children from the home where much of her childhood had been spent, was her need to please her sister and disregard the years there, forget the kindnesses and the love they were shown. Maude only remembered the bad – she coped better if she had an excuse for her unhappiness.

In the moments before sleep, when she thought about her life and dreamed of some time in the future when everything had magically changed and she was living it in a different way, she made excuses for her loneliness. She told herself that living the artificial life sharing a dormitory filled with other orphans had been the reason she had failed to develop the enviable skills of friendship. And now, the noisy, smelly factory gave little chance to converse. Being a newcomer had made it hard to break into the circle of long established friends. She wasn't forceful enough and besides, she didn't think she had anything to add to the lively chatter that went on around her, the girls shouting to make themselves heard above the machinery and the clanging of metal.

You had to be confident to shout. Sometimes she thought she would try, but the idea of everyone turning and looking at her questioningly stamped out the idea before it was formed. How could she ever be a part of the crowd? Friendships were long established and there was no chink to allow her to slide into a group of laughing girls whose conversation travelled back and forward over experiences they had shared.

If only the doctor would persuade those in authority that she needed fresh air, then she would work at the beach instead of a noisy, foul-smelling factory. Perhaps she would go to ask if Bleddyn had managed to see the doctor and speak on her behalf. Or maybe, if she went to see the doctor again herself, and exaggerated the pain she sometimes felt in her chest, he might relent and arrange for her to change her occupation.

Without telling the family, she had re-applied for the Land Army, trying to convince them that she was well enough for some of the less energetic work, but a glance at her medical records had been followed by the expected shaking of heads.

She looked out of the window. The day was gloomy, the clouds low and full of rain. The house was warm and she knew it was sensible to stay in, but suddenly she couldn't. The house was mocking her in its emptiness, echoing around her, and it would be hours before she could expect to see Myrtle. Anger swelled up towards her sister. Myrtle was being unfair; she had been ill and deserved a little consideration.

She reached for a raincoat and hat, picked up Uncle Wilf's huge umbrella and, prepared for whatever the weather decided to throw at her, she set off. She had no particular goal in mind. She just needed to run away from the silence and the fear that her life might continue its lonely path until she was as old as Auntie Audrey. She wished she knew where to find her sister. She was sure to be with the irritating Stanley Love, who acted as though he were twenty, and his boring brothers would probably be with them. If she knew where they'd gone, she would try and find them. The company of the three boys was better than nothing.

Filled with melancholy, she walked through the streets, indifferent to people pushing past her, ignoring them if they spoke, wrapped in her own thoughts, none of them happy. She tried to face the truth that she lacked the ability to make friends, and at that moment it was a serious disability to which she saw no end. Telling herself it was because she was more particular about whom she chose as a friend, she convinced herself for a while that one or two true friends were better than a host of acquaintances.

Her mind drifted back to her childhood with Mam and Dad who loved her and a baby sister who needed her. It was a time grown more rosy in hindsight, a time when everything was perfect. Then, she trawled miserably through all that had happened to them since. Surely she deserved something more than this?

She reminded herself how the staff in the home dealt with

her periods of melancholy by telling her to remember and list the wonderful things in her life. There were wonderful things and the best had been their good fortune ending up as part of the generous and loving Castle family. She cheered up a little and began listing the good things in her life. It was a good thing to remember the best rather than the worst sometimes. They had been right about that.

Although they had seen little of her at first, Hetty had relented her initial fury at her discovery that they were her errant husband's children, and she now treated them kindly. They would never be close, but after believing they were alone in the world, having Hetty, Shirley and Bleddyn was greatly valued by Maude and Myrtle.

These thoughts cheered her and she wanted to talk to Myrtle and tell her about her happier mood. But soon the rain began to fall, the air grew cold, she had no idea where to find her sister, and slowly melancholy settled once again.

Myrtle was out with Stanley, Harold and Percival Love. Eirlys had made them a picnic and with the two older boys carrying paper carriers containing all they could scrounge, they had set off for the small rocky inlet, hardly large enough to be called a beach, not far from the more popular sandy stretch of St David's Well Bay with its hordes of visitors. Before they had reached the outskirts of the town, it began to rain. The spots were gentle at first but within a few minutes had increased to a heavy downpour which threatened to soak them, so, turning away from the beach, Myrtle led them down a lane behind some dilapidated shop premises, with broken-down buildings on either side, walking across concrete which was old and worn. There were cracks through which plants and even a few small trees grew. The rain shushed around them and the place had an eerie atmosphere that made Percival hurry to Myrtle's side and grab her hand. With an arm around his shoulders, she pushed open the door of what had once been a stable.

They stood in the doorway, waiting for the rain to ease, their backs to the interior.

'Phew, it stinks a bit,' Stanley complained after a glance inside. 'How did you know about the place?'

'This is where Maude and I lived one winter,' she said softly.
'What, on your own? Just you and Maude?' Harold gasped.
'Wow! No one to nag you. Do what you like. Great! Why did
you leave?'

'Sick and starving we were and if Beth Castle hadn't found
us, and if Marged and Huw and Granny Molly Piper and
Auntie Audrey hadn't taken us in, I don't know what would
have happened. Maude would almost certainly have died.'

'I'd be too scared to sleep here,' the ten-year-old Percival
muttered, in his low, slow monotone. 'Creepy-crawlies, no
proper bed and all this dark.'

'And food with lumps in it – when you could get any,'
Stanley teased.

'I wouldn't like it neither,' Harold said soberly. 'Not really.'

Aware that Myrtle was feeling embarrassed by the revela-
tion, Stanley said, 'Come on, brovers. Our place wasn't all
that grand. Ma did her best, but we lived in a room smaller
than this, four to a bed and first up best dressed. I remember
if you don't!'

Driven by the rain, forgetting their intention to spend a few
hours on the beach, they went inside. As their eyes became
accustomed to the poor light, they saw a manger with a few
rotting wisps of hay inside, and in a corner, a pile of clothes
and a few empty tins. Then something moved and the three
boys gave a shriek of fear. A figure stood up and in disbelief
Myrtle stared at her sister.

'Maude! What are you doing here? I thought I'd seen a
ghost!'

'Me too an' all,' muttered a trembling Percival. 'You've
given us all nightmares, Maude.'

As confidence returned, Stanley demanded, 'What the 'ell
you playing at, Maude? Eh?'

'I was feeling miserable and I thought that by coming here,
remembering how we had lived after running away from the
children's home, I might realize how lucky Myrtle and I now
are.'

'Why did you run away?' Percival wanted to know.

'We thought we had a brother-in-law and we wanted to find
him,' Maude said.

'Instead we found Hetty and Shirley Downs,' Myrtle added.

'Shirley's a sister, our dad was her dad, too. Hetty didn't like us at first, but now she's like another auntie. And we've got all the Castle family and lots of friends.' Myrtle turned to her sister. 'So, what have you got to be miserable about, our Maude?'

'Nothing, I suppose. I feel lonely now you're out so much. Auntie Audrey and Wilf away, everyone busy, I'm neglected, and I want to work at the beach like I used to.'

'Jealous, she is,' Stanley whispered to Myrtle as they left the sad building and set off once more for the beach. 'You having a nice bloke like me to go out with.'

She grinned and gave him a push. She turned to her sister. 'Why don't you come with us?' she asked, but Maude shook her head.

'I'll go home with her,' Myrtle said, handing Harold the soggy paper bag she was holding. 'I dare say you lot will manage to eat my share.'

'Don't do that, Myrtle,' Stanley whispered urgently. 'It's what she wants, to spoil things.'

'Don't be daft! She isn't well, that's all.'

'Spoils things, that's what she does. Jealous of you and the friends you make and the fun you have, so she spoils it.'

Angrily, Myrtle pushed him away and hurried after Maude. She was aware that what he was saying was true but she wasn't ready to face it.

As they walked home, Maude said, 'D'you think if I brought the man from the employment office here, showed him where we had lived, he might be more sympathetic?'

'Worth a try,' Myrtle said. 'Talk to Uncle Huw about it, he'd know how to get them to come.' She patted her sister's arm. 'Sorry you were miserable and I wasn't there to talk you out of it.'

'I'm on my own so much lately. You always off with that daft Stanley, Auntie Audrey and Uncle Wilf in Devon.'

'You don't have to stay in. Why don't you go out? You never know who you'll meet if you go out instead of locking yourself away.'

'I don't know anyone.'

''Course you do, there's them for a start!' Myrtle pointed to where Mr Gregory and his donkeys were coming around

67

the corner of the lane, returning from their day on the beach.

They turned and walked beside the dainty-footed creatures, Maude touching the rough wet coats, taking pleasure at being with the sturdy animals. They waited while Mr Gregory collected the animals' feed and a bale of hay which the lead donkey, Charlie, carried, and went with him to the stables where they were sheltered at night.

The sound of the donkeys as they chewed their meal, the smell of their wet coats, the companionable feeling they gave, comforted Maude in a way she was unable to describe. They gave comfort and asked nothing in return. Mr Gregory studied her changing expression, the frown lines easing away, the jaw softening and, clenching his pipe in his strong teeth, he smiled and nodded slightly to show he understood.

When Maude left the factory at two o'clock one afternoon, she remembered Myrtle's words and, instead of going home she went for a walk. Her feet took her along the lane leading to Mr Gregory's smallholding, and at a junction where two lanes crossed, she saw a young man standing looking at a piece of paper, turning it this way and that in a puzzled manner, shuffling his feet, looking in one direction then another, obviously lost. She called out offering help and walked towards him.

'I'm looking for a Mr Gregory,' he explained. 'I have an appointment to talk about a job.'

'I'm heading that way, I'll show you where he lives but he might not be there. He's probably on the beach with the donkeys for a couple of hours yet,' Maude said.

'I have an appointment with him,' he explained, waving a piece of paper vaguely.

'In that case, he'll have left someone in charge.'

After pointing the way she looked at him curiously. He looked about her own age, so why was he job hunting when he was at the age for being called up?

As though reading her mind, he said, 'I was offered the chance of doing work on the land instead of the army. My parents have a farm and I'm experienced in growing things.'

'I thought they employed girls to do that sort of thing,' she said with a hint of disapproval. She was immediately resentful

68

at her own unchosen placement. 'The Land Army is supposed to be for girls, to release men to fight. I tried to join but they wouldn't have me because I have a few health problems. I had no choice,' she said pointedly. 'I was told to work in a factory and I hate it. I'd love the chance to work on the beach with the rest of my family. How come you were able to choose?'

'Things change. I'm needed here apparently. But in a few months I'll be told to join the forces. I've only been given a deferment.'

'You don't think the war will end this year then?' she asked, softening her tone.

'Unlikely, I'd say, but we can hope.' He smiled then and asked, 'Why the beach? What can you do to help win the war working on the beach?'

'Entertainment is important. People need some fun as much now as in peace time. More perhaps, and the Castle family do a lot to keep people entertained.'

They had reached the gate of the smallholding, and walking to meet them was Bernard Gregory, his pipe in his hand, waving towards them.

'Hello, Maude, coming in for a drink? I've made some tea and Beth brought some cakes home yesterday, left over from her cafe.' Turning to the young man, he said, 'You must be Reginald, come in and I'll show you around.'

An hour later, Maude and Reginald left Bernard leaning on his gate, waving his pipe at them, as they set off back to the town.

'Never without his pipe or that old hat of his,' Maude whispered.

'Where are you off to now?' Reggie asked. 'I don't have to rush back, so if you want to show me the beach where these wonderful entertainments take place, I'll be pleased to see it.'

Maude was hungry. The small cakes Bernard had offered them had not been enough, so she hesitated.

'It's all right, Maude, I understand if you want to get home,' the young man continued.

She shook her head. She didn't want to say goodbye to this pleasant young man. Taller than her by a head and strongly built, with hair that was wiry and long, a thick black frame for his rugged face with its surprisingly dark blue eyes. With an instant change of mind, she said, 'No, not home. I was wondering if we could go to the Castle's cafe. I'm starving.'

'The cafe it is.' He pulled some coins out of his pocket and examined them. 'Four and sixpence I've got, is that enough d'you think?'

'We'll go Dutch,' she insisted, taking out a purse and shaking it encouragingly.

Myrtle was there and she looked up in surprise when her sister walked in with the young man and introduced him rather casually, as though they were long time friends. 'My baby sister,' she announced as she waved towards Myrtle.

'Nearly sixteen,' Myrtle hissed.

Marged filled two plates with chips and a slice of spam and handed it to the young couple just as Huw was asking Reggie if he was looking for work. Reggie laughed and shook his head.

'If I started work here I'd be in the army faster than Maude can eat this plate of chips.' He explained his position.

'So, we'll be seeing you then, if you're living at Bernard's place with our daughter Beth,' Marged said and further explanations ensued on the Castle family members.

When Reggie walked back to the station, he was bemused with the information that had been hurled at him and begged Maude to meet him at the weekend and help him to sort it out. Maude walked home filled with excitement. Her feet wanted to dance. It was the first time she had made any kind of arrangement to meet a boy and Reginald was one of the nicest she had ever met.

That evening, Shirley was taking part in a concert not far from the town of Newport. Because of the late finish, she had been given accommodation in a small bed and breakfast in the town and a taxi had been arranged to take her there at the end of her performance.

She was quite used to staying away from home now. She enjoyed the camaraderie of other performers and had no fears about waiting for taxis to take her to unknown places to spend the night. That evening she had been asked to join with a

70

small group and sing a few choruses at the hospital where they had given a small concert for injured soldiers, sailors and airmen. She was touched to see how the familiar choruses cheered them.

They overran their time and when she went for the taxi it had gone. Using the telephone in one of the nurse's rooms she was disappointed to be told that she would have to wait for almost an hour.

'That will make it late for my landlady,' she said with a worried frown. 'She doesn't have a phone, so I can't let her know.'

A young man who had been helping with the mock-up stage asked where she was staying and, when she told him the address, offered to take her home.

'I've got Dad's car and enough petrol to get me home and I go past your digs anyway,' he assured her. The taxi was cancelled and amid grateful thanks, the young man, who said his name was James Thorby, helped her and her stick and small makeup bag into the Austin Seven with pride.

Shirley didn't know the area and had never been to the address where she was to stay, so when ten minutes had passed in polite conversation and she looked out to see fields and woodland she didn't feel any alarm. The town couldn't be far and with the continuing restriction of lights being shown at night, she wasn't likely to see it until they had arrived.

It was as the road became a lane and appeared to peter out into what was no more than a track, that she asked, 'Is this a short cut, James?'

He turned to smile at her and gave a slow chuckle. 'We aren't in a hurry to get there, are we? Why would we want a short cut? There's a nice little patch of grass up here just outside the wood, we can sit there and get to know each other.'

A chill drenched her in sweat, she felt it running down her sides. Her bowels churned and muscles stiffened as fear gripped her. Trying to sound calm and in control, she said, 'I think you've made a mistake, James. I am very tired and I need to get to sleep.'

His hand left the wheel and he began to caress her thigh, moving higher until she lifted her handbag and brought it down heavily on his roaming hand, making him gasp.

'What did you do that for?'

'Please, just take me to my digs, will you?'

'What's the m-m-matter, Shirley? You've been g-g-giving me the eye all evening and the way you accepted my offer of a lift, well, we know how many b-b-b-beans make five, don't we?'

His stutter and the way he was glancing at her showed he was as nervous as herself and her panic increased. 'Stop the car! I insist you turn around and take me back to town as you promised.'

'S-s-stop the c-car,' he mocked. 'T-t-t-ake me home! All right, I don't mind playing your games and having some fun first.' He stopped the car and she backed away from him as he leaned towards her. She realized with increasing alarm, that he thought her demands, her reticence, were part of the game in which he believed they were involved.

She opened the door of the car and threatened, 'I'll scream if you come near me. D'you understand?' She reached towards him to rescue her stick but he caught hold of her arm in a strong grip, pulling her until they were face to face.

'Tease,' he hissed. 'Worse than tarts they are.' With frightening speed he leaned across and pushed her so she fell from the car onto the gravelly surface, then he drove off. The tail lights disappeared and she was alone in complete darkness, miles from anywhere. Surely he'd come back? He wouldn't abandon her without cause? She felt panic rising as she realized she knew nothing about him and neither would anyone else. She hadn't even noticed the man until she was phoning for the taxi. Her presumption that he was one of the hospital staff was almost certainly wrong.

The sound of the engine which had almost faded, grew louder and she sighed with relief. He was coming back. Thank goodness. He'd only intended to frighten her. He was coming back and everything would be all right. She knew she would never accept the offer of a lift ever again, particularly in an area she didn't know.

As the red lights reappeared, she began to prepare words to apologize without appearing too forward – she didn't want to face more embarrassment. The car skidded on the gravel, the door opened but as she stepped forward to get in, first her stick was thrown out then her handbag, open, its contents, including the torch without which she never travelled, falling in a scatter. Then the door slammed shut and he drove off once again. The silence settled around her and she fought back tears of helplessness. Lowering herself painfully to her knees, she began to feel around trying to gather her belongings, her fingers searching for the round, shiny torch with urgency.

She collected what she could then sat wondering what to do. It couldn't be more than midnight and she didn't fancy sitting there until morning in the faint hope of someone passing. She got up, wishing she was wearing something more sensible than a thin dress decorated with sequins. Heading back the way they had come seemed the wisest thing to do and as she walked, picking her way in the darkness with only the narrow beam of light from the torch to guide her way, she tried to remember how long it had been since they had made the last turn.

A man was leaning against a tree, a couple of dead rabbits hanging on his shoulder, a ferret in his pocket. His eyesight was keen as he was used to being out at night and he saw and heard the woman approaching long before she reached the bend in the track. He moved quietly around to the other side of the trunk and waited.

The person was walking unevenly and when he saw the long clothes and heard her sobs, he realized it was a woman and didn't want to frighten her. He ran quietly and swiftly until he was some distance away from her, then he began singing. Approaching her slowly would worry her less.

'"Kiss me goodnight Sergeant Major",' he sang, '"Tuck me in my little wooden bed". Here, who's that wandering around at this time of night?' he asked as though he'd just heard her.

'Go away!'

'Certainly, but if you're lost, I'm the bloke to help you. I know this area like a pigeon knows his way home. He stepped out from the bushes and Shirley raised her stick threateningly. 'All right, I'll leave you to find your own way. How did you get out here? No buses and we're a long way from a railway. Car?' he suggested, head on one side. 'Bicycle? Broomstick?'

'I was offered a lift but, well it might sound like a joke to

73

you, but he got fresh and I've ended up having to walk.'

The man laughed and she turned and walked on. He ran to catch her up. 'Sorry, I'm real sorry, but you have to admit it's funny. It's like a music hall joke.'

She admitted she needed help and he led her, keeping well away from her, aware of the speed with which she could raise that formidable stick, until they came to a small cottage.

Leaving her at the gate, he knocked on the door until a window opened and a voice called out angrily. Shirley heard a whispered exchange of words and soon a man and a woman came to the door.

She had a fleeting thought that this might be an experience similar to the first, but she was exhausted, her leg was aching badly and she accepted the invitation to sleep on their sofa.

'You bin poachin' again, young Andy?'

'Poaching? Me? Never! But I've left a rabbit on your doorstep. If anyone asked, he gave himself up.'

The following morning, after a good sleep and a huge break-fast, Shirley was taken into Newport on a hay cart, where she collected her overnight bag and caught the train back to St David's Well, wondering whether she would ever again have the nerve to leave it.

Audrey and Wilf came home from Devon and when Huw met them at the station, it was immediately apparent to him that something was wrong. Audrey was flushed, as though hold-ing back anger, Wilf solemn and uneasy. They answered the usual questions about the few days away automatically, as though the holiday was already forgotten and irrelevant. Huw's good-natured smile faded and he was reduced to silence as he drove them through the streets in the late evening glow. The day had been a pleasant one, but these two had brought clouds and gloom, Huw thought curiously. He glanced at them in the rear view mirror wondering if they had been quarrelling – a most unlikely event.

Marged opened the door to them and ushered them inside, while Huw carried their luggage to their own house a few doors further on. Audrey refused her sister's invitation to stay for a meal, insisting they went straight to their own home. 'You can come if you wish, we have something to tell you both.'

'It's only salad and baked potatoes with a scrap of cheese,' Marged announced, 'so I'll bring it up.' She placed all they needed on a tray and took the supper to where her sister and Wilf were sitting silently, one each side of the table.

'I won't be opening the shop as I promised,' Audrey announced when they were sitting down to the meal Marged had prepared for them. Maude and Myrtle were both out and the four of them were sitting uneasily around the table.

'Good,' Marged said. 'I'm sure you'd rather be home with Wilf. I must confess, I'm relieved. I've been at my wit's end wondering how to fit it all in, the laundry and the cooking and the rest. Marvellous, you are, Audrey, isn't she, Huw?'

'Hush, Marged. Let's listen to what Audrey's got to say,' Huw said, his hand on his wife's arm. Something in Audrey's expression prepared him for some bad news.

'Wilf's very ill,' Audrey said quietly. 'He knew before we went away, but he didn't tell me. He knew we would need time alone to get used to it.' She reached out a hand and Wilf held it tightly.

'I tried to persuade Audrey that it's best for us both for life to go on as normal, but she isn't willing,' Wilf said. 'We're going to get out and about, build a few memories while we can.'

Marged and Huw looked at each other, unable to decide what to say. It didn't seem appropriate to offer sympathy, that would come later. The words wouldn't come when Marged tried to ask the nature of the illness. Eventually, Huw said. 'Whatever you want us to do, just ask and we'll do it. Anything.'

'When are you going to tell the others?' Marged wanted to know. 'Myrtle and Maude? Bleddyn, Hetty and the rest?' She was looking at Wilf and was surprised and embarrassed at the mild irritation she felt when Audrey answered for him.

'Not yet. We want things to go on as normal for as long as we can manage.'

'What about you, Wilf?' Marged said, pointedly. 'What do you want?'

His answer, so lightly said, chilled her. 'I want to stay well long enough to see the boys safely home, but I doubt I'll manage that.'

'Now, we're going out,' Audrey said, rising from the table and helping to pull Wilf's chair out as he followed.

'But it's now you're back! You haven't unpacked yet! Where are you rushing off to at this time of day? It'll be dark in a couple of hours.'

This time it was Wilf who answered. 'We're going to visit our son's grave,' he said with a glance at his wife. 'I know he can't possibly know, but we want to tell him anyway.'

Marged and Huw watched them leave, speechless with the sadness that had unexpectedly accompanied the homecoming. 'Should we go with them?' Marged whispered as they heard the front door close behind them.

'No, Marged. I think they need to be on their own.'

In silence, they gathered together the dishes and went home.

Somehow things settled down and after a few days, the news of Wilf's illness was rarely referred to, Audrey making it clear that discussion was not something she wanted. Two girls were found to run the shop in half-daily shifts, and at Bleddyn's suggestion, Myrtle proudly dealt with the books and also worked in the shop on the occasions when the girls were unable to be there.

It was apparent that Myrtle had a gift for figures and Bleddyn invited her to visit himself and Hetty for them to explain a little about keeping the books for a small business. Shirley was there, packing her clothes ready to leave for a two week concert tour.

'I admit that apart from totalling the weekly accounts for newspaper deliveries when I worked in the newsagent's, adding up is something I'm happy to leave for someone else to do,' Shirley admitted.

'Go on, Shirley, clever you are. Sums are easy.'

'Don't underestimate yourself, Myrtle. You're good at them. I can't keep my mind on the figures for long enough to complete a task.' She smiled at Hetty. 'Left it to you, didn't I, Mam?'

'It's a gift,' Hetty said, 'and you, Myrtle, have it in plenty.'

Maude met Reginald once or twice and she began calling at the smallholding after her early shift, and sometimes before the late one. Bernard willingly accepted her offer to work an hour or two, and she began to enjoy the physical effort needed to pull weeds, hoe the ground, plant seedling lettuce and the other tedious work. Whenever she could she helped carry food for the donkeys' evening feed.

Bernard blithely ignored the requests from the Ministry to spend all his time on the land, and continued to take his string of donkeys to the beach, insisting that they needed the exercise and the children needed the fun of riding them. There were always boys willing to help on days when he was unable to stay. Stanley still found excuses to avoid going in to the shop to help out on the beach and he was delighted on the occasions when he was given Bernard's donkeys to look after.

In the busy month of July, Stanley, Harold and Percival found reasons to meet Myrtle and she forgot Stanley's youth, attracted by his spurious adulthood, which was noticeable in the way he looked after Harold and Percival as though he were their father. Although, she reminded him frequently of her own maturity, as she was now, she insisted – having recently passed her fifteenth birthday – almost sixteen years old.

At the end of July, Maude was told that following the request of Bleddyn Castle, she was excused from factory work and would be employed by him and Bleddyn in the cafe or on the sands. She was enormously relieved and certain that this summer would be better for her.

With an increasing number of day trippers as well as the summer visitors staying at the guest houses and the dozens of private houses that took the opportunity to make some extra money, the pavements in the town became blocked with the tourists who were content to stand and stare whilst the locals tried desperately to do their daily shopping.

It seemed there was no room for one more family on the crowded beach, but still they came and squeezed into the smallest patch of sand or grass and made a space to call their own for the few hours of their stay. The trippers, cheerful on their precious day out, brought a gaiety that almost made some of them forget the war, except those with a member of their family serving in one of the armed forces. For those, the smiles were false, the laughter a pretence, an attempt to persuade others that all would be well, or convince the bereaved that life would go on and get slowly better.

Marged believed that what the Castles did to help the town and its visitors enjoy the warm summer days was a valuable addition to the battle against the enemy. She was proud of her family's reputation and guarded them all against the occasional remarks suggesting that for the Castles, making money was the only priority.

Summer wore on, the number of visitors to the town increased. The summer activities organized by Eirlys, most of which were a repeat of the previous year, brought even more from other areas, defeating the idea of persuading people to stay at home and not travel. 'Holidays at Home' was not of concern to St David's Well; they had a reputation for drawing crowds to share in their holiday fun which they intended to keep.

The government had requested that every town should provide entertainment to encourage their citizens to stay home for their holidays to ease the pressure on public transport and leave it free for urgent deliveries and the armed forces. The attitude to this in St David's Well was, let other towns do what they could, but if people wanted to ignore what their own towns offered and instead travel to St David's Well, there was nothing they were going to do to stop them. If the natural amenities of the popular town, plus the council's efforts, succeeded in attracting visitors from other places, it was hardly likely they would discourage them.

The town was renowned for its welcome and the fun it provided. It continued to attract people from miles away, visitors filling the trains and the buses and blocking the roads with bicycles and the pavements with those on foot.

There was a great deal of entertainment arranged. Open air concerts were rarely cancelled because of inclement weather, the crowds insisting on ignoring the cold winds and even the rain. There were sand castle competitions and cricket matches, giant chess tournaments – the variety was endless. Many events were planned to raise money for the war charities. Every activity from dolls' picnics to community singing brought the crowds, and the cafes were busy for most of the daylight hours.

Only Audrey seemed unable to enjoy that bright, lively summer. She and Wilf went out on day trips to other places, their smiles forced, avoiding the usual family gatherings, making excuses whenever one was suggested. Maude had left the factory, but with Myrtle they also ran the household and did what they could to assist in the various businesses. Since meeting Reginald, Myrtle thought her sister had become a different person, rarely complaining and if she still suffered symptoms from earlier illnesses, they were never mentioned. Best of all, Myrtle could go out without being accused of neglecting her.

'Hopping about like fleas on a griddle, we are,' Myrtle told Mr Gregory. 'That busy, you'd never believe. Great, isn't it?' She had called to help with the harvesting of tomatoes and beans. She loved to work in the fields, as well as going with Mr Gregory on his horse and cart to distribute his orders. It was a surprise therefore to see Reginald sitting on the loaded cart, the reins held loosely in his hands.

'You? I thought Mr Gregory was taking me?'

'Sorry to disappoint you.' He laughed at her surprise.

'Can you manage the horse? It isn't as easy as it looks, mind,' she said in a warning tone, hands on hips.

'I can manage.'

'And have you put the boxes in the order we deliver them? Saves ages that does.'

Reggie looked suitably solemn. 'Yes, Miss. I've done every-thing as per instructions.' He offered his hand for her to climb up, and pushing it away impatiently, she jumped on and fell into his lap. Blushing madly, and muttering about her stupid shoes, insisting they had caused her to trip, she settled into her seat and gestured for him to drive on, which he did, turn-ing away in an effort to hide his laughter.

Shirley Downs came home from the tour feeling tired and edgy, trying in vain to concentrate her mind on the success of the performances she had given. She hadn't told her mother and Bleddyn what had happened after the concert in Newport. There was no point in alarming them and causing them worry every time she went away. The stress and the fright she had received by being abandoned far from her accommodation, made the thought of a rest on her comfortable bed very tempt-ing, but she was unable to resist looking through the post that awaited her. There were five letters from Freddy Clements and it was these she read first.

Shirley had written to Freddy ever since he had joined the army. They had enjoyed a friendship which they had kept secret at first as he had been engaged to marry Marged's daughter, Beth. The friendship that had started as a bit of fun had quickly grown into an affair which neither had taken seriously nor regretted. It had been pure devilment on Shirley's part at first to coax him away from Beth, but since he had gone away, their friendship and liking for each other had grown in a surprising way. Shirley looked forward to his letters with great excitement. She wrote to him twice each week and it was a point of honour not to let him down by missing one of her regular days.

In civvy street, Freddy had always had a problem with money. As soon as he touched it, it seemed to melt away. When he and Beth were engaged, he had used most of the money they had saved, and now, serving in the army, facing danger on a daily basis and with a maturity he had not previously possessed, he felt ashamed. He was still interested in money, but now he didn't spend it with the same carelessness. He wanted to come out of the fighting with a bank balance that would set him up in a business of his own. Making money was now the obsession, and making it was easier than he had imagined.

Soldiers were easily bored. So far from home and with little to do when they had precious time to themselves, he organized card games, he acquired food and even cigarettes and sold them. He was an expert at finding local people to supply his needs and he earned a reputation for being able to supply practically anything. He even managed to smuggle some girls into the camp and, when caught, insisted they were for the officers and the whole thing was hushed up. He didn't make any money on that occasion, but he wasn't court-martialled either. He wished he could put that story in one of Shirley's letters, but with the censors reading every line he decided that the story had to wait until he got home.

In odd moments he thought he might be able to earn a good living after the war if he ignored the rules and played it boldly like many who hovered on street corners with cases full of illegally bought merchandise. Wide boys or spivs they were called and he envied them. He was here earning a pittance and they were at home making fortunes. It wasn't fair, but he didn't waste time or energy worrying about it. After the war, he intended to redress the balance more than a little. There was certain to be plenty of opportunity for making money fast.

It was only dreams though. Thoughts of Shirley made him realize he would never succumb to blatant dishonesty. He would lose her if he went down that road. He had never told her how much she meant to him, their relationship had always been light-hearted and he wanted it to stay that way until he was home and could show her just how he felt about her. Shirley Downs was the reason he wanted money.

Licking his pencil he sat down and wrote to her, telling her he was well and couldn't wait to get home. He ended it in a way he hadn't done before; glancing around to make sure none of his mates were looking and able to tease him, he signed it, 'Love you for ever, Freddy.'

One day, Myrtle saw a notice on the board outside the town hall asking for objects that were surplus to requirements, to pass on to families from the big cities who had lost their homes in bombing raids. There was a list of the items needed which at first surprised her, but quickly made sense. Pictures, photograph frames, vases, ornaments, cushions, flower pots, small things that make a home. These were things that would be hard to replace. She went straight home to tell Audrey.

The poster explained that the essentials were provided: beds and cupboards, tables and chairs, but it was these small items that made a home a home.

Audrey ransacked the house, piling up what had once been treasures and were now rarely seen. In her distressed state, with Wilf being seriously ill, there was no value placed on the things she packed into boxes ready for collection. Ornaments that had belonged to her mother, kitchen utensils that were duplicated by the things they had brought from Wilf's home when they had sold his mother's house and married.

Thinking of how little time Wilf and she had left, more and more went into the boxes, throwing things in with less and less care as she abandoned so many things she had once loved.

81

Tearfully she looked at it all and wondered why they had once been so important.

With petrol so scarce it was no surprise to see the man collecting it all, and writing it down in a notebook, travelling by horse and cart. The collector, who called himself Derek, appeared to be in his late thirties and walked with a pronounced limp. He wore a solemn expression and seemed almost tearful when Audrey opened the door to him and showed what she was contributing.

'God bless you, lady. This is a town with a good heart,' he said. 'Every piece will go to a good home, that I promise you.'

'Who is going to distribute it?' Audrey asked curiously.

'A special task force set up by the Women's Voluntary Service, lady. Another fine band of good hearts.'

Audrey helped him load her boxes and saw that several people had given rugs. Running up to what had been her mother's bedroom, she came down and handed him a brand new rug handmade by Eirlys Ward.

'I'll have to go straight to the depot with this lot, lady. I'll be back to call on your neighbours tomorrow,' he explained as he set off down the street.

Reginald was passing Sidney Street on his way from the corn merchants when he saw Audrey handing the last of the boxes onto the cart. At first he didn't notice the driver, he was looking at the door half expecting Maude to appear. When the cart drove slowly past him, he looked at the man who was clicking to the horse to encourage him to hurry, and gasped in shock as the man winked at him.

'Hi there, Reggie, doing all right are you?'

'Andy!'

Without slowing the horse, the man leaned forward and shook his fair head. 'Not Andy. Not anymore. It's Derek now. Derek Hanbury, sounds posh, eh? Impresses people no end.'

'Come back, Andy. Give it back, please! Andy!'

As the horse heaved then picked up speed, the man called back, 'Andy? Never heard of him.' His laughter left a slipstream behind him accompanied by the rhythmic clopping of the horse's feet. Reginald turned and walked away from Sidney Street. There was no point in meeting Maude now. Andy's unwelcome appearance had ruined everything once again.

Maude had arranged to meet Reginald when he finished work at five. She cycled down the lanes towards Mr Gregory's smallholding and was surprised to see him walking towards her before she reached the crossroads where they had first met.

'You're early, why don't you come back and have something to eat with us, then we can go to the pictures, if you like,' she said as she dismounted and raised her face for his kiss.

'Sorry Maude, but I won't be coming.'

'Oh, you have to work, do you? I know what a busy time of year this is.'

'It's more than that. I won't be seeing you again. I'll probably get a transfer to another farm quite soon. Sorry, but it's something I can't change.'

'But we can write? You won't be going that far, will you?'

He shrugged. 'I don't know. I might be called up now the work here is finished. It was only a temporary arrangement, getting a few people trained to help Mr Gregory grow extra food.'

'So, when will I see you?'

Again he shrugged.

Maude turned away and without another word, cycled away, tears temporarily blinding her. She blinked them away until she was out of sight of Reginald who was standing in the middle of the road watching her go. Then she stopped and wiped her eyes, reminded herself angrily that he was boring anyway, always talking about his job, and cycled on.

Thankfully, the house was empty and she held off tears until she was inside. She sat on the stairs and sobbed her disappointment into a succession of handkerchiefs. How could life be so unfair?

Myrtle came home and found Maude red-faced from crying. At once concerned she asked if Wilf was all right. Then she wondered if it was Reginald who had upset her.

'He doesn't want to see me anymore and won't tell me why,' Maude told her, in a choking voice sounding unlike her own.

'It happens,' Myrtle said in a worldly way. 'Girls have lots of boyfriends before they find the one they stay with forever.

If he's the one for you he'll be back. Beth told me there are often quarrels when you first meet a boy. Adjusting to each other, she said it was. This is probably what this is. Don't cry, Maude, it makes you look awful blotchy, and he might be on his way to see you, now this minute.'

Myrtle was filled with disappointment. Reggie and Maude being friends had eased the responsibility she felt for her sister. With Reggie and Maude becoming close friends, she had been more free to go out without having to ask whether Maude minded, or worse, wanted to come.

It was six o'clock and they had promised to cook the evening meal for Audrey and Wilf, who had gone to keep a doctor's appointment. Myrtle had picked some wild flowers, some red and white valerian and a few scabious from the wall of an old church nearby. While Maude stifled her tears and set the table, she went to collect a vase to arrange them, but the pantry shelf on which such things were stored was empty. She was curious, but not unduly so as Auntie Audrey was always sorting things out and changing things around these days. A symptom of her distress about Wilf's illness, she supposed, keeping herself busy. She filled a milk bottle, arranged the flowers, and put it in the centre of the table.

'Don't go out again tonight,' Maude begged. 'I don't want to be on my own.'

'Please Maude, don't ask me to stay in. Stanley and I are going to the concert. Shirley is singing and there's a troupe of dancers who're supposed to be really good. There's a comedian, too. Come with us,' she pleaded.

'I can't. I'm too miserable.'

'All right,' Myrtle said stifling a sigh of disappointment, 'I'll offer my ticket to Eirlys. Stanley won't mind, and if he does he'll have to lump it.'

'He'll be pleased, I expect. He's real fond of Eirlys, she's almost a mother to him, whereas you're just a casual friend.'

Knowing the remark was brought on by her sister's misery and fully intended to hurt, Myrtle only smiled and agreed. 'Yes, Eirlys and her father are all the family Stanley and his brothers have. A bit like us, really, which is why we have to be their friends.'

'All right, go if you want to. I'll go and see Beth and Mr

Gregory. Perhaps Reginald will be there and we can sort out the problem.'

'Good idea. Thanks, Maude.'

Happily, Myrtle washed lettuce and the rest of the salad, chopped potatoes and mixed them with the soft boiled egg – the last of their ration – and spread the thinly cut corned beef on the four plates. 'All ready for when Auntie Audrey and Wilf come in,' she said, flopping into a chair and glancing at the clock.

It was almost seven o'clock before the meal was over and the dishes dealt with. During the meal, Audrey had explained about the collection for the homeless and the items she had contributed. Myrtle and Maude looked surprised. All Granny Moll's things had remained untouched since her death. This was a very sudden change of mind. They said nothing, but while they washed up they whispered to each other, wondering if the clearance was part of a larger plan, perhaps to sell the house and move somewhere else. As always, their first thought was about their own future. Where would they live? Would Marged and Huw take them in? Or would they be left to find a place for themselves?

'After all,' Myrtle whispered, ' we can't expect them to look after us for always, can we?'

'I suppose not, but where would we go?'

'If that Reggie asks you to marry him, I think you should say yes,' Myrtle joked. A glance at her sister's face told her it was not funny.

'His name is Reginald. He doesn't like to be called Reggie.'

'All right, but it's a bit of a mouthful, mind.'

Myrtle went to the concert with the three boys. Eirlys's father came too. Afterwards, Morgan promised the ever hungry boys some chips. Percival looked less pleased than his brothers. 'I won't have to eat one of them rissoles, will I, Uncle Morgan? I 'ates them, I do.' His brothers glared at him. If he'd kept quiet they'd have been able to share his between them.

Maude went on her bicycle to talk to Reginald but it was Beth who answered the door and when Maude asked to speak to Reginald, Beth shook her head.

'Sorry Maude, he's out, I've no idea where. I'll tell him you called and perhaps he'll see you tomorrow.'

85

To a disappointed Maude, it was the word *perhaps* that seemed the loudest. *Perhaps* he would see her tomorrow. It was clear to her that he would not.

Beth closed the door and turned to where Reginald was standing close behind her. 'Don't ask me to do that again, Reginald, please. I hate lying and I hate it even more when it's on behalf of someone else.'

'Sorry, I know it was cowardly, Beth, but I find it hard to hurt her.'

'And you think I don't? You have to grow up and deal with your mistakes yourself, it seems to me.'

It wasn't a mistake, he wanted to tell her. The mistake was in thinking he could avoid seeing Andy who was calling himself Derek Hanbury and who wore a pious expression that fooled people and had once fooled him.

Five

Bernard Gregory was always up early in the mornings. With animals to care for there was no Sunday morning lie-in, every day began the same. Now that Beth lived with him, she too usually rose at the same time, spending the hours before leaving to open her cafe in small household tasks and occasionally some cooking. Peter was rarely at home. He spent most of his time in enemy-held territory helping to organize and run safe shelter and escape routes for prisoners and airmen shot down and on the run.

On this Sunday, early in August, Bernard went downstairs, and after making a cup of tea he opened the door intending to sit outside to drink it before starting his day. He heard Beth coming down the stairs and poured a second cup of tea, holding it ready to hand to her as she opened the door.

'What's all that smoke over near the field where the donkeys are?' she asked, taking the tea and hurrying to the door. When they stepped outside, the smell of burning was strong. Smoke billowed on the morning breeze and, from the amount of it, the fire was a large one.

'Damn me, Beth, I didn't see that. Or smell it. Come on, we'd better go and see. It looks dangerously close to Sally's cottage.'

Before they had swallowed a few mouthfuls of tea and reached for a jacket, they heard another sound. Fire engines were already on the way. 'We'd better hurry, Beth, in case Sally's in trouble.'

They called to Reginald, who was sleeping in the back room that had once been an outhouse but which had been joined on to the main building. He hastily dressed, apologized for oversleeping and followed them up onto the hill.

The vehicles were at the entrance to the field where the

donkeys spent their nights, and their anxious braying could be heard as the trio ran to Sally's house, which thankfully seemed safe from the fire. A fireman had already banged on her door, and as they approached a sleepy figure in a pink dressing gown with the addition of a coat held around her, opened the door. Her white hair was tucked around a band of material, which went around her head, as though she had hastily attempted to tidy its long, uneven tresses. Short-sightedly she peered at them and asked what was wrong.

Leaving the fire officers to explain, and promising to come back, Bernard went to check on his donkeys. The smoke was frightening and confusing them and, running through it, ignoring the shouts of the firemen, Bernard, Beth and Reginald went to the stables. At the gate, Bernard stopped and sighed with relief. The blaze was in the corner of the next field, close to the hedge. A cart was burning, its silhouette visible now and then as eddies of smoke moved around, teased by a light breeze.

Bernard and Reginald went into the stables and led the anxious donkeys out and Beth guided the frightened creatures to the far side of the field. As a precaution – sparks had been known to fly high and over surprising distances – Bernard went inside to make sure all was well, and gasped in surprise. Behind the door, grazing peacefully on hay from a string hay bale hanging against a wall, was a cart horse.

'A cart burned and a horse stabled with the donkeys? I hope you don't think this is my doing?' Bernard said to the police. 'Donkeys for the beach and a horse for my small cart is all I need. This one is a handsome fellow, big and strong.'

'He's that all right, Bernard.'

'He can stay here until you find the owner, if you like,' Bernard offered, patting the animal's powerful shoulders.

Beth went back to reassure Sally that her house was not in any danger, and once the fire had been extinguished, they all stood there for a while, wondering what had happened, and discussing the possibilities. Reginald had not slept well that night, and added to the tiredness a wave of dismay spread over him. An admiration for and an interest in horses gave him a keen observation and he had recognized the horse at once. It was the one his brother had been using the previous day. He was thankful that this time Andy hadn't involved him, but burning the stolen cart in a field close to where he lived had clearly been a deliberate act, taunting him, telling him he could easily connect him to his illegal and criminal activities and lose him the place he had worked so hard to earn.

He had probably stolen the horse when he needed one to beg householders for unwanted items in the area. He had always had an affinity with the creatures and would have no difficulty persuading one to follow him. With the horse a willing partner, stealing the cart would have been easy. With his charm and the 'little-boy-lost' expression he used so effectively, Andy had no difficulty getting money out of gullible, kind-hearted people. If only he would choose somewhere far away from here, Reginald could go on pretending he didn't have a brother.

Later that day, a policeman called at the smallholding and told Bernard that they had found the owner of the horse and the burnt out cart. Both had been stolen a week previously.

'Someone too lazy to walk home, maybe?' Bernard surmised. It had been known for one of his donkeys to be used by a drunken reveller to help him return home – although the unpredictable donkey was more likely to tip the rider into a ditch.

Once Beth reached the beach cafe that morning, Maude and Myrtle were there and she entertained them all with the story of the unlikely start to her day.

'Is the horse all right?' Myrtle asked and reassured she turned away content.

'The cart was a loss, it's a valuable thing to own these days. It's surprising how many businesses depend on horses now there's so little petrol,' Huw remarked.

'Like the man who called at our house to collect for bombed out families,' Myrtle added and at once, Marged was curious.

'What man?' she demanded. Maude explained abut Audrey handing over many of her possessions to the polite man with the horse and cart. At once Marged was angry. 'Some of those things belonged to my mother and I should have been consulted before she gave them to a stranger, good deed or not!'

Huw irritably told her to hush. Turning to Maude he said,

'You'd better find Audrey and go at once to tell the police. I heard yesterday that the man was a fraud. He's pretending to collect for the people made homeless, but is selling the stuff at markets miles away.'

Maude and Myrtle went to the police station with Audrey, who gave a description of the man whom she knew as Derek Hanbury, and also wrote down a list of the items she could remember giving him. On their return, Myrtle went onto the sands where she was in charge of the swingboats, and Maude returned to the beach cafe, proud of being able to help.

What an exciting day it had been so far. Although, she knew Audrey was far from pleased at the way she had been duped. But it was still exciting, being mixed up with criminals. She couldn't wait to discuss it with Reginald, if he still wanted to see her. A niggle of disappointment shadowed the day. Beth had seemed doubtful when she had said perhaps they would meet today. Even sleeping on it, changing the emphasis on the remembered words, trying to convince herself she had been mistaken, hadn't driven away the sad thought that he might not want to see her again.

At the police station, Police Constable Charlie Groves stared at a picture of Andy Cain and wondered. Audrey hadn't recognized him from the photograph they had shown on a poster, but that might be because she hadn't looked at him properly, busy handing out all she could spare, it was often the case that people didn't really look at each other, not strangers anyway. According to the information available, this was just the sort of scam Andy Cain would dream up. There was a second photograph of Andy Cain in the file, this time under his proper name and standing beside his brother, Reggie Probert.

He remembered seeing Reggie helping at the smallholding and notified his superiors about what had happened. He remembered Reggie and presumed the boy had once again been helping his brother to steal from good-hearted house-holders. The thought saddened him. He had believed that Reggie had stood a chance of going straight, if he could stay away from Andy.

He had said nothing about the man's brother to Audrey and

90

the sisters. Best not risk Reggie being warned. He had to be stopped. It was a mean trick, to accept gifts so willingly given and make money out of people's generosity and the tragedies of others, although he knew that disaster suffered by someone else was no barrier to greed.

St David's Well was so full of visitors, this busiest month of the year, that it would be impossible to check on every one of them, and the Probert brothers would have changed since the photograph had been taken. Imprinting the picture of the two men on his mind, he determined to try and find them. If they were still in the town that is, and that was extremely unlikely, he thought with dismay. He decided to call at the smallholding first. Perhaps Reggie was confident enough to stay put, bluff it out and swear he wasn't involved.

Beth had arranged to help at Castle's cafe for the whole day. Being a Sunday, her market cafe didn't open and her parents were grateful for her help. For Marged it was a breath of happy memories of a time when her daughter and she had worked alongside each other summer after summer.

Beth told several customers about their early morning adventure. It made a change from repetitive remarks about the weather and the war. When she saw Reginald approaching with the eggs and potatoes Marged had asked Bernard to supply, she turned to him and gestured to the lady who was listening to her story and asked him to verify what she was telling her. To her surprise, the lady turned away and appeared to lose interest in what she had been relating. Later, she realized the woman had been hiding her face from Reginald.

When Reginald had gone, the lady turned around and asked, 'Who is that young man?' When Beth told her his name was Reginald and explained that he worked for her father-in-law, she was alarmed when the lady then said she was on her way to the police station. 'If there's been any thieving going on, like this you've been telling me about, I think they should know where he is. I know him, his name is Reggie Probert and he's a thief. He's been in prison for theft and if you know what's good for you, you'll make sure he stays away from you.'

Alarmed but unable to decide what to do, Beth said nothing. The woman could have been mistaken and with his sun-bronzed face and the open, honest expression in his blue eyes, Reginald didn't look like a man with a secret past.

It wasn't always possible to arrange transport when Shirley was booked to sing, and she was tolerant of using public transport when the distances weren't great. But although she willingly accepted the inconvenience, she dreamed of the day when she would be so famous she would never again have to suffer a delayed or broken-down bus or a taxi that failed to arrive on time.

Bleddyn had planned to take her one evening when she was singing at a church a few miles from St David's Well, but the van suffered a puncture and a damaged tyre which made it impossible. So, it was train and a short bus journey, where, she was promised, the church would be only a few steps away.

She stood waiting for the bus, the warm sun making the delay a pleasant one, helping to overcome the nerves which still affected her sometimes. The pleasant sound of clopping hooves sounded in the distance and gradually came nearer. She looked along the quiet road curiously and a man appeared leading a large shire horse. He was dressed in corduroys and an open-necked blue shirt. He was clucking and talking to the horse as he walked, holding the head harness, as companionably as two old men, Shirley thought with a chuckle. The bus appeared and it looked full. She stepped forward irritated at the thought of a crush of people spoiling the dress she carried in a small bag, but with a regretful shake of the conductor's head, it went past without stopping. Shirley gasped in disbelief as it disappeared around the next bend.

'Hello again!' the young man with the horse called, coaxing the heavy animal to a halt. 'Don't tell me you've got yourself stranded again!'

She didn't recognize him, but the voice was familiar, low and slightly husky, and as the words penetrated she realized it was her rescuer from the night she had been abandoned miles from home.

'Captain will take you where you want to go if you don't

mind a two mile an hour stroll,' he offered. Cheekily he added, 'Better than hopping about on sticks, eh?'

'I can't . . .' she hesitated.

'Rubbish! A young woman like you can do anything she wants. Come on, hop up.' He joined his hands and indicated for her to use them as a step. She glanced at her watch; the time was flying past and the next bus might not be for a long time and she prided herself on never being late. It was cowboys or nothing. Laughing, she put a left foot on his hands and he heaved her up so that she could lift her right leg across the unbelievably wide back. Instead of her calves gripping the sides of the animal, her legs seemed to be almost straight out. She relaxed once the horse began to move at a slow steady pace. So much for a dignified arrival, she thought.

'I'll fall!' she said in alarm but he shook his head.

'No chance of that. He's as safe as a baby's cot, our Captain.'

A group of people stood outside the church looking anxiously along the road. When she called to them they applauded loudly. 'We were afraid you wouldn't make it,' one man said. 'We saw the bus go past and there isn't another for an hour.'

Thanking the man and patting the huge horse, she was helped down, her bag with her dress apparently unharmed, and ushered into the church hall to change. When she turned to repeat her thanks to the man and the horse they were already clopping off and were out of hearing.

Marged had promised Maude that she could finish work early that Sunday. They had been very busy, many families coming in for early lunches, and others had brought food from home, on which they picnicked either on the headland or the sand. Many of these came in for a late meal before setting off home. At two she had arranged for others to come and give Maude the afternoon off.

Maude finished washing the trays on which pasties had been cooked, and looked down at the sands. In the fading sunshine, Mr Gregory had arrived for the last hours of giving donkey rides to children. The young boys who helped during the day were leaving and as Maude watched, Bernard helped the parents lift a group of toddlers on to the animals, then walked them up and down, talking to them, the patient donkeys plodding the well worn route on their dainty unshod feet, taking their riders safely around the wide oval track marked in the sand by many such journeys, to return to their applauding parents.

There was a rush of customers in the cafe and a need for help preparing the trays for the sand. Maude forgot her promised afternoon off and began to prepare more sandwiches and set another batch of Welshcakes to cook on the hotplate. It was nearer four o'clock before she was free to leave. Marged apologized and promised her a few hours later in the week. Maude didn't mind. She wanted to catch Reginald just as he was finishing for the day, and she walked at a leisurely stroll through the lanes to Gregory's smallholding.

She hadn't mentioned her plan to Beth. She didn't want to be told again that he was not at home and perhaps he would see her tomorrow. If Reginald didn't want to meet her anymore he had to tell her to her face, not hide behind Beth.

Tensing herself for disappointment, prepared for embarrassment, she hurried down the lanes to the smallholding. The house appeared to be empty. One of the dogs was in the yard and came towards her barking furiously. She leaned over the gate, tickled his ear and as a pretence she called out for Mr Gregory. She knew he wasn't around, but she needed an excuse to be there. There was no response and no sign that Reginald was there either, so she walked on up the lane towards the donkeys' field, which she thought a likely place to find him.

She heard voices before she saw them; voices and laughter as Mr Gregory and Reginald approached her from behind. She waited as the small troupe of donkeys, Charlie in the lead, followed by Mr Gregory and Reginald who were laughing at some private joke, came towards her. The older man lifted his trilby politely and walked on, leaving Reginald to talk to her.

'Maude! What are you doing out here? Looking for me, I hope?'

'I felt like a walk,' she said.

'I was coming to see you later. Sorry about the other day. I got caught up in something unexpected. Are you coming in for a bite to eat? Beth will be home soon and she'd be pleased to see you.'

94

'I doubt that,' she said with a laugh. 'I've worked with her all day!'

There was nothing in his manner to suggest he had been anything but pleased to see her and she relaxed, took his proffered hand and walked with him at the steady pace of the donkeys. It was as she asked him about the fire that his mood changed. He was unwilling to discuss it. She was puzzled. Since it had happened, it was something on which everyone had an opinion. She glanced at him, about to add something more, but his face was set determinedly closed. From the moment she had mentioned the fire, it was as though she wasn't there, his early comments based only in her imagination. She didn't know what to say to retrieve the situation.

The donkeys picked up speed as though suddenly aware that they were almost home and food awaited them. Hurrying with them, laughing at their haste was a fortunate way of hiding their unease at the mention of the subject that Reginald clearly did not want to discuss.

Beth arrived an hour later and she and Maude helped Bernard prepare a meal. Fresh vegetables, a tin of casserole meat, which Beth had earlier managed to make into two pies, and a rich gravy. Maude ate with enthusiasm, filling up with bread and damson jam on to which some illegally made clotted cream was piled. Full and contented, she helped clear away then sat with Bernard and Reginald as they talked about the day at the beach.

The sun was dropping below the line of trees and the room was filled with the gentler light of evening, the fire burned brightly, a pleasant addition to the room even in the middle of summer, with its kettle singing on the hob. Maude felt unwilling to move but knew she had to get home soon. She was thankful she no longer worked in the factory and had to face leaving the house at five thirty in the morning – which, Bernard told her, was not *that* early, as he and Reginald often began their day at four to get the chores done when he had to work the day on the beach with the donkeys.

Aware that they too needed to get to bed, Maude stood to leave.

'I'll walk you home,' Reginald said.

The knock at the door was answered by Beth as they stood to gather their coats.

'Father-in-law,' she said turning to look at them in surprise, 'it's the police. They want to talk to Reginald.'

There was a brief conversation between the two policemen and Mr Gregory, then he turned to Maude. 'Sorry my dear, but I think I'll be the lucky man walking you home. Reginald is needed to help with some information. Me, too,' he added to reassure her, 'but I can make them wait.'

'No, Father-in-law,' Beth said. 'Best we get it over and done with. If you lend Maude your bike, I'll ride halfway with her, and you can pick up your bike tomorrow.'

Alarmed by the sudden tension in the small room where moments before everything had been peaceful, Maude longed to be allowed to stay. It was clear Reginald was in some sort of trouble. The look on the faces of the two policemen left her in no doubt of that. It was also clear that they didn't intend asking their questions until she was gone.

The two girls set off in silence, each wondering whether the police visit was a general enquiry or whether there was something more serious. Beth said nothing about the customer who thought she recognized Reginald. The least said the better at this stage, she thought, concern creasing her brow.

Back at home in their joint bedroom – where they normally shared every thought, although that had changed in recent months with Myrtle avoiding telling Maude about the time she spent with Stanley – Maude was unwilling to share her worries over Reginald. Myrtle knew there was something not right between her sister and the young man who had brought her brief happiness, but she didn't feel able to ask. They lay there both unable to sleep, each wanting to talk but held back with a newly discovered need for privacy.

In the next bedroom, Audrey was also unable to sleep and like Maude and Myrtle, she was thinking about her sister and wishing she could confide in Marged, share everything with her as she once had. They had been close enough to tell each other most of their thoughts but of late that had changed. Audrey remembered their earlier closeness with regret; a few doors away, Marged thought about it with simmering anger.

*   *   *

Unable to sleep that night, she slid out of the bed without disturbing Huw and went down to make a cup of tea. The night was warm, a moon riding in the sky making the garden bright enough to see around her. As she waited for the tea to brew, she walked down to the end and looked up at the window of her sister and Wilf's bedroom, surprised to see a chink of light shining through carelessly pulled blackout blinds. She was not the only one unable to attract sleep, she thought with unkind satisfaction.

She poured herself a cup of tea and carried it back into the silent garden. The bedroom curtain was now tightly drawn but the window was open and leaning out clearly visible was a figure looking out.

'Audrey?' Marged called in a stage whisper and she saw her sister's head turn. 'Want a cuppa, do you?' With an exaggerated movement of her arm, she waved towards the back gate and as her sister closed the window, she went down and unlocked the gate leading into the back lane. When she came out of the kitchen with a second cup of tea, the gate opened and her sister came in.

'You couldn't sleep either then,' Audrey stated.

'Worries about your Wilf?' Marged asked.

'I wish Mam was here, she was a pain at times, so insistent on what we had to do, when and how we had to do it, but she was so comforting when things went wrong. I miss her so much.'

'You don't hate her for the way she spoilt things for you?' Marged asked in surprise.

For a moment there was harshness in Audrey's voice as she said, 'You and her both.'

'All right, I know I was as much to blame as Mam for stopping you marrying Wilf all those years ago, I admit it. But Mam was strong and she convinced me you were in the wrong. I wasn't old enough to think for myself, Audrey.' She reached out and patted her sister's arm and was horrified at the way Audrey shrank from her touch.

'No, Mam didn't encourage either of us to think different from what she told us to think.'

'I'm sorry, I'm not stupid and I should have been stronger for you back then. But isn't it time to forget the misery and remember the good things?'

'There were plenty of good times for you but not so many for Wilf and me.'

'Come on, Audrey, don't you remember when we climbed that tree in our best new Sunday dresses? We had a wallop from Mam and an ice cream to cheer us up from our dad. And the time you and Wilf, Huw and I went to the pictures and the fog came down and we had to walk all the way home? Mam hit us first and asked questions after in those days, remember?'

'She didn't know Wilf was with us, did she? Forbidden to meet we were.'

'And Huw and I never told her.'

Having to whisper for fear of disturbing those around them gave the mood confidentiality and when Marged reminded Audrey of other incidents in their younger years, the atmosphere between them eased and muted laughter began to fill the garden.

Memory revived memory and soon they were unaware of the late hour or the need to keep their laughter low. After a while, Audrey turned to her sister, Marged's face pale and heavily shadowed by the moonlight, and complained: ' I'm hungry. What about some toast?'

'It's three in the morning!'

'So?'

Smiling contentedly they went into the kitchen, leaving the door open to the fresh, sweet night air and Marged turned on the grill. 'No butter of course,' she sighed, 'but I'll mix some margarine with the top of the milk and we can pretend.'

They didn't hear the footsteps coming down the back garden path and when the door opened and Maude appeared, surprise quickly turned to laughter. 'Not a minute's peace do we get, even in the middle of the night,' Marged complained with mock severity.

'What's been keeping you awake, young Maude?' Audrey asked. 'And how did you know where to find us?'

'I heard you laughing and came to see what there was to amuse you at such an unlikely hour. As for what's keeping me awake, well, when I was at Mr Gregory's the police came wanting to talk to Reginald. Reggie they called him and they appeared to know him rather well. D'you think he was involved with the collection of gifts for the bombed out families? It was a terrible thing to do if he was.'

'Surely not, love,' Audrey said at once. 'It was probably something far less important. He delivers wood and other stuff on that horse and cart. They were bound to ask if he'd seen the other cart.'

They looked serious and Audrey warned, 'Don't make judgements until you have the facts, Maude. It's so easy to say something you'll regret.'

'I hope they catch the man. Wicked it was, him benefiting from the troubles of others,' Marged added, whipping furiously at the cream and margarine as the toast browned under the grill.

They sat and talked for a while, the sisters coaxing Maude gently to tell what she knew.

'I was ushered out before anything much was said, but it was clear they knew Reggie, as they called him. He must have been in trouble before and I wondered whether he and this other man had worked together, you know, Reginald telling him the best places to try and perhaps finding the horse and cart for him. Good with horses, he is.'

'Oh yes, and bringing the stolen horse home with him and putting it with Mr Gregory's donkeys. Bright boy he is to have thought of that, eh?' Sarcasm made Audrey smile but it wasn't reflected on the sad face of Maude.

'He might be clever enough to think it would convince them he couldn't be involved, mightn't he?'

'Oh dear, all this is getting too complicated for this time of the morning,' Audrey sighed. 'Go and see him tomorrow and you'll have a full explanation,' she advised.

'Heavens!' Maude said as she jumped up. 'It *is* tomorrow and almost time for us to get to work!'

A glance at the clock told them it was pointless to try and sleep: there was less than an hour before Marged and Maude had to rise. Marged pushed Maude back into her chair and made another pot of tea. 'At least you've had some breakfast,' she said.

It was clear to her that Maude was attracted to the young man and she did what she could to reassure her before sending her back home, replete with toast and several cups of tea.

'I'd better go, too,' Audrey said, yawning as she placed the dishes in the bowl for washing. 'A short doze is all I can hope for before Wilf wakes.'

'It's hardly worth me bothering,' Marged sighed. 'I might as well stay up and start on the cakes, I wouldn't sleep now anyway.'

'I'll go and put a note by the bed for Wilf in case he wakes and worries, then I'll come back and help.'

Marged thought those words were the best she could hear, apart from being told her young son, Eynon, was alive and on his way home.

Myrtle was awake when Maude went back into the house. She sat up and asked where Maude had been. 'Did I wake you?' Maude asked.

'No, I was disturbed by some thoughtless people having a party and making sure everyone knew it!' Myrtle said.

Maude gave a brief explanation and Myrtle protested at being allowed to sleep instead of being invited to join. 'A promise to stay together works both ways, our Maude,' she complained. 'How could you miss me out of a midnight feast?'

On tiptoe, Maude went down the stairs and made cups of cocoa as an apology. She wished Myrtle had slept. She didn't want to talk to her about Reginald and there was always the danger of letting something slip as they were usually so open and honest with each other. She was glad when Myrtle discussed something different.

'I've been thinking of Bleddyn's suggestion that I go to night school and learn accounts, you know, bookkeeping,' Myrtle said as they sipped the hot drink companionably.

Fear of her sister drifting away from her flared up again. Book learning changed people. Everyone knew that. Working in an office would mean Myrtle mixing with different people from those on the beach. Very soon they would have nothing to say to each other. There wouldn't be anything to share.

'Don't be daft, our Myrtle. You couldn't manage anything like that! What schooling have you had? Less than me and I didn't manage much. Remember the times we moved house and started at different schools? Remember how hard it was to keep up with the others? And then those months living wherever we could find shelter, including that filthy stable. They'd laugh at you if you tried something like bookkeeping.'

'You're probably right,' Myrtle said.

'Of course I'm right and Uncle Bleddyn is unkind to pretend you could do something like accounts. Work like that isn't for people like us and it's best you remember that.'

Maude went down to wash out the cups. Myrtle opened a box containing some of her treasures and took out one of the notebooks in which she had first started to learn to write and do simple calculations. Marged, Audrey and later, Bleddyn had all helped and they had agreed that she had an ability possessed by few. Numbers danced across her brain and the pictures they created were as exciting as any an artist could create. She smiled at the ugly distorted letters she had then formed and compared them to more recent work. Surely she could make use of her ability, even if only to help the Castles with their business?

Leaving the box on her lap, she took out a piece of paper and began to write to Marged and Huw's son Eynon. She didn't know him very well but perhaps explaining it to him would help her to sort out her own feelings. Sometimes it took a stranger to help see things clearly.

During that August in 1943, the war continued in its destructive, bloodthirsty way. Letters were still greeted and read with relief and the movements of the telegram boys were followed with eyes filled with dread.

In a lull in the fighting, Eynon Castle too was writing letters. As always his first was to his wife, Alice. His letter was loving and reassuring, telling her nothing of the fearsome fighting that had taken place in the battle for Sicily or how many friends he had lost. The Americans were strong and with the rest of the British allies, progress was being made, and that was what was important. No looking back was the unwritten law of the exhausted men.

German cities were being devastated by bombing raids both day and night. Italy was slowly giving way to the efforts of the combined forces. The brave Norwegians were refusing to obey orders given by their German invaders, and in Denmark the number of cases of sabotage was rising, demonstrating an increased defiance against their aggressors. There was, running through the armies and those at home, an air of cautious optimism.

For the serving soldiers these hopeful signs were fused with fears that with the tide beginning to turn, fate might be whimsical in her choice of whose life would be forfeited. To have survived four years was making their chances thinner.

None of these morbid thoughts appeared in letters home. Eynon and thousands like them wrote home to their various countries telling the people waiting for them there was nothing to worry about and they were fine.

A few miles away from Eynon Castle another man sat also writing a letter to St David's Well. Freddy Clements wrote the usual brief duty letter to his parents, then he settled to write to singer and one-time dancer, Shirley Downs.

He knew about her accident and made light of it, presuming that she would have to face plenty of negative sympathy and didn't want more from him. He joked about her inability to dance, and insisted that he would put up with her poor performances when he took her on to the dance floor when he got home. He reminded her, very lightly, that she could still sing and hinted that there were other things that weren't limited by a damaged leg. He knew she would chuckle as she read his words. Not one to be sorry for herself for long, was Shirley Downs. He signed it, 'with all my love', but apart from that, any hope of a more than casual friendship when war ended he kept to himself.

Both men placed their fountain pens at the side of their writing pads and sat to dream about their girls, imagining them as they read the words they had penned and hoped they would know how much they had left out, and how much they were loved.

For Beth, there was never the comfort of letters from Peter. She would know nothing about what was happening to him until he walked in, smiling and weary, for a brief respite before returning to his dangerous work.

Maude didn't visit Mr Gregory's cottage when, on Marged's insistence, she finished work at two o'clock the day after the midnight tea party. For one thing, she was too tired after the disturbed night. For another, she felt it was Reginald's place to come to her and explain what was going on.

It was very warm, the sun shone harshly and, following a mainly sleepless night, was making her even more tired. She thought she might sit in the garden for an hour or two. She turned her key in the door and stepped inside the cool hallway, calling to see whether either Audrey or Wilf were home. Silence greeted her and she sighed with relief.

She threw down her handbag and the lightweight jacket she wore, and went into the kitchen to search for food. While the kettle boiled she washed her face and started to prepare a sandwich. A knock at the door surprised her. People rarely called during the day as most of the Castle family were at the beach until the evening. It was Reginald.

'Can I come in, Maude?' he asked politely.

'I was just going to eat my lunch,' she told him.

He smiled and showed her a package tucked into his jacket pocket. 'That's all right, I've brought mine with me.' He tilted his head towards the corner. 'The horse is tied to the lamp post and tucking into his,' he added.

She stepped back to allow him to enter and followed him through to the living room. He watched as she took a second cup and saucer from the dresser and placed it next to her own on the table beside the teapot, sugar and milk.

'Well?' she demanded as they sat down. 'You have an explanation about being so well known to the police that they call you Reggie?'

'If I tell you something, will you promise not to tell anyone else?'

'How can I promise until I know what it is? If it's against the law or something—'

'It isn't against the law, I promise you that. It involves my family.'

She waited, chewing on a mouthful of food that threatened to choke her.

Reginald looked equally incapable of eating the food he had brought. After hesitating as though deciding whether or not to trust her, he said, 'The man who took the things from your Auntie Audrey is Andy Probert. He's my brother.'

'He said his name was Derek Hanbury,' she said, unable to think of anything more original.

'I know. He's been in trouble a few times and my parents don't know how to stop him. He won't work, he prefers to steal and insists it's for the fun of it, the risks making life less boring than keeping to the straight and narrow. The truth is, he's terrified of going to war. That's the reason he's always running. The police are looking for him and so are the military police. He was called up and he ran away. He's been on the move ever since, taking a job, finding somewhere to live but moving on before someone realizes he's a draft-dodger and gives him away.'

'Is that why the police wanted to speak to you, because of your brother?'

'Partly, but I've been in prison, too.'

'You've been in prison?'

'He left a trail that led to me and I couldn't convince the police I was innocent without telling them it was Andy. He'd have gone down for a good stretch and I got off lightly as it was a first offence.'

'You must have been crazy to do that! It hasn't stopped him thieving, has it? So what was the point? Now you have a criminal record and he's carrying on as before.'

'I suppose this means you won't come out with me again,' he said sadly.

'Where's your brother now?'

He shrugged. 'A long way off, I hope.'

'Are the police satisfied that you weren't involved?'

'They thought I might have acted as lookout or was perhaps involved in another way – transport or helping him to choose the victims. I don't know whether I convinced them, but if they believe me and my words are backed up by Mr Gregory, I should be all right.' He pushed his long hair back using his fingers like a comb. 'It's so unfair. I left home hoping to stay clear of him and he found me. Of all the towns to choose, he managed to come here and mess everything up for me.'

'Not everything, Reginald. I'm still here, and Mr Gregory and most of your friends will give you their support.'

Sandwiches forgotten, he stood and pulled her gently to her feet and kissed her. They stayed for a long time, holding each other tightly, exchanging words of love.

Until the door opened and Audrey shouted, 'Anyone home?'

104

Separating hastily, Maude shouted a reply, adding that Reginald had just called and they were going to eat their sandwiches together.

'Call me Reg,' he whispered. 'Reggie was accused of theft and Reginald sounds as though I'm fifty!'

'I like Reggie best,' Maude whispered back.

'You haven't started on your sandwiches then,' Audrey remarked pointedly. 'And this full pot of tea's gone cold.'

Reggie left and Maude watched him untie the horse before she went back inside. As she was about to tell Audrey that he was not suspected of the theft, Audrey interrupted her by handing her a letter.

Opening it, Maude danced with excitement. She was told that there was no need for a medical in a few months time when the season ended, as she was permanently excused from factory work to help on the beach.

'You won't earn as much money, mind,' Audrey warned her.

'I don't care. It's good news all the way today. Reggie came to tell me he isn't suspected of being involved in the theft of household goods.'

'That's good. Do they know who did it?'

Maude shook her head. She hated lying to Audrey but in this instance her loyalty had to be with Reggie. She repeated the name several times in her head. Reggie Probert. It sounded fine to her. As she lifted the dishes from the table, she thought Maude Probert sounded good too.

Six

'You were up early yesterday morning, Marged,' Huw commented as they prepared and ate the breakfast of toast and a scraping of butter. 'What kept you awake? Thinking about our Eynon and Johnny?'

'Partly, they're never really out of our thoughts, are they? So far away and us not knowing what's happening to them. I came down and made a cup of tea and, well, you'd hardly believe it, but Audrey was awake too and we sat here drinking tea and talking.'

'Talking? Not quarrelling?'

'No, no quarrel. I tried to get her to open up and tell me about Wilf's heart trouble but she wouldn't. Young Maude came, too. Funny night all round it was.'

'Maude as well? That explains why you and Audrey didn't come to blows,' he said teasingly. 'What did you discuss? It must have been something unlikely for you two to avoid having a row!' He looked at Marged but she didn't answer. Her face had a closed look he knew well. She would tell him when she was ready, unless she had angered her sister with her unfeeling manner. Marged was not one to dwell on sympathy, her way of helping was on a practical level and she was often misunderstood, and people considered her to be hard.

He watched her, wondering if she and Audrey would ever get back to the closeness they had once had. Marrying Wilf had been good for Audrey, but not for the relationship with her sister.

Marged packed up the boxes with the clean laundry, the cakes and pasties, which once again her sister had helped her to make, and the other items needed for the day. 'Come on, Huw,' she chivvied, 'we'll be late.'

Huw continued to wonder about Marged and Audrey's

midnight conversation throughout the busy morning. Marged had been remarkably cheerful. There was no sign of the usual solemn disapproval she showed, always looking for some imperfection in the way the customers were dealt with or the food was prepared. She even sang at times, while she served customers, and allowed herself time to ask them about their plans and wish them well.

When Wilf arrived mid-morning with three letters, two bearing the army's stamp, she almost hugged her startled brother-in-law. Something strange was happening, Huw thought, as they left Myrtle to serve and went into the kitchen to read the news from their soldier son.

The letters were read and re-read before Marged put them in her pocket, ready to show Eynon's wife, Alice. Now her cheerfulness had a reason. At least when he had written them, Eynon was safe and well, although Huw feared he was in the thick of the fighting in Italy. Being happy at the receipt of a letter was a false mood. Anything might have happened in the time it had taken to reach them, but they pretended and tried not to think any further than holding the letter in their hand and imagining him sitting and writing another. Huw said nothing about his fears to Marged. He didn't want to ruin her happy mood.

The weather was very warm and people came into the cafe with red, sunburned faces, their clothes patched with perspiration, the women bedecked in pretty dresses which looked crumpled and in many cases very worn. The men wore handkerchiefs on their head, the corners knotted to form a simple hat, their shirts wet with sweat, sleeves rolled up. The men's trousers were as crumpled as the women's dresses where they too had been rolled up to the knees to allow the men the simple pleasure of paddling at the edge of the waves. Most of the children still wore their bathing costumes, and it made Maude and Myrtle envious seeing them tripping in with their bathers still wet and sandy.

Maude and Myrtle made faces to each other, miming their wish to go into the sea and cool off. At four o'clock, Myrtle could stand it no longer.

'Auntie Marged, can we have a half hour break to flop in the sea? I'm about to burst into flames, I'm so hot. Just me and Maude, can we?'

107

'Ask Uncle Huw to leave the swingboats to one of the boys and come and help me here and you can have twenty minutes, no more, right?'

They had worn their dippers under their clothes, which was one reason they were feeling so uncomfortably hot, and running down to the edge of the waves, Maude asked, 'What made you so sure she'd agree, our Myrtle?'

'I knew she was in a good mood when she called to pick us up for work, and it's lasted all day. What did you talk about in your midnight meeting that made her forget to be miserable, our Maude? She and Auntie Audrey are speaking like they're the best of friends.'

'Perhaps she thinks Auntie Audrey's going back to doing the housekeeping. She helped again this morning.'

'I don't think so, she . . .'

There was no time for more as they ran into the sparkling water and dived headlong into an approaching wave.

Although St David's Well Bay had been kept open through-out the threat of invasion and since, there were limits to its use. Inside a line between the two headlands was a barrier which prevented boats entering or leaving the bay and a further line closer to the beach warned bathers to stay clear. Maud and Myrtle swam out as far as they dared and circled lazily around, the constant hum of shouting and laughing a summer melody around them. A sound that lived on in memory from one summer to the next, the sound of happy days spent in innocent fun.

At the end of the day, while they were collecting the things they had to take home, which included the usual tea towels and tablecloths for laundering, Marged relaxed and suggested they went to Bleddyn's cafe for fish and chips instead of rush-ing home.

'But I thought you had to get straight on with the laundry?' Huw queried.

'Not anymore, Huw. Audrey has come to her senses and she'll be doing the washing and the cooking again from now on. It's only right. Castles is a family business and we each have to do our share.'

'Damn me, no wonder you're happy today. It's been a lot of extra work for you since Audrey told you she was finished.'

Leaving the van outside the house, the four of them went to Castle's Fish and Chip restaurant and enjoyed a leisurely meal, and when they walked back to the house it was past eight o'clock. Opening the back of the van, Marged picked up the bundle of washing and took it to Audrey's door. As usual, she knocked then opened the door to walk in, but the door was locked. She knocked again, and called out, politely at first but with increasing irritation. There was no reply.

'It's all right, Auntie Marged,' Maude called. 'I've got the key. They must be out.'

Maude and Myrtle, who had been unloading the van came up, and Maude thrust the key into the lock. They went in, but it was soon apparent there was no one at home. On the table, propped against the teapot was a note: 'We are spending a few days in Tenby. Look out for a postcard. Love from Auntie Audrey and Uncle Wilf.'

'But they can't! Audrey said everything was all right. When she helped with the baking yesterday morning and today, and helped fold the tablecloths, I thought she was going back to doing the housekeeping,' Marged said, throwing down the washing.

'Seems you were wrong,' Maude pointed out.

'Seems I'll be up half the night trying to catch up!' Marged snapped, bending down and retrieving the tablecloths. 'How could she do this? Why is she being so spiteful? She more or less promised.'

'Perhaps you misunderstood,' Myrtle said.

'Perhaps that was what she wanted me to do! This was deliberate and you won't tell me no different!'

In her anger, she seemed unaware of Maude getting ready to go out. Then as Maude picked up her shoulder bag, she demanded, 'Where d'you think you're going at this time of night? You have to stay in with your sister.'

'I'll be all right, I'm almost sixteen, remember,' Myrtle protested.

'I promised to see Reggie,' Maude said. 'Only half an hour, I'll be.'

In her disappointment, hurt by what she saw as Audrey's deliberately misleading friendliness, followed by her unexplained absence, she turned on Maude. 'You're going nowhere with that criminal. He's been in prison for thieving *and* he was questioned about the stuff that was stolen from your Auntie Audrey. How can you think of meeting a boy like that?'

'He was innocent, Auntie Marged, and the police only wanted to talk to him because his brother's a suspect and . . . I mean . . .' Too late she remembered Reggie's plea to keep his brother's involvement a secret.

'His brother! So the whole family are bad and you want to go and meet him after he stole from Audrey? A woman who's been a second mother to you and Myrtle?'

'Please forget I said that. I promised Reggie I wouldn't tell anyone.' Maude was tearful and she reached for Myrtle's hand as she had done when they were children.

'You stay in this house, and if this Reggie knocks on the door, you don't answer it. Right?'

Maude put away the coat she was about to put on and nodded. She couldn't speak, she was too afraid of collapsing into tears.

Marged took the washing and stormed out. When she went into her kitchen and lit the large boiler to heat water for washing, banging things about, muttering about her selfish sister, Huw sighed. Her happy mood hadn't lasted very long.

Marged was calm and easy-going once the season ended, but when life was so busy, she was edgy and nothing he did was right. Without giving her the chance to disagree, he put on a coat and went out, calling from the door seconds before he closed it. Better to drink a pint of beer with friends than sit listening to her going on and on about Audrey.

In Audrey and Wilf's house, Myrtle was saying to her sister, 'Go on, Maude, go and meet Reggie and tell him what happened. You don't want him to think you just forgot, do you? I'll listen to the wireless for a while. I'm quite all right on my own. Ronnie and Olive are up in the flat if I set fire to the house or anything,' she added with a grin. 'Go on, you know you want to. If Auntie Marged comes back, I'll say you're in bed with a headache.'

Reggie Probert was waiting where they had arranged to meet, sitting on the park wall not far from the shops. He had seen Maude and the others walk past on their way back from the cafe and had smiled, contented to wait until she could get away. It was a very warm night and there were several couples strolling around, enjoying the balmy summer night, unwilling to go inside where the air was stuffy.

She was later than they had arranged, but he understood, having seen them walking back so recently. She was running when he saw her and he went to meet her, urging her to take her time. 'You know I'll wait for you,' he assured her.

'I can't stay,' she panted. 'Auntie Marged has forbidden me to meet you and I've slipped out to tell you.'

'Forbidden you?' He frowned. 'How can she do that? Eighteen you are, Maude, not eight!'

'She knows about the police questioning you and, well, she's over-protective I suppose. It's difficult for me, Reggie. Myrtle and I owe them so much and to be honest, I don't know where we'd go or how we'd manage if we had to leave the Castles. They're our family now and we depend on them so much we can't risk upsetting them.'

'How long will this go on? How long will you be dependent on them and have to do as they say?'

'Myrtle's not yet sixteen, even though she pretends to be. I couldn't face being on our own again, even though I'm well enough to work and keep us fed. Not like last time. But it would still be miserable not having a family.'

'They won't throw you out. And besides, you're old enough to think about a family of your own,' he said softly and as she glanced at him, she knew he was thinking of the two of them as a married couple with children and a home built around them.

There was a need for honesty and she said, 'I'm real sorry, but in the heat of the argument I let it slip that your brother was the suspect.'

He pulled away from her and stared at her. She could not read his expression, his eyes were dark pools in the fading light. She knew they would have shown hurt and disappointment, but his reaction was greater than expected.

'The military police came today. Did you know he's supposed to be in the army? Hiding he is, using different names and moving around so they can't catch him. Blamed me they did, convinced I know where he is, but I don't. He's been living away from home since he was about twelve and we've rarely seen him.'

111

'I'm sorry, I didn't help telling Auntie Marged, but she wasn't the reason they called on you. He's been cheating people out of their belongings, and stealing that horse and cart then burning the cart, well, it isn't a very secretive way to go on, is it?'

'You promised not to tell anyone.'

'Auntie Marged and Auntie Audrey are different. Myrtle and I don't keep secrets from them, or the uncles.'

'Even when I ask you to?'

'Sorry, but you can't blame me for the military being after your brother. He's got the fault, not me!" Her voice became shrill as the stupidity of the argument increased. 'Your brother Andy is a crook so why are you trying to blame me?'

'At least I know where your loyalties are,' he retorted angrily. 'The Castles, with their dogmatic rules and unreasonable demands, are more important to you than I am.' Without another word he turned and hurried off, through the park and out of the furthest gate. He didn't look back.

'Of course they are, stupid! We've only known each other a few weeks!' she shouted after him, then, as he showed no sign of stopping, she pleaded, 'Reggie, please wait.' She stood there and listened as his footsteps faded.

In the small hotel in Tenby, Audrey and Wilf sat at one of the tables overlooking the sea, and held hands. 'I hope Maude or Myrtle tells Marged about our little holiday,' Audrey said. 'This was so unexpected, your friend inviting us to spend these few days with them, there wasn't time to do anything except pack.'

'That's how life should be for us, never two days alike, taking impromptu decisions with no planning for a future that's precarious, to put it mildly,' he replied.

'Marged won't be very pleased.'

'That problem is Marged's. Our only problem is whether to have the lamb or the beef. Not that there'll be much of either,' he added with a laugh. He waved as their two friends appeared and Audrey forced any thought of her sister out of her mind. This time was for Wilf and no one else.

Myrtle had arranged to meet Stanley and his brothers to go back to the beach after work for a late swim. None of the brothers were good swimmers but that didn't matter. The weather was so hot that no excuse was needed to get into bathing costumes, and splash about in the refreshing foam.

After a busy day in the cafe, Myrtle was looking forward to her swim. With the meal dealt with and her offer to help with the ironing thankfully refused, she picked up a towel and headed for the door.

'Myrtle! You aren't going out and leaving me on my own, are you?' Maude said in astonishment. 'How can you be so mean? Reggie and I have quarrelled, and you know how miserable I am.'

'But I'm only going for a swim. I've been looking forward to it all day, our Maude.'

'With Auntie Audrey and Wilf away I'll be on my own.'

'Come with us then, the three boys need some help with their swimming, with two of us they might learn quicker.'

'I can't. It's too cold. You promised you'd never leave me when I need you and I need you tonight. I'm so miserable, I liked Reggie so much and now I won't see him again.'

In momentary defiance, Myrtle said, 'So you want me to stay home and be miserable with you, do you? And disappoint Stanley, Harold and Percival.'

'Oh, go if you want to. Your promises aren't worth much, are they?'

Myrtle got as far as the front door, then threw the rolled up towel on to the bottom stair and went up to her room.

Later on, she went down to the sitting room where Maude was struggling with a khaki sock she was knitting. 'This isn't the best way of dealing with it, Maude, sitting here being miserable. Best you show Reggie you don't care, then he'll want to come back to you.'

'You're right,' was the unexpected answer. 'In fact, I think we should go to the dance on Saturday, just you and me.'

'The dance? But we've never been to a dance. I don't know how to and neither do you!'

'Best we start learning then!' Maude declined to add that she believed that Reggie was going, with Beth and a few friends.

There was dance music on the wireless and they plodded around the room to a one-two-three beat or whatever rhythm

113

the band played, laughing and planning what they would wear. Myrtle laughing loudest of all, pretending she didn't mind missing her planned trip to the beach.

In Morgan's house in Conroy Street, the three boys waited, sitting clutching their dippers and watching the clock. The heat was intense, pressing down on them, making the thought of a swim change from happy anticipation to urgent necessity. Anthony was restless, and crying, unable to sleep. Eirlys pleaded in mime to her father and eventually, Morgan offered to take the boys himself down to the sea. 'If Myrtle comes, I'll tell her to follow you,' Eirlys promised.

'She won't come. That sister of hers has called up some promise to stop her,' Stanley grumbled. 'Wicked old witch.'

'Old? She isn't more than eighteen.'

'That,' Stanley said with great authority, 'is old!'

'In that case, why don't I come, too? Anthony might go off to sleep in his pram.'

The sands were surprisingly full considering the lateness of the hour, many people thinking the same as Eirlys and taking children out into the cooler air instead of forcing them to stay in too warm bedrooms and expecting them to sleep. Shirley was there with her mother and Hetty took over the pram, giving Eirlys a chance to go to the water's edge with the three boys. Stanley managed a few strokes but failed to make any real progress in the water, Harold struggled too, and young Percival was satisfied with kneeling down in the shallow water, and shuffling along pretending to do impressive strokes with his skinny arms.

Beth was there too, and her brother Ronnie with Olive and their little girl. 'Lucky our Mam doesn't know,' Ronnie joked, 'or she'd have us opening the cafe!' Although the enjoyment was the same, the mood was different from the sands during the day. The excitement was muted, voices less raucous, as though they had no right to be there and were afraid of being caught.

Myrtle slipped out, leaving her sister still struggling with the sock she was knitting, and on her bicycle rode to Conroy Street. To her disappointment, there was no one in and she went home dejected and discarded her dippers in disgusted disappointment.

* * *

When it came to the moment, Maude wanted to forget their plan to go to the dance. She had never been keen on dancing, she lacked the ability to let herself go and enjoy moving to the music. On the rare occasions she had tried, she had come away hating herself for her shyness and swearing never to do it again.

She stopped at the doorway where they had to pay for their ticket and would have gone back home, but Myrtle saw someone she knew and went straight in and she had no choice but to follow. They stayed a long time in the cloakroom as Maude was worried that once they got into the hall she'd be asked to dance when she didn't know a waltz from a foxtrot.

Marged had guessed that it would be difficult and she had explained her predicament to their daughter Beth, who rounded up a few extra friends and planned to help the two girls enjoy their evening out. On hearing about the arrangement, Stanley had asked to borrow a tie from Morgan Price and said he was going too.

'They'll never let you in,' Harold jeered. 'You're only fourteen.'

'I'm almost fifteen!'

'An' you look eleven!'

'All right you two,' Morgan said. 'You and I will go, Stanley. Eirlys and Ken will keep an eye on you two. They'll be home anyway, with the baby.'

'I'm not sure I want to go with an old man,' Stanley looked doubtful. A hand aimed at his cheeky face made him duck but in a consenting tone, he added, 'All right, Uncle Morgan. Just this once and make sure you be'ave and don't embarrass me.'

Eirlys's husband Ken was home and they arranged a babysitter and came too.

The hall was crowded and it was like walking into an oven, Maude thought, as they joined the dance in the hall. Finding a corner, Myrtle and Maude thought they would be brave and make an attempt to become part of the chattering people moving around like a giant, lethargic Catherine wheel. However, the band was very loud, the people so sure of where they were going and what they were doing, that the girls soon

115

lost their nerve and decided to stand and watch until it was time to leave.

When Eirlys, Ken, Mr Morgan and the others walked in everything changed.

'We're only here to watch,' Maude said at once.

Stanley had no such ideas. He pulled Myrtle on to the floor and with great enthusiasm and little skill, moved to the music with such abandon that they found themselves with a space around them in no time.

He had taken a few lessons from Morgan and Ken, and loudly chanted the one, two, three of the waltz, oblivious to the stares of amusement and disapproval that were pointed their way. Unable to be serious, Myrtle relaxed and enjoyed the experience, shouting as loudly as Stanley, when Eirlys and Ken, then Maude and Morgan, moved sedately past them.

With a group of friends with whom she felt easy, Maude relaxed and the evening became a pleasant one. If only Reggie had turned up as she had hoped, it would have been perfect.

That Saturday dance was the first of many that were attended by Maude and Myrtle and the others. There were dances each Wednesday and Saturday, although it was a rush to get there on Saturday as it was always the busiest day of the week on the sands, and when some extra entertainment was taking place the day could be even longer.

Reggie knew about these outings but was nursing his hurt over the way Maude had refused to ignore what Marged had told her, so he didn't try to see her. Instead he went out with one of the other boys he knew from college and stayed away from places where he might expect to see Maude.

Then Huw met Constable Charlie Groves and was told that there was no evidence to suggest Reggie had been helping his brother to rob local people.

'But you questioned him and acted as though he were guilty,' Huw said.

'The police and the military are looking for Andy and there's been no contact between them or he'd have been caught. The military police are diligent and they don't relax their search for a man who should be serving in the army. If Reggie had been setting up the thefts by pointing out the best houses to

116

call on, he'd have been caught. There are plenty of people looking for him.'

'Young Maude likes the boy and we've sort of stopped her seeing him. You know what it's like. Marged worries about them.'

'To be honest, Mr Castle, we don't think he even did the burglaries he went to prison for. Andy allowed his brother to take punishment for something he did. Nasty piece of work. Charming, mind, but a man without morals, a character who doesn't care who he steps on to get what he wants.'

Later that evening, Huw repeated what Charlie Groves had told him, to Marged.

'Do we have to tell her we were wrong?' Marged asked.

'I don't think it would do any harm to admit we were mistaken, do you?'

When they next met Bernard Gregory they explained the doubts about Reggie and their change of heart and he promised to tell the boy that he was welcome to call if he still wanted to see Maude.

'After all,' Marged said as they left Bernard, 'he won't be here for much longer, he'll be going into the army as soon as he's finished at the smallholding, so the friendship will die a natural death.'

'You still aren't convinced, are you?'

'Not really. There's bad blood in the family, if you ask me.'

Beth was struggling to finish the day at the cafe. She stacked the last of the dishes and was tempted to leave them until the following morning, but she knew that starting 'all behind like a cow's tail,' as her mother would have said, was not a good idea. Following her mother for efficiency and speed, she normally ran the place with ease, but the last week she had found it hard to keep going after the middle of the afternoon. On Sunday, instead of the usual chores, she fell asleep and Bernard let her stay deeply sleeping on the couch under the open window until five o'clock, quietly dealing with the dinner dishes and setting the table for their light tea.

The realization that she might be expecting a child brought dismay and a feeling of vulnerability upon her. It was as though her greater need of Peter was daring fate to intervene. She

117

knew she was going to cry and, rising from the couch, she hurried to her room and hid her sobs in her pillow.

Peter knew she was not her usual self and when he went back to his work his thoughts were of her, wishing his travelling was over and he could stay and look after her. Then he deliberately pushed useless worrying aside. To survive over the next few months he needed a clear mind, uncluttered with worries about which he could do nothing. Concentration on the moment kept him and others alive and staying alive was the best way of helping her. That she might be carrying their child did not occur to him.

Audrey and Wilf had returned from their visit to Tenby and Audrey was surprised to be greeted by her sister with less than delight. Whenever they met, Marged gave the impression she was in a hurry, reminding her sister wordlessly that life was hard without her help and trying to make her feel guilty.

Discussing it with Wilf, they decided it was best to ignore what they saw as Marged's latest attempts to make her change her mind about helping in the business, and concentrate on enjoying the last few weeks of summer.

Marged had a set routine and as soon as she reached home each evening, her first job would be to light the boiler ready to start the washing. While the water was heating, they ate a meal and the girls would clear the dishes and get everything ready to begin cooking. Myrtle and Maude were both competent cooks by this time and it was they who usually dealt with the dry mixtures for Welshcakes and scones ready to be finished and then cooked the following morning.

On a night when the sisters had gone to the dance, Marged found herself alone. Huw had gone to help at the fish and chip cafe to give Bleddyn and Hetty an evening off, and feeling more irritable and put upon than ever, she went into the kitchen to discover that the boiler had begun to leak. The kitchen floor was flooded with soapy water. Where was Huw when she needed him? Why were Maude and Myrtle never there to help? A part of her mind told her she was being unreasonable, but her frustration was so great she felt that the whole world was against her and she was standing alone.

Ronnie and Olive might be in, but to reach them she would

have to disturb her sister and suddenly that was too much. Having to face Audrey and show her she wasn't coping – something she had been trying to point out ever since she and Wilf had returned from Tenby – was now the very last straw. Pride made her want Audrey to understand how badly she had let her down, but not allow her to think she couldn't cope.

She was ladling out the last of the water from the boiler when Huw came in. It was almost eleven thirty and he had expected her to be in bed. He listened as she angrily told him about the latest disaster, then he made her sit down while he dried the floor and examined the boiler.

'I can fix it in the morning, it's only a small job,' he told her. 'But tomorrow you are having a day off. You aren't going to the cafe, and you aren't going to deal with the washing.'

'Oh, and how will we manage when tomorrow's washing has to be done and with today's not seen to?'

'I'll take this pile to the laundry and do the same with tomorrow's lot. Take a day off, Marged, you're worn out.' He took a deep breath, preparing to argue with her, but she nodded and agreed.

'You're right, I'm tired, Huw. A day at home will give me the chance to give the bedrooms a good sorting.'

'No, Marged. You're to relax and enjoy a quiet few hours. We all have time off except you, and it's time you did.'

That she agreed was evidence of how exhausted and ill-used she was feeling.

A few hours before, Audrey and Wilf had returned from a picnic in the park, where a performance of *Midsummer Night's Dream* had been performed by a local school. Audrey was in a happy mood. Wilf's illness had settled and although he became tired if he did more than common sense told him he should, he was able to enjoy most days in gentle pleasure.

Putting down the bag containing the remnants of their supper picnic, she was humming cheerfully to herself as she went to revive the fire and persuade the silent kettle to sing. The house was empty: Ronnie and Olive were asleep in the flat at the top of the house, Maude and Myrtle were probably out with friends, she presumed.

They sat and listened to the wireless, content to relax, unworried about early rising and a frantic tomorrow. Maude

119

and Myrtle came in, chatted and went to bed. Still they sat, unwilling to disturb themselves.

The knock at the door made her sigh in mock irritation. 'That girl has forgotten her key again,' she said to Wilf, who had sat close to her on a chair near the fire. 'I've threatened to tie it round her neck on a big red ribbon.'

'Don't be daft, they're both in bed. Who can it be?'

It was Marged. Huw had gone to bed, content that he had dealt with the problem and eased Marged's mind. But Marged had sat there in her kitchen quietly fuming until she could sit no longer.

'Where's our Ronnie? I need him to come and sort out a problem with the washing boiler.'

'I think they're asleep, there aren't any lights on and it is rather late, Marged.'

Needing someone to blame, Marged glared at her sister. 'How could you, our Audrey? Leading me to think you were going to help as before, then going off to Tenby like that without a word.'

'What are you talking about? That was ages ago and I did leave a note to tell you all where we were going.'

Wilf pulled himself out of the chair and crossed the room towards the hall door. He had never been involved in the regular disagreements between the sisters and he didn't want to start. He had hoped, that once Marged realized Audrey was no longer willing to help with the business, she would calm down, but by the look on her face it seemed she had been storing her resentment and, like an unpredictable volcano, it was about to erupt.

'I need our Ronnie to help fix the boiler,' Marged repeated. 'It overflowed all over the kitchen and the mess was terrible.'

'It's too late to bother Ronnie tonight and I don't see what this has to do with Wilf and me going to Tenby,'

'You've let me down. In the middle of the busiest month you've walked away from your responsibilities.'

Audrey smiled and in a quiet voice said, 'I'm putting my husband first, for once.'

As Wilf reached the door, suddenly it seemed difficult for him to draw breath and a severe pain forced him to cry out. Audrey ran to him and made him sit at the end of the couch

120

and slowly lean back against the arm. Marged ran to the door. 'I'll go and fetch the doctor,' she said, full of remorse for her outburst.

'You do that!' Audrey snapped, helping Wilf to a comfortable position.

Marged stayed at the house while the doctor attended to Wilf, then said to Audrey. 'I'm sorry. I didn't realize how ill he is. You won't talk about it so how could I?' she added, in defence of her behaviour.

'I don't want to discuss it, Marged. You just have to accept that he and I need all the time we have to spend together. You robbed me of so much, surely you can't fail to understand that?'

Most of the night hours had flown. The curtains were opened on to a fresh, summer morning and Marged looked around for something to do to ease her conscience. So much for a day off, she thought. She'd have to stay in case Audrey needed her help.

Automatically, she made tea, prepared a breakfast and placed it in front of her sister. 'Eat, Audrey. To help Wilf you have to stay healthy and fit.' Obediently, Audrey ate the slice of bacon she had intended for their lunch that day with fried tomatoes and a few potatoes, and the egg she had been saving for Wilf's breakfast. There had been no point in trying to stop Marged from doing what she thought best.

When there was nothing more she could do, Marged went home and told Huw what had happened.

'Leave them to themselves,' Huw advised. 'Go out, have a few hours of relaxation. Audrey will tell us if she wants help.'

Too weary and upset to argue, Marged agreed.

Huw, with only momentary guilt, called at 78 Conroy Street and asked Stanley to call in sick and help on the sands, something for which Stanley needed no persuasion.

Marged, meanwhile, walked through the park but she couldn't take her mind off the business. Her thoughts wandered over the day's needs, wondering whether Huw had bought what he needed to fix the boiler and arranged for the laundry to be done, and whether the cakes would last the day. Then she remembered the potatoes. Huw wouldn't give the potatoes a thought. Bernard Gregory delivered an order each week but they had been extra busy and they were short of potatoes. The day was sunny and pleasantly warm so she decided to go to the smallholding and place the extra order, glad to have a purpose to her walk.

She was so used to rushing that it wasn't until she was breathless that she slowed down and remembered there was nothing to hurry for. She looked around her at the fullness of the summer flowers, the boldness of the last few poppies in the corn and the scent of meadowsweet where it had survived the cutting of the hay, tall and elegant in the hedgerow. The unexpected delight of freedom for a whole day filled her with a joy she had almost forgotten how to cherish.

How many others were the same as herself, rushing, trying to cope with life in wartime, with shortages and worries about their loved ones? There were weary faces everywhere you looked. The way she felt, weighed down with weariness, was the same for everyone, the redeeming factor was the way everyone helped each other and no one took advantage of the situation and allowed greed to take over. How will we all survive it, she wondered.

She sat on a stile near the edge of the town and the sound of the clattering hooves of a stationary and impatient horse made her turn her head curiously. Further along the lane Mr Gregory's horse and cart was tied to a gate. Perhaps she wouldn't have to walk all the way to the smallholding after all. She walked towards the cart and then stopped. There was a man climbing in through a bedroom window and, unless she was mistaken, that man was Reggie Probert. 'I knew it!' she muttered.

As he disappeared inside the house, she turned away and began to hurry back to the town, while below him, holding the ladder, Mrs Franks stood waiting patiently for Reggie to let her through the front door for which she had forgotten the key.

Marged didn't go to the police. Like many others she avoided the complications of being involved. Instead, she caught the bus over to the cafe where Maude and Myrtle were busy serving a queue of hot and sunburnt visitors with drinks. An irate customer came in and waved a plate under Huw's face. 'This isn't a proper sausage,' he complained angrily. 'The one you gave to the last customer was twice as big!'

Calling Maude aside and leaving Huw to deal with the customer, Marged told her what she had seen. 'Now d'you believe me when I say you should keep away from him?'

'Perhaps there's an explanation,' Maude stuttered.

Too tense and angry to walk away, Marged went to the cafe's kitchen, pushed Huw aside and began dealing with the dishes. 'We want more potatoes,' she reminded him brusquely.

'On their way!' he snapped in reply.

'How was I to know you'd remembered?' she retorted, reason fading fast.

In her fury she dropped and broke a jug filled with milk, and in stretching out to save it, Huw knocked over a tray of cups and saucers.

At that moment, Reggie delivered potatoes and some tomatoes and told them cheerfully about Mrs Franks forgetting her key and how he came to the rescue. Huw looked at his wife, waiting for her to apologize to Maude, but before she could say a word, a red-faced Stanley came in, escorted by a man even more red-faced, who said he was Stanley's ex-employer.

'Sacked he is and not before time. Calling in sick and giving graphic descriptions of his symptoms, then coming here and working for you. Well, you can have him! He's sacked!'

'Dammit all, Marged, everything was all right until you came in,' Huw groaned in dismay. Then, grinning widely, he said, 'Well done, Stanley, lad. Welcome to the mad house!'

Wilf, meanwhile had been advised to rest for a few days and this he did. Marged called daily to make sure they had all they needed and the washing went to the laundry until Huw fixed a washer over the hole in the boiler. The tablecloths didn't look as good as when she or Audrey did them, but she didn't complain. She was honest enough to face the fact that complaining had become a habit. She was tired and worn down by having too much to do, but so was everyone else.

One Saturday towards the end of the season, there was a beauty contest being held on the promenade followed by dancing by moonlight. When Marged mentioned it to Audrey, Wilf suggested they went along to watch.

'What about you two?' Audrey asked Maude and Myrtle.

123

'You're getting fond of dancing, and in the open air, dancing by the light of the moon will be fun.'

'I'll ask Beth and Eirlys if they'll come.' Myrtle was immediately enthusiastic about the plan.

'Eirlys'll be there, stupid! She's organizing it like she did before. She'll want to see if it's as good as last time.'

'Stanley will come,' Myrtle said, thinking aloud.

'Oh no, Myrtle. What d'you want to ask him for? We don't want him hanging around.'

'I haven't seen that Reggie who works for Mr Gregory lately. Had another quarrel, have you?' Audrey asked.

Maude didn't answer. She was still unhappy about their parting. But Myrtle had no qualms about telling Audrey that it had been Marged's decision. 'Him being questioned about the stuff taken from you by a man who turned out to be Reggie's brother.'

'Why did that stop you seeing Reggie?'

Myrtle shrugged. 'Crooks the lot of 'em. Or so Auntie Marged thinks.'

'Oh, does she.'

Audrey used Myrtle's bicycle and went to see Mr Gregory and when she came back she went straight to see her sister.

'Why have you stopped Maude seeing Reggie?' she demanded.

Huw jumped out of his chair. 'Damn it all, if you two are arguing again, I'm going for a pint!'

To Audrey's surprise, Marged admitted she had been hasty accusing Reggie of housebreaking and she promised to explain her error to Maude.

When Maude went to the smallholding to see Reggie and try to sort out their differences, Mr Gregory told her he had gone.

Seven

Shirley Downs stared around the street of the busy town and wondered how to fill the next few hours. Although Ken had promised her she wouldn't be stranded between a couple of concerts, here she was again. He had persuaded her to sing at three concerts on consecutive evenings and this meant that once more she was in a town she didn't know, with five hours to wait before she was due to arrive at the concert venue – in this instance the local school hall.

It was three o'clock and she had used as much time as possible by eating lunch in a small restaurant and had explored all the shops in the main road several times. Many more times and I'll be suspected of being a thief waiting for an opportunity, she mused. Although, I'm not made for swift actions, with a gammy leg and a walking stick.

The town was a small one and so far as she could see there was nothing else with which to fill her time. There was only one possibility; the library beckoned.

When she stopped a lady to ask the whereabouts of the library she was advised to walk through the indoor market as this was the quickest way. Shirley thanked her but thought that the longest way would have been better, it would have used up more of her unwanted leisure time.

She still needed a walking stick since the injury to her legs, but the discomfort was easing and she strolled along to the market entrance, which she had not noticed before. It was a surprisingly large market for such a small town. The first stalls were the usual mixture of fruit, vegetables, fish, bread and cakes, plus whatever else people found to sell that was not rationed. There was a small cafe there, similar to the one in St David's Well market owned by Beth. Although it was not long since she had eaten lunch, she sat and ordered a cup of tea. She wasn't sightseeing, she was filling time.

She sat there, sipping the weak brew and watching the chattering shoppers wander past, when she became aware of the chanting sound of a seller. She moved her chair slightly until she could see a young man who was attracting an audience by his enthusiasm and humour. Some people who were ready for some fun, were adding to his remarks, responding to insult with insult, encouraging his bantering spiel. She finished her tea and stood up. He might be a way of passing a few more minutes.

The young man was dressed in extremely smart clothes. Good quality, well cut slacks and a neatly ironed short-sleeved shirt. His black hair was worn longer than was fashionable, swinging across his face as he bent to pick up his wares and as he turned to encompass his widening audience. His dark eyes were everywhere, watching for the hesitant customer and directing his words to encourage her. There was a gleam in his eye, a promise of fun in his half-smile, giving him an air of devilish attraction to which even the older members of the crowd were not immune.

Having studied him for an unnecessarily long time, Shirley looked to see what he was offering. Then his voice changed and something about the softly spoken, slightly husky tone seemed familiar. She looked at him again and no recognition came. His voice could hardly be unique, it must have reminded her of someone she knew.

Beside him were boxes of china and from what she could see, he was concentrating on selling cups and saucers. All were patterned but nothing matched which, he was insisting, would be the new fashion.

'Everything a mishmash, it's what all the smart people are doing, ladies,' he assured them earnestly. 'Honestly, no one bothers about matching sets anymore. Hitler's seen to that and now everyone who's anyone mixes patterns and colours and as long as they're good bone china, like these – as you expert ladies will recognize – well, anything goes. Just look at the quality of that, ladies. It'll be a pleasure to drink even common old tap water out of a cup of that quality.' He offered a cup and saucer to a young woman standing close to him. 'I bet you haven't see anything as good for years, but I'm in a good

126

mood today and I'm promising you that if you buy one cup and saucer for a shilling, I'll give you a spoon for nothing. Now, can I say fairer? First half a dozen only, then the price goes up. Come on, this is something you can't afford to miss. Forget the rabbit you were going to buy for dinner and give the kids beans on toast instead. Come on, treat yourselves while I'm in a generous mood.'

Shirley watched in amusement as a forest of arms reached out offering their shillings and were handed a cup and saucer plus spoon. Six only, he'd said, but she saw at least twenty sets change hands. 'That's right, ladies, sick of plain white china, aren't we? Bored to death with it. A bit of colour'll cheer up them marvellous meals you make for your ungrateful families. I know what it's like. Do your heart good, a bit of cheerful colour will. Look at this one. Roses! I ask you, could you get better anywhere?'

The chattering, smiling crowd dispersed and more began to gather as he once more began his encouraging chanting. His dark eyes scanned the crowd as though assessing his chances and when his eyes met hers they gave a wide wink. Startled, she backed away.

'Here, don't go, you're bringing me luck standing there,' he called and still amused, still curious about the half remembered voice, Shirley returned to her place.

There was a repeat of his performance and this time she counted twenty-two sales, most women buying more than one set. At a shilling a time, he had taken more than two pounds in twenty minutes. Again, she began to move away but again he stopped her.

'I'm stopping for a cuppa in a minute, just one more session. I'll buy you tea and a sticky bun if you hang on while I do my last spiel then pack this lot away safe.'

'Pack up? But you aren't finished selling already are you?' She glanced at her watch. 'It isn't half past three yet.'

He was grinning widely and again she felt that half-remembered familiarity but the identity of the smartly dressed young man eluded her.

'Knowing when to stop is part of the skill in this job,' he said. 'No, they're all making their way home now, kids coming out of school, the family wanting their tea, selling's over for today. This next lot will be down on numbers, ten if I'm lucky, you watch.'

He was correct as the selling was less frenzied, and he succeeded in getting rid of just eight sets. 'Just as well,' he said cheerfully. 'I'm almost out of cups and saucers. Tomorrow I'll be somewhere else and selling dinner plates. Want to buy a couple?'

Laughing, Shirley shook her head.

Packing the last of his wares into boxes and tea chests, he staggered with them out through the market entrance. 'Pity about your leg,' he said nodding towards the stick. 'You could give me a hand if you weren't injured.'

Shirley followed, bemused by him, curious to see how he managed his unwieldy stock, and saw him push them into the back of a van.

'Now then, I'm Larry Carver, and what about that cuppa, eh?'

'I'm Shirley and if drink another cup of tea today I'll explode.'

Unperturbed, he took her hand and led her along the street. 'Then you'd better just sit and watch me. I don't know how to deal with exploding women.'

He took her to a cafe called The Copper Pot, with the eponymous pot in the window which was clearly made of something other than copper but which had been painted a cheerful coppery red. He pointed to a notice behind the counter which stated that The Copper Pot offered the best coffee in town. 'That's a lie, too,' he whispered when she remarked on the falseness of the name.

'Lying, eh? You should know about that,' she said, smiling to take the sting out of her words. 'Your speciality telling "Tom Pepper", isn't it?'

'Selling has to be lying by the very nature of the thing,' he replied with a wink. 'I wouldn't get very far if I said the odds and sods I've got for sale are a mis-matched disaster, now would I? But all those ladies will go home pleased that they've found a real bargain and their tea will taste sweeter because of it. Now, we've talked about me for long enough, what about you? Waiting for a boyfriend, or a bus to take you home or something? You're always lost when I meet you.'

'I am lost, in a way. I'm taking part in the concert tonight and until then I'm at a loss to know how to fill the hours,' she told him, puzzled by his remark.

'Good at rescuing damsels in distress, I am.' He stared at her, quirking an eyebrow as he waited for her to see him in another guise.

She recognized him then. 'You're the man with the horse? And the man who helped when I was stranded in that lane? You're dressed so differently and seeing you selling china, I didn't recognize you, although I knew there was something familiar about the voice. Andy, isn't it?'

'Not today I'm not! In this suit I'm Larry Carver, entrepreneur.'

'And besides wandering around at night gathering suicidal rabbits, you sell china.'

'And you're a singer, or is it a comedienne? A juggler?' he went on as though she hadn't spoken. 'Not many of us restrict our talents to one thing these days.'

'As I think you know, I sing,' she managed to say in the fast flow of words.

'What time are you on? If we were nearer I'd take you to meet my mum, she'd be real impressed, meeting a singer. But there isn't time. So, we'll go for a swim. The baths are open for a couple of hours and what better way to pass the time than swimming.'

'Swimming? But I can't.'

'Can't swim or can't come with me? Your leg doesn't stop you getting into the water surely? So, it must be me. All right, I'll wait outside and walk you to the hall when you've finished your swim.'

He spoke so fast, his mind was so quick, she didn't know how to answer him and laughter overcame her once more. He began to speak again and in desperation she reached over and pressed a finger to his lips to stop him.

'I don't have my bathers or a towel, I don't want to mess up my hair as I've just had it done, and most importantly, I don't want to swim.' She was disconcerted by the look in his dark eyes – which she now realized were not brown, but a deep blue – and the way he was lightly kissing her fingers. She pulled them away hastily.

129

'My mum says I talk too much. Do I?'

'Yes! Drink your tea.'

'You sound just like her. Prettier though. Much prettier.'

Shirley knew she had to get away. She imagined that Andy, or Larry Carver in a suit, was the kind to sit in the front row and watch her performance and that was something she didn't think she could manage. Telling a lie was something she would now have to resort to. She told him the concert was in the town hall building, where she knew there was a concert hall having seen notices to that effect, and she managed to get away from him before he realized her untruth.

Arriving at the school hall early, she found a room where she could sit and compose herself. What a whirlwind of a man. When it was time to go on stage she had managed to forget the interlude and was able to concentrate on her music. She did two spots with three songs in each, and came off happy that she had performed well.

When the concert ended, the whole cast were called back on stage to sing the national anthem with the audience. The lights went up, and there sitting in the front row was Andy. He grinned at her then, shaking his finger in an admonishing way, mouthed, 'You told me a Tom Pepper, didn't you?'

The serious tone of the anthem was difficult to achieve.

He was waiting at the stage door and walked her back to the guest house where she was staying.

'Meet me tomorrow? I'll be free in the morning, then I have to move on,' he said.

'Sorry, but I have to be on the nine o'clock train. I'm singing in Cardiff for three nights, then I'm going home.'

'And where would that be?'

'Oh, a small seaside town you won't have heard of. It's called St David's Well.'

'You're right, never heard of it.' Andy hoped his alarm didn't show. Larry Carver he might be at the moment, but the police in St David's Well knew him as Derek Hanbury and also under his real name of Andy Probert. It was a small town and as such it was extremely likely that Shirley had met his brother Reggie. Such a shame, but sadly, it was time to say goodbye to the attractive and interesting Shirley Downs.

Leaving her at her door he kissed her hand and suggested

they met at the station and exchanged addresses. 'I'm all over the place,' he said, 'and so are you, but if we keep in touch we might meet again. I hope so, Shirley.'

'So do I – maybe,' Shirley said, frowning as she closed the door.

She went slowly up to her room still smiling, aware that she had enjoyed the few hours spent with him more than any for a long time. It was unlikely they would meet again, in fact she didn't think she really wanted to – there was something dangerous about Andy, not danger of physical harm, but danger to her peace of mind. It had been fun and a most unlikely way to have spent the empty hours, but some things are better being left unfinished, a brief cameo to be remembered and nothing more. Accepting that their surprising third meeting was destined to be nothing more than an amusing memory, she was nevertheless disappointed when he was not at the station the following morning.

Later that day, again with hours to spare, Shirley tried to write to Freddy Clements and describe the market trader, but although she remembered him clearly, she found him impossible to put into words.

Andy Probert, alias Larry Carver, was fifty miles away. Setting up a stall alongside a small roadside market, he brought out the goods he had collected the previous night from his lockup. Scattered among the remnants of his china sale was the stuff he had been given in St David's Well by Audrey Thomas and others. It was far enough from home not to be recognized. At a time when luxury was little more than a dream, items such as those given by Audrey were snatched up as soon as they were placed on display.

He'd had a good week and it was fun work and certainly better than joining the army. The story he had told his family about being unsuitable, was not really the truth. He had been on the move, changing his name and even his appearance, and so far had evaded being dragged protestingly into custody and dressed in khaki. He had to stay one step ahead all the time, but instead of being tedious it only added to the excitement of his life.

The basis of his determination to stay out of the army was

131

pure, inexcusable fear. He'd had a recurring dream since before he had become eligible for conscription. He saw himself in khaki uniform and drowning in a sea filled with men unable to see him or hear his cries for help. He had been startled out of sleep – sweating, gasping for breath, his heart pumping – many times and every time the dream ended with his slipping below the water.

Whatever happened and whatever he had to do, he was determined to stay out of uniform, even though his brother Reggie, the one person he'd confided in, had told him it was not a premonition, only a dream brought on by apprehension and fear.

Packing the few goods he hadn't sold into his van, changing the number plate to a local one, he drove off to find a place to sleep. Perhaps he'd sleep in the van tonight if he could find a quiet lane somewhere. Then he would travel north to another of his contacts to buy some fresh stock. This time he had been promised some food. He'd have to be particularly careful where he sold that, with so many people employed to look out for anyone selling black market foodstuffs and too ready to inform the police. He wouldn't get away with it a second time and he promised himself he would never again allow his brother Reggie to take the blame.

He parked in a lane which led to a disused church and, after changing out of his smart 'selling' clothes and into a jumper and a pair of dungarees, he slept the sleep of the innocent and pure minded, undisturbed by guilt. The world was filled with the 'haves' and the 'have nots'. He was simply balancing the levels a bit, that's all.

In the town where he and Shirley had met for the third time, the market manager was trying to trace him. The man who had called himself Larry Carver had booked a stall for two weeks and had left after one day's trading, without paying any rent.

By sheer coincidence, Andy saw a poster advertising a variety show as he drove through Cardiff some days later. On the list of performers was the name Shirley Downs. He was tempted to arrange a meeting but survival warnings rattled. He knew he should avoid seeing her again. Once only was the rule and he had seen Shirley three times. Familiarity

132

brought danger. And regrettably, he had told her his real name. To keep one step ahead of the law and the military, he had to steer clear of involvement. A woman could ruin everything and he liked the way his life was going.

The van had been painted a dull brown, an assorted collection of part used tins of paints he'd bought from a scrap yard dealer had been mixed together. The number plate had been changed for one he had found on a rubbish heap near a garage. Everything was set for another collection of items for the unfortunates in some imagined city. He'd be foolish to risk seeing Shirley again, especially as she was from the town where his brother and he were known.

The concert programme was made up mainly of amateur performers. Shirley sat in the room which passed as a dressing room and wished she were home. Her leg ached, she hadn't slept comfortably since leaving home, and the accommodation had been far from pleasant; small rooms often several flights up, and with poor washing facilities such as she hadn't experienced in a long time.

Ken Ward did his best and until this recent tour he had been insistent on getting comfortable rooms and friendly managers in the places where she was performing. This week long tour, with unattractive digs and hours to kill in strange towns, made her want to forget singing and stay at home indefinitely. Instead of feeling like the successful woman she had become, she felt second-rate and that was something she couldn't accept.

When she went out to sing her numbers, Ken Ward was at the side of the stage and at once he apologized. 'Sorry about this, Shirley, you shouldn't be here. I agreed to you accepting this tour to help a friend but it wasn't what he promised – or described.'

'Are all the seats filled?' she asked, and when he nodded, and showed her his notebook with the expected profit to be spent on parcels for prisoners of war, she said, 'Then it's all right, I'll do it, but Ken, I don't want a long tour like this for a while. Just one night bookings and not so far from home, all right?'

'I understand, and thanks Shirley. In fact, I don't like being away too long myself, not now Eirlys and I have the baby. Being a father has changed me. I have even learned to tolerate Stanley, Harold and Percival!' He looked thoughtful, then suggested, 'What about catching the last train instead of waiting for the morning? You'll be late home but at least you'll wake up in your own bed.' This was agreed and Ken ordered a taxi to be waiting when the show ended.

They talked about young Anthony Ward for a while and when she stepped on to the stage, Shirley's mood was sunny. The lighting in the hall was poor, the spotlight supposed to circle her in a glow was weak and she could see the audience clearly. There, in the centre of the front row, was Andy.

He had decided that just for an hour or so, seeing her would not be much of a risk, especially as he would be leaving the area again the following day. He was waiting at the exit afterwards, and it was with disappointment that she explained that she was leaving for home immediately. A display of melancholy and the calling down of curses on a fickle fate, hid Andy's relief that the decision had been made for him and his dangerous risk had been aborted.

Freddy Clements had received a letter from Shirley recently which had sparked the fear of doubt about the future of which he had dreamed. She had spoken three times of a stranger who had miraculously appeared when she was in trouble and helped her, then turned up in a town where she was booked to sing. Jealousy filled him every time he thought of the man. Out here with no chance at all of getting home, how could he fight him off? Shirley hadn't told him any more than the basic facts. She had told him about being left stranded by the man who had offered her a lift and thinking about the man who had done that to her increased Freddy's desperate urge to fight. Not the enemy, but the men who spent time with her when he could not, an anger based on jealousy.

He opened the pages and re-read the relevant section with disbelief about the man selling goods in a market. Three times was too much of a coincidence. The words quivered before his eyes and he had difficulty reading. When he had calmed down he re-read the whole letter, and to his relief the rest of the letter was as affectionate as always, and she had signed it 'love from Shirley' and added a line of kisses.

134

He gave his oppo a friendly shove and said, 'Fancy a game of football? I have a need to kick something very, very hard.'

Eynon, Marged and Huw's son, was less sure about Alice. They had only been married for a few days when he'd had to leave. And although her letters were filled with love and plans for their future, he wondered how she would be when they met again. Perhaps she would look at him and see a stranger. After all, it was a stranger who looked back at him from his mirror when he shaved. He wasn't the man she had known. Dangers and unimagined tensions had added fatigue and age to his once boyish features.

They hadn't spent enough time together for her to really know him. He wrote a letter telling her that if she had any doubts when they met at the end of the war, she mustn't feel tied to him. Their marriage was what he wanted and she was the most important thing in his life and always would be, but he realized it was unfair to expect her to feel the same. He read it through, then tore it up and burned it on the fire.

In the middle of September the weather turned sultry; there had been rain for several days then the temperature rose and the town suffered under stifling heat that made them unable to sleep. Windows were left open in the hope that the rooms would become cooler, women sat on doorsteps and chatted to each other along the street as they struggled to knit with hands that were damp with perspiration. Small children were restless and uncomfortable in their beds. They fidgeted until they were tangled in the sheets, then woke wailing for someone to make them feel better. Older children cried out and pleaded to be allowed to get up.

Audrey and Wilf were sitting in the garden where they were pestered by flying insects and a few doors down Marged and Huw suffered in the same way.

'Come on, Huw, let's go and persuade Audrey and Wilf to come for a walk, it might be cooler up in the park,' Marged said.

'The only place where there'll be a breeze is the beach,' Huw replied. They went through the back lane and leaned over Audrey's gate. 'We're going for a walk, do you fancy coming? It's too hot to sleep.'

135

'I can't leave Maude and Myrtle,' Audrey began.

Then voices from above shouted, 'We'll come, Auntie Marged. Our clothes are sticking to us and I long for a paddle in the waves.' The sisters were hanging out of the window, their damp hair pulled up into a bun on top of their heads, their nightdresses floating around them as they flapped their arms to create a breeze.

'A paddle? That's for cissies. I'm taking my dippers,' Huw said.

It didn't take more than a few minutes for them all to be ready and in a chattering group they walked to the main road and caught a late bus that took them most of the way, and walked the rest. To their surprise the pavements were crowded.

Living in a town alongside the sea, people were used to enjoying its pleasures and the fact that it was late at night was no deterrent. Whole families were there, babies in prams wearing only napkins, mothers in summer dresses with a cardigan over their arms – just in case. People smiled and greeted each other as though they were sharing some giant party. Buses brought more overheated families to the nearest bus stop and they all came in a chattering excited group along the pavements towards the tempting waves.

Myrtle pointed as she recognized Eirlys with baby Anthony in his pram followed by Morgan and the three boys. 'Hi yer, Stanley,' she shouted. 'Got your dippers?'

'You bet!'

The noise from the beach revealed the presence of a crowd of bathers long before they were seen. The tide was high, creaming around the outcrop of rock not far from the metal steps leading to Castle's cafe. Rich foam was rising and falling at its edge, breaking on the rocks. It looked very tempting. Even though the air was cooler here, the need for a bathe hadn't lessened.

The heat and sluggish weather had made them expect a flat millpond sea, but this turbulence, which Huw said was probably from a storm far out to sea, was wonderful. Kneeling down in the doorway of a closed shop, Myrtle pulled off her dress to reveal her bathers. With Maude following, she ran over the warm sand, in and out of the now closed stalls and rides, and into the welcoming waves.

Stanley looked doubtful. 'I don't think I fancy them big breakers,' he said to Wilf.

'Not a strong swimmer yet?' Wilf asked in surprise. 'All the hours you've spent on the beach I thought you'd be able to swim to France. Not that I'd recommend that just at present, mind,' he added with a laugh. To encourage the boy to where others were having fun, he added, 'You don't have to swim, Stanley, it isn't very deep. Walk to the rocks and just mess about and cool off. I wish I could.'

'Don't tell me you can't swim!' Stanley jeered. 'And you telling me off for not going in.'

'I can swim, lad, but because I have this heart problem, I'm advised not to.'

'Oh, sorry, Mr Thomas.'

'When the tide drops back a bit I might paddle, mind. Come on, I'll walk across with you, shall I?'

Stanley looked at the water foaming around the bottom of the cliffs before exploding and bouncing back in a creamy shower and the temptation was too much. Harold followed him but Percival refused.

'No, our Stanley, it'll be over my head and I'll drown,' he said, backing away before Stanley could insist. Stanley could be a bit of a bully sometimes, making him do things he didn't want to do. 'I'll watch and cheer when you dive through the waves,' he promised. With Harold beside him, Wilf coaxing Percival to at least come and sit on the rocks and dabble his feet, Stanley walked down and sat on a rocky shelf where the waves foamed over his feet. Audrey waved and came after them.

The rocks on which they found a place to sit were quite high above the waves and the water was deep as it swirled around them. After calling to tell Wilf what he was doing, Stanley made his way across the rocks to where he could make his way down to the water to join the others who were standing in a row, holding hands and jumping up and down chanting rhymes.

Wilf found a convenient spot where he and Audrey could lean against the rock and they sat looking down at the children having fun. He turned to Audrey and said sadly, 'We're so extravagant with the years when we're young. There seems

137

to be plenty of time for anything we want to do, until something happens to remind us that time isn't for ever.'

'I know, dear. So many times we've said wait till next year and now we aren't sure how many next years we'll have.'

'There'll be plenty. We must think so or we'll waste the time we have.' He patted her arm affectionately. 'What is important, Audrey, dear, is that you don't waste the time you'll have after I'm gone. You promise to do what you've planned? Not waste time regretting the past? Being angry about how much we lost?'

'I promise, dear.'

He looked at her strangely, 'And you won't hate me if I've done something you don't fully agree with?'

'Hate you? You aren't capable of doing anything to make me feel anything but love, Wilf dear.'

Shaking off the melancholy of their conversation, Wilf turned to see Percival standing on the rock not far from him. He was leaning over precariously, exchanging insults with his brother. Below, the tide was at its fullest, the water creaming high against the rocky outcrop with the added turbulence that accompanied the change from flow to ebb. The bathers were more than waist high in the foam, still holding hands, still chanting their rhymes.

'Step back from the edge, Percival,' Audrey warned.

'I want Stanley to go and get that kite for me,' Percival complained. He pointed up at the cliff near the cafe where, with its string caught on a jagged piece of rock, a red kite fluttered in the thermals rising up the cliff face.

'Don't worry about that one, it's probably damaged. It's better if I buy you a new one tomorrow,' Wilf said. 'It isn't worth risking a fall.'

'Thanks, Mr Thomas.' Percival turned to call again to his brother and, when Stanley didn't appear to hear him, he leaned over and shouted in what was for him a loud voice. 'Our Stanley, I'm having a new one so you can forget the stupid kite. Right?'

A piece of sharp rock hurt Percival's foot and put him off balance. Wilf shouted for him to be careful, 'Look out, Percival!'

As Percival turned in the direction of the voice, he lost his balance, teetered, cried out and fell. In horror, Wilf jumped up and looked down at the water, but there was no sign of Percival. The foaming waves had swallowed him up.

The crowd in the water hadn't seen the boy fall and no one seemed to be doing anything to help. Wilf ran across the rocks and jumped down into the sea. His heart was racing with the fear of the boy drowning and his own guilt for distracting him when he was so precariously balanced. Still no one reacted. Wilf dived in and headed for the place where he had seen Percival disappear.

Audrey stood, unable to call, her breath tight and her head filled with panic. She looked around but no member of her family was near enough to have seen what had happened. She took a deep breath and called to the bathers nearest to her, but her voice sounded puny, the noise of the waves and the singing of the youngsters made it impossible to make herself heard.

When Wilf hit the water the pain in his chest all but overcame him. He managed a few strokes and found he could stand up. He looked around, but in the turmoil of the white waves hitting the wall and bouncing off, it was impossible to see anything that might be among them.

He shouted for help but no one responded. He called the boy's name and walked around, his hands and legs searching for him below the surface, and still no one realized his distress. 'Stanley!' he called but Stanley waved cheerfully and went on with the game they were playing, leapfrogging in the water and falling about like demented clowns.

The pain in his chest became unbearable and he clutched his body and struggled a few paces trying to reach out for the rocks. They seemed a long way off and as he struggled to reach them, they seemed to recede from his outstretched arms and grasping fingers. Slowly he became unaware of everything happening around him. Sounds became muted and it was as though he were in a dream, with people far away, no longer a part of the moment, like memories of other days and other places.

He felt hands reach under his arms and voices murmured unrecognizable words and he felt himself being dragged along in the water, with the pain pressing and everything whirling.

Then he was being carried and was carefully lowered until he was lying on the concrete and a soft, soothing voice was talking to him, a face close to his own. A dear face; a loved face. 'Audrey,' he gasped. 'What have I done?' Then the darkness came and he relaxed into its welcoming, painfree arms.

Dripping wet, but unharmed, Percival stood and looked down at the man and cried. 'He was nice to me,' he wailed. 'He was going to buy me a kite an' all.'

'He still will, Percival,' Audrey said in a choked voice. 'As soon as he's well, you will have your kite.'

Wilf woke up in hospital and was declared a hero. He spoke very little, only to Audrey and then simply to apologize for his foolishness. He touched her arm and whispered, 'Forgive me, my darling.' Then, 'Such a surprise planned.' Then he murmured something unintelligible. Leaning over him Audrey caught a few words, like: 'our son,' and 'little Bobbie.' The words 'forgive me' were repeated several times and once, he said clearly, 'I tried to tell . . .' The rest was just a jumble. Three days later he died.

The day after his death, ignoring the pleas of Marged and Hetty to rest, Audrey tried every shop in the town searching for a red kite. Every other consideration was blocked out. She had to keep Wilf's promise for him. She found one at last and presented it to Percival, who was on the edge of tears.

'I'm sorry, Auntie Audrey,' he sobbed.

She guessed that he was feeling at least partly responsible. 'Don't upset yourself, Percival. He died because he was an elderly man and was very ill, so ill the doctors couldn't help him. It was nothing to do with you falling in. Remember that, will you?'

There had to be an inquest and once that had been dealt with, Marged arranged the funeral. Audrey was locked in grief and unable to think of anything but the briefness of her happiness. In her heart she kept thinking that if Percival hadn't been so foolish, leaning out so precariously, Wilf would still be alive. She would never speak her thoughts aloud. The boy hadn't intended such a thing to happen and no one should have to carry such guilt. Giving him the kite had been important. It was a sign that Wilf didn't blame him either.

'Why did he have to die?' she moaned softly to Marged.

'As if there haven't been enough deaths. All he wanted was to see Eynon and Johnny come home, but this damned war goes on and on and every tragedy is made worse because of it.'

Marged crossed her fingers superstitiously. Talk about the boys coming home in the same breath as talk about Wilf dying frightened her. The war was a long way from over and her son and her nephew were in daily risk of their lives. 'I've written to tell Eynon,' she said, 'and Bleddyn will write to Johnny. They have to be told.'

'Will you close the cafe on the day of the funeral, Marged?' Audrey asked.

With only two more weeks before the season officially ended, Marged had intended to employ help and keep the place open rather than miss a day's takings, but looking at her sister's face and the accusation there in her eyes, she nodded. 'We'll close,' she said. 'Of course we'll close.' It was what Huw and Bleddyn wanted, and besides, her sister's wishes were paramount at this time.

There were three flower shops in St David's Well but the most popular one was Chapel's Flowers. Mrs Chapel was assisted by Maldwyn Perkins who when he first came to town had worked in Marged and Huw's cafe and on the stalls on the beach. But he had been unhappy there and when Mrs Chapel offered him a job in the florist, he had accepted with relief. Flowers were what he knew and preparing bouquets to sell and filling the window of the shop with tempting displays gave him a lot of pleasure.

It was Maldwyn who spoke to Marged when she came to order flowers for the funeral of Wilf Thomas.

'Sorry, I am to hear of your loss, Mrs Castle,' he said at once. 'Read it in the paper, I did. Brave man, going in to rescue young Percival when he knew he shouldn't dive into cold water. Instinct, isn't it, to help someone in trouble? Everyone's talking about it.'

'I hope the talk fades once the funeral is over. Brave he was indeed, but there's Percival to consider in this. We have to look after the living, the dead are beyond our help.'

'I don't know what you mean, Mrs Castle. You don't think he was a courageous man?'

'Of course we do. What he did was unthinking bravery. We're trying to keep the paper reports from Percival though, in case he thinks he's to blame. He's only a boy and if we aren't careful he'll never get it out of his head. There's no point in him being upset.'

'No, indeed,' he said, still not quite understanding her concerns.

Maldwyn watched Marged go after he had taken a note of her requirements. It was strange how grief changed a person. He'd noted it before, lines appearing on their faces, the stooped walk, the lowered voice and brief sentences leaving some things unexplained.

Seven wreaths were ordered. He went into the back room to check they had the bases mossed and ready. Mrs Chapel was sitting beside the small work table and she began to select evergreen leaves from those she had recently gathered from the garden of a neighbour. Pruning the fir trees in the gardens of friends gave them all the evergreen they needed. Once they were fastened into place, the flowers would be quickly done on the morning of the funeral. Looking at Maldwyn's neatly written list, she scribbled down the flowers she would need.

'Better phone them to make sure we get what we want, Maldwyn dear. This will be a big occasion and we don't want to have to make do with anything but the best.'

She had to speak twice as Maldwyn was daydreaming.

'Thinking about your wedding, are you, Maldwyn?'

'Sorry, Mrs Chapel, it's hard to imagine that I'll have a wife in a couple of months.' He turned to her and smiled. 'I'm so lucky. Delyth will soon be my wife, I'm here working with you, doing what I enjoy, and even my poor eyesight was a sort of blessing, keeping me out of the army.'

'Phone through and get the order booked then you can go back to your daydream,' she said with a chuckle. 'I don't think I'll get much sense out of you over the next few weeks.'

Maldwyn picked up the phone and as always, she marvelled at the efficient way he forgot everything else and attended to the order. Whatever happened, he had never neglected his work, in fact he did much more than he was paid for.

*   *   *

142

Shirley Downs came home to find the Castle family in mourning. She had been away for four nights having again given in to Ken's pleading, and had heard nothing about the tragedy. Wilf had not been a relation for very long. Her mother, Hetty, had married Bleddyn Castle the previous year and the fact that Wilf had been married to Bleddyn's brother's wife's sister, was too tenuous a connection for her to feel a great sadness.

She wrote to tell Freddy Clements and also told him a little more about her latest brief encounter with the man she now knew as Andy, making light of the man's attractiveness and youth. A serving soldier did not like being reminded of those safe at home, making money.

In a distant town, Andy, who now called himself Kenneth Durham, was taking out some home-made forms purporting to give him permission to collect items for distribution among families who were being rehoused after being made homeless by the bombing. A borrowed handcart was all he had by way of transport and that was worrying. There was no chance of a fast getaway, even leaving all his stock he might be caught. He'd discovered a shed in the large garden of an empty house, in which to store the goods and provide a place to sleep. He looked around him, the cart was loaded with all he could manage and the shed was filled with stuff he had brought ready for the next market town. He would need to steal a van to get the stuff to a market – the last one, having become too well known, had been abandoned in an old quarry.

At the funeral, Maude and Myrtle comforted Audrey. Marged's briskness hid her grief as she concentrated on making sure the arrangements went well. While Huw was carrying in extra chairs for the people who were arriving at the house, she was talking in low tones to Hetty and Bleddyn discussing the end of the season, 'By the time the next one starts, Audrey will be recovered and back into her usual routine,' she sighed. 'Thank goodness. This year has been very hard for us all. It will be good for Audrey to get back to normal, won't it?'

Overhearing, Audrey thought differently. 'Don't think you can count on me coming back now I'm widowed. I'm not suddenly helpless, unable to decide what to do with the rest of my life.'

'Oh, Audrey, I was just saying—'

'I heard you and you can forget me helping next year or the year after that. I have other plans.'

'What plans? Surely you aren't going to keep up this resentment? You promised our mam that you'd always be a part of the family business. And with the boys away it's even more urgent for us all to do what we can.'

'I'll be busy,' Audrey snapped.

'Doing what, for heaven's sake?'

Huw came in struggling with a pile of chairs and shouted for them to stop. 'We're in mourning. This is a day for remembering Wilf and you two can't stop rowing? You should be ashamed of yourselves.'

'Yes, tell your wife to leave me alone, why don't you?' Audrey sobbed as she ran from the room.

Eight

Audrey and Wilf had discussed what she would do after Wilf's death many times in the weeks since they had learned about his serious illness, but now the time had come Audrey was at a loss. Half thought out ideas, plus doubts about her ability to carry them out filled her mind with confusion. To those who knew her, she appeared vague and occasionally Maude and Myrtle would worry. Grief did strange things to people, and her vacant expression and the moments when she appeared not to hear them were frightening. They declined to speak to Marged about it in case they offended Audrey or made her worse.

For Audrey, the days running up to the funeral and the service itself were a blur and in the week since the final goodbye, she hadn't left the house apart from her determined search for the red kite. All the brave words had come to nothing, she didn't know how to cope without him. They had been married for less than two years, but had been loving friends since they were at school, neither wanting anyone else, even though Audrey's mother had forbidden them to marry.

She knew Wilf had left a will but she was in no mood to care. Coaxed by their solicitor, she sat while he went over the carefully worded sentences, her mind drifting. She wasn't interested in the contents. She knew there was enough money for her to live comfortably. She knew that, so she didn't listen to the droning voice as it read the two page document. Her needs were simple enough and she had no great ambitions to surround herself with luxuries even if she could get them.

'Do you have any questions, Mrs Thomas?' he asked and coming to her senses she smiled and said no, there were no questions.

'None?' he asked with a frown. 'You aren't curious?'

'Thank you for your help. If you'll send me a bill for your services I'll pop in sometime and pay it,' she said, hurrying from the room.

His perplexed question: 'But, Mrs Thomas?' went unheeded.

It wasn't until she reached home and looked at the document carefully that she realized that there was no money. That was a huge shock and she stared at the walls for an age, wondering how Wilf could have spent such a large sum. The shocking thought occurred to her that although they had been together, as friends, for most of their lives, perhaps she hadn't known him at all. That thought upset her more than anything that had happened since his death. She became more withdrawn than ever.

Maude and Myrtle dealt with the cleaning and cooked meals to coax back Audrey's appetite but she ate little and seemed unaware of the hours and days as they passed. They didn't know what to do. They had tried talking to Marged, but Audrey was unwilling for her sister to come into the house – in fact she wouldn't see anyone, insisting that she needed to face the emptiness on her own before she could allow others back into her life. The truth was partly the need for privacy and partly her unwillingness to impart the news of the lost money.

The sisters didn't go out either. When Stanley called to invite them to go for a final swim before the weather became too cold Audrey cried, the mention of the beach a harsh reminder of Wilf's death. Myrtle pushed Stanley away from the door and slammed it shut.

'I didn't hurt him,' he protested angrily through the letter box. 'It isn't my fault!'

'Go away, you're stupid,' Maude hissed through the door.

'Stupid yourself!' he shouted. 'Myrtle, open the door, I want to talk to you.' The door remained closed and he went back and asked Eirlys and Ken why he was treated like the enemy.

'You aren't the enemy, Stanley,' Eirlys comforted. 'Myrtle is looking after Audrey until she recovers. For a while she is Myrtle's priority, then everything will go back to normal.' As she said the words, Eirlys doubted the truth of them. How

146

could Audrey's life return to normal after a marriage that had followed years of waiting and had ended so soon?

'I wanted us to go for that swim,' Stanley grumbled, pushing his brothers without need as he crossed the room. 'Percival needs more practice or he'll have forgotten by next summer.'

'I ain't going,' Percival whimpered. 'I 'ates the sea.'

'Rubbish, Percival, you always say that, then have more fun than the rest of us!' Eirlys said with a laugh.

'Go to the beach and have your swim,' Ken coaxed. 'I'll stay with the baby and Eirlys can go with you.'

'I ain't coming, Stanley. It's too cold.' Percival gave a very impressive shiver and looked mournfully at Eirlys.

'You're coming, so stop acting like you're dying and get your dippers!' Stanley said sternly, pulling him out of his chair and pushing him towards the cupboard.

'I can't go, my dippers ain't here.' The protest was stopped by Stanley pulling the dark green bathers from a pile of clothes and waving them in front of Percival's face.

When they had gathered what they needed, they set off. Stanley was, if not cheerful, less miserable than before. Ken slipped a few shillings into Eirlys's pocket, 'Chips after their swim and they'll forget Myrtle's rudeness.'

'Thank goodness they're still young enough for their problems to be sorted by their constant hunger,' she whispered to Ken as she kissed him before closing the door.

Stanley stared down into the water, fighting his own fears. He imagined falling in and being unable to swim, which was what had happened to Wilf. His heart had weakened and he didn't have the strength to save himself. If someone hadn't dived in and hauled him out he would have died right there with all those people about; crowds laughing and fooling about and him dying within their reach. Then there would have been some who would have blamed Percival.

He looked up to where his brother was struggling with his clothes. 'Come on, you lazy sod,' he said, helping his young brother to pull his feet out of his trousers. 'Why don't you take your boots off first like everyone else?' Taking a firm hold of his hand, he ran with him and jumped into the waves. He understood why Percival had been reluctant to come and he was the real reason Stanley wanted this swim. He had to kill off the demons that might invade Percival's mind if he didn't overlay the tragedy with laughter and fun.

Audrey began going out for walks, but she went at night, strolling around the dark streets where the blackout was still in force although cars were allowed to display a little more light than in the early years of the war. Shops were in darkness, and not all of the blank windows were due to blackout restrictions. Many businesses had failed since the shortages of so many items and the rationing of others meant there was little to sell.

At a corner near Chapel's Flowers, she stopped on a few occasions and tried to peer through the windows of the silent premises. She began thinking about a plan she and Wilf had once discussed, but at the time had decided it was too soon for the idea to gel. Although, she mused, perhaps now, while she was stinging with the hurt of his secrecy, was the moment to take the first step? She still had this painful ache inside and her head was filled with a confusion of memories that jostled with resentment and anger. The loss of the large sum of money was puzzling. Wilf should have been quite wealthy, but it wasn't the money that disturbed her peace of mind, it was the mystery. Until her mind could think calmly about his death and she could face her future knowing she would be forever alone, she would be unable to keep her promise to him. A good promise, one Wilf had asked her to keep because it was right for her, not a selfish promise like the one her mother had forced her make all those years ago when she had been an ashamed and obedient child.

One morning, as she made her way to the shops to buy her ration of corned beef, she met Mrs Denver. Although Lilly had married Sam Edwards, Lilly's daughter had been fathered by Mrs Denver's son who had died in battle. Lilly had kept in touch with the child's grandmother and Mrs Denver was grateful. Not wanting to talk, Audrey tried to avoid her but she couldn't ignore her cheerful greeting.

'I've just been to see your Lilly,' she told Audrey. 'Lovely child and Lilly cares for her so well.' She paused then, remembering the news of Wilf's death. 'Sorry I am about your dear husband. I hope you find plenty to fill your time, it helps, doesn't it, to be busy?'

148

'Thank you, yes. Once I gather my thoughts I'll find a way of occupying myself.' Tears threatened and at once Mrs Denver was sympathetic. 'At least you won't have money troubles. I was left with a little boy and no money. No husband, really, if the truth's known. We never married.' She chattered on, allowing Audrey time to recover. 'Cooking saved me. I've always loved cooking and I found jobs cooking for cafes. Apple turnovers were my specials. Then there were my lodgers. Maldwyn, him at Chapel's flower shop, and poor Vera, they were the most recent. Don't worry, Mrs Thomas, dear. Something will turn up for you. Although,' she added, 'sometimes you have to do a bit of searching – it doesn't always come to you, you have to find it.'

Summer 1943 drifted to its close, and as the crowds stayed away the beach returned to its quiet winter mood. With the season at an end, Maude and Myrtle were looking for work. It had to be something temporary as they wanted to return to the beach again in the spring.

'What about that night school course?' Hetty said to Myrtle when Myrtle applied for a job in the children's home where she had worked before. 'You'll still enrol for that, won't you?'

'I'll be working shifts so I don't know whether I can,' she said. She wanted to go, there was a pleasure in dealing with numbers that she couldn't explain: precision, no doubts, no halfway between what was correct and what was wrong. But Maude had discouraged her, convinced her she would be humiliated and teased once her lack of education was revealed.

'I want to go as well,' Audrey said when she explained her fears. She counted in her head before adding, 'It's more than thirty-eight years since I went to school, you can't be more embarrassed in front of the other students than me!'

Bleddyn and Hetty had tried to persuade Maude to take shorthand and typing lessons but she had declined. Office work did not appeal and when would she need to type?

'Myrtle and I missed our chances and it's too late,' she insisted.

'Only if you want it to be,' Hetty coaxed.

With her sister's warnings of disillusionment ringing in her ears, Myrtle went to enrol with Audrey. Both booked to take a course in accountancy and business. Maude looked at the list of courses on offer and decided there was nothing to suit her.

It was as they were walking home from their first lesson that Audrey told Myrtle of her plan, swearing her to complete secrecy. The idea she imparted, plus the secrecy, seemed to lift Audrey's spirits. The studying, now with a legitimate purpose in mind, added to her enjoyment. Slowly, she began going out and picking up the threads of her life.

Marged crossed her fingers and hoped that after a winter to grieve, her sister would return to supporting the family business by doing the laundry and housekeeping once the summer of 1944 began. Besides Audrey herself, only Myrtle knew this was not going to happen and she said nothing.

Beth left the market cafe one afternoon, as the day closed in for a cold clear night. The stars were bright in the sky, the air was chill but clean and refreshing, and as she cycled along the lanes toward Bernard Gregory's smallholding she felt at peace. If only Peter were home the day would be a perfect one.

When she saw two figures standing near the front gate her heart leapt – for a moment, she thought the soldier standing there was in fact her husband. There was a fleeting moment when she believed her wishes and thoughts had been realized because she had sensed he was near. Her feet pressed hard on the pedals, the wheels crackled over the gravelly surface as she increased her speed, but as she realized the man was not tall enough and was too heavily built to be Peter, the pedals became stationary as her joy died and the wheels freewheeled and slowed.

'Hello Beth, remember Reggie?' Mr Gregory called as she dismounted. 'He's in the army and with a few days leave he managed to call and see us, isn't that nice?'

'Reggie, how are you?' Beth hid her disappointment well, adding, 'Can you stay for something to eat? I made a casserole this morning and there's plenty for an extra person.'

'Thank you, I'd like that. Mr Gregory's been showing me the fields. The fresh ground has done well for a first year, hasn't it?' Leaving the men discussing the crops Beth went into the kitchen and prepared the food. She wondered whether or not to mention Maude, but decided it best if they ate first. It might make Reggie feel uncomfortable and spoil the meal.

The decision was taken out of her hands. A knock at the door as she was setting out the plates was answered by Bernard, and Maude stood there.

'Mr Gregory, I've been wondering if you have a vacancy for an unqualified but willing worker this winter,' she said.

'Hello, Maude,' he said unnecessarily loudly. 'You'd better come in.'

'Hello, Maude,' Reggie said.

Leaving them together, Bernard scuttled into the kitchen to assist Beth. 'Better make that four plates,' he said, showing firmly crossed fingers.

There had been a small deception. Maude had received a letter from Reggie in which he told her he planned to be there. Being left alone for a little while, they began to revive a promising friendship. Talking fast, they told each other their news, snatching a few kisses, always with a wary ear listening to the activities in the kitchen. They were rosy-faced and their eyes were glowing when Beth and Bernard rejoined them.

Audrey and Marged were still saying very little to each other and it seemed impossible to imagine things would ever return to their once close working partnership. Marged confided in Huw her fears that the estrangement, whatever its cause, was becoming harder to heal.

'I know it's six months before we need to think about the new season, but the weeks fly past and if Audrey and I don't start talking soon, I'll have to find a way of dealing with it without her help once again. This year was hard and I don't know whether I could cope with another one like it'

'I know, Marged. Even someone as insensitive as me could see you were exhausted. You can't manage another year without reliable help. Best if you get something sorted just in case, but say nothing. Then if she doesn't want to help, you won't be left without anyone. You can't leave it and end up doing it all yourself, in the hope she'll suddenly change her mind.'

'Perhaps if I asked her?'

'Best you wait, Marged.' Huw knew how easily Marged could say the wrong thing and start an argument. 'There's plenty of time. Give Audrey a chance to think about it. I'm sure she'll want to go back to how things were before Wilf's illness changed things, but if you push her too soon she might think we're insensitive, and refuse.'

Marged nodded, but as soon as Huw left to work in the chip shop with his brother, she called to see Audrey. She was in a gentle mood, concern for her sister giving her an air of compassion. But Audrey's first words changed that to irritation.

'Before you say anything, Marged, I'm not going back to working on the beach next summer.'

'I only called to see how you are!'

'I'm fine, but I still don't intend to deal with the house-keeping.'

'How can you say that? It's months away. How can you know how you'll feel next spring?'

'Why not? You know how you'll feel.'

'Yes, I'll feel duty bound to help in the family business!' Too late Marged wished she had kept her voice calm.

'I've had a lifetime of duty. I'm ready for something different. Plans Wilf and I were making. I'm starting something new.'

'At your age? Don't talk daft, Audrey. Past fifty you are, how can you think of starting anything? What are you talking about?'

'Something for myself. Something that doesn't involve my being at your beck and call.'

'All right, we can work out other ways for you to help. You don't have to do the washing and the cooking. What about the cafe? You and I could do that between us without having to employ more than a part-time assistant. Maude and Myrtle can help on the sands and in the shop and we can manage the cooking between us, we'll manage fine.' She looked away and admitted, 'I'm desperate, our Audrey, this summer was hard and I'd be so glad if you'd help us like you always have.'

Audrey softened and guilt made her stomach churn, but she strengthened her will and refused. 'Get some help arranged

152

as soon as you can. Don't expect everyone to feel as strongly about the business as you do,' she advised. 'You shouldn't depend on anyone anymore. People have to make up their own minds.'

'That's rot. We've always managed and until the boys come back and everything settles down again, we all have to do what we can.'

'No, Marged. You can manage without me, and anyone else who refuses to help. There are people out there who'd love working on the sands and you have to find them. If Wilf had lived, I'd have been looking after him but as he isn't alive anymore, I'm going to look after myself.'

'But what will you do? You can't sit in a chair and do nothing for the rest of your life. You're only fifty-one, Audrey, not ninety!'

'First I'm too old and now I'm too young, what an awkward age fifty-one has turned out to be!'

Marged didn't stay long. There was a gleam in Audrey's eyes that observed her with something suspiciously like humour as she struggled to persuade her sister of her family duty, and Marged knew that if she didn't leave she would lose her temper and say more than she should.

'I don't know what's got into you,' was her parting shot. 'You're acting like a child!'

Audrey took out the estate agent's leaflet she had been studying before her sister's visit and began to make notes in the margin.

Maude came in an hour later and with her was Reggie Probert.

'Do you mind my coming in?' Reggie asked apologetically. 'After what my brother did I'd understand if you didn't want to see me.'

'We can't be responsible for our family, Reggie,' she assured him. 'We have to follow our own path and try to be understanding about how others follow theirs.'

Reggie had a late train to catch but after sharing a hot drink and a few biscuits, he and Maude stayed on the doorstep and talked for a while, then she walked with him to the corner. He took out a piece of paper, made her kiss it and added his own kiss on top. It was there that Marged saw them.

'Was that the man who stole from Audrey?' she asked, as Reggie waved and ran towards the station.

'No, Auntie Marged, it was his brother, you know, Reggie, who worked for Mr Gregory.'

'I hope you told him to stay away.'

'Oh yes, of course I did,' Maude lied with a smile.

Audrey searched through Wilf's papers in an effort to find out what had gone wrong and caused him to lose so much money. His mother's house had been sold and the money should have been in their building society account. All that was left was money she had saved and some left to her by her mother. Distressed by the mystery, and after going through everything once more, she went to the cemetery to grieve all over again. She stood for a long time beside the small grave of their son, who had been born and died in November the same year, then reminded herself that whereas grief was normal, excessive grief was nothing more than an indulgence, or self-pity, something Wilf would not have liked to see. She had to do something, talking about it to Myrtle was not enough. Mrs Denver's words echoed as she stood there, reminding her that solutions didn't always come, they had to be searched for.

Leaving the quiet cemetery, she called at the estate agents and asked to see a property that had once, a long time ago, been a cafe where shoppers had paused between their shopping and their bus ride home, to drink tea and share some gossip. It was next to Elliot's fashion emporium, not far from Chapel's Flowers. It was a corner site, and inside several large mirrors were fixed to the walls, which were decorated with worn and poorly hung yellow wallpaper.

Unable to find anything around which to build his enthusiastic sales patter, the agent nodded and smiled, occasionally saying, 'Just a bit of tidying, Mrs Thomas, just a bit of tidying. That's all the place needs, isn't it?'

The shop area had once been two rooms and the fireplaces were still in situ, covered untidily by brick-built screening. Cellar steps led down behind the chimney breast into a dark basement room which opened into the yard. The cellar had been used for storage and once the door had been forced open, was revealed as a fairly large room.

Upstairs were two bedrooms, a living room and a tiny kitchen. A box room had been made into a simple bathroom. Everything was grubby and dirty, with abandoned oddments lying everywhere. It was difficult to imagine it as a smart and attractive place which could entice people in. Half-peeled wallpaper and scuffed paintwork, a couple of broken windows and dirt encrusted floors added to the gloomy impression of sad neglect.

'Just a bit of tidying, Mrs Thomas,' the estate agent muttered hopefully.

'It's a mess, Mr Carter,' Audrey said firmly, when they stood once more at the doorway. 'I hope the price will be commensurate with the condition?'

'I'm sure we can meet at a price to please us all, Mrs Thomas.' He tried to hide his disbelief at the prospect of getting rid of the property. It had been on his books for so long he had all but given up hope. As Audrey was one of the wealthy Castle family, this had the smell of a good prospect.

The following day, Audrey went for a second look. This time, swearing them both to secrecy, she took Myrtle and Maude. After measuring each room and discussing the way the space could be used, they drew plan after plan, huddled over their diagrams like true conspirators, then went together to see a builder, although no builder seemed willing to take on the job. However, before anything could be begun, the first problem was her need for a small loan, which she quickly found, as a woman, was not going to be easy. Taking Bleddyn and Hetty into her confidence, she asked for their help. A loan was arranged with Bleddyn acting as guarantor. Two weeks later, in the middle of October, the property belonged to Audrey. But there was still the need for a builder.

Keith Kent had done work for Audrey and Wilf before and when he knocked on her door and asked if he could quote for the work at the corner shop, she welcomed him.

'I'm working at the hospital at present as you know,' he said. Audrey didn't know, and wondered why he thought she might, but she ignored the remark and asked him to go with her to look at the place she now owned.

'I'll be finished at the hospital in a few weeks and then I'll be able to start as soon as you like,' he went on after looking at what was needed.

Audrey still said nothing to Marged, and the girls went about their daily routine without allowing their excitement to show. Maude stopped looking for winter work and Myrtle turned down the job she had been offered at the children's home. On the day before the conversion work began, while the council officers were stamping their final approval on her plans, Audrey invited Marged and Huw, Bleddyn and Hetty to see what she had bought.

Huw warned Marged before they left that she was to say nothing derogatory. 'Whatever she's doing, it's her money and her life, remember. Nothing to do with you.'

'What if she's done something really stupid? Am I to smile and say well done?'

'Yes!' he insisted.

The place looked almost as bad as when Audrey first saw it, but she showed no concern about its dilapidated state. 'I want you to see it at its worst, so you'll see how well we judged it when the work is completed. We've thought it out with great care.'

'We?' Marged asked. 'Who's been advising you on this? Why didn't you talk to Huw and Bleddyn before you bought this . . .' A warning nudge from Huw made her hesitate over the critical words she intended to use and instead she said, 'this place?'

'Maude and Myrtle have been involved and as for advice, well, I knew what I wanted and I've had my own instincts to rely on, and the long discussions Wilf and I had over the past months.'

The two men wandered around tapping walls, kicking skirting boards and declared it 'Basically sound.'

Bursting with questions, Marged asked, 'What are you going to sell, Audrey? It isn't really sensible to start a business at this time.'

'We're going to open a cafe,' was the reply that widened her eyes with shock.

'I thought you hated the work?'

'This will be different, it will be mine.'

'You won't get permission.'

'Got it!' Audrey replied.

'It'll be months to get the work done before you can open.'

'The builder has promised three weeks.'

'That's reasonable, there aren't any materials to buy except some wood and most of that can be bought second hand,' Bleddyn said.

'Chairs? Tables? Boiler? Cooker?' Marged was finding it increasingly difficult to avoid a sarcastic tone.

'Bought and ready for delivery. All second-hand, of course, but good quality.'

'You don't seem to want our help with anything,' Marged said.

'This is all for me,' Audrey replied softly. 'It's what Wilf and I often talked about and this is my chance to make it happen.'

'Come on, Audrey, let's go and get a couple of flagons. This is something to celebrate.' Huw led Marged towards the door seeing the hurt and disappointment on her face.

'There'll be plenty of help from us all if and when you need it,' Bleddyn added. 'Marged will be pleased to be involved, and Hetty too.' He looked at his wife and she nodded agreement.

'Just ask, Audrey. We're here if needed.'

'We'll manage, me and Maude and Myrtle,' Audrey said, placing an arm around the girls affectionately.

It was not until Marged reached home that she wondered just how long the girls intended to help Audrey with her foolish venture. Surely they would be on the beach when the 1944 season began? Audrey wouldn't entice them away from the sands next summer and leave her with hardly any help at all, would she?

Audrey intended to do exactly that. She called on her sister the following day and confessed that Maude and Myrtle had asked if they could help her, and she had agreed, on condition Marged didn't object. She said this apologetically and with a feeling of shame at the way she was making it more difficult for her hard working sister. 'I'll refuse if you think I should, Marged. They'd understand. It's just that it's an exciting new start and they want to be involved. Anyway,' she added, 'no one knows whether the cafe will succeed and if it doesn't the girls will be glad to help next summer.'

'We'll see then, but thanks for telling me so quickly. I'll

157

prepare a list of possibles in plenty of time for May opening.' Marged looked so disappointed that Audrey felt ashamed. 'I'll help you to find someone, I promise,' she said.

'Your promises don't last, do they, Audrey?'

Without much hope, Marged went to see Lilly. Sam answered the door with the little girl beside him holding his hand.

'Lilly's out,' Sam told her. 'She's meeting a friend and they've gone to the pictures.' He invited her into the neat, orderly little house where he had obviously been reading stories to the two and a half year-old Phyllis.

'Lucky Lilly,' Marged sniffed as she noticed the table set for a meal, the appetizing smell of cooking wafting in from the kitchen.

'I came to ask if there's a chance of her helping in the cafe next summer. Phyllis will be three next May and she could come with her if there's no one to look after her. Desperate we are, with the boys away fighting and Audrey unwilling to help anymore.' She glared at the calm quiet man and added fiercely. 'Married or not, she ought to do something to help us. We all have to do our share.'

Sam tilted the kettle and poured boiling water onto leaves in the teapot. 'You'll have a cup of tea?'

'Our Lilly's lazy, doesn't it bother you? Taking advantage of you she is.'

'She makes me happy,' was his brief reply.

Keith Kent began work on the refurbishment of the cafe Audrey planned to call the Corner Cafe, and he was very enthusiastic. Before employing him she had been beginning to face the prospect of asking Huw or Bleddyn for help after being turned down by the other builders she approached. When he had come to the door uninvited and told her of his keenness for the job, she had been relieved.

'I know the place and fully understand what's needed,' he had told her. 'I did some work for the previous owners and I can tell you here and now what needs to be done. Not a lot structurally,' he went on.

That pleased Audrey. As a woman on her own she had been prepared for him to cheat and tell her work was needed when it was unnecessary. His opinions were the same as Huw and Bleddyn, cleaning and decorating being the most important.

'I'll begin as soon as the work on the hospital is finished,' he promised. He looked at her expectantly, waiting for a comment but she made none except to thank him.

Keith Kent was in his late forties but looked older due to an accident that gave him a stoop and had whitened his hair. His mature look and patient demeanour endeared him to prospective customers and he had worked steadily since leaving school. The reason he wasn't in the forces was a crooked shoulder, caused when he fell from the roof of a cottage on to concrete. The breaks had healed but because they hadn't been set properly, due to his own negligence, the bones were distorted. Unable to obtain insurance for building work, he had considered other occupations but found none as enjoyable as the work he knew. He continued to work on buildings but tried to concentrate on jobs that didn't entail working at a great height.

He still suffered some pain and his solution to his discomfort was alcohol, although few realized the extent of that therapy. Tall, white-haired and tanned to an attractive bronze that emphasized the brightness of his blue eyes below thick white eyebrows, he was an attractive man who had little difficulty finding female company, although he avoided more than brief friendships.

He had a way of smiling that made the recipient believe his smile was meant for her alone. Widows were his speciality. He found that working for women who were alone and doing more than the work for which he was paid, often meant valuable recommendations and, occasionally, a generous tip as well.

He turned up on time at the corner premises on the first morning with three young boys who were unemployed, expecting to be called up any day. Unable to find permanent work they welcomed the three or four days of casual labour offered by Keith and were prepared to do anything he asked of them.

In several places walls needed repair, and they knocked out weak areas and replastered them. A fireplace was bricked up and another became a set of shelves. The rubble was cleared and the rooms brushed clear. It wasn't until the floors had been cleaned with wet sawdust and a long handled scrubbing brush to settle the dust, that Keith allowed Audrey to check on their progress.

Rubbing down the paintwork, sizing the walls for fresh paper, all these were accomplished for the whole of the ground floor in the first week. When Maude and Myrtle went with Audrey for the second visit, they were impressed.

'You certainly chose the right man for the work, Auntie Audrey,' Myrtle said. 'I didn't expect to see such a change.'

'I didn't choose him, really, he chose me,' Audrey said with a laugh. 'He knocked on the door and promised me a good job, giving me a good price, and he was so much more enthusiastic than the others, that I said yes, straightaway.' She didn't add that with his white hair and blue eyes he reminded her of Wilf.

Myrtle went to see Stanley when they left the soon-to-be cafe. Morgan was at work, but Ken Ward was home and he and Eirlys were listening to the wireless with the three boys playing Ludo on the table behind them.

'Auntie Audrey has bought a cafe and me and Maude are going to work there,' Myrtle announced as soon as she had found a seat.

'Another cafe for the Castles?' Ken replied. 'I'd have thought they had enough to do with what they've got.'

'No, this is Auntie Audrey on her own. She's going to live there, too'

'They've had a falling out?' Eirlys asked. 'I'm not surprised, mind. Working so closely together and practically living in the same house, it's a miracle they haven't quarrelled before this.'

'There's no quarrel, but something's up,' Myrtle said. 'Auntie Audrey isn't the same since Uncle Wilf died. She says she isn't going to be Auntie Marged's obedient slave anymore. I don't understand it really. But I'm excited about working in the cafe because it'll be open all the year round, not just the summer.'

'You'll have to be careful, Myrtle, or they'll be bringing you into the family quarrel,' Stanley warned as he threw the two dice and walked another counter up the straight to home. 'I'd make sure not to take sides or you'll be in the middle of a family feud and then where will you be?'

160

'In Sidney Street where I am now! They aren't going to throw me out because I'm working for one and not the other.'

'Your lot are a family fond of promises. I've warned you before. Marged expected Audrey to stay with the family firm and she won't like it now Audrey's left. Specially as she's taking you and Maude with her. Stands to reason you'll be in trouble.'

'You're stupid,' Myrtle retorted.

'So are you if you can't see what will happen.'

'Now, now, you two, let's calm down, shall we?' Eirlys said, standing up and beckoning for Ken to go with her into the kitchen. 'We'll have a bite to eat then you'd better get home before Audrey starts worrying. Marmite on toast, everyone?'

'Can I have mine with the crusts off?' Percival pleaded.

'No,' Eirlys and Ken said in chorus.

'Sorry, Myrtle,' Stanley said when the young people were alone. 'I'm probably worrying about nothing.'

'I wouldn't want to work in a boring cafe when I could be on the sands,' Harold said.

'It isn't going to be a boring cafe.' Myrtle almost blurted out the secret plans Audrey had revealed, but stopped in time, saved by Ken coming in with a plate of sliced bread ready to toast against the fire. Secrets and promises could make life very exciting and she wasn't going to risk disappointing Audrey on either.

Maude was writing to Reggie. She couldn't reveal the extent of what she knew about the new cafe but she was able to describe it and explain about the work that was entailed. The letter covered six pages before she had finished, and then came the difficult part. How should she end it? 'With love' was too forward; 'affectionately' was almost as bad.

When Myrtle came in she was still undecided and, risking a rude response, she asked her.

'If I was writing to Stanley, I'd sign it, "your friend". Won't that do?' Myrtle stared at her sister. 'Of course,' she added tilting her head with curiosity, 'if you've kissed, then perhaps you could say something more.' She grinned as Maude began to blush. '"Loving friend", then. Wouldn't that be better?' She stood near the door miming kisses.

161

'Oh, go away, Myrtle.'

Audrey sat in the dark kitchen staring out at the night sky through the open door, amused by the banter. They were growing up and one day they would be gone. The thought didn't make her sad. Children were only borrowed, you enjoyed them and helped to build their confidence preparing them for the day they would leave you. That was right and proper.

She was so glad to have the girls in her life. Having no children herself apart from poor little Bobbie, they had been an unexpected and valued gift. Sitting there, she felt her heart swelling with happiness. With Wilf gone she would have been so lonely and although she knew they were only with her until they found husbands and began to build homes of their own, she was grateful that they had been sent to her at a time when she needed someone so badly.

Next week they would be moving in to the flat above the Corner Cafe and a new stage of her life would begin. She dreaded the actual moment when she closed the door of this house behind them, but was determined not to show it. She was fulfilling a dream she and Wilf had dreamed and knowing it was what he had wanted for her was enough to sustain her through the pangs of leaving.

'Cup of cocoa, Auntie Audrey?' Maude called.

'That would be lovely,' she said, closing the door on the cool and calm night and pulling the curtain across.

Nine

Shirley met Andy Probert several times when she was away from St David's Well taking part in concerts. She had asked Ken to book her for local venues only, but he was often desperate to find someone to top the bill and she usually agreed to perform out of town. So, many of her bookings still entailed an overnight stay and Andy seemed able to learn where and when she would appear. He would be in the audience and when she left he would be there to accompany her to the guesthouse where she was staying.

He began to hint that he might stay with her and share her room and although she was flattered and even momentarily tempted, she knew that a casual affair was not what she wanted. At first she pretended not to understand the innuendo, then she displayed outrage although that didn't discourage him. When he kissed her too passionately and insisted that she wanted him as much as he wanted her, she hit him – hard.

'Sorry, Andy, but I don't do what you're asking.'

'You mean you never have?' he asked in surprise.

She slapped him again, but didn't answer. She and Freddy Clements had enjoyed a few secret visits to a small hotel called The Grantham, in the village of Gorsebank, but she didn't want to tell him about those occasions; he might have thought it was an invitation for him to persist. She went into the house where the landlady had left a tray of food and the makings of tea for her. As she ate, she wondered why Freddy had been special and Andy was not. It wasn't as though she and Freddy were engaged, they hadn't even talked about what would happen after the war, apart from an occasional joking reference to their continuing friendship.

Knowing Andy was dishonest wasn't the reason either. He had told her his real name and admitted to some of his 'deals'

163

as he euphemistically called them. She didn't think getting hold of some china to sell at the market was terrible. And certainly didn't consider taking a few unwanted goods from foolish women a serious crime. She had no evidence to suggest he did anything worse. He was what many called a spiv, a wideboy, out to earn a few shillings whenever he could. No, the reason he would never be more than a casual friend was simply that he wasn't important enough. Regarding Freddy, she wouldn't know how important he was to her, until they met again, and with the war going on endlessly that day was likely to be a long way off. Suddenly she had a strong, aching desire to see Freddy again.

She was still thinking of Freddy as she prepared for bed and, as she relaxed into sleep, she decided that she would call and see Freddy's parents on the following day. She visited them occasionally, mainly so she could share the little news they had, but she hadn't been for a while. Her career meant she was increasingly in demand and her time was full of rehearsals and concerts beside the many other events she was invited to attend, like handing out prizes at churches and schools, or opening various exhibitions and even jumble sales. Being a local celebrity was very exciting but it took up a lot of her time even though it was time she didn't begrudge.

The Clements's house was small and rather gloomy with curtains almost closed, and, whatever time of day she called, it never smelled of food cooking, or flowers, just polish and soap. Everything was neatly arranged and the semi darkness and excessive tidiness made her nervous. Remembering how particular Freddy had been about his clothes she imagined that the tending of them had been a joy to his mother, and guessed that his shoes had been given a regular polish by his equally orderly father. She sat on a high-backed dining chair and tucked her own, scruffy, shoes out of sight. This was not a home in which to relax, rather a place to expect frowns and criticism.

Both parents had been quite old when Freddy was born. His father was now seventy-three and his mother just ten years younger. On that day she looked older, her face was puffy and there were rosy patches high on her cheeks giving her an artificially healthy appearance not borne out by the weariness in her eyes or the breathless heaving of her chest.

She had been there a couple of minutes and politenesses had been dealt with, before Shirley suggested they had a cup of tea. She went into the kitchen but there was no food, not even a bottle of milk. All the cupboards had been scrubbed clean and it looked as though the occupants had moved away. She did find a few spoonfuls of tea and she made a potful and poured it, weak, warm and uninviting.

Mrs Clements's hands didn't seem to work, her fingers unable to grip the cup. Shirley held it to her lips and coaxed the woman to take a few sips. Shirley noticed her eyes were glassy and she seemed to be lost in sad memories. 'Have you heard from Freddy this week, Mrs Clements?' she asked as she turned to place the cup on the corner of a highly polished table.

'Not for more than two weeks. He's dead, I know it.'

Shirley spun round to stare at her. 'What d'you mean?' The expression on Mrs Clements's face frightened her. Was this the cause of the woman's depression? It was so easy to imagine the worst.

'Of course Freddy isn't dead,' she almost shouted, her fears spiralling. 'Look . . .' She fumbled in her handbag and produced three letters. They were dated three weeks previously but she had to convince his mother he was all right. If they stopped believing he was safe, their fears would come true. 'These came only last week,' she lied.

Mrs Clements said almost casually, 'Freddy's father is quite ill, you know.'

'Ill? What is it? Where is he?'

'He's in hospital. You can go and see him if you wish, but I should hurry if I were you. We've reached our time. It's time for us to go.'

'Go where?'

Mrs Clements didn't reply.

'Of course I wish to see him! What's the matter with him? Does Freddy know?' She felt exasperated at the lack of information, angered by the woman's strange attitude. Then as she looked at the woman she saw how depressed she was and at once her anger changed to sympathy. 'If you'd told me I'd have come sooner,' she said softly. 'I'm Freddy's friend and I want to help you if I can.'

165

'We didn't want to worry Freddy, not when he was out there in the fighting. And now of course, it's too late, he's dead, I know he's dead.'

'Of course he isn't. Freddy will be fine.'

Shirley didn't know how to cope with this strange defeatist mood. Then a thought struck her. Perhaps it wasn't a fancy. Perhaps she had received the dreaded telegram telling her Freddy had been killed. 'You haven't heard bad news, have you?' A voice inside her pleaded with the fates for her to answer in the negative.

'I'm a mother and I don't need telling,' she replied.

'It isn't true. You're wrong. Freddy's fine. He'll be fine.'

'His father's always been chesty. His lungs are failing him,' she went on. 'A mother doesn't want to outlive her child. The vicar has warned me that it's time. God is calling us home.'

Shirley gulped the unpleasant tea as though it were a life-giving elixir. She had been badly frightened both by the woman's appearance and her conviction that Freddy was dead. After coaxing the sad woman to take a few more sips of tea, she placed the cup in front of her and looked around the neat, soulless room. She marvelled that Freddy hadn't been subdued into a nervous wreck living in this house, or become so boring he could have faded into the furnishings, as unnoticeable as the wallpaper.

Three times she tried to change the subject and persuade Freddy's mother to talk about something else but the words always returned to the subject that her husband was dying and her son was already dead.

Unable to decide how best to help and in the hope of a more encouraging conversation, Shirley went to the local hospital where she found Mr Clements being attended by nurses and a doctor. Before she could approach him, the curtains around the bed were closed and she was told to wait. Murmuring voices were heard but she was unable to glean any clue to what was happening. Three people stepped out but the curtains remained closed.

Minutes passed and glances darted her way from a group of doctors and a nurse standing near the enclosed bed, and she knew she was being discussed. Finally she demanded to know what was happening.

'I'm a friend of his son and I've just left his mother feeling extremely depressed. Will you please tell me when I can see Mr Clements?' After more murmured discussion, Shirley was told the man had died. She sat on one of the chairs and stared at them. What should she do? A few minutes later, as she sat there undecided whether she should leave or go back to Mrs Clements, or, wishful thinking, go home, two policemen arrived. There were more discussions held in low voices and more glances towards her. If only someone would tell her what she should do!

A nurse smiled encouragement and eventually asked, 'Would you be willing to go with the police to tell his wife?' She shuffled a few pages of notes. 'There doesn't appear to be any relation apart from their soldier son, not even a particularly close friend we can ask.' Shirley nodded sadly.

She returned to the house accompanied by two constables. This was not going to be a pleasant task, Shirley thought to herself, but remembering it was Freddy's mother, she determined to do her best. The policeman knocked on the door, then as there was no response, he pushed it open and they called to ask if anyone was home.

'She has to be here, I was talking to her less than an hour ago.'

They found her sitting in a chair, a cup of cold tea near her hand, empty tablet bottles in her lap, and she was quite dead. Shirley's instinct was to put her arms around the woman, but the constable forbade it.

While they waited for the doctor and extra police to arrive, Shirley's hands shook as she thought about the almost empty kitchen. She gave the police Freddy's army number and most recent postal address and wondered whether the deaths of both parents would entitle him to some leave. She knew little about the couple, they having been very private people who discouraged regular visits. She told the police the few facts she remembered, then left them to their melancholy task.

She wondered then, if the woman had already taken pills when she had visited. She thought of the weakness in her hands, and the strange listless state of her and the glassy look in her eyes. Her legs ached dreadfully as she set off home, she felt trembly and tearful, more for Freddy than for his parents. He was so far away and would have to be told yet be unable to do anything.

She walked a little, sat on a bench and walked some more. A bus came and she got on, thankful not to face the walk back to Brook Lane.

'If I'd realized, if I'd called a doctor,' she said to Hetty when she told her and Bleddyn what had happened. 'If only I'd known, recognized the symptoms, got help, I might have saved her.'

'How could you have known, dear? It would take a doctor to recognize what had happened. Don't start blaming yourself. There was nothing you could have done.'

'If only I'd gone for help or—'

'"If only" is a bad bedfellow. "If only" brings nightmares,' her mother soothed.

'Freddy can't get home in time and there's no one else, so I promised I'd see to the funerals,' she said. Hetty and Bleddyn agreed to help.

'Freddy would want me to do that for him,' Shirley said. If he's alive, her mind insisted on reminding her. If he's not dead as well. His mother was so convinced when she said their time had come.

In all the tragedies that had filled the newspapers, of death and wounding and capture, she had never once imagined Freddy in any of those scenarios. She had always believed he would come home and thinking of their reunion had been so often a part of her dreams both day and night, it had to come true.

Her own doctor was called and he gave her a sedative and put her to bed. Her last thought before sleep overcame her was that Mrs Clements must surely be right, Freddy had been killed. She cried for Freddy and his parents and most of all for herself. Until Mrs Clements had uttered those words, she had hardly been aware of just how much she was looking forward to Freddy's return.

Audrey worked at her new premises for most of each day. With Maude and Myrtle's help she cleaned the place thoroughly and the painting and wallpapering soon transformed it from grubby and inhospitable to clean and welcoming. Keith

Kent was there for most of the time, unwilling to leave the finer points of the decorating to the inexperienced boys. During the second week, when he was touching up the mirrors with some gold paint he had found in a builder's yard, Audrey invited him to go back to Sidney Street with them for a meal.

'Nothing special, mind,' she warned. 'Yesterday's leftover vegetables fried up into a bubble and squeak with a bit of cold meat.'

'It sounds all right to me,' he said, thanking her. 'I'd better go back to the lodgings and change.'

'No need to bother, we won't be dressing for dinner, Mr Kent,' Myrtle said smiling in amusement.

He was very quiet for the first part of the evening. He seemed uneasy in their company, on edge and jumpy. He missed the point of several remarks, his mind vague as though he were not interested, but waiting for something to happen. An excuse to leave, Myrtle thought curiously.

Then he began to explain about the work he had to fit in during the following weeks, remarking on the variety of his days almost complainingly.

'Hang on, I'll show you what I mean,' he said. He went into the hall and fished out something from his pocket. Audrey and the two girls took the opportunity to remove the dishes and stack them ready for washing. When they returned to the table he was smiling. 'Look at this, a few of the things I've been asked to do in the past couple of weeks,' he said, pointing to his notebook. 'Washing and painting a ceiling, unblocking a drain, rescuing a cat from a tree, digging a vegetable patch ready for autumn planting, and, believe this or not, someone called and asked me to get a spare bed down from the loft when an auntie was coming to stay – and there's me believing I'm a builder, painter and decorator.

'It's the war, see,' he went on. 'There are so many households without the menfolk, I'm asked to do the few jobs women can't manage.'

'You're very kind,' Audrey said.

'Go on with you,' he said with a self-deprecatory shrug. 'I'm glad to do what little I can.'

From then on, he entertained them with stories of his varied jobs and difficult customers until half past ten. Apologizing

169

for keeping them up so late, he left, joking that he wouldn't make it an excuse to be late in the morning.

'He's nice,' Maude said. Myrtle didn't add any enthusiastic agreement. There was something a bit false about Mr Kent that worried her a little. He tried just a little too hard. His mood had changed so suddenly that she wondered whether his geniality and willingness to help was all an act.

Hearing about the deaths of Mr and Mrs Clements made Hannah Castle feel sad. She had very little contact with her own parents and the thought that a couple could die so suddenly made her want to try again to repair the rift.

Hannah had been married to Laurie Wilcox, who was a violent man. She had suffered bruises and broken bones, yet when she left him, her mother refused to support her. Both parents insisted that a promise given in the sight of God was a promise for life. A marriage couldn't be ended except by death. The fact that they had been warned that the death of their daughter was a strong possibility, didn't alter their attitude.

Hannah and her two girls, Josie and Marie, had been allowed to live in their house after the divorce, which they refused to recognize, but using the front room and the middle room with limited access to the kitchen had been a difficult period for them. There had been no financial help offered and Hannah had worked long into the nights on her sewing machine to earn enough to keep them all . When she had married Johnny Castle, Bleddyn's son, everything had changed. She and the girls had been accepted as members of the Castle clan and for the first time in their lives, Josie and Marie, now seven and six years old, were a part of a close, loving family.

They had a garden to play in and adults who loved to share their games. Hugs, once a rarity apart from those from their mother, were now a daily delight. There were books to read, stories told, people to talk to and always a loving smile whenever they met one of the family. Frowns and disapproval and demands to be quiet had been left behind.

They couldn't have been happier, but for Hannah there was always an underlying disappointment that she had never managed to persuade her parents to forgive her and understand.

With the thought of Mr and Mrs Clements's deaths fresh

170

in her mind, and while the girls were at school, Hannah walked up to the house near the park and knocked on the door. Her mother opened the door a crack and as though she were a stranger, asked what she wanted.

'Nothing, Mother. I just wondered how you are and whether there's anything I can do for you.'

'Unless you're going to leave that man you think you're married to and repent of your sins, there's nothing I want from you.'

'And Dad? Is he well?' she asked, trying to ignore the repetition of the old, stupid hostility. 'I haven't see him for such a long time.'

'And you won't see him either. Living in sin is not something we want to be seen to be supporting.'

'And Rosie and Marie? Are they to be punished as well?'

'The children suffer because of what you chose to do.'

The door closed and Hannah walked slowly away, hiding her tears from passers-by, bending down as though admiring the bedraggled and forlorn late roses and fuchsias in the park gardens.

For a while she had thought her mother was going to relent and visit the children, but the momentary mood of reconciliation had quickly ended. Her mother had retreated from the attempt, which she had described as a weakness, in shame and embarrassment, and respect for her rigid interpretation of the attitude of the church she attended. She had called at the shop where Hannah worked with Beth and Eirlys, and the girls – her granddaughters – had hardly remembered her, and she had walked away.

Hannah went home and wrote to Johnny but said nothing about her latest attempt to coax her mother back into their lives. She had been so fortunate, loving Johnny and being loved in return. Why should the loss of her parents make her miserable? If she were honest, Bleddyn and his second wife, Hetty, plus Hetty's daughter Shirley, more than compensated. It was just that children always stayed close to their parents, it was difficult to think of anyone else where this didn't apply.

Johnny's response when she mentioned it was always to tell her that her parents were the losers, missing out on a daughter like Hannah and two delightful granddaughters.

Sometimes it helped to think like that, but at other times it didn't help at all.

Freddy was informed about the death of his parents and was told he could have ten days leave to go home and settle their affairs. He wrote to Shirley, but their letters crossed, hers telling him she would arrange the funeral and his asking her to do just that, but his never arrived. Shirley and Hetty dealt with everything they could, hoping Freddy would write and let her know what he wanted them to do, but there was no word. Shirley hid her fears, trying to forget his mother's solemn conviction.

The funeral was a quiet affair with few people present. Shirley and her mother had arranged it with Bleddyn's help, and the house was locked up to await a decision on its fate. She went every day to pick up the post and separate it into piles of bills, receipts and personal letters, hoping for one from Freddy.

Every time the post was checked and there was no letter from him, her heart gave a lurch of disappointment. The sad words his mother had spoken filled her mind, echoing around, becoming distorted and louder until she thought she was going mad. Our time has come, she had said. She had been right about Mr Clements and had made sure she had been right about herself, so why should Freddy be safe? Didn't sad things and bad things always go in threes?

All through each day she tried to tell herself his mother had been wrong, but receiving no word, watching the postman walking past as he delivered to Brook Lane each morning, made her confidence weaken. He must be dead. He was certain to have been told and if he were alive he would have been in touch.

She was closing his parents' front door one morning two days after the funeral, having collected the single letter from the doormat, when the gate creaked and she turned to see him standing there.

'Freddy!'

'Hello, Shirley, have you missed me?'

They ran towards each other, tears streaming down Shirley's cheeks. The strength of him, the rough touch of his greatcoat, the soft coldness of his cheek against hers, and his lips claiming hers, hungrily, memories revived of how dear he was. Then arm in arm, shyly glancing at each other as though in disbelief, they went back into the house. In a dream they kissed, fears fading, the war a million miles away, the months of separation drifting as he led her up the cold, linoleum-covered stairs. Succumbing to each other in a house that still echoed with the presence of the oh, so neat, oh so orderly couple had a tinge of wickedness to it. There was the piquancy of believing they could be seen at any moment, that his parents would walk in and find them making love on the pristine sheets, creasing the immaculate pillows.

It was some time later when Freddy walked from room to room and faced the fact that he wouldn't see his parents again. Shirley sat in the hall and waited while he said his silent goodbyes.

'It doesn't seem real,' he said when he returned to her. 'All those weeks without seeing them, it's easy to convince myself that their absence is continuing, that when the war's over they'll be here and everything will be as it was.'

'Like Max Moon's song,' she reminded him. *Waiting for Yesterday* was one of her most requested songs, one which had been written by a friend of Ken Ward, who had been killed in an air raid in London.

Freddy stayed at the house and met Shirley every day, going with her to her concerts and seeing her on stage singing sentimental songs and knowing she was singing them for him. If he'd had any doubts about what he wanted to do when he finally came home, they had gone. He knew he wanted to settle back into this warm-hearted town of St David's Well, with Shirley Downs as his wife.

'The house is rented,' he told her, 'and the rent is paid until the end of the year. If you can, will you sell the contents? I won't be coming back here and I don't want to pay to store stuff I won't want.'

'What about some of the china and linen? It'll be difficult to get new for a long time yet.'

'Can I leave it to you? You know more about these things than me. If there's anything you think we should save,' he added emphasis to the word 'we' and looked at her oddly, as

173

though wanting to say something but unable to decide on the words. 'Take anything you think we'll use – things you like – and store them.' There was that word again. 'The rest can be sold. Will you look after the money for when I come home?'

'Of course I will, Freddy.'

'I want to start a shop selling gentlemen's clothes,' he told her. 'Something like the one I worked in before I joined up, but with a bit more dash.'

'Dash?' she asked curiously.

'Bespoke tailoring, expensive suits and jackets and over-coats. Clothes for the wealthy – who will always be with us – sports clothes: golf shoes and plus fours, riding macs, cricket trousers, pullovers and shoes. Walking shoes and outdoor all weather gear. I've seen shops like that in London and other big towns and I think that once this war's over, the top people, the wealthy, will rise to the top again and want the best.'

'It's a gamble in a seaside town like this,' she warned. 'And besides, it's likely to be a long time before those things are obtainable.'

'Perhaps, but they will be back and I'll be ready to sell them.' He handed her a thick envelope. 'Talking about a gamble, here's what I managed to make while I was overseas. Gambling was a way of passing time so I provided it. Luxuries like extra food were there too if you knew how to find them and they sold easily enough. I trundled around and found gifts for the men to give their families when they get home. Nothing really illegal, mind, but the money came rolling in.'

'What d'you want me to do with it, Freddy?'

'Mind it for me until I come home. Put whatever you get for the furniture with it and there'll be enough to make a start.'

There was a momentary doubt in her mind about the unethical way the money had been earned and she mentioned Andy. As she would have guessed, he laughed and made it clear he approved. 'There's a lot who have made money during this war, and I can't blame anyone for doing what they can, so long as it doesn't harm anyone.'

'Some of what he stole came from Auntie Audrey,' she said.

'What? Stealing from your family? I'll kill'im!'

'What's good for the goose is good for the gander?' she teased.

174

'It isn't good for him if the goose is someone I know!' he warned. He looked at her then turned away and asked, 'Important, was he, this bloke Andy?'

'Not in the slightest, although he was useful by giving me stories to tell in my letters to you.'

He held her close and whispered, 'Glad I am that he wasn't important to you, because, you, Shirley Downs, are very important to me.'

Making an excuse that she was singing and would be away over night, they went to the Grantham Hotel and booked a room as Mr and Mrs Clements. Shirley was a little nervous as, being quite well known, she knew the chances of her being seen were stronger than when they had stayed there on previous occasions. The place hadn't changed in the couple of years since their last visit but everything was more shabby. The towels were threadbare, the curtains faded, the food was less exciting, but they loved every moment. Until, at breakfast, which they were unable to take in their room owing to the shortage of staff, they were greeted by one of the cafe owners from St David's Well Bay.

'Damn,' Freddy muttered, 'I'm real sorry that happened, didn't want to embarrass you.'

Shirley shrugged, 'I don't suppose he'll mention having seen me. I don't think that woman he was with was his wife!' Laughter, a constant companion during those precious days, rang out unabated.

The ten days passed too quickly and it seemed only hours before Shirley was standing on the railway platform waving at the train taking Freddy back to the hell of battle. She turned as the train disappeared from her sight and went back home. Her leg ached a little and she marvelled over the fact that she hadn't been aware of its discomfort all the time Freddy had been home.

Using the Castles' van, Huw, Bleddyn and Keith Kent moved the furniture Audrey needed from the house in Sidney Street into the flat above the cafe. Maude and Myrtle helped too and the girls and the three men were cheerful and wishing her well as the moment she dreaded, when she closed the door behind her, was eased into light-hearted fun.

When Bleddyn and Huw had gone, Audrey and the two girls walked proudly around the premises which now had a cheerfully painted green shop front with the name, Corner Cafe, in cream with an edging of gold. The furnishings had arrived, bought from a cafe that had closed its door permanently, and the kitchen fittings were installed. The plan was to open for business in November, but this idea was criticized by Marged.

'November isn't a time for women to sit in cafes, Audrey. They want to get straight home after their shopping and get in by the fire. You'd do better to wait, really you would.'

'We'll be busy, just wait and see,' Audrey said. Myrtle giggled and covered her mouth with her hands and Marged began to wonder what they had planned.

'There's hardly anything they can do that I haven't thought of. I can't imagine why they have to pretend the opening is such a secret. It's a cafe, that's all it is, and even if they get a few curious people going in for a coffee and a look around, there isn't anything to make it different from all the other cafes in the town. I don't know what Audrey's thinking of,' she complained to Huw.

'Let her have her fun, Marged. It's certainly helped her to get over the death of poor Wilf.'

'And that's another thing. She's seeing far too much of that builder of hers, Keith what'shisname. She's invited him back to the house for meals and everything.'

'Yes, with Myrtle and Maude there as well! Give over, Marged. Let the woman alone.' He could see by her expression that his plea was landing on deaf ears.

'Have you seen the chairs and tables in that cafe Audrey's supposed to be opening?' she asked a few days later.

'All painted green, with touches of gold. Yes. Smart isn't it? I wonder where Keith managed to get that gold paint?'

'No tablecloths, just some bits of cork she's picked up somewhere and how smart is that?'

'She's opening it on November 13th, so you'll be able to see how well it works.'

'That's another thing. The thirteenth is a Saturday.'

'More people about on Saturdays. Our Beth'll tell you that. Her cafe is always busy on Saturdays.'

176

'And that's another thing—'

'Leave it, Marged.' Huw gave an exaggerated sigh. 'You have to face it. Your Audrey has stopped working for Castle's and has started a business on her own. It's only the same as our Beth has done, after all.'

'Audrey promised our mam that she would never leave the family firm.'

'An unwise promise that your mother had no right to ask of her.' Huw raised his voice and Marged said no more. She would have to wait until the opening, then her views would be proved correct. She imagined how magnanimous she would be when Audrey asked if she could come back to work for Castle's. Not a mention of 'told you so'. She would behave impeccably.

It was Bleddyn and Huw who dealt with the sale of the furniture in Freddy's home, advertising the better items, delivering chosen items in the firm's van and arranging with a house clearance firm to take the remainder. When Shirley and Hetty went to do the final cleaning they made sure every cupboard had been checked and nothing remained. As they left, they closed the doors and locked them firmly, but one of the back windows was left unintentionally unlatched.

Maldwyn Perkins, who worked in the flower shop, was engaged to be married. He had originally lived in the town of Bryn Teg and before he moved to the seaside town, Maldwyn had known Delyth slightly but their friendship had grown into love during the previous summer when they'd both worked in St David's Well. Now, all that was stopping them from marrying was finding a place to live which they could afford.

'Heard about the deaths of Mr and Mrs Clements?' Mrs Chapel asked one morning as Maldwyn returned from the early morning market. 'Now there's a strange thing. Both of them on the same day.'

'Seems she couldn't face life without him.'

'And that poor Freddy having to come home and sort out the house and everything.'

'Sad, but I bet he was glad to get home for a few days, and from what I've heard, that Shirley Downs was glad to help him enjoy it,' he said with a chuckle. 'I confess that I enjoy listening to the gossip when two or three of the local ladies spout their opinions as they choose flowers,' he confessed. 'I'm getting to know all the families and about the skeletons rattling in their cupboards.'

'Maldwyn,' she asked curiously, 'how would you feel about living in a house where there's been a death?'

He laughed. 'I doubt if there are many houses in the town where there hasn't been a death. Old places, many lifetimes,' he said, coaxing a bloom to stay where he wanted it in the window display. 'Why, were you wondering about the Clements's house? It'll be sold and I can't afford to buy just yet. Delyth and I thought we'd start in a nice little flat or a couple of rooms, and one day we'll buy a house of our own.'

'I think it might be for rent, and if you hurry you might be lucky.'

He stared at her for a while then said, 'Too expensive.'

'You won't know unless you try.' She handed him a piece of paper. 'Here's the man you have to see, there's his phone number and you can take an hour off while I finish the window.'

He came back an hour later to tell her that he and Delyth were seeing it on Sunday morning.

Andy Probert was having a tiring night. In a borrowed van he had driven to Hereford and during the hours of darkness, with the aid of a friend, he had loaded up the van with some potatoes and greenstuffs stolen from a barn where they had been packed and labelled ready to be collected and taken to the early morning market the following day. A crate of eggs was also removed from a shed. A dog barked, a door opened and they heard footsteps scuffling on the yard, but the dog was soothed with a piece of liver, and no one disturbed them during the short time it took to fill the van.

'Not a very profitable load,' Andy said as they drove quietly away, 'but they'll sell quick enough.' The two men discussed the possibilities and decided on a small town where they knew they would be able to find a stallholder willing to buy at a low price and not ask questions.

When the transaction was done and the money shared, the

van was abandoned for the day in a field, hidden by a rotting hay stack that had been partially burnt. No one would see it and it would be there when they next needed it. They went their separate ways, the man who helped him back to his wife and Andy to search for a place where he could get some sleep. The weather was mild for November and he slept the sleep of the innocent on the back of a lorry heading for South Wales with a load of wood.

A few days after the Clements's house had been cleared out, Andy had made a comfortable bed for himself in the corner, and he was hoping this would still be there so he could rest until he went in search of another deal. He had changed his appearance again. This time his hair was black and a beard covered his face. The beard would be strictly temporary but it might confuse his followers for a while longer.

Audrey put the finishing touches to the cafe. Maldwyn had advised her about floral decoration and had recommended dried grasses and painted twigs, those mainstays of the flower sellers during the times of year when flowers were scarce and expensive. He built up quite large displays with just a few artificial flowers to brighten them, and filled high corners and edged the doorway and the windows, giving the cheerful cafe a feeling of spaciousness without using any precious floor room. There were mirrors on the walls and in front of them narrow shelves on which smaller displays were placed. By the end of the first day the shelves would have been put to a better use.

'Two more days and we open,' Audrey said to Myrtle and Maude as they closed the door one Wednesday evening. 'Today the advertisements go in the newspaper, and it will be shown on posters from tonight. Our secret will be out.'

They went up to the flat above, filled with excitement, planning to go back down to the cafe later that evening to stick their posters on the windows telling people what kind of cafe it would be.

'I'll never sleep again,' declared Myrtle.

'What will Auntie Marged think?' Maude wondered.

'Will anyone come?' Audrey wailed.

The posters described the new cafe as a place to meet

179

friends, sit and talk, listen to music, and patrons could stay as long as they liked.

'That can't work,' Marged said when she and Huw were told by Bleddyn what the posters offered. 'Having people sitting for hours on end just talking doesn't make money. It's just a scheme to get people in, she'll soon change the rules.'

'We'll go up in the afternoon and see how she's getting on, just before it closes, about four,' Huw suggested.

'You're wrong there, Huw,' Bleddyn said. 'It says on the posters that she's staying open until nine o'clock to give young people somewhere to sit and talk and meet each other. Good idea, eh?'

Opening day began slowly, with people wandering past looking in but few entering. However, as news spread more came and by lunchtime, when they offered drinks, sandwiches and cakes and nothing else, they were kept busy serving them all. The tables were filled and a queue formed as people waited to be seated.

When Huw and Marged arrived, Huw brought in a few extra chairs from the yard where surplus furniture had been left. They were unpainted, but in between settling newcomers, and smiling encouragement at those still waiting, he promised that he would deal with that the following day. There were customers unable to find a chair leaning on the wall and using the shelves in front of the mirrors as somewhere to put their cups and plates. He offered them chairs which were accepted with delight and he thought that it was more like a party than a cafe opening its doors for the first time.

Marged went into the kitchen and began making extra sandwiches. When Stanley, Harold and Percival appeared, she sent them to buy extra bread.

'Can we have a cake for free?' Harold asked.

'You'd better ask Auntie Audrey, this is her place not mine.'

As she heard the words, Audrey glanced across at her sister expecting to see animosity, but instead she saw a smile.

'Audrey, you have done something wonderful here. I'm sure it will be a success.'

'Are you saying you were wrong?' Audrey asked with a wide smile.

'I was wrong and I have never been more pleased to say

180

it. Giving young people a meeting place where they aren't hassled to move on as soon as their cup's empty, is a brilliant idea. Congratulations.'

Audrey hid her tearful joy. If only Wilf were here. She still wondered about the money, thinking of the better premises she could have bought if it had been found, and the better position, and being able to employ waitresses instead of stealing Maude and Myrtle from her sister.

'Sorry about Maude and Myrtle,' she said, 'but by the time the new season begins they might well have changed their minds and ask to join you on the sands.'

'Let them be. I'll find help, don't worry. Just enjoy your success, Audrey.' She meant it and for the first time in months, the sisters hugged each other affectionately.

Hetty came with Shirley, Eirlys came with Beth, and Hannah walked in with the two little girls who had been given a special late night to attend the new cafe's opening. Keith Kent called in just as they were closing to offer his congratulations.

When the doors closed at nine o'clock, the whole family fell into chairs exhausted, and stared at each other. Praise for Audrey for her vision, and Maude and Myrtle for their hard work echoed around the now quiet room.

'And don't forget Keith,' Maude said. 'He kept his promise and allowed us to open on time, remember.' Myrtle nodded but said nothing. She still had reservations about him.

'It will be a great success,' Keith said, 'and it's all down to you, Audrey. We only helped you to follow your dream, didn't we girls?'

'I hope next week isn't a disappointment,' Audrey said.

Huw gave a groan. 'You mean there's more?' In a mock frail voice, he added, 'Thank goodness tomorrow's Sunday and all I have to do is paint about eight chairs!'

Audrey said, her eyes sparkling, 'Oh, how Wilf would have loved this.' At the doorway Keith waved at her and quietly left.

Ten

A ndy Probert knew he had been foolish to go back to St
David's Well, especially as it was in the hope of seeing
Shirley. He had been at one of the concerts where he'd noticed
her with a young soldier, and had guessed correctly that this
must be the Freddy he'd heard so much about. He didn't really
know her that well anyway, and although she seemed friendly
and even attracted to him, he couldn't be sure that she wouldn't
report him to the police – particularly now her young chap
was back – and get him arrested then handed over to the army,
who would not deal with him lightly.

After all, she was involved with a serving soldier and might
easily be resentful about his avoidance of being called up. She
had seemed sympathetic when he had tried to explain about
his nightmares and fears of drowning while in uniform among
others who seemed unable to help him. But things changed
and having spent a short time with her Freddy Clements, she
might easily decide to report him.

It was with these gloomy thoughts that he awoke in his
temporary shelter in the Clements's empty house that Sunday
morning. After washing at the kitchen sink with cold water
and a sliver of soap he carried in a tobacco tin, he looked
carefully around him then slipped out through the back lane.
He had left the back door unlocked but as a precaution he
pocketed the key. Head down, collar of his overcoat pulled
up around his ears, he was thankful that it was winter, and
the darkness and chill air made it easy to hide behind thick
clothing.

He knew where Shirley lived, having taken her home on a
couple of occasions, and as he was approaching the house on
Brook Lane he saw the paperboy with his sack of papers on
a small bogie cart.

'Got anything for the Castles, have you?' he asked. When the boy nodded, he offered to take them for him and with the newspapers in his hand he knocked on the door. He would explain that he was helping but wasn't sure of the number if anyone but Shirley answered the door, but he was in luck.

'Hello, Shirley, I'm your new paperboy, handsome, eh?'

'What are you doing here? Will you come in for a cup of tea and some toast? Mam's just making some.'

'I won't come in, but if you can bring some with you, that'll be great. Starving I am, and cold beans is all I've got to eat.'

'Bring some? Where are we going?'

'I'll show you where I'm living.'

Wrapping a couple of slices of toast in some greaseproof paper, she went out and saw him waiting at the end of the lane.

'Living here in St David's Well permanently then, are you?'

'I'll be around for a while. A big risk, mind, me being in such demand – by the police and the army – but worth it to see you, Shirley Downs.'

He took her via the lanes and after checking that no one was in sight, he pushed her through the gate of the Clements's house and closed it behind them.

'Andy! What are you doing here?' she demanded. 'This is Freddy's house!'

'Hardly. Not anymore. He won't be paying the rent on it out of his army pay for the pleasure of returning after the war, will he?'

'But you can't stay here!'

'What harm am I doing? I slip in and out without disturbing a thing and sleeping in a corner won't offend his parents or their ghosts, will it?'

He was grinning widely as he showed her a small collection of tins and a vacuum flask. 'Fancy a cup? I can't offer you anything to eat, unless you fancy some sardines? I have to go to a cafe for food and to get this filled.'

Disapproval flared but quickly died. He made her laugh and he didn't appear to be doing any harm by using an empty house. He put a hand on her arm, but she shrugged it off, a warning look in her eyes.

'All right, but you can't blame me for trying,' he said, grinning.

183

She looked at the clothes which he used as bedding in a corner of the kitchen and frowned. This was one story Freddy wouldn't like to read in a letter.

'If I keep my hands in my pockets and my eyes on the ground, will you come upstairs and look at the garden? I think it was once very nice, but the lawn is about three feet high and the flowers are hidden by weeds. Isn't it amazing how well weeds grow without attention?' Andy said as he gently persuaded Shirley to follow him upstairs.

Today was also the day that Maldwyn had planned to take his fiancée to see the Clements's house with a view to renting it. Delyth arrived by train at ten o'clock on that dark, damp November Sunday morning, filled with excitement. Most of her friends had begun married life living either with their parents, or in two rooms in the house of a neighbour. Maldwyn had promised her a house.

Hand in hand they walked to the house and Maldwyn unlocked the door. They were met with a draught that puzzled Maldwyn. 'Wait here while I check that there's no one else around,' he said. He was extra protective of Delyth as she had been involved in a menacing situation the last summer, and was still nervous when something unexpected happened.

He went inside and quietly looked into the two living rooms and the kitchen. The back door opened when he turned the handle and he looked at the bunch of keys the estate agent had given him and found one to fit. Locking the door, he called to Delyth, 'Someone must have left the back door open, I think, and the draught when we came in must have closed it. Come on, there's no one here, love.'

Upstairs, where they had been looking out of the window into the neglected garden, Shirley heard voices and suddenly looked at Andy, alarmed. Andy, however, just stifled a laugh.

'It sounds like that Maldwyn from the flower shop,' Shirley whispered. 'He must be here with his fiancée. Delyth, she's called. She was kidnapped last year and nearly died. I don't want to give her another fright. We have to get away. But how?'

'Pity they didn't leave a wardrobe here, it would have been fun snuggled in there with you.'

'Shut up and think of a way to get us out of this!'

Maldwyn and Delyth looked around the ground floor. The linoleum had been left in the rooms, the hall and on the stairs. It was highly polished, the brass rods across each stair still shining brightly.

'That's lucky, we won't have to buy floor covering,' Delyth said. 'Whatever we bought wouldn't be better than this.' The kitchen with its red tiled floor was again spotlessly clean. It contained a cooker and a sink with a well scrubbed wooden draining board. As they commented on the various items downstairs, Andy was mimicking them upstairs.

Shirley was less amused. 'How do we get out?' she hissed. 'You might be able to get out of a window and run away, but I can't!'

'It'll be easy as long as you can put on a bit of an act, and I bet that's something you can do real well, you being on the stage an' all. Just go downstairs all bold and tell them you were looking at the place for a friend. You found the back door open and walked in.'

'What about you?'

'I'll take the rest of the toast and scarper out the window, what else?'

Once Andy had slipped out of the window and with the support of the drainpipe had slid to the ground, she shuffled her feet and coughed, to alert Maldwyn and Delyth of her presence.

'Who's that?' Maldwyn called, pushing Delyth behind him.

'And who's that?' Shirley demanded like an extra loud echo, having decided that the best form of defence is attack. She came down the stairs holding on to the banister, her stick raised threateningly in the other hand.

'Shirley Downs?' Delyth gasped. 'I didn't know there was anyone here.'

'Maldwyn? Delyth? Hi yer. I hope I didn't give you a fright. Tell the truth I shouldn't be here. I was looking at it for a friend and when I found the back door open I came in. I didn't know what to do when I heard you come in.'

They were in the hall and from where Shirley was standing she looked into the kitchen. Outside the window, Andy was clearly finding the situation very amusing. He was waving, his laughter inaudible but no doubt genuine. Shirley found it difficult not to join in. He really was an idiot. When the others turned around he ducked down out of sight only to reappear in the window beside the front door making a silly face.

'Who was that?' Maldwyn asked.

'Just some stupid child having a laugh,' Shirley replied.

Andy was leaning on the wall at the end of Brook Lane when she reached home.

'Go away. I've had enough of your stupid games,' she said.

'Meet me later? We could go for a walk?'

'So you can embarrass me again? Sorry, but once is enough.'

'Somewhere private, only me and you.'

'Go away or I'll call the police. You should be in the army not conning a living out of others.'

'Oh dear, we are high and mighty today, aren't we?'

Audrey was on her way to see Bleddyn, and hearing voices she looked down the lane. Recognizing Andy, she decided to call the police. They came quickly and as Andy was walking away, he was met by two constables who grabbed an arm each and hauled him away. He looked back at Shirley who stared in disbelief. She wanted to tell him it was not she who had called the police, but suddenly she realized it didn't matter. He was going where he belonged and a thief and cheat for a friend wasn't the best way to cope with missing Freddy. She went in and wrote to Freddy telling him everything. She told it humorously, giving Maldwyn and Delyth's involvement a greater part in the story than was true.

Marged guessed that the new cafe would be busy with people coming to look out of curiosity; a temporary burst of activity that might not last. In this she had been correct. The week began with the tables constantly occupied, but by Thursday the numbers had decreased as customers returned to their usual meeting places.

'It's nice to see it so busy and I'm thrilled for you but don't be too complacent, Audrey,' she warned when the week was ending and they were cleaning the place ready to close.

'I didn't expect anything more than nosy parkers at first,' Audrey replied. 'In fact, the people I'm hoping for haven't started to find the place yet.'

'You don't want shoppers and office girls? But they will be

your mainstay. You have to cater for them or you'll fail.'

'I want the young people. I want the busiest time to be after the shops close. This is a place for them to meet and chat and flirt a little. I want them to gather here between finishing work and going to the pictures, that's the sort of place I want this to be. Not a gossip shop for bored women. Apart from dances and the pictures, there's nowhere for the young to go. Wilf and I often talked about opening a place like this, a place where the young will congregate. There are plenty of places for shoppers and I don't want this to be just another one.'

Marged said nothing but her face spoke clearly of her doubts.

During the week, she had called each day and helped when necessary. Sometimes moving a few things then sighing as she watched her sister put them back as they were. Mid morning and again at lunchtime, the place filled up with shoppers and office girls, as Marged had predicted, but the evenings when Audrey had hoped to see young people occupying every chair, filling the air with their chatter and laughter, remained her quietest time.

Keith Kent had long ago finished all the work that needed doing in the cafe, but he still found excuses to call. Once it was a pair of chairs he had found and painted in the green Audrey had chosen for her cafe. Another time it had been a wide elegant container that had once held flowers. He cleaned it up, painted it and took it to Chapel's Flowers for Maldwyn to fill with a dried flower arrangement to stand near the cafe doorway. His visits were usually after he had finished his day's work and he always stayed and found some small job to do. He often went up to the flat with Audrey, Maude and Myrtle for a late supper but always left before ten o'clock. He came more and more frequently, no longer needing a reason, and on days when he failed to appear Audrey found herself looking for him and wondering where he was.

'You want to watch it,' Marged warned, when someone remarked on the late night visits. 'A rich widow you are and rich pickings might be what he's after.'

'You don't think he could like me for myself then?'

'Of course he could, Audrey, don't be so touchy. I'm just warning you to be careful, that's all.'

'Thank you, I will.'

The friction between them had eased. With the beach activities long ago closed down, Marged called at the Corner Cafe most days and helped in the kitchen. When she saw something that needed doing, she tried to persuade Huw or Bleddyn to deal with it, hoping that Keith would eventually be squeezed out of the cafe for good. The Castle family needed no outsiders. Keith was very good at finding an excuse to call. Audrey was in a strange mood of late and she didn't want the man taking advantage of her.

The winter was a quiet time for the Castle family and Marged was glad to pass a few hours working beside her sister. After all, she had worked at Castle's Cafe on the beach since she was a child and knew the business better than most. 'Audrey ought to be grateful,' she told Huw, 'but she hardly says thank you. There's something bothering her, I know it.'

'Wait, be patient, help her when you can, and she'll tell you when she's ready,' Huw advised.

'I do help, don't I?'

Huw guessed that part of Marged's way of helping would be to tell her sister how things should be done. 'Perhaps it would be better if you don't go so often, love,' he said. 'Let her do it her way, sort out her own problems, is it? You can't have her becoming dependent on you, then leave her as soon as the season starts, can you?'

Marged didn't appear to listen to him. 'I'll clean those mirrors again tomorrow,' she said. 'Fingermarks all over them. Now that was a mistake, having mirrors like that just tempts people to mess them up.'

With Christmas drawing near the town did its best to add a sparkle to the shops and the streets. A few windows displayed Christmas trees and if the ornaments were tattered and had seen better days, no one complained. Whatever happened, the festival would be marked with as much joy as possible.

Stanley, Harold and Percival went out with Myrtle to gather holly from the fields around Mr Gregory's smallholding. He had taken what he needed to fill the orders from market stall-holders to sell as a welcome addition to the fruit and vegetables they managed to acquire, and had given them permission to take any that was left. Small bunches of the rich green, shiny leaves with a few berries, were used to fill pots and vases in Audrey's cafe and candles were placed in jars and would be lit to add to the atmosphere during the last couple of weeks before everything closed down on Christmas Eve.

Audrey found it strange not to be involved in the usual family arrangements. In the house where she had lived all her life, the house in which she and Marged had been born, the family had gathered and the house had rung with reminiscences, singsongs and laughter. Now the house was empty apart from Marged and Huw's son Ronnie and his family, who still lived in the top rooms. Audrey knew she would have to do something soon about finding a tenant, but she couldn't let it go, not yet, in case the cafe failed and she had to go back.

The flat above the cafe was comfortable and with Maude and Myrtle sharing it, she was beginning to feel at home there, but if she had to sell the cafe the flat would be sold with it and she would have to go back to Sidney Street. The thought saddened her. This place was completely her own; for the first time in her life she had made the decisions with no thought of trying to please others. She had chosen a home and everything that went into it, she didn't want to give it up.

She promised to go to Marged and Huw's on Christmas evening, but the lunchtime meal would be here in her new home with Maude and Myrtle and perhaps, if the girls had no objection, she might invite Keith to share it with them. As the thought developed she laughed aloud. Still locked into her brain was the compulsion to ask if her plans met with approval. First by her mother, then Marged. Now, when she thought she was free to please herself, she was worrying about Maude and Myrtle being upset.

She called them and announced her intention. 'About Christmas lunch. I'm inviting Keith to join us.'

'Great,' Maude said. 'Just the person to make the day special.'

'Lovely,' Myrtle said in a tone that sounded anything but pleased.

For a moment the worry returned, then Audrey smiled and said, 'Now, shall we buy him a little gift for under the tree?'

Audrey had never seen the place where Keith lived; he had been reticent about telling her his address. It was Marged who found out and there was something in the way she shared the information that made Audrey curious. On impulse one afternoon, while Maude and Myrtle managed the cafe, she went to find it. The name was charming, tempting the imagination to paint beautiful pictures. The Dingle sounded quaint and pretty and countrified, but the reality was a shock.

The Dingle was a rundown row of cottages that had become little more than a slum. In one there was a family of eight children, two other cottages were abandoned and open to the elements, and in another, where Keith lived, the owner had rented out three sad rooms to lodgers whom she boastfully called 'her gentlemen'. Audrey didn't go in. She had intended to knock and see if Keith was at home but on seeing the place she changed her mind. He would be embarrassed if she met him there. Puzzled, she walked away.

She said nothing to Marged or the girls, and she didn't tell Keith she had been there. He seemed to have a good business, he was certainly busy with work in the town, so why did he live in such a dreadful place? She knew he had been married and wondered if he were still having to pay maintenance to an ex-wife or perhaps there were children to support? She realized with a shock that she knew very little about him. Their conversations had seemed to range widely, but they had been mostly about the work he was doing on her cafe. But surely that was only because she hadn't been curious enough to ask? He didn't seem a secretive man.

She made a pledge to herself: before she invited him to spend Christmas Day with her and the girls, she would find out about his family and why he no longer lived with them.

Marged found it strange to have her sister no longer living a few doors away. Audrey still used the house to keep stores in and one day they met there. These days they greeted each other more affectionately than of late but on occasions there was still an edge of unease. Anything to do with the cafe was discussed in a tentative way, but Marged began to relax and hope that they might become really close friends again, and Christmas was the perfect time to achieve it.

'Why don't you all come to us for Christmas lunch as well as in the evening?' Marged asked.

'I can't, Marged. We've invited Keith.'

'Still hanging around, is he?' she said.

'Yes, he's "still hanging around", Marged. He's become a good friend to me and the girls.'

'You know he's married, don't you?'

'Divorced,' Audrey retorted, hoping it was true.

'All right then, divorced. He's still paying for that ex-wife of his, mind, and the two children.' Knowing he had children was a shock, but Audrey hoped it hadn't shown.

'That's why he's working so hard and that's why we're lucky to have his help free and for nothing!' Audrey retorted. 'Stop trying to make trouble, Marged. Leave me alone.' Audrey picked up the extra linen she had called to collect and was on her way out when Ronnie and Olive came down the stairs and called to her.

'Auntie Audrey, we know you won't be here for Christmas and we want us all to go out for a meal a few days before, say Wednesday the 22nd? The market closes at one and Beth will be free. She doesn't think Peter will be home, but it will be lovely if the rest of us can be together.'

Seeing his enthusiastic face and with Olive adding her coaxing, Audrey had to agree. 'Thank you, Ronnie and Olive, dears, of course we'll be there. I'll tell the girls and they'll be delighted. We'll meet you at eight, if that's all right It won't be a problem, and,' she added, glancing at Marged, 'Keith is sure to offer to help.'

When he was told, Keith at once offered to deal with the cleaning.

'You three go off and get dolled up and enjoy yourselves,' he said. 'Just leave everything and when you come back you'll think the fairies have been.'

As the Christmas festivites were drawing closer, the town had decided that although a tree with lights was too much of an extravagance with the country struggling to survive, and with lighting still prohibited after dark, they would still have a Christmas tree outside the town hall. A tree was duly felled and placed in a central spot and decorated with all the tinsel, now dreadfully tarnished, that they could beg or borrow. Instead of lights, a circle of candles was placed around the tree and these were lit during the afternoon and doused officiously by the wardens at nightfall. It wasn't much, but it cheered the inhabitants to see it standing there, where others had stood over past years. It seemed a beacon of hope, an augury of good news to come. Perhaps this Christmas really would be the final one celebrated in wartime? They were three months into the fifth year of the conflict.

On the day of the family meal to which Ronnie had invited Audrey and Maude and Myrtle, there was a complication. Wednesday was half-day closing in the cafe as well as most of the shops in the town and it was on this day they were asked to accommodate a birthday party. Eirlys and Ken wanted to make a special occasion of Stanley's fifteenth birthday which was a slight embarrassment as he had been telling Myrtle he was fifteen for several months.

Having accepted the invitation to go out with Ronnie and Olive and the rest of the family on the same evening, Myrtle decided she couldn't go and for this Stanley was grateful. Please don't tell her it's my fifteenth,' he pleaded. ' I told her it was a party for Percival so she wouldn't think she was missing much.'

Without hesitation Audrey agreed to keep the cafe open for the afternoon and to her surprise they were quite busy. Shop girls on their half day off and with nowhere to go, learned of the opening and arrived with friends to enjoy a comfortable hour to talk about Christmas. Older people joined them, pleased to find a place to sit and dream of Christmases that had gone and those to come.

The takings were better than most afternoons and Audrey decided that if regulations allowed, she would continue to open on the town's half day to give the young people a place to meet and hopefully instil in them the idea of meeting there in the evenings as well. It might be just what was needed to get the business on track.

'What about Ronnie's dinner with the family, Auntie Audrey?' Maude asked when at five o'clock there was no sign of the place closing.

'Go and find Keith and we'll ask him to close up for us as he offered to clean up anyway,' Audrey suggested. 'I'm sure he won't mind. He's working in the butcher's shop yard, fixing the broken fence at the back.'

192

'Is that why we haven't seen him for a few days?' Maude asked.

'He's very kind, helping us when he can, but he does have his own work and that must come first,' Audrey reminded her. 'But I'm sure he'll come when he knows we're running late for the family meal.'

It was Myrtle who went to the butcher's shop to find him, and she was told that Keith had packed up the job a couple of days previously and had gone home feeling unwell. Given his address and an offer to use the big delivery bike, she set off for The Dingle. When she found it she was as shocked as Audrey had been.

'Not well,' was the answer to her query about his whereabouts. The overweight, underwashed woman whom she presumed was his landlady stood at the doorway, arms folded, suspicion creasing her brow. 'Who wants to know?' she asked. Myrtle was saved from answering by Keith coming to the door looking quite cheerful and smiling a greeting.

He was very carelessly dressed in dirty overalls and shirt, and a paint-splashed jumper, all of which were creased as though they had been slept in. By the look of him Myrtle thought he hadn't shaved for a couple of days and looked as though washing was something he hadn't got around to either.

Doubtfully, Myrtle explained the situation at the cafe and he promised to come within the hour.

'It was a migraine,' he explained. 'I get them now and then and they make me feel quite ill for a while. I have to lie down in a dark room till they pass. It's going now and as soon as I've had a hot cup of tea I'll be fine.'

'Are you sure?' Myrtle asked. She didn't want Audrey to see him in this state or she wouldn't leave him to look after the cafe while they went out, and she did so want to go. She missed the Castle family dreadfully and, even though her loyalty was to Audrey, she wanted to see the rest of them, remind them of their importance to her and Maude. 'Don't come if you aren't well,' she said crossing her fingers. 'You don't look—'

'Don't worry, Myrtle. I'll smarten myself up before I report for duty. Don't say anything about the migraine to your auntie, there's no point in her worrying. I'm going to be fine.'

Wondering about the unpleasant place in which he lived, undecided about whether or not she should tell Audrey, she cycled back to return the carrier bike and then ran back to the cafe, where business was still hectic. Between clearing tables and dealing with dishes, she told Audrey about the terrible place called The Dingle.

'I know,' Audrey said. 'I went to see it myself a while ago.'

'You know? Then tell me, why does he live in such an awful place? He works, he can't be so poor he's unable to find something better. Maude and I were destitute and we didn't have any way of getting somewhere decent to live, so why does he accept that place and have that awful woman looking after him?'

'Apparently there are several lodgers living there and some of them are little better than tramps, begging on the street for money, so I've heard. But I can't offer to help, can I? He's never told me much about himself so it's a question of pride.'

'He's in debt or something?'

'Maybe. Whatever it is, it's his business and private. We can't ask,' Audrey said. 'It's best he thinks we don't know.' She hesitated then decided to tell Myrtle what she knew. 'Marged told me he's married and has two children. He's probably divorced but still paying most of his wages to them.'

There was no chance to discuss it further as the cafe needed their attention, and a few minutes later Keith arrived. He had washed, shaved, changed his clothes and he looked perfectly well. As he had been involved with the cafe so often before, he saw what was needed and began to sort out the chaos that followed a busy few hours with efficiency and in good humour. Myrtle watched and wondered.

At seven, leaving Keith to close the cafe and clean up ready for the following day, the three went up to the flat to get ready. Maude had treated herself to a new winter dress and she put it on, while Myrtle chose to wear a skirt and a blouse on to which Hannah had sewn a few sequins and lent her a rhinestone necklace which caught the light beautifully and added a touch of glamour. Audrey wore a dress she had bought years before when she and Wilf had first married. In a soft blue, with an edging of lace and some silver buttons, she felt smart enough to feel confident in front of the family she had all but abandoned.

She felt a bit uneasy, aware that if Marged chose she could make the evening a tense one for her, but as soon as they went inside the hotel where their meal was booked, everything went well. Ronnie and Olive, with a sleepy Rhiannon ready to settle to sleep in her pram beside them, acted as host and hostess for the evening and welcomed each one as they arrived. Their places were marked and Audrey found herself next to her sister with Hetty on her other side. Bleddyn and Huw had been placed outside the three of them.

'Maybe not formally correct,' Olive whispered, 'but we thought it would be nice for you two to sit together. You and Marged have always been such close friends as well as loving sisters.'

Audrey hoped Olive would be of the same opinion when the evening ended. Aloud she said, 'What a wonderful idea this was, thank you Olive dear and you Ronnie. It will start Christmas perfectly.'

Others joined in their approval and the hum of conversation began to swell. Two and a half year-old Rhiannon slept through most of the evening and seemed unaware of the noisy chatter and laughter billowing around her amid the smoke of cigars and the chinking of glasses.

In the Corner Cafe things were not as orderly. With the blinds closed and the lights reduced to one overhead light by which to see what he was doing, Keith had started to gather the last of the china and on the final load, which was too unwieldy a load for the tray, he tripped, and fell against the counter before falling to the floor. All around him lay shattered glass and china, the contents of the tray having been joined by the broken glass falling from one of the counter display units.

He sat there for a moment and gradually dared to stare at his hands. In one a large piece of glass was embedded. As he watched, thick dark blood oozed around the glass. Carefully he removed the circle of glass and pressed a tea towel against the cut to staunch the blood. Slowly he got up and made his way into the kitchen.

Fixing the tea towel more firmly, he looked for a brush and shovel to start clearing up the mess. He couldn't find the small hand brush, and the long sweeping brush handle was a nuisance, getting caught against chairs, the door and against the counter. He struggled but seemed incapable of judging distances and repeatedly knocked into things or pushed them over with the brush. He glanced at the time. Audrey and the others would be back soon.

Trying to hurry he pushed harder with the brush, tugging as it snagged again behind a chair. It came free and out of control, jerked up to hit the window blind. It came away from its fastenings and hit the window and, as though in slow motion, he watched as the glass cracked, loosened, then slid down, some to land on the floor, most piling up on the pavement outside.

Some wag passing by shouted, 'Put that light out.' And for a moment it was funny. His face creased into hysterical laughter and he had no strength in his arms.

The laughter ended as suddenly as it began. He was finding it difficult to concentrate but decided that the first thing to do was find some way of covering the broken window. A blanket and some tacks were quickly found and he fastened the blanket over the gap to provide, if not security, then at least some protection against someone falling against the glass.

The smashed glass went into the ash bins and the bins were left as a barrier beside what was left of the window. Going back inside he thought it would be wise to remove anything of value up to the flat in case an opportunist burglar should happen to pass. Illogically, bearing in mind its size, he decided that the undamaged glass counter display units were something it would be difficult to replace, so he staggered with one as far as the bottom of the stairs then decided that the coffee maker was more important.

Having turned off the main light, he lit a few candles to help him see where he was going. He was struggling up the stairs with the chrome coffee maker when he realised his hand was still bleeding. He stopped halfway up the stairs, supported the heavy coffee maker on his bent knee to re-fix the tea towel, and lost his grip on it. The blood made it slippery and although he tried to save it, handling it at an awkward angle gave him no chance of holding its weight and he cried out in dismay as he saw it roll down the stairs. It hit the glass display unit and he sat down on the stairs and covered his face with his hands. What was the matter with him? He couldn't think straight. Why had he come? He had known when Myrtle had asked him that he wasn't well enough, so why hadn't he said so?

He was still asking himself those questions when Audrey, Maude and Myrtle walked in.

Eleven

A udrey and the girls stared at the ruin of the cafe, now lit with a couple of candles, in disbelief.

'Keith! What's happened here?'

He didn't reply, he just sat on the stair looking at her, and in the wavering light of the candles he looked like a whipped boy. She saw that he was shaking. Shock and the icy cold of the unheated place, which was practically open to the chill of the night, had made him intensely cold and when he tried to speak, he shivered so much the words were inaudible.

Behind the three women, first Marged and Hetty, then Huw and the burly, bearded figure of Bleddyn appeared.

'What the hell?' Huw and Bleddyn gasped in unison. Their words broke the spell of disbelief and Audrey went up the stairs to where Keith sat.

'I wanted it to be perfect,' he finally muttered, 'but I couldn't find the hand brush.'

'And you lost your temper?' she asked in alarm. 'You lost your temper and did all this?'

'No, I never lose my temper. You can ask anyone, they'll tell you I'm the mildest of men. No, Audrey, I couldn't find it and I had to use the floor brush.'

The others looked around them as Audrey stood waiting patiently for an explanation of how the lack of a hand brush could cause such damage.

'Because I couldn't find the small brush,' he went on, 'I used the long handled one and it got stuck and I jerked it free and broke the glass display case and then, when I was clearing that up, the handle hit the window.'

He was shivering uncontrollably and Audrey helped him up and guided him to the flat and into the equally cold sitting room. She sat him on a chair and lit the electric fire. Maude and Myrtle had followed and they began reviving the coal fire which had all but died while they were out.

'I bought flowers to leave on the stairs for you,' Keith said almost tearfully. 'I called on Mrs Chapel at the flower shop and persuaded her to sell me a nice bunch of late chrysanths. I wanted it to be perfect. I wanted to please you, Audrey.'

Downstairs a bewildered Huw and Bleddyn examined the damage, while Marged whispered to Hetty that Audrey must be out of her mind allowing such a maniac anywhere near her.

Huw went upstairs to find notepaper, ruler and pencil, and he and Bleddyn measured up what was needed to repair the window. 'I don't know what we can do about the broken cabinet,' Bleddyn said. 'They're hard to find.'

'And costly. She'll have to manage with one for now.'

At the bottom of the stairs Marged was still whispering to Hetty, who tried to calm down her excessive outrage. 'Come on, Marged, we don't know what happened here and we have to get the facts before we can accuse Keith of wild behaviour. Let's go and see what's happening. But please, wait until we know the facts before sounding off.'

'Who d'you think you're talking to? Five minutes you've been a part of this family!' Marged snapped.

'Long enough to know you speak too quickly and say things you later regret!' Hetty retorted. She led the way, making sure Marged was behind her and when she went into the living room, she quickly asked, 'Can Marged and I make us all a cup of tea, Audrey?'

'Thanks,' Audrey said. 'Keith has had a terrible shock and a cup of hot tea with plenty of sugar is what he needs.'

'What about a brandy? I can slip home and get some,' Bleddyn said, having followed them up.

'No thanks,' Keith replied. 'I'm not much for drink and the thought of brandy makes me feel a bit sick. Tea'll be fine.'

'You'd better tell us what happened,' Bleddyn demanded.

Keith, with interruptions from an anxious Audrey, explained the sequence of events.

'It's this headache,' Keith told them. 'I thought it was passing but it came back worse than before. Migraine, it is. I should have told Audrey I couldn't do it, but I wanted to please her and she rarely asks for help.'

Bleddyn nodded. 'I've heard about migraines. Bad they are, by all accounts.'

There was no sleep that night. With the aid of candles and a low wattage bulb on the stairs they cleaned up the last of the damage and the coffee urn was restored, battered but still useable, into its place. By six o'clock the next morning, the place looked quite orderly and apart from the lack of glass in the front window, and the freezing temperature, it was ready for business as usual.

Because of staying open so late in the evenings, Audrey didn't start serving until ten o'clock in the morning and by that time, the glass had been replaced, and apart from some fingermarks from the putty, the cafe opened with few visible signs of the night's disasters.

Marged, busy making sandwiches while the girls made cakes, managed to keep her tongue still, but every time she looked at Keith, who was clearly unwell, she glared fiercely enough to melt him into oblivion. Keith avoided her as much as was possible, keeping busy, helping Bleddyn and Huw prepare the visible damage around the new glass.

After Keith had drunk the cup of sweet tea the previous evening, Audrey had persuaded him to take a bath to warm himself and when he came out of the bathroom he had looked a different man. The headache had apparently cleared and he was cheerful and deeply apologetic. He set to and worked with the others to get everything straight, insisting on scrubbing the floor in case there were remnants of glass that might cut someone else. 'If anyone is cut I deserve for it to be me,' he said.

'I'm going to make a few enquiries about Keith Kent,' Marged muttered to Hetty when they walked home through the gloomy, frost bound morning.

'Fine, but if you find out something unpleasant, don't expect Audrey to be pleased,' Hetty warned.

Keith stayed all that day, and when the cafe closed at nine o'clock, Audrey persuaded him to spend the second night with them. 'Maude can make you up a bed on the sofa. You'll be comfortable there and we'll keep the fire going so you won't be cold. You've had a bad shock, and I'd feel happier if you didn't go back to those lodgings.'

'I'm sorry you saw where I live,' he said. 'It was only going

200

to be temporary. I took it in a hurry after I was told to leave the room I had in Church Street. The woman's son was coming home, invalided out of the army, poor lad, so she wanted the room back. I took the room in The Dingle just for a week or two, but I've been too busy to do anything about moving on.'

'Don't worry about it now, stay here for a few days until you feel stronger and we'll all help you to find a better place.'

'But I can't! It's Christmas, you have your family around you and I'd be intruding.'

'Nonsense. If you'd rather go back to your room we won't stop you, but we'd like to have you here to share our Christmas, so it's up to you.'

'Thank you. I'd love to stay.'

Maude smiled her approval but Myrtle frowned. Somehow it was a little too contrived. And as for the headache, that was convenient too. A cup of tea and a hot bath had been a miraculous cure for the migraine he complained of and she doubted whether such a headache could be so easily cleared. She said nothing. Auntie Audrey was no fool and she wouldn't be taken in for long if the man was as dishonest as she was beginning to suspect.

Audrey was tired, but inexplicably she was happy too. Having someone to look after was comforting. She'd always thrived on being needed by someone, in the past her mother and Marged, and then more recently dear Wilf. After Wilf had died, she had missed being important to someone. To the rest of the family she had never been anything more than good old Audrey, always willing to do what no one else wanted to do. Having Keith to fuss over had lightened her spirits as nothing else had done. She day-dreamed about him staying with her and the girls, looking after them all; life could be very good.

That night, sleeping in Audrey's living room, Keith couldn't sleep. So, he slipped out of bed when he thought he wouldn't be heard and went to his jacket hanging on the door. He knew he wouldn't sleep unless he had some help. There was a small bottle of whisky in an inside pocket and he drank thirstily. He had refused the brandy when it had been offered because he didn't want Audrey to think he was weak and needed support, as he'd made enough of a fool of himself, but after the bizarre events of the past twenty-four hours, he needed something to

201

settle his nerves. The drink did the trick and he slept immediately.

The story of the series of disasters that had befallen Keith brought publicity and a flood of customers to the Corner Cafe in the two days before Christmas. He went back to The Dingle after breakfast on Christmas Eve, but at Audrey's invitation, he stayed only to gather a few necessities, including his bicycle and trailer on which he travelled between home and his place of work, and came back to the flat.

He insisted on helping, apologizing repeatedly for his unfortunate clumsiness until Audrey told him to stop. 'You were ill, it was an accident. None of it was intended,' she said. 'If you want to do something to make up, just help us today and we'll never mention it again, right?'

Christmas Eve was the busiest day yet and the place was filled right up to closing, leaving them little time to sort out the cleaning between serving and preparing more food. Marged arrived, glared at Keith, smiled rather grimly towards her sister and began clearing the tables and stacking the dishes ready for washing.

'What's he still here for?' she asked and Audrey replied that he was a guest and it was no business of hers.

Without exchanging another word the two sisters worked in unison, sorting the chaos of a hectic day like the team they had always been.

On that most unusual of Christmas Eves they finally climbed back up to the flat at ten thirty after cleaning up, leaving everything empty and clear for the few days they would be closed over Christmas.

Marged saw that Keith had settled in, much to the family's disapproval. Huw and Bleddyn considered him a scrounger and Marged was convinced there was something they hadn't been told. She couldn't resist voicing her doubts once again, and she and Audrey were again unable to be civil to each other. They spoke only when they had to and in a stiff and formal tone, disapproval hovering around every word.

Meanwhile, Andy was on the run again. The police had been quite relaxed by his apparent willingness to accept his fate.

He told them he'd had his fun and now wanted to pay for it. 'I dreaded serving in the army,' he told them. 'I've never resorted to violence and can't imagine ever wanting to hurt another human being. Expecting me to kill someone because he's on the other side is something I can't do. Conscientious objectors are treated like criminals and I couldn't cope with that either, so I thought I'd ride out the war by keeping a couple of steps ahead of blokes like you, but you were too quick for me this time, eh?'

The two constables felt sympathy for him. After all, they had sons serving and would have helped them to avoid the call up if an opportunity had arisen, they admitted to each other. They were waiting for the custody sergeant to bring the relevant papers and when Andy offered them a cigarette and asked to go to the lavatory, they didn't rush to accompany him, but pointed the way and waited for their cigarettes to draw before standing outside the door and waiting for him to reappear.

Boldly, Andy walked calmly through the front door of the police station, he even paused for a moment, appearing completely confident, then walked to the nearest lane, cut across some gardens, through the park, and caught a bus.

Shirley Downs was looking forward to a few weeks rest. She had been busy both locally and on tours over the past months and with no concerts booked until the end of January, she settled down to enjoy an idle few weeks.

Her leg ached still, but she was determined to stop using her stick before her next booking at the end of January at the town hall. Walking on level ground was the best way to strengthen the muscles and it was while walking along the windswept cold and abandoned promenade on the morning of Christmas Eve that she met Andy Probert.

'I thought you'd been arrested!' she gasped. 'And before you say anything, it wasn't me who called the police, right?'

'Right. I never thought you did, not for a minute.' He laughed and his eyes held such warmth, and such delight at seeing her, that she relaxed and took the arm he offered her.

'Where are you living this time? Found another empty house so you can frighten some poor young couple again?'

'I've got a room in the most awful place you could imagine,' he told her. 'It's called The Dingle, which sounds quaint, but in fact it's a rundown house in a rundown row, and if the landlady isn't rundown, it's because she's always been a mess!'

As they walked along the cliff path, Shirley pulling up a shawl to protect her head from the icy wind that worsened as they climbed up on to the headland, he told her about the room he had accepted. 'It's such a terrible place that no one would go there unless they had to. I'll be as safe there as anywhere, at least through the Christmas weekend. As for what I'll do then, I don't know. I'm broke apart from the cost of the disgusting room and a few meals, and with having to lie low and it being Christmas and all, means I can't earn.'

'Give yourself up,' Shirley said. 'You can serve your time and come out with a clear conscience to start again when the war ends. It can't go on much longer.'

'Oh yeh? Go off to fight and have me head blown off? Sod that for a lark. I'm staying well clear.'

'What will you do? You must have some plans?'

'Right now, I plan to go on the bus to a pub I know where we might get a bit of steak and kidney pie, which to be truthful is more paste and mystery than steak and kidney, but the gravy's good. Coming?'

'I wouldn't say no if you're offering.'

'Good! I'm starving.'

'Are you still having those bad dreams, Andy?' she asked as they walked away from the seafront.

'They're what give me the speed I need when the police are about to grab my collar. They're so real, Shirley. I can't help thinking they're a premonition.'

'Don't think like that. It's probably only nerves. I'm sure I'd have worse dreams if I had to face the thought of going into battle.'

'I've been lucky so far, the police have been very casual about my arrest. They've been more interested in nabbing me for a few robberies, rather than my invitation to serve in His Majesty's army. But if I was caught by the military it would be a different story. Hard and cold they are, and I wouldn't stand a chance of getting away from them once they had their great big mitts on me.'

204

It was later that evening when she was helping Hetty to prepare a chicken and a piece of pork Bleddyn had managed to buy illegally, that Shirley heard her mother mention The Dingle.

'That's a coincidence,' she said. 'I was talking to someone today who has just taken a room in one of the houses there. It sounds a terrible place. Do you know it, Bleddyn?' she asked.

'Who do you know living in a place like that?' Bleddyn asked. 'It's where that Keith Kent has been living. Him that's always hanging around Audrey.'

'Oh, someone who I've met a few times. He travels a lot and he's got a room there at the moment.'

'He can't be up to much if he's settled for a place like that!'

'Will you take me there, Bleddyn?' Shirley asked. 'I'm curious to see it. I don't want to talk to the person I met earlier, I just want to see if his description was an exaggeration.'

'Go on,' Hetty urged. 'You know you want to find out something about this Keith Kent. Now's your chance while he's still at Audrey's.'

The place was approached by a narrow lane over which few vehicles passed. Grasses and wild flowers, now nothing more than dead stalks, grew out of the surface and the trees hadn't been trimmed for several seasons, leaving the place almost cut off from view.

While Shirley waited just out of sight of the row of houses, Bleddyn went boldly to the first door, and when a slovenly woman answered, he asked for Keith.

'Gave notice he did,' he was told. 'Said he'd found somewhere better and cheaper. Well, you can tell him that if he wants to come back he's too late, the room's taken.'

Bleddyn was quiet on the way home. It appeared that Keith was so sure of being offered a permanent home with Audrey and the girls, that he had left himself with nowhere else to go. His thoughts followed those of Myrtle: the migraine headache had been very convenient.

Out of a growing concern for Audrey, Huw and Bleddyn made a few more enquiries. Apparently, Keith worked hard and there were only a few who complained about his occasional lapses when he went off for a few days and was slow finishing a job. Yet, he never seemed to have any money.

'I spoke to Charlie Groves, the policeman, and he told me there's an ex-wife and a couple of children somewhere,' Bleddyn told his brother.

Huw had heard the same and he added, 'The two boys are working and it seems unlikely the wife demands much from him; she's re-married and quite comfortable, I believe.'

'We have to tread careful here. If we say too much, Audrey will stop talking to us and we need to be on hand, to keep an eye on him,' Bleddyn said. He and Huw agreed to say nothing, but watch and wait.

Christmas exaggerated joy and sadness more during war time than at any other. Letters were unfolded, discussed and analysed, people trying to read more into the few facts they contained, inventing opinions and struggling to understand what their loved ones were going through. For Shirley, an unexpected delivery of letters that arrived from Freddy was a joy. The mail had obviously been delayed and having three within a couple of days and just before Christmas was the best gift she could have received.

She took them to her room and wallowed over his affectionate words, sharing only a little of what he had written with her mother and Bleddyn. His words were light-hearted but they warmed her more than any attempt at romantic flummery. 'If only this war would end and he could come home,' she said with a trembling sigh. Then a burst of frustrated anger overcame her. She needed him home. She wanted to know how they really felt about each other, not live this half-life, not knowing how their story would end. She was tired of trying to guess how he truly felt and even after his ten days leave she wasn't sure of her own feelings. It was like standing on the edge of a precipice: would she fall this way or that? Would their love be stronger once they could spend time together and really talk? Or would the return of Freddy tilt her down into the abyss? The endless wondering was so cruel. To Hetty's alarm, she burst into noisy tears.

Christmas Day was quiet for the Castles. Bleddyn took Hetty and his daughter-in-law, Hannah, with her girls, for a walk and called in to Huw and Marged's after lunch. He knew the emptiness would be distressing for Marged, who had always shared the work with Audrey and provided for them all. Ronnie and Olive and little Rhiannon were there and Eynon's wife Alice. Maude and Myrtle called later, leaving Audrey at the flat with Keith.

Like Audrey, Marged's daughter Lilly, her husband and baby Phyllis had declined the invitation to join them. Somehow the empty chairs lined along the walls were reminders of those other absentees: Bleddyn's son Taff, who would never come home, and his other son Johnny who hadn't been home for such an age, as well as Marged and Huw's son Eynon, whose wife Alice was so determinedly confident and cheered them all. To compensate for the emptiness of the chairs, as in so many homes that Christmas, recent letters were read and discussed. Johnny and Eynon would celebrate another Christmas away from their family but they were here where they were loved, safe in everyone's heart.

The children helped to liven up the atmosphere, but there was none of the usual camaraderie. Huw knew that for Marged, the absence of Audrey was the worst. Eynon and Johnny couldn't be there, but Audrey was less than ten minutes' walk away and it was distressing for her.

It was a strange Christmas Day for Audrey and her thoughts kept winging towards Sidney Street, where she imagined there would be the usual noise and laughter. In her mind she envisaged previous Christmases, so far removed from today's subdued echo of those times. Once, she even stood and began to suggest that she and Keith called in, but she changed her mind. If she arrived with Keith, she and Marged would be sure to quarrel and why spoil it for the rest?

In Sidney Street, Marged was promising herself that if Audrey walked in with Keith she would be as welcoming as she could. There were several knocks on the door but each time she was disappointed when neighbours walked in to exchange seasonal greetings.

Christmas was more cheerful at the home of Morgan Price. His daughter Eirlys and her husband Ken with their little boy made it a Christmas that he would always remember as one of the best. The three boys added to the atmosphere with their excitement. As they had outgrown their earlier ones, he had bought them second hand bicycles and painted them. With Ken's help he had polished the chrome and added a few refinements like a new bell and a saddle bag – for which he had queued for more than an hour, having been told of their imminent arrival at the local bicycle shop.

Dependent on pocket money, Harold and Percival hadn't been able to buy more than a few cards, but Stanley, having found a job in a shoe shop, had bought one or two small gifts. Perfume with an unknown name and strange scent for Eirlys. A toy train for the baby and for Myrtle a handmade handkerchief box which he had found in the hand craft shop. He knew women liked fancy jewellery and toiletries that made them smell nice, but he didn't want a girl he liked to have any of these. His mother, with her fancy clothes and heavy makeup and strong perfume, had been beautiful, he knew that, but he was mature enough to know that she didn't dress up for him and his brothers, but for the men she went to meet, while they waited in their sad little room for her to return – often very hungry and hoping she would bring them back some supper.

Peter Gregory was absent from home and, trying to stop their minds constantly returning to the danger he was undoubtedly facing, Beth and Mr Gregory decided they had a need for company. They knocked on Morgan's door carrying a couple of flagons and some mince pies, sure of a welcome. Myrtle had brought a new game of Monopoly, which kept them amused for the whole evening and which Percival surprised them – and himself – by winning.

Stanley loved it when Myrtle came to see him. As she was leaving, Ken having promised to walk her home, he asked, 'Uncle Morgan, can I leave the shop at Easter and work over the beach again next summer?'

'Why? I thought you liked the shop?'

'Selling shoes to fussy old women? Not as much as I like the sands.'

'It's only for six months, what will you do when the season's over again? No, son. It isn't a good idea at all. Stay in the shop and you'll do well.'

'Will you think about it?' Stanley pleaded.

'I'll think about it but I don't think I'll change my mind.'

Optimistically, Stanley felt cheered by his reply. 'He didn't say no, did he? Not for definite.'

Morgan, rosy-faced from drink, replete with too much dinner and Christmas pudding, and in love with the whole world, winked at Myrtle and said, 'Mind you, it wouldn't do any harm to have a word with Bleddyn and Huw.'

Shirley refused to go to Marged and Huw's with her mother and Bleddyn. Instead she went for a walk. The Dingle was a long way for her and Andy had promised to be at the end of the lane at four and would walk towards town, in case she was able to join him. She set out intending to go part of the way, leaving it to fate whether or not she met him. It was already getting dark and she knew she couldn't face the eerie gloom of the dreary lane on her own, especially with those unwelcoming cottages that seemed to be inhabited by threatening people. She would go to the edge of town and turn back. Perhaps I'll go to Marged and Huw's after all, she thought.

She wasn't far from Castle's fish and chip shop when she saw him. He ran to greet her, and at first she didn't recognize him. He was wearing a heavy overcoat that was far too large for him and which disguised his slim figure. He had allowed his beard to grow again, giving him a wild piratical look and, from what she remembered of the row of dilapidated cottages, his appearance suited the place perfectly.

They walked slowly around the empty streets, passing houses where the sounds of laughter, singing and chatter revealed family celebrations behind darkened windows.

'Does it make you sad, not being able to go home at Christmastime?' she asked. 'If the circumstances were different I could have invited you to share ours, but I don't think you'd like to bump into some of your victims, or my step-father.'

'I wish I could have seen Reggie and my parents. It's not like Christmas at all, living in a house filled with strangers.' He turned to her with a grin. 'And The Dingle certainly attracts some very strange people! The bloke who used to have my room was a builder apparently, but although he worked he never had any money. Now that's a lesson I take to heart. I don't have any money either, but I don't graft day after day only to go home to a place like that.'

'Was that Keith Kent?' Shirley asked. 'He's staying with Auntie Audrey at the moment.'

'Then tell her to get rid, and fast. He's had people looking for him to pay money he owes. He's been kicked out of several places for not paying rent and even the bike, ladders and trailer he uses belong to someone else. The man's a loser and people like that pull other people down with them.' He didn't tell her all he had heard about Keith, he had other things on his mind. Slipping an arm around her shoulders, he pulled her towards him and pressed his cheek against hers. Gently she moved away.

'Only a hug, surely that's not much to ask on Christmas Day?' he complained mildly.

'If this coat smelled a bit sweeter you might be able to persuade me,' she said, laughing as she walked away. 'Come on, I've got some chocolate in my pocket and a couple of Mam's mince pies.'

'Smashing, we'll have a picnic,' he said as he caught her up.

'Andy, why are you staying around here? It isn't safe,' she admonished. 'Do you want to get caught?'

He looked thoughtful for a while, then answered, 'In a way I suppose I do. My running a few steps ahead of the authorities has to end sometime, and there are moments when I wish it was over and I could relax and accept my fate. I ran away scared when I realized I'd have to join up. I mean really scared, unable to sleep until it's almost morning, then waking up sweating after the same, terrifying dream.

'I've been telling myself that outwitting the police and the army is fun, but it gets wearying after years of it. The Dingle is the very worst place to live. I've known barns that are better. I'm broke and I need new socks, my bed smells and, on top of that, it's Christmas! Don't call the cops, mind. I'll give myself up when I'm ready, when I've really had enough and that isn't just yet. I'd miss you too much.'

'Idiot.'

He walked her home and as they turned into Brook Lane she saw her mother and Bleddyn coming towards them. Andy dissolved into the darkness with a whispered, 'Goodbye, Shirley, Happy New Year.'

'Who was that?' Hetty asked.

'Someone asking for a light,' she lied. 'He's been warning me against Keith Kent. What do we tell Auntie Audrey?'

'You can tell her what you've been told if you like, Shirley, but Bleddyn and I won't say a word.'

'If I stay out of it and avoid arguments, she might be able to talk to me if things turn unpleasant,' Bleddyn said. 'I have a feeling she'll need someone if she continues to befriend him.'

A few days later Shirley went into the cafe, and when Audrey brought her tea she waited as the rest of the tray was unloaded on to the table before asking her if she knew about the awful place called The Dingle. 'I went there recently to try and find someone and—'

'If you're going to tell me Keith lived there, I already know,' Audrey replied. She was smiling but there was a threat, a warning in her eyes for Shirley not to continue.

'Then you know something about his debts? His inability to pay his rent at the other places he's lived?'

The only response was for Audrey to return the cups and plates to the tray and walk away with it. After sitting there for a few moments staring at the empty table, Shirley left, her face red with embarrassment.

Delyth Owen and Maldwyn Perkins having found the Clements's old house to rent, had brought their wedding plans forward. Maldwyn dealt with the few things that needed doing, including tidying the garden and cleaning the shed, and it was Delyth's delight to leave Bryn Teg and go there on her half day and on Sundays to rearrange the furniture they had acquired, and clean and polish, making sure everything was perfect for when they returned from their brief honeymoon.

She was alone in the house that would soon be her home one afternoon, and decided the top cupboards needed just one more wash. They were high, but she tried not to bother Maldwyn with things that needed doing, determined to cope with as much as possible without asking him for help. So, while Maldwyn was busy with other things, she climbed a stepladder to wash out a kitchen cupboard before filling it with dishes given to her by a neighbour, when she suddenly lost her footing on the stepladder and fell.

Andy Probert happened to be passing and he went into the house having heard her calling for help. He was in a dilemma. If he helped her to the hospital he would be seen and probably caught. He would be sent to certain punishment before joining the army. He didn't know the situation. She might be all alone and, if he didn't help her, she could be there all night in an unheated house and who knows what could happen to her.

There was no choice and he went in. Her knee was painful and she was trying to hold back the panic she was feeling. 'I was so stupid,' she repeated several times. He made her comfortable and, after calling a neighbour to help, went with her to the hospital, promising to call at Maldwyn's lodgings to tell him what had happened.

He was arrested as he was knocking on the door of Mrs Denver's house in Queen Street and as Mrs Denver called to let Maldwyn know what had happened, Andy shrugged philosophically and went off with the police constable without complaint.

Maldwyn ran to the hospital and found Delyth waiting for him, hobbling around with the aid of a stick.

'Nothing broken,' she assured him. 'I have to rest and come back in a week's time.'

For Andy, the outcome was more serious. The police came as he was knocking on Mrs Denver's door. He shrugged philosophically and went without complaint.

The night school classes began again and Audrey and Myrtle started their second term. They had both completed homework during the holiday and were anxious to hand it in and learn of their progress. Having run the cafe for several weeks, Audrey had learned that Mondays, the day on which their classes were held, were usually quiet and she had chosen that day to close for a half day and remain open late instead on Wednesdays when the shop girls liked to call.

Keith continued to stay. He went out every day to the work he had found, and every week he handed Audrey the money to pay for his food. At first she had been tempted to refuse, but aware that his pride might suffer, she accepted and even wrote the amount down in a notebook each week. However, the amounts tended to dwindle: two pounds on the first Friday, then one pound ten shillings, then nothing at all. She didn't ask but felt a searing disappointment when he didn't offer any more.

'I ought to go back to the lodgings,' he said occasionally. Audrey knew he no longer had a room but she feigned ignorance and persuaded him to stay, just for another week or so, and he finally stopped offering.

On several evenings a week he went out to meet friends. It was on one of those evenings, a Saturday on which Maude and Myrtle had gone to a dance with Stanley and a few friends, that Audrey felt the loneliness hit her badly. She had tried to ignore what she had been told by family and well meaning friends about him failing to pay rent and being told to leave his lodgings. She had been so sure it would be different if she gave him her unquestioning support. He was a friend and if he didn't want to pay she didn't mind. He helped in the cafe, and he was a companion, someone to talk to and laugh with, and that was payment enough.

She looked around her at a room empty of memories. She listened to the silence and felt fear. Marged and Hetty never came now, Shirley walked past without a glance, Maude and Myrtle were finding friends and enjoying a lively social life, and Keith, she knew, was using her.

He kept his friends separate from his life here with her. He never invited her to join him when he went out, and when he came back, often with one of his headaches, he would go straight away to the sofa they had put in Maude's room (the girls now sharing) without a word of how he had spent his time.

She was past fifty and soon she would be alone. The years stretched out in front of her, a silent, empty path into old age, her hands with no one to touch, her voice silent in the echoing flat, a cruel contrast to the people she served in the cafe, who took their chatter and laughter home with them, leaving her with only the emptiness.

Like many wartime weddings, the marriage of Delyth Owen

to Maldwyn Perkins was a small affair. They needed every penny they could scrape together to furnish their home and were determined not to spend more than they needed on a large celebration. The small town of Bryn Teg had different ideas and the ceremony was followed by a party which included most of the neighbours amongst its guests. As many as possible crowded into the home of her parents. They had all brought gifts, usually things they had been able to spare from their own stores and the pile of linen and china grew until Delyth thought they would be unable to find transport for it all.

It was delivered on a cart and stored in their front room until they returned from honeymoon. Mrs Chapel and Mrs Denver saw to its unloading and spent an afternoon finding room for it all.

'It isn't money that makes a wedding a successful occasion,' Mrs Denver said as she admired the gifts the young couple had received, 'it's goodwill. And thank goodness there's still plenty of that.'

Reggie Probert came home on leave and went to see Bernard Gregory where he had been invited to stay. They talked enthusiastically about the work planned for the coming year.

Maude had been told of his leave and Audrey invited him to Sunday dinner at the flat above the Corner Cafe. She prepared a meal which had been augmented by a rabbit sent by Bernard Gregory which he had delivered the day before. Audrey grasped the excuse to fill the flat, give it some life and perhaps start to build a few memories, by inviting Beth and Bernard Gregory to join them.

'It's about time this place had a few people to liven it up,' she said.

Bernard accepted and he and Beth arrived with Reggie at twelve o'clock, Bernard bringing a few leeks and some sprouts from his fields, Beth bringing a bowl of daffodils bought from Maldwyn at Chapel's flower shop.

Keith had gone to visit a friend – name not supplied – but he had prepared the vegetables before he left and promised not to be too long. Audrey set the table for seven but only six ate. Keith failed to arrive. His meal was keeping warm on top of a saucepan full of hot water, but it wasn't until

Bernard and Beth had gone that he appeared.

Reggie, Maude and Myrtle made their excuses and went out, Audrey stood and waited for Keith to speak.

'Sorry, Audrey. I thought, as they were your friends I'd do better to stay away. I don't really belong.' Avoiding her eyes he added softly, 'It's best that I go.'

The silence was back. The visitors had filled the hollow places for a while but now the echoes were fading. The house wrapped her around with the sense of isolation that wouldn't go away. The prospect of years of loneliness ahead saddened her. So what if Keith wasn't the wonderful man every woman dreamed of? She'd had her share of that kind of happiness already with Wilf. Life with Keith would be different, but his companionship would take the edges away, soothe the silences, and who knows how long she might wait for someone else to come into her life? Her mind made up, she touched his arm gently.

'You can be a part of the family if you wish,' she said softly. 'There's a place for you here. A place you never need to leave, if you want it.' She held her breath, alarmed at her temerity, fearful of rejection.

'You mean you want me to stay? Always?'

'Always, Keith. So long as it's what you want.'

'What I want? Audrey, it's the answer to my prayers.' They stared at each other for a long moment then he gave a kind of a sob and opened his arms. Their kiss charmed away her fears and the path ahead of her was flower-strewn and no longer empty.

Shirley finally had a letter from Andy. It said very little except that it would be a long time before he was given leave, and he hoped to see her when he did. She didn't keep it like the ones she received from Freddy. She re-read it sadly and threw it away. She didn't reply, but instead wrote to Freddy and told him the end of the story.

When she learned that Andy's brother was staying at the smallholding, she went to see him and told him what she knew about his brother.

'If you write to him, give him my regards,' she said. She didn't want to give any false impressions, no wrong ideas

215

about her feelings. To make sure he understood, she added, 'Over the weeks, I've written to Freddy and told him all about Andy's adventures, ever since he took that stuff from Audrey Thomas, and today I sent off the final instalment.'

'Thanks for being his friend,' Reggie said. 'I don't think he has many of them.'

'Oh, it wasn't as strong as friendship. Just curiosity and something to fill my letters to Freddy,' she said to reinforce her point.

When Audrey went to the house that had been her home in Sidney Street, she found her sister there.

'Hello, Audrey,' Marged said. 'I'm just looking through the tablecloths and tea towels, seeing if there's any mending to be done. Better do it now than have to rush nearer the start of the season.'

'There's months yet, Marged. It isn't even February.'

'Only weeks away and you know how quick the weeks pass once Christmas is over.' They spoke formally and it crossed Marged's mind that they would be more relaxed talking to strangers in a bus queue.

'February will be a busy month for me,' Audrey said, helping her sister to check the linen.

'Oh?' Marged was bursting with curiosity but managed not to show it.

'Keith and I are getting married on the twelfth. We'd like you and Huw to come.'

'Marrying him? Audrey, what are you thinking of? You hardly know the man!'

'I know him well enough to want to share the rest of my life with him.'

'You know he has two sons? Have you met them?'

'Not yet. But I will.'

'And a wife who divorced him?'

'Oh Marged, don't start raking up every little thing. I'm marrying him and if you want to come to the wedding you'll be welcome, if not, well, it won't spoil our day.'

Forcing herself to speak calmly, Marged pleaded, 'At least wait. What's the rush?'

'Last time I waited thirty years.'

'I might have known you'd bring that up! Mam stopped you marrying Wilf because he'd taken advantage of you. She thought it was for the best.'

'Whatever. This time I don't intend to waste any time.'

'Waste time? You haven't forgotten that a week ago it was your anniversary? You and Wilf would have been married for three years. The poor man hasn't been dead a year. Show some respect.'

'The twelfth it is,' Audrey replied calmly. 'Will you let me know whether you and Huw will be coming? We thought we'd have the reception at the Seaview Hotel.'

'You don't want me to do it then.'

'Just come if you want to wish me well.'

'Of course I do, you know I do. The wedding will be a small one I suppose, like when you married Wilf?'

'Not this time. Not a white wedding, of course, but quite grand in its way. One for the town to remember.'

'We'll be there,' Marged promised.

There had been several falls of snow during January and when Audrey woke on her wedding morning, she knew immediately there had been another. The light from outside was weird, the clouds, when she looked out of her bedroom window, were dark and with that odd purple-greyness that came with the startling brightness of the snow. She got out of bed and wondered how people would get to the ceremony. Smart dresses and wellington boots probably. She smiled happily – it was going to be a white wedding after all.

The pavement outside the register office was crowded with well-wishers and the curious. Audrey smiled and accepted the good wishes as she passed through the throng for the brief ceremony that would change her name to Mrs Keith Kent. In spite of the snow that lay on the ground and was still falling at intervals, they walked in procession to the hotel. A generous spread awaited them and twenty people sat down for the wedding breakfast and an imitation wedding cake.

At three o'clock, Audrey and Keith had arranged to leave in a taxi for the station to go away for a long weekend, while the cafe remained open with Maude, Myrtle and the promise of help from Hetty.

At the reception Keith was uneasy with the guests, and a concerned Audrey asked if he had one of his headaches coming on.

'I'll be all right, love,' he said. 'It's often brought on by stressful situations.'

'Stressful? I'm so sorry, Keith. I asked for your approval before arranging anything, you should have told me if you wanted a different kind of day. It could have been anything you wanted it to be.'

'I wanted what you wanted, Audrey. I always want you to have what you desire.'

'There are some Aspros in my handbag, go and take a couple. I know they don't really help, but it's all I can suggest. It won't be long now. Everyone's leaving early because of the weather, so we'll soon be on our way and then you'll relax.'

Clutching the strip of tablets he left the room as the last of the guests were leaving; some intending to wait at the railway station to wave them on their way, others to make their way home before the snow and the approaching night's freezing temperatures made it impossible to travel.

When the waitresses cleared the tables and the imitation wedding cake was packed away to be used for photographs at another wedding, Marged and Huw, Bleddyn and Hetty waited with the happy bride for Keith to return. Maude and Myrtle had gone to take over the cafe from friends who were filling in for the afternoon, and everyone else had gone.

Minutes passed and Huw went to find Keith but came back looking worried. 'He isn't here,' he said. 'I've searched the place and asked the staff to look too. There isn't a sign of him.'

Audrey smiled. 'He's cooking up a surprise, I'm sure of it.'

'Of course he is,' Marged said with a forced smile.

'We'll wait with you,' Hetty said. 'We don't want to miss this, do we Bleddyn?'

The hotel offered tea while they waited but Audrey refused. This was ridiculous, there wouldn't be time to drink tea. As soon as Keith came back they would be on their way home. When an uncomfortable hour had passed, Huw ordered a taxi, and they went back to the flat.

The cafe was open and Maude and Myrtle had changed out

of their smart clothes and were busy keeping the customers fed. They hadn't seen Keith and were alarmed at the news of his disappearance.

While Audrey stood being comforted by Marged and Hetty, the men went to look in the flat. There was no sign of his having been there.

'What about the cellar?' Myrtle suggested.

'Don't be ridiculous, what would he be doing down there?' Marged asked.

'No reason, but it's the only place you haven't looked.'

Without a word Bleddyn and Huw went down to the room where the laundry was done and the stores were kept. The door to the garden was open and lying on the floor was Keith. Behind them, Myrtle watched as they leaned over him to check on his condition. Audrey pushed her aside to look down at the prostrate man.

'Had another migraine and fallen, has he?' she whispered, her hands over her mouth in horror.

Marged instinctively reached out and hugged her sister, and for once, Audrey didn't push her away.

'Migraine, my arse,' Bleddyn said. 'He's drunk!'

Twelve

Bleddyn and Huw carried Keith upstairs without a word to Audrey, who was hovering around them sobbing but trying not to. She helped them put him into the bed he had recently used, unable to consider having him in her own bed, at least until he was recovered enough to know where he was. Marged hugged her and managed not to say anything and Maude and Myrtle ran the cafe and smiled as though nothing untoward was happening.

The guests who had walked to the railway station hoping to see them off on their honeymoon waited in vain. No one thought to let them know.

'In fact,' Huw muttered, 'the fewer who know the better. Audrey will have enough to worry about with having to face us.'

'We could just say the honeymoon was cancelled because of the weather,' Bleddyn suggested. 'No one would find that hard to believe.'

While Keith slept and Audrey sat watching him, Marged helped in the cafe and Huw washed dishes. Bleddyn and Hetty went home. When the cafe closed at nine, Marged and Huw left, and Maude and Myrtle took their time finishing off the clearing up.

'What shall we do?' Maude whispered. 'I don't want to go upstairs and talk to Auntie Audrey, I wouldn't know what to say.'

'We could go to Auntie Marged's I suppose, but we'll have to face Audrey some time, won't we?'

'Best we don't go up just yet. We could stay and wash the front of the counters and set the tables ready for Monday morning, that'll keep us down here a while longer.'

They worked quickly, anxiety giving them a need for speed,

220

and as they dealt with the cleaning, they changed their minds every few minutes about whether to go or stay.

'It'll be best we go and give her time on her own,' Maude would decide.

Myrtle would agree, but then frown and say, 'What if she's lonely and needs someone to talk to?'

The two sides of the discussion were repeated in different words for all the time they were working, finding extra things to do to avoid making that final decision. When there was no reason for them to stay in the cafe any longer, Maude crept upstairs and seeing Audrey like a statue, watching the sleeping Keith, she tip-toed back down and, writing a note to tell Audrey where they had gone, they let themselves out quietly and hurried through the dark, snow-covered streets to Sidney Street to see Marged and Huw.

When Keith woke and looked around him, Audrey saw his face change as realization of what had happened reached his brain.

'Don't say you're sorry, Keith,' Audrey admonished in a whisper. 'Sorry isn't enough.'

'I'm no good with a lot of strangers.'

'I gathered that much.'

'I took a drink of whisky to help me over a difficult few hours, that's all. I'm not family, they're all strangers. I'm hopeless with strangers.'

'So you said.'

'It won't happen again.'

Ignoring the promise, Audrey asked, 'Would you like something to eat? It might help make you feel better.'

'A slice of toast?'

She went to the kitchen and when she came back with the toast he was once more fast asleep. As she adjusted the covers more neatly around him, she found gripped firmly in his hands a quarter bottle of whisky which was empty.

Audrey ate the toast, watching the man she had married who was sweating slightly, and rosy-cheeked, lying peacefully in his bed, while hers was cold and empty and for the foreseeable future was likely to remain that way. It was after midnight when she heard Maude and Myrtle come in, stamping the snow from their boots, calling goodnight to Huw who

221

had presumably walked them back, and giggling as they tip-toed up the stairs, but she stayed in her room. She wasn't ready to do the cheerful, in control, capable Auntie Audrey act just yet. When everything was quiet, she went to bed.

Snow continued to fall throughout the night. She woke very early, to a silent world. She reached over and opened the curtains and the room was filled with that strange light that attends the presence of snow. She had no idea of the time as the morning activities were muted by the insulating effect of the snow. Sunday morning sounds slowly began to make pictures in her mind, of ordinary people starting their ordinary days. Dogs barking, doors grating as they opened, and slamming shut. The sound of shovels, scraping as they removed the snow from paths to allow access to lavatories in the yards and to gather fuel from the coal sheds. The scraping was followed by the rattle as the coal fell into coal buckets, a rhythmical scrape and clatter, scrape and clatter. She thought vaguely that she would soon have to do the same.

She slid out of bed and sat looking out of the window as the day slowly began. Across the road, at the side of the radio repair shop, she saw a shrouded figure in the yard looking for sticks, the man wearing a sack around his shoulders to protect him from the gentle flakes. He chopped a bundle and took them inside. Women off to their cleaning jobs walked along the pavement with socks over their shoes to prevent them falling. The paperboy went past, whistling cheerfully, dragging his load on a sled behind him, a dog following, jumping playfully through the deep snow and stopping occasionally to cock his leg.

She was so engrossed in watching others, forcing thoughts of her wedding day away, she only gradually became aware of sounds within the house. Someone was moving about. Her heart began to race. It must be Keith. What would she say to him?

She heard a kettle being filled, then the rattle of china. Still, she waited. Her thoughts wouldn't gel, she felt a swelling of self-pity and when Myrtle knocked and came in with just one cup, making it clear she knew Audrey was alone, she couldn't speak at all.

'I'll put it down on the table, shall I, Auntie Audrey?' Myrtle said, kissing her.

Audrey could only nod. Ten minutes later, she forced herself to rise and go into the small room where Keith had slept. She hesitated before knocking on the door and going in. The covers were thrown back and the bed was empty, and it was then that the tears came.

Maude and Myrtle promised to find him and at first Audrey told them not to bother. Hurt, humiliated, she felt the onus was on Keith. He was the one who had gone away and it was up to him to decide when to return. 'How could he do this to me?' she asked again and again, and after repeating the usual platitudes a dozen times, Maude and Myrtle could offer no answer. They could only hug her and promise to help in any way they could.

'What shall we do?' Marged asked Huw, on that Sunday morning, when Maude had come to tell them Keith was again missing. 'Nothing until we're asked,' Huw replied.

'I think I should go to the cafe tomorrow morning and do what I can there,' Marged offered.

'Only if you promise to say nothing,' Huw warned. 'This is Audrey's mess and only she can solve it. Even offering help will only make her feel worse. This is a time for silent sympathy.'

All through that Sunday, Audrey's anxiety grew and finally she asked the girls to help her search for him.

'There can't be many places where he could go. Perhaps he's gone back to The Dingle?'

'We'll go there,' Myrtle said. 'You go back to other places where he's stayed, and it wouldn't hurt to tell the police,' she added trying to sound casual. 'He might have got himself arrested or something.'

A shiver went through Audrey, the 'or something' hung in the air, an augury of disaster. He could be dead, or dying, alone and with no possibility of help. Finding himself with nowhere to go was serious in such weather.

'You make sure you two stay together, mind. No wandering off. It isn't safe to be out there alone in this weather. Whatever happens today, I don't want any harm to come to you two.'

Maude and Myrtle wrapped up warmly and, carrying a blanket although not quite sure why, they set off. 'I hope we aren't the ones to find him, mind,' Maude said. 'What can we say to him if we do? Come home, Auntie Audrey wants a little chat? He clearly doesn't want to come home or that's where he'd be.'

'We can reassure him I suppose, tell him he won't get a row.'

'Say we need him to help with the cafe blinds?'

Myrtle giggled, 'Tell him his breakfast is on the table?' she suggested. 'That would do the trick for me!'

Their searches were unsuccessful, and by Monday morning they had heard nothing from him. The police told them that no accident or vagrant answering Keith's description had been reported.

'He isn't a vagrant!' Audrey shouted at them. 'Vagrant indeed! He's my husband.'

'If he'd been found sleeping rough, or without visible means of finding food and shelter, that's how he'd have been described, Mrs Thomas, er, Kent. There was no offence intended.'

When Marged reached the corner where the cafe stood on that Monday morning, she was surprised to see that it was open. Myrtle was attending to customers and Audrey was setting flowers on the tables as though nothing had happened.

'What d'you want me to do first, Audrey?' she asked and, with few instructions necessary, the morning continued just like any other. The day was busier than usual and Audrey's only comment was that the disaster had increased the business more efficiently than a rumour that they were serving fresh cream cakes. There was no sign of Keith.

Monday's post brought Shirley another letter from Andy Probert and it was the strangest letter she had ever received. It said only that he was well and would be in the military prison for several weeks, then posted to where they thought he would be useful. 'Somewhere from where I can't run home like the coward I am, you can be sure of that,' he added as a postscript. It was written on a piece of newspaper, using the borders and few empty spaces around paragraphs and advertisements. The newspaper was from Leicester and the postmark on the envelope was Scotland. There was no address and Shirley wondered if he had written it and given it to someone else who was being released to post for him. She wasn't sure how she felt about Andy: pleased he had written to her, thankful he was safe and at the same time worried about the danger for which he was undoubtedly heading. Dangers, she reminded herself that Johnny and Eynon Castle, and Freddy Clements had been facing day after day for years. He had been a cheat, and as he so rightly said, a coward too. But there was something about him that made her wish he was still in St David's Well and it was possible for him to appear again without warning, and make her smile and feel happier for seeing him.

Beth Gregory had a letter that same morning from her husband. Peter simply stated that he probably wouldn't be home for some time but that she wasn't to worry. She showed it to Peter's father, who nodded, sucked on his pipe and said, 'An impossible thing to ask!'

For the past weeks writing had been scrawled on walls demanding a 'Second Front Now'. The demands were increasing and appeared over night on railway bridges, factory walls, on shop windows and across the entrance to the school playground. Rumours sped from group to group creating an atmosphere of hope that the end of the war was in sight. Most were secretly afraid that the second front meant taking men and women across the Channel to fight on German-held land and that would mean more deaths and an increase in the visits of the telegram boy on his bicycle bringing tragedy in a small yellow envelope.

'D'you think these rumours about the "Second Front" will mean Peter going abroad again?' Beth asked her father-in-law anxiously.

'No, my dear. He'll be somewhere in England training others.'

Peter's expertise was in behind-the-lines support for escaped prisoners and assistance for those helping the allies by sabotaging enemy communications. Neither said it, but they knew it was likely that Peter was already in France. Trying not to think of him in enemy-held territory was impossible. With no hope of him receiving letters, they still decided to write as frequently as they could to show him, when he finally got the letters, that he had been constantly in their thoughts. If what they suspected was true, their letters wouldn't reach him until he was out of danger back in Britain.

At once, they sat to write long, cheerful letters telling him about the happenings in the town, including the non-marriage of Audrey and Keith, about which they had heard even before the milkman had called with the morning's delivery. News travelled fast and a story touching on the edge of scandal and concerning such a well known family as the Castles, this one had wings.

Myrtle had told Stanley who had passed it on to Morgan, who shared it with others at the allotment and in the pub. And to Eirlys and Ken, who had met others, who told others and the story went out like ripples in a pool. There was a lot of sympathy for Audrey and wry amusement too. Jokes about 'the one who got away' spread through the town, becoming distorted and soaking up guesses and opinions and transforming them into what passed as the truth.

Eirlys didn't go into work that day. She had been awake most of the night sitting beside Anthony who had a cough. She knew Alice and Hannah looked after him as well as she did, but the cough was distressing and she wanted to watch him and make sure he was comfortable and took the medicine the doctor had given him at regular times. Again, she knew she could trust Alice and Hannah, but her need to look after him herself was strong.

Thank goodness the office was quiet. It was a long time before she needed to think about next summer and the routine tasks were dealt with in her usual efficient way and there was nothing urgent needing her attention. From the phone box outside she telephoned and promised to be there on the following morning. Faced with a clear day and a listless child who didn't need much entertaining, she settled to making a couple of rag dolls for the shop. Skinny Sarahs, made in patchwork from oddments of material, were popular with little girls and always sold quickly. Taking some curtain remnants, she began with the body.

Anthony slept most of the day, and when Harold and Percival came in from school she had completed four of them. She was a little concerned about the little boy. It seemed to be more than a cold. The cough was lasting a long time. Perhaps she would go to the doctors tomorrow if he was no better.

The snow made deliveries difficult and Beth wondered if it was worth her making the effort to go in to open her cafe on that Monday morning. But the thought of the walk through the snow across fields and the beautiful countryside, along lanes where her wellington boots would be the first to mark the smooth, glistening white surface was irresistible. She dressed warmly and pushed her way through the banked up snow against the hedge and walked across fields to the market.

She didn't hurry, the childlike enjoyment made every moment a happy one and she stopped occasionally to look around her at the beauty that would be short-lived and would end with a chaos of muddy slush. She relished the loveliness of the trees that were already shedding their white mantle with gentle shushing sounds. Birds flew agitatedly around, their wings fluttering, their calls filling the air, branches creaked occasionally as the weight of the snow caused a shift: a winter symphony.

The tranquillity and the silence that wasn't a silence at all calmed her, and she thought of future days like this which she would share with Peter. She was constantly afraid for him, but at that moment she was confident that he would come home to her. She was smiling as she reached the entrance to the market and saw to her surprise that others were too. Laughter surrounded the early shoppers, dressed in ungainly boots and heavy coats, they were treating it as a gift, a pleasant interlude rather than a problem.

She didn't expect to see many customers but to her surprise she was kept very busy, although she soon realized that most were there in the hope of gleaning more information about the disastrous wedding of Audrey and Keith.

She played dumb, even though she had been told by Ronnie on the nearby stall what had really happened. 'Lovely wedding,' she told everyone who asked. 'They looked so happy we all wanted to cry.'

The happy newly-weds, Maldwyn and Delyth, had been given so many presents there were still some waiting at Delyth's home. Her mother and stepfather, the man she still called Uncle Trev, had invited them to go back for an overnight stay and collect them.

It was an ordeal for Delyth, who had been very shy about going home and sharing a bed with her new husband in the house where she had lived as a child. They had sat up very late, she ignoring all Maldwyn's hints about getting to bed. She was too embarrassed and too afraid of the teasing – with which she found it hard to cope – to declare herself ready for bed.

On the following day, Maldwyn had taken the opportunity to see his stepmother, and it was there they had eaten their midday meal. Back to Delyth's parents for tea and a quick visit to her friend Madge next door then, thankful it was over, they struggled, loaded with gifts, to the station for the seven o'clock train back to St David's Well.

Everything about being married was still a thrill. The congratulations, the kind offers of help, the presents and being called Mr and Mrs. The homecoming on Monday evening was no different.

'Look, Maldwyn, there's the milk we ordered standing on the doorstep. Isn't it exciting?' She struggled with the parcels and bags she carried and picked up the pint bottle.

'Oh, look,' Maldwyn gasped. 'A flower arrangement on the table to greet us. That's the work of Mrs Chapel, bless her.' On the doormat they found some letters, which again was considered very exciting, addressed as they were to Mr and Mrs Maldwyn Perkins. Some contained cards from well-wishers, one offered the services of a window cleaner, another a belated letter of welcome from the local church.

Hand in hand they stepped into the kitchen where they found a basket of provisions including a week's ration from the grocer shop, plus vegetables, a loaf of bread, a home-made cake and a tin of stewed steak, a gift from Marged and Huw.

'With everyone so kind, and wishing us luck, we can't be anything else but happy,' Delyth said as she hugged her husband.

'Who wouldn't be happy surrounded as we are by such wonderful friends, eh?'

The snow was still falling and when they had taken their

luggage inside, Delyth filled the kettle for a cup of tea while Maldwyn went the shed to gather wood and coal to start a fire.

In the coal shed he found the two hundredweight of coal they had been allotted – and Keith Kent.

Maldwyn went at once to help the man up, but he couldn't move him. He was stiff and as cold as marble. He appeared to be dead and apart from wanting to run away, Maldwyn's first thought was how to tell Delyth. She had been badly frightened the previous summer by a man who had kidnapped her and put her in fear for her life, and this could start her fears overwhelming her again. For it to happen here, in their home, was disastrous. Without knowing why, he took off his thick overcoat and placed it around the man, tucking it in as though comforting a child.

He went inside, and although he was far from calm, he put his arms around Delyth and told her as gently as he could what he had found.

'Now I want you to come with me and we'll go and call the police and although I think he is dead, we'll want an ambulance as well. The poor man was probably lost. And our coal shed his only hope.'

'I think you should stay with him,' Delyth said shakily. 'Even if he's dead it isn't right that he's left alone.'

'I'm so proud of you,' he said when he saw her on her way. 'Ask for Charlie Groves. It will be a help if we talk to someone we know.'

Constable Charlie Groves was engaged to Delyth's friend, Madge, and the two couples had spent a lot of time together, both having been involved in the wedding, so it was with some relief to them that he was one of the policemen who arrived.

'He isn't dead, but he's suffering from severe hypothermia,' they were told as Keith was lifted on to a stretcher, wrapped in blankets and taken away.

'But I thought . . .' Anguished, Maldwyn thought of the time between his finding the man and help being given. 'He could have died because of my ignorance and stupidity.'

'Stiff and icy cold, it wasn't surprising you made that mistake,' the ambulance driver comforted. 'And warming him too fast wouldn't have been the best thing for him. No, you

did the best you could, covering him with your coat and calling us. Just be thankful you found him before tomorrow morning. He certainly wouldn't have survived the night, at least
now there's a chance he might.'

'What was he doing in our shed? I thought he was getting
married last Saturday?'

It was late, and forgetting about lighting a fire, Maldwyn
and Delyth filled hot water bottles to warm the sheets and went
to bed, where they held each other tightly until they slept.

Over the following days Audrey went into the hospital every
visiting time and sat beside Keith's bed. The doctor had
explained that he had been warmed slowly, as too much heat
too soon could have been fatal. The only humorous moment
was when Audrey said, 'Yes, I believe that when they found
someone suffering from exposure, the American Indians used
to get into a bed-sack with them, stark naked, as it was the
safest way to warm them.'

'Don't think of doing anything like that in my ward!' was
matron's hot reaction.

Audrey and Keith said very little as he grew stronger. She
demanded no explanation and he offered none. She would sit
there for the allotted time, then after a brief word with one
of the nurses, would leave without looking back.

When she was closing the cafe a week later, a man in army
uniform, aged about thirty, knocked on the door loudly and
continued to knock, refusing to accept that the place was
closed. When Audrey opened the door to explain, he said, 'I'm
Keith Kent's son, Alwyn.' He stepped inside and she quickly
adjusted the curtains. Then he held out his identity card for
verification, although she didn't doubt him. He was very like
his father. It was nothing but shock after shock, she thought
as she invited him inside.

He followed her up the stairs where he was introduced to
Maude and Myrtle who at once announced that they were
expected at Marged and Huw's for supper. They dressed for
the dismal weather where melting snow and steady rain were
making it unpleasant to be outside, and stood at the door.

'We can't go yet, can we?' Maude hissed. 'We can't leave
her up there with a complete stranger even if he is Keith's
son.'

'The kitchen needs clearing,' Myrtle said. They took off their coats and washed the last of the pots and dishes as noisily as they could. They wanted Audrey to know they were there but not think they were listening to what was being said. While Myrtle continued to bang and rattle the dishes and talk as though in conversation, Maude crept up the stairs to the flat and stood for a while until she was reassured that the discussion was amicable.

Audrey appeared at the top of the stairs a few minutes later and told them they could go out if they wished. 'Alwyn and I have a few things to discuss.' She smiled reassuringly and watched as they let themselves out.

'A polite way to tell us to clear off,' Myrtle muttered, as they hurried through the dismal streets to tell Audrey's sister of the latest development.

'What exactly happened?' Alwyn asked Audrey when they were alone. 'I was told only that Dad is in hospital suffering from exposure and that he was married to you.' He faced her with a frown. 'Did you throw him out? Did you know he was living rough? In this weather?' His voice was soft, the words held no real threat, but Audrey at once hotly denied the implied accusation of neglect.

'He went missing overnight with no word to tell me where he was going, or why. He married me then got drunk and when I thought he was sleeping it off, he left his bed and disappeared. The police were informed and we searched every place we could think of, but it wasn't until Monday evening that he was found, unconscious, frozen almost to death, in someone else's coal shed.'

'Sorry, I didn't mean to accuse you.'

'Yes you did! It's a strange fact of life that the less people know, the easier they find it to condemn.'

'Mam threw him out, you see,' he said then. 'Years ago, when I was five and my brother was three.'

'Can you tell me why?'

'Only what we were told – which wasn't much – plus what I've learned since. He worked as a builder but Mam wanted him to be something better than what she called an odd-job man. She was rather embarrassed by him wandering around the town with a wooden trailer behind his bike. She had dreams

231

of a big business with Dad in an office and others doing the work. She found someone else who offered her something closer to her dream, so she threw Dad out.' He looked around him at the comfortably furnished room and again Audrey sprang to her own defence.

'I wasn't ashamed of what he did. He was good at his work and honest too. He helped us here and did much more than we asked of him. Why should I marry him then complain about who he was?'

'I'm sorry.' Alwyn stood to go and he handed Audrey a piece of paper. 'This is where you can reach me,' he said. 'I might not be near enough to visit after the next few days, but this address will find me wherever I am.' With self-conscious formality he held out his hand and wished her good luck.

After she had shown him out, she went upstairs and sat in the big chair she had bought for Wilf and wondered how she had reached such a predicament. For the first time for weeks she thought again about the money in Wilf's account that had been lost. If he hadn't spent it and left her with just her own small savings, she wouldn't have opened the cafe, she wouldn't have approached Keith to do the alterations she needed and she would still be living in Sidney Street near the rest of her family.

What could he have spent it on? Most puzzling of all, *how* could he have spent it? They had hardly been apart, so when had he found the time to get rid of the money left to him by his mother and grandparents? It was more than a thousand pounds.

She felt let down by the man she had trusted all her life and because of it, sympathy swelled towards Keith. His only fault was shyness. He hadn't cheated her out of a penny. He hadn't lied. She had known about his ex-wife and their sons, while Wilf had stolen money that would have made working through her middle and old age unnecessary.

For the first time, Audrey went that evening and sat beside Keith's bed with something other than disappointment and anger.

'I'm sorry, Keith. The fault for all of this is mine. I think I rushed you into marriage.'

'Two women,' he said sadly, 'and I let you both down. I knew I would.'

When she had been there a few minutes, Alwyn came and

she patted Keith's shoulder; a reconciliatory gesture, an attempt at showing affection, and left them to talk.

When he was discharged from hospital, Keith didn't go to the flat above the cafe. His son gave him some money and he found a room in a different part of the town. One of the first things he did was to go and see Maldwyn and Delyth to apologize for the fright he had given them and to thank them for their help.

Over the following weeks, he and Audrey met a few times, always on neutral ground: a cafe or on the bus that took them into another town where they could wander and talk undisturbed. They would exchange news like polite strangers, then part, to go their separate ways, both hoping that one day they would be able to try again. But that time was a long way in the future, they both understood that. Most of his work was in St David's Well and sometimes he would see a member of the Castle family and they would wave but never stop to speak to him. They all knew that if he and Audrey were ever to recover from the disaster of the wedding that wasn't, they needed to stay well clear.

Eirlys was still a little concerned about her son. The following morning she left baby Anthony with Alice and went to the office feeling shaky and unhappy about leaving him. On that morning her emotions wavered between forcing herself to deal with the work demanding her attention at the council offices, and running through the town to rescue Anthony from Alice, who might not understand his needs and cause him unnecessary distress.

Somehow she managed to stay until lunchtime, when she caught a bus and went to see how he was coping without her. She found him cheerful, clean and obviously unaffected by his hours away from her.

He cried as she handed him back to Alice after a final cuddle. That afternoon she found it even more difficult to settle down to the work that faced her. Over the next few days, she went to check up on him every lunchtime and during the change over from Alice to Hannah, she even left work in the middle of the morning on the pretext of calling to inspect a hall to be used for a dance parade.

233

'He's got a bit of a cough,' she excused herself as Hannah opened the door to her with Anthony in her arms. 'I just wanted to be sure he was all right.'

'We know, and if there's any cause to worry either Alice or I will take him to the doctor, so don't worry, he's in safe hands.'

After a week, Alice and Hannah cautiously suggested she might be better to stay away at lunchtimes so he didn't become accustomed to her visits, which, they dared to say, were beginning to upset him. Eirlys knew she had to make up her mind quickly whether to give up her job and concentrate on her child, or be sensible and leave him with her friends, where she had to admit he seemed perfectly content.

When another week had passed and apart from the cough and a slight cold, Anthony was safe and content, she relaxed and began to concentrate on the busy months ahead of her, organizing the holidays at home for the town of St David's Well.

Although the season didn't begin until May there was already plenty to do. Requests for local concerts during the out of season months she handed to Ken. Others, pencilled in for the summer were her concern and her diary began to fill up.

A letter came for Ken which he showed her. He was asked to tour with a small group of actors who performed a three act play and alternated it with a song and dance routine interspersed with a few comedy acts. Apart from a few small items which they would beg, borrow or steal locally, the group carried all their needs on a clumsy looking vehicle that had once been used for coal deliveries and to which a cover had been amateurishly added.

'What d'you think?' he asked. 'Two bookings in Scotland, one in an unspecified dockyard, then in Lincolnshire a bomber drome – not specified, and back to somewhere in Kent, again not specified. It will mean being away from home for weeks.'

They discussed it and agreed that he should go. Rumours were gathering strength about a gradual build up of men and equipment in the south, and demands for the Second Front were increasing. They knew the men and women needed relaxation and it was right for Ken to do what he could to help.

Travelling was extremely difficult. The stations were crowded with weary servicemen and civilians. Trains were late or didn't come at all, and many went through the stations full of servicemen and didn't even stop. Food was hard to find and he wondered why he had agreed. Scotland might have been the other side of the world the time it took to get there.

He spent hours hanging around waiting for trains and buses but eventually met up with the rest of the group and they set off in a convoy of a car and the strange-looking lorry to their first performance in the north west of Scotland. He was feeling miserable and wished he hadn't agreed to come. It was so far from home and he couldn't even telephone Eirlys unless she was at the office. He concentrated on the concert party, but the loneliness wouldn't go away.

Everything went well and they stayed for a third evening, the cast arranging a sing-song on the last night before setting off south.

It was at the bomber airfield that things became really difficult. Almost as soon as they had been shown to their accommodation, Ken heard the name Janet, referring to someone who worked in the Naafi canteen. He knew the chances of it being Janet Copp were minute, but he had to find out.

He and Janet had once been lovers but the affair had ended and his marriage to Eirlys was secure. But the prospect of talking to her was extremely tempting. Meeting someone from St David's Well, someone from home, was just what he needed at that time. Common sense warned him not to go, but after they had all settled in for a night's sleep, he went out and innocently passing behind a guard who had moved from his position to stare across the field at something, he walked into a restricted area and approached the canteen.

A hand touched his shoulder suddenly, and he looked up and saw two very tall, powerfully built soldiers barring his way. He turned and silently two others appeared behind him. By their stance he knew they were holding guns and as his night sight improved, he saw they were aimed at his chest.

Thirteen

Ken was interrogated several times and the sessions were exhausting. Several men at once threw questions and accusations at him, then two of them left and there was only one man who, while still suspicious, seemed to gradually accept what he was saying was the truth. He was left in a locked room while enquiries were made and it was dawn before he saw anyone again. A cup of tea and a piece of toast, then the questioning continued.

All the time, whenever he had the chance, he begged them not to tell his wife. 'I was looking for an ex-girl friend,' he insisted, 'and Eirlys might misunderstand and would be hurt.'

'So, you've been a naughty boy, have you?' one asked jocularly. Ken smiled and the next question made it vanish.

'Who do you pass your information to?' And so it went on through most of the next day.

When two military policemen called to speak to Eirlys, she was alarmed. She tried to think of someone she knew who might be a victim of war, but she had no relations serving. They came in and sat rather stiffly on chairs and politely asked her a few questions. They told her nothing about Ken but asked instead about Janet.

'Is she all right?'

'So far as we know, yes.'

'She's serving abroad with Naafi, I believe.'

No reply. Then, 'Is she a friend of yours?'

She didn't answer straightaway, wondering whether to be completely honest, wishing she knew the reason for the questions to help her decide. From the way the two men were staring, they were suspicious of her hesitation. Better, she thought, to be honest.

236

'I knew Janet, but my husband was closer. She sang and as he organizes concerts they worked together.' Another uneasy silence, then she went on. 'They had an affair.' Still no reaction. 'I have no reason to think it is still going on. She's abroad and out of touch. My husband and I have sorted it out and we're very happy.'

'He wouldn't try to see her?'

'Definitely not.'

They looked at each other, thanked her and left.

Ken was kept in a prison cell for three days and then allowed to leave. Shaking, looking pale and ill, he checked to make sure the drama group had gone, and caught a train home. He wondered if he would ever feel confident enough to leave it again.

He couldn't decide what to tell Eirlys, if anything. She broached the subject and he told her everything at first, except that he had been hoping to see Janet.

'You were just going to the Naafi for something to eat? But isn't the Naafi for servicemen?'

Seeing the expectant look on her face, he knew he had to be truthful. 'Don't take this the wrong way, Eirlys, but I heard the name Janet and I admit I went to see if it was Janet Copp. It wasn't with a hope of starting something between us, that's well and truly over, but to talk to someone from home, who remembers so much of what has happened since this war began. I was tempted. That's all.'

Eirlys smiled. 'Ken, I believe you. I just hoped you would tell me. You will tell me everything that happens, won't you?'

'Yes, specially as I missed you so much whilst I was away.'

She slipped into his arms and a low, slow voice that could only be Percival, came from upstairs, 'Look out brovers, they're kissin' again.'

Their laughter was fresh and natural, a shared joy, and they both knew they had turned yet another dangerous corner in their marriage and were still together.

As winter eased its grip and the days grew longer and warmer, business at Audrey's cafe increased. News of its unique attractions for young people spread, and the place was filled right up to nine o'clock when she closed. Although she was pleased with its success, proud of her conceptual skill, in truth she had little heart for the enterprise.

Preparations for the start of the new summer season were underway as March turned into April, and she wondered if Maude and Myrtle were feeling regret at not being included in Marged's plans for the beach. They seemed to be enjoying life, going out more and gathering a group of friends around them. They were out most evenings when they weren't needed at the cafe, to the pictures, concerts and dances, and to visit friends.

When they were working, the cafe became a meeting place for their friends as well as others who were attracted to its welcoming atmosphere to meet away from the suspicious gaze of their mothers. A place where they could meet boys and taunt them with insults and persuade them to buy them an extra coffee when pocket money day was too far away.

She smiled at the confident way the two girls coped with the badinage, remembering their withdrawn and sickly demeanour when they had been rescued from the tumbledown stable in which they had been living. It would have been impossible then to imagine them coping with the cafe, giving their tormenting friends as good as they got and being capable and hard working members of the Castle family.

How she regretted ever separating them from that close circle and bringing them to this place. Successful it undoubtedly was, but it had hardly brought her happiness and Maude and Myrtle would have been more content if they had remained in Sidney Street with Marged and with Huw and Hetty and Bleddyn close by.

A roar of laughter filled the air and she looked across to where Myrtle was collecting dishes and her sister was offering a plate of biscuits to a crowd of young people. She was in a melancholy mood and the laughter didn't make her smile as it usually did. Perhaps she should sell up and go back to Sidney Street?

'Audrey?' a voice called, and she looked up to see Keith at the door. 'Can you come out for an hour, there's someone I want you to meet.'

Her first instinct was to refuse. She was on the defensive most of the time these days. So many disappointments, it was

238

easier to say no to whatever was offered.

'Go on, Auntie Audrey,' Myrtle said. 'We'll rope some of these in to help with the cleaning up if you aren't back.'

'I'll just clear the tables first,' she said, unwilling to capitulate too soon.

Keith helped and they stacked the dishes and cutlery in the orderly kitchen and he took her winter coat from the hook and helped her put it on. Slowly, deliberately delaying, she added a scarf and a hat.

'Where are we going?' she asked.

'Not far. We'll be back to deal with the dishes.'

The evening was milder than of late, the end of a day when the air was warm, and everyone had been touched by the joy of the strengthening sun. Summer dresses had been brought out and could be seen hung on washing lines to freshen them ready for the attention of an iron. The early preparations for summer were frowned on by many, young people were warned to 'not cast a clout till May be out'. No one hurried, the pace was leisurely, the extra hours of daylight giving everyone more time.

Incurious, too unhappy to feel the pleasure of anticipation, Audrey walked with Keith to the park in the centre of the town. There were children playing on the swings and from the size of them she guessed it was past their bedtime, but the mothers had sensibly decided that they deserved an extra hour of outdoor activity.

Keith walked towards the family and beckoned to Audrey to follow. 'These are my five grandchildren,' he said. 'Alwyn's two boys and Geraint's two girls and a boy. Their fathers are away but my daughters-in-law are over there and they want to meet you.'

Whatever she had imagined, it wasn't this. She looked towards the two young women who approached her, smiling in a friendly way. She hardly heard as Keith introduced them as Frances and Gillian.

'Audrey? Can we call you Audrey? Stepmother-in-law is a bit of a mouthful,' the one called Frances said.

They asked very few questions, and spoke more as strangers might, knowing they wouldn't meet again. They were polite and friendly but didn't fuss; no gushing, no crowding her with

239

questions or facts, they just sat beside her and Keith and watched the children playing.

Casually, very casually, Gillian suggested that if she wished, she could come to the twins' birthday party a few weeks hence. No pressure, they were skilled enough to make her feel she was wanted but would understand if she refused.

Gradually, Audrey realized that they were welcoming her into the family with gentle coaxing and she warmed to them. An hour later, she was pushing two-year-old James on the small swing and talking freely to the others as they came and went between games and friendly arguments.

Keith walked her back to the cafe from where the sounds of laughter and shrieks told her that Maude and Myrtle's friends were supposedly helping to clear up. Keith stood hesitantly before she nodded for him to follow her and they tiptoed past the kitchen door and up to the flat.

'I hope you didn't mind. It was a bit like throwing you in at the deep end,' Keith said ruefully. 'But I didn't know how to introduce you and the park is a good place for meeting children.'

'I had a lovely couple of hours and your daughters-in-law are kind and charming, Keith.'

He looked slightly embarrassed. 'Does this mean we can talk properly, as friends?'

'As friends?' she queried.

'For a while, but I hope one day you'll forgive me and we can be more.'

She waited for him to continue, it was clear he had more to say.

'About the drinking. I only drink when I'm worrying about something over which I seem to have no control. If we can make a fresh start . . . ?' he hesitated, then reached out and took her hand in his. 'Audrey, I can't promise I'll never drink again. I'd be terrified of breaking that promise and that alone would make it difficult. But I do promise I'll fight it if it threatens, seek help, do anything to avoid hurting you again.'

'I'm not a great one for promises, an unwise promise can ruin lives. I would ask only that you tell me when something is bothering you. That way, if there's any fighting to be done we'll deal with it together.'

240

'Then I can stay?'

'If you are sure it's what you want.'

His arms slid around her shoulders and he pulled her so close she could feel the beating of his heart. They sat for a long time without another word.

Eirlys was troubled. Ken seemed to have lost direction. He was delegating more of his work and, worse, seemed unaware that Anthony was unwell.

'Will you be at home tomorrow?' she asked one morning as she cleared the breakfast table. 'I have to go to the office, I have several meetings arranged with people promising help in the summer. But if you're home, I think I'll leave Anthony with you, he still has that cough and it's better to keep him indoors, I think.'

He looked up at her as though he hadn't listened to a word. Irritably she repeated them. 'Anthony isn't well and I think you ought to stay at home with him.'

'Darling, it's only a cough. Everyone's assured you it's nothing more.'

'But it's gone on too long, and he's listless and too willing to sit still and listen to a story, during which he usually falls asleep. At two years old he should be full of energy, always finding mischief, and for the past weeks he's been neither of those things. He doesn't get excited when I suggest a walk to the park or to the beach or to the shop to buy sweets, or anything else I've suggested.'

'Hannah will cope,' he replied.

Eirlys accepted that but promised herself that they would talk that evening until she found the reason for his self-absorption.

Hannah had been true to her word and had taken him to the doctor, but typically, Anthony had chosen that time to be chatty, and lively, curious about the new surroundings and keen to investigate. The doctor had smiled as he retrieved various items from the child's determined grasp and could find no cause for concern. But Eirlys was unconvinced.

Taking him to stay with Hannah, she reiterated her worries and Hannah assured her the little boy was in safe hands. When she reached the office she tried to relax, reminding herself that Hannah and Alice were good friends who both loved

241

Anthony and gave him the best possible care.

The list of things needing her attention was a long one as she battled to make arrangements for the various entertainments that would take place throughout the approaching summer of 1944. Her mind was not as concentrated as normal. Anthony was on her mind and so was Ken. His work was similar to her own although he worked far away from St David's Well on most occasions, but since his return from his terrifying arrest, he appeared to have little to do. When she questioned him, he said he was resting before planning a new tour.

When she collected Anthony he was brighter than he'd been that morning and had enjoyed a few hours watching school-children playing in the park with Hannah and Alice providing a picnic in the shelter of the pavilion. He chattered to his mother on the way home and had clearly enjoyed his day. Eirlys hoped that the irritating cough which had plagued him for so long was at last leaving him.

Her talk to Ken took place as they pushed Anthony in his pushchair through the lanes to call on Beth and Mr Gregory. At first he assured her there was nothing wrong, but she said, 'No secrets, Ken. We share everything good and bad.'

'I suppose I've lost my nerve. The thought of going into another army camp or walking through the guard house of an airfield is the stuff nightmares are made of.'

'Go back to what you do best; after a week your fears will have vanished. Please, Ken, just think about when the war ends. You'll need all the contacts you have made. If you don't use them someone else will and you'll spend the rest of your life aching with regrets.'

They discussed it for a while and by the time they reached the smallholding and the cup of tea certain to be offered, Ken had made up his mind.

'I'll need a pile of pennies,' he said. 'Mr Gregory's bound to have plenty, he gets change ready for when he gives donkey rides on the beach. Tomorrow I'll need them for phoning around and getting a concert party ready for the next tour.'

'I'm so happy, Dadda,' she said to her father that evening as she lifted Anthony out of his pushchair. 'Ken and I are very happy now. We have a wonderful son, we truly love each other, and we are working together in perfect partnership.'

'There's pleased I am, Eirlys. You deserve it,' Morgan replied.

'After the war, Ken plans to build up an agency through which acts can be booked and he realized what a valuable help I'll be to him with my organizational skills and the knowledge I'm gaining. I know he didn't want me to leave Anthony and go back to full-time work but now he understands my need to do something besides running a home.'

'You have to do what you think is best for you, he knows that. But I understand how he felt. I hated your mother working, it made me feel I was a failure.' Eirlys didn't hear his words, she was still filled with the euphoria of her happiness.

'The future looks so good, Dadda, in fact, everything is just perfect.

She had no qualms about tempting the Fates by feeling so content, but, as Morgan knew only too well, perfection had a way of falling apart with devastating speed.

Once the summer season began in earnest, Marged knew she would have little time for cleaning her own house, so she spent the next few weeks doing her spring cleaning. Pulling out furniture and cleaning hidden places, freshening the curtains, were tasks she quite enjoyed, but this year she worked alone and she missed the companionship of her sister.

They all missed Audrey. Marged still wondered how they would manage once the season began. She couldn't do it all and this year she wouldn't have Maude and Myrtle to help either. If only this damned war would end and the boys could come home, she moaned. She didn't say the words aloud in case it sounded like help on the beach was the reason she wanted them back.

It was one way of dealing with their absence, the fear of them being killed. Looking ahead and imagining everything returning to normal was a pretence that no danger threatened them. Soon Eynon and Johnny would be home and everything would slot neatly back into place.

From time to time they heard of the loss of a neighbour's son or husband, and sometimes a doorway was decorated to welcome home a wounded dear one. Fleetingly, she wished Eynon would be wounded so he too could return. Then, ashamed of admitting to a loss of faith in the happiest outcome, she pushed the shameful thought aside. She wanted them home well and strong.

She dusted Eynon's photograph and replaced it on a newly polished table. As she struggled to move the heavy sideboard, her thoughts returned again to the problem of staffing the beach activities. She had hinted several times but her sister showed no sign of coming back, even though her marriage to Keith had ended so disastrously. She had not been told of Keith's return, so she still clung to hope of Audrey admitting failure and abandoning the cafe. Something would have to be arranged soon. Day trippers started coming as soon as the evenings were light enough to make the trip worthwhile.

Leaving the problem of moving the sideboard, and with little hope of success, she called to see her daughter Lilly, and found her sitting in the garden reading a copy of *John Bull* magazine while the little girl, Phyllis, played happily beside her.

'Mam? Everything all right?' Lilly threw down the magazine and smiled at her husband who had opened the door to Marged. She tilted her head and Sam nodded and smiled. 'I'll put the kettle on, shall I?'

'Thank you dear,' Lilly said, clearing some toys from a seat and inviting her mother to sit down.

'I've come to ask if you'll come and help at the cafe for a few days a week,' Marged said as she hugged her grand-daughter. 'Only for a while, until we can find someone to help on a permanent basis.'

'Sorry Mam, but Sam and Phyllis need me.'

Marged swallowed a retort. What did Lilly possibly do that made her indispensable, she wondered, looking at her over-weight, carelessly dressed daughter.

'I won't stay then,' she said, biting back her anger. 'Sorry about the tea, Sam, I'll come again when I have more time. Whenever that will be,' she couldn't resist adding.

Walking back to Sidney Street she thought about her daughter and wondered why she had turned out to be so lazy. Marrying a man the same age as her father after first courting

244

his son, had been a sure way of being spoilt. She was ashamed at the way Lilly allowed the man to wait on her and wondered what it had been about her daughter that had attracted him. Vanity perhaps? Walking along with a woman half his age on his arm giving his ego a boost? She suspected Sam paid a heavy price for such pride, although he seemed content with his side of the bargain.

Marged didn't go straight home, she was disappointed knowing her visit had been a wasted couple of hours and she was still no nearer getting help. She detoured along the lanes and as she passed the cafe she saw Audrey coming out with Keith beside her. Hesitating, she watched until her sister saw her and beckoned her over. Ill at ease, she smiled at Keith and said a casual, 'How are you'. Not expecting a reply, she looked at Audrey and saw at once that something had happened.

'We're fine,' Keith said.

Audrey added, 'Back together and happier than before.'

Marged felt tears sting her eyes as she hugged her sister. 'Audrey, I'm so glad.' She moved and gathered Keith into her embrace. Perhaps, she thought guiltily, this might mean Audrey would come back and take her part in the business. To her credit she managed to say nothing.

She ran to the bus stop and went to the beach cafe to tell Huw, Bleddyn and Hetty the good news, then reluctantly returned to her cleaning. Audrey was happy, Lilly was happy but the family was falling apart.

She had pulled some of the furniture away from the walls and it would have to be put back in place before they could eat as the table was covered with the contents of the sideboard, which itself still had to be moved. Why had she started this? Her heart really wasn't in it. Her thoughts were dwelling on the problem of the help they needed on the beach.

A letter rack stood on the sideboard and it was the place where accounts and invoices were habitually kept. Sometimes letters fell behind and landed on the floor, but as far as she could tell, none had fallen recently. Even empty the thing was too heavy for her to shift, but she didn't want to leave it until Huw came home as she wanted the room finished that day, so she slowly, painfully moved it inch by inch from its corner. Stuck between the back of it and the wall, held there by a drawing pin, was a letter. Curiously she examined it and saw it was addressed to Audrey and the writing was undoubtedly Wilf's.

She stared at it for a long time wondering whether to throw it away for fear of upsetting Audrey now she and Keith had overcome their problems, or hand it to her when she was alone. She decided that whatever the outcome, it was Audrey's to deal with. She would hand it to Audrey the next time they met. It could hardly be important enough for her to go over immediately and she really did have to get this room cleaned and straight.

Hannah watched Anthony playing listlessly with a toy she had given him. She had spent most of the morning nursing him between serving customers and she was concerned. He needed to see the doctor again. She knew that Alice was at home, having worked the early morning shift and she called to a woman passing the shop and asked her to knock on Alice's door and tell her she was needed.

When he fell asleep, she wrapped Anthony in a shawl and was holding him, ready to leave the moment Alice arrived. She looked at the clock, and at the flushed and feverish child, deciding to give her friend another five minutes before she shut the shop and left without her. Fingers crossed, she hoped Alice would come. She knew the situation might need two people. One to stay with the child and one to find Eirlys.

Alice arrived, dealt with the customers who were there, then they closed the shop and together they went to the surgery. Anxious now, wishing she had made the decision earlier, Hannah ran, carrying the sleeping child, afraid to let go of him and put him into his pushchair. They arrived at the surgery breathless and fearful of what the doctor would say.

When they were told the child needed to be in hospital, Alice stayed with Anthony whilst Hannah phoned Eirlys's office, but unfortunately she wasn't there. She left a message, trying to word it carefully, to avoid panic, and ran to 78 Conroy Street hoping to find Ken at home. No luck. She left a message with a neighbour and hurried next to the factory where Morgan worked. He came straight away and together they went to the hospital to see what was happening to the child.

* * *

246

Marged stared at the letter and wondered. Leaving the side-board still at an angle from the wall, she picked up her coat and went to find Audrey. The letter must have been written months ago, yet there was a sudden urgency. If Wilf had written to his wife before his final illness it must be important.

When she reached the cafe, Audrey was just going out.

'I can't stop, Marged. We've just heard that young Anthony Ward is ill. Suspected TB. I'm off to the hospital to see what I can do to help. Neither Eirlys nor Ken can be found.'

'I found this letter, it's in Wilf's handwriting,' Marged said. She waited as her sister examined the envelope, hoping she would read it and perhaps divulge the contents, but Audrey pushed it into her handbag and hurried out. 'Hang on,' Marged shouted, 'I'll come with you.'

Reggie was looking for Shirley Downs. He found her with Ken, discussing arrangements for a charity concert to be held in aid of comforts for prisoners. Ken had booked a pianist, a small local choir and a comedian as compère. It would be a popular event, the kind of thing he enjoyed putting together.

Reggie saw them when he called into Audrey's cafe. They had just sat down near the window with fresh cups of tea on the table in front of them almost hidden by sheets of paper.

'Shirley, can I have a word?' he asked.

She looked up and from the expression on his face guessed something was wrong.

'What's happened?' she demanded, as Ken went up to the counter to look at the cakes.

'It's our Andy.'

'He's not—'

'He died as his dream had foretold. He was on a ship which was torpedoed.'

'I can't believe it! Poor Andy!' Sadness and guilt enveloped her. 'That awful dream that worried him so much came true! Oh, Reggie, what a terrible way to die!'

'One of his friends called to tell Mam and Dad what had happened and it was exactly as he said, he was in the water, surrounded by others and no one was able to help him.'

'I persuaded him to give himself up,' Shirley moaned. 'I told him it was the best way. I promised him he'd be glad to

247

get everything settled. Glad! And now he's gone. I feel so sad and so terribly guilty.'

'Try not to be, Shirley. You were only saying what everyone else was saying. Mam and Dad pleaded with him to give himself up and so did I.'

'He was such fun. I can't believe he's gone.'

'The awful thing was that he was quite close to the beach when it happened, but he wasn't a good swimmer and as his friend watched, he disappeared.'

'When is the funeral?'

'There isn't one. They haven't found the body.'

For a moment hope shot through her and she half smiled at Reggie.

Reggie shook his head. 'There's no hope of him being alive, don't think it.'

Shirley asked for his parents' address and promised to write, but in her heart she wondered if, even at the moment of truth, Andy had somehow managed to escape from the death his dreams had predicted. The death of someone so young and so lively was impossible to accept.

As Audrey and Marged walked towards the hospital, a group of women hid their mouths with a hand, to gossip and stare as they followed their progress with disapproving eyes. From the way their bodies curled and the angle of their heads, close together sharing whispered words, Audrey knew they were talking about her.

Some had been sympathetic about her misfortunes, but there were many who laughed and considered her to be a foolish old lady. 'Past fifty and looking for romance,' she'd heard some sneer. Romance was for the young and she'd missed out. She had loved Wilf most of her life but he had spent all his money without explanation. Keith getting drunk rather than face her on their wedding day. She had been a gift for gossips over the years.

She wondered what further shocks Wilf's letter would contain and was tempted to tear it into pieces and throw it into a wastebin. It was only the presence of Marged that stopped her.

At the hospital they had to wait for a few minutes outside

the children's ward as it was not quite visiting time. Audrey heard someone call her.

'Mrs Kent. At last!' Matron came towards her, both hands out to grab her own, smiling a welcome. 'Mrs Kent, my dear, I'm so pleased you've come. We thought you were never coming to see us.' She gestured with her hand and Audrey looked up and above the door she saw the name of the ward, Bobbie's Ward.

'That was the name of our son,' she said.

'We know, and it was a name your dear husband didn't want forgotten. He was so generous, wasn't he? When you have finished your visit, come to my office and I'll show you what he achieved.'

Dazed and tearful, Audrey decided now was the time to open the letter:

My darling Audrey
I hope you will forgive me for this and understand my need to do it. I gave all the money my mother left to the hospital for the refurbishment of a ward in the name of our son. I feel sure you will understand and approve and so have kept it from you in the hope that the surprise will be a pleasant one. I love you and thank you for the oh, so happy years we shared,
    Your loving
     Wilf

'Your husband planned a little ceremony to which you were to be invited as honoured guest, but sadly it wasn't to be,' Matron told her softly.

When Audrey told Marged, her sister looked at her glowing face and asked, 'You don't mind?'

'Of course I don't mind! I'm thrilled by his gift and by his certainty that I would understand and approve. Our marriage was brief, Marged, but it was one of perfect understanding. How many can say that?'

'It was too short. Mam was terribly wrong and so was I not to realize that you two should have been together always.' Marged hesitated as the door opened and people began to shuffle into the ward. 'Will you tell Keith?'

249

'Of course, and he'll understand too.'

Marged went with Audrey to see Anthony, and soon after, Eirlys and Ken came and they left them there, arms around each other, discussing the care of their child. Then, while Audrey went to see Matron to hear the extent of Wilf's gift, Marged went home.

She was smiling. There was nothing to make her miserable. Petty worries were a waste of precious days. Hadn't she read somewhere that it used more muscles to frown than to smile? This was a town for smiles. People would be found to fill the places on the rides and stalls and in the cafe. Summer would come and go and the Castle family would do all they could to make sure that people who came to St David's Well Bay had the happiest and best time that the town could offer.

A van approached heading for the beach. Bleddyn, Huw and Hetty moved over to make room for her. 'Jump in, Marged, we're going to make sure everything is in readiness for the best and happiest season yet.'

Audrey talked to the Matron for a long time and she told Audrey that it was Keith who had done much of the work in the ward. 'And,' Matron added, having learned of Audrey's second marriage, 'when Keith Kent heard about the generous, secret benefactor, he worked for many hours without pay, to keep the job under budget. You have been most fortunate in the men who love you, Mrs Kent. Many would envy you.'

Audrey smiled and agreed.